I08178931

# Flowers Island

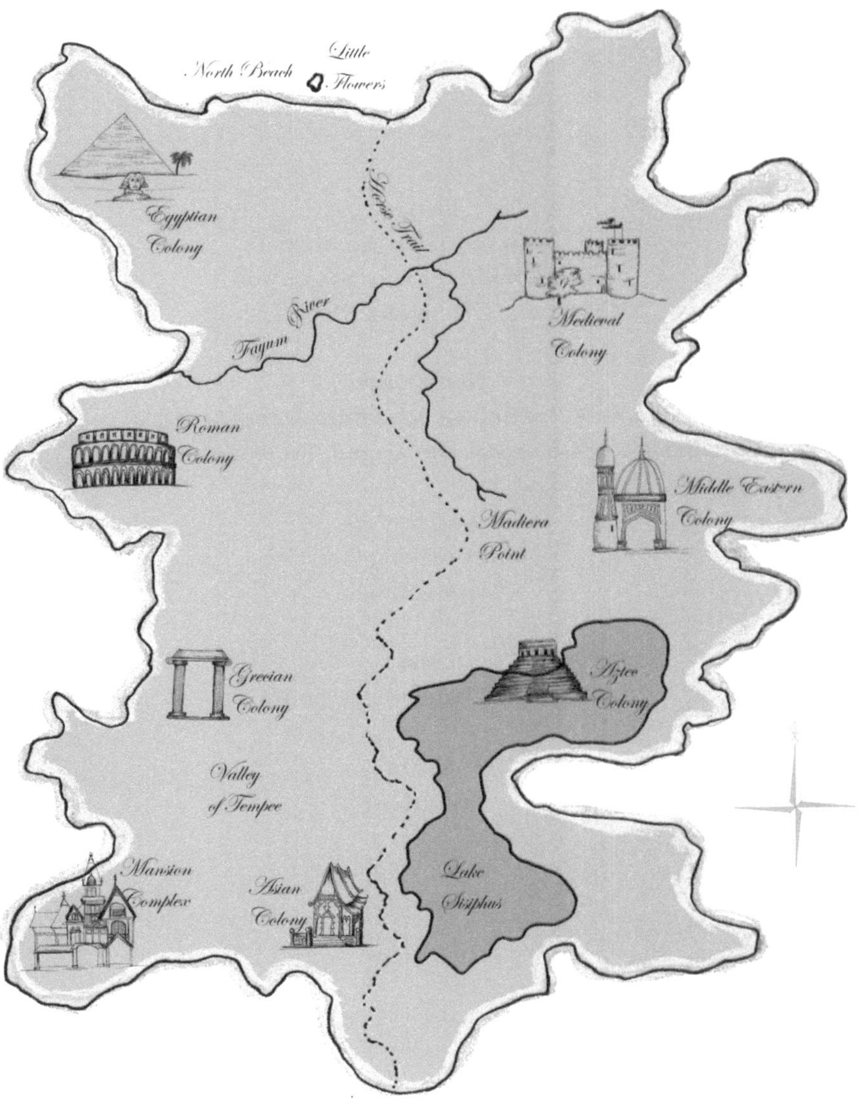

## Other Titles by William Northey

**Fiction**

The Grand Trine (Book One)
The Grand Triumph (Book Two)
The Grand Triangulum (Book Three)

**Non-Fiction**

88 Pianos: A Recumbent Adventure Across America
Radiant Floor Company: Design and Installation Manual

**Short Stories**

The Creaking Plot
Game Animals

**Essays**

Turning Litter into Literature

**Satire**

Everything

# The Grand Trine

William Northey

The Grand Trine
Radiant Press



For more information about this title, please contact:
William Northey
bill@radiantcompany.com

Cover design by Pierce and John Lockwood

Printed in USA

William Northey
The Grand Trine
2nd Author's Edition

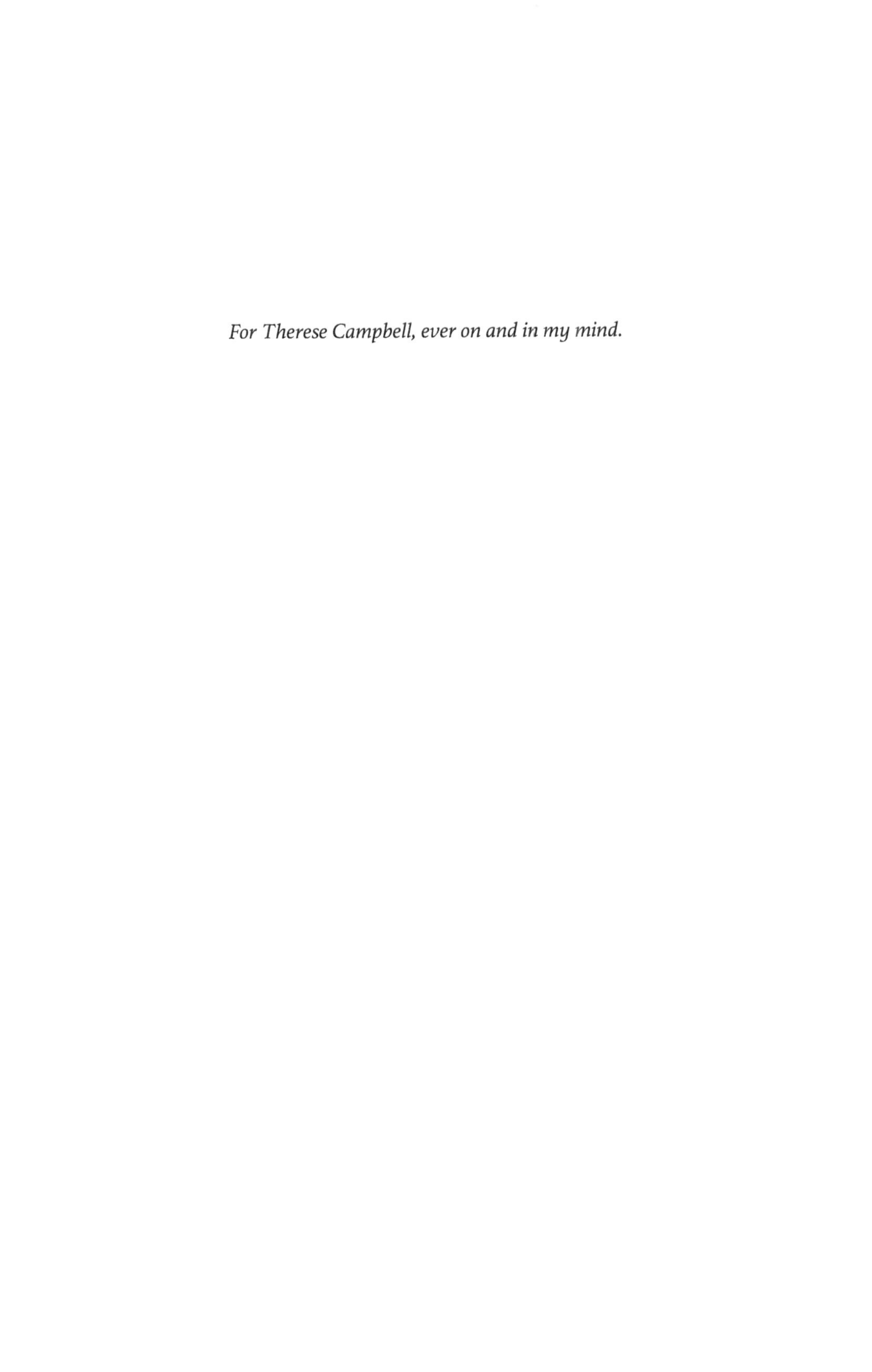

*For Therese Campbell, ever on and in my mind.*

# Book 1

# Flowers Island

...musical training is a more potent instrument than any other, because rhythm and harmony find their way into the inward places of the soul...

PLATO, *The Republic*

# The Grand Trine

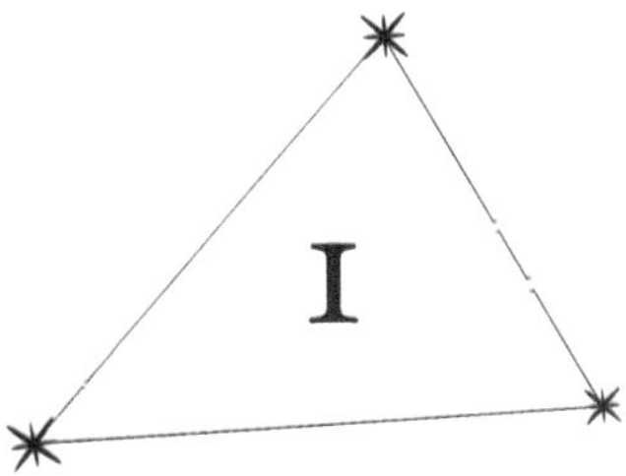


Some days were grand.

But on this birthday, August 9th, in a year that spoiled the past like an unwelcomed present, George Flowers died. The occasion ruined eighteen years of ignorance, education, bliss, and misery. And though this was a death of previous life, neither physical nor moral, it pillaged a million trivial, but dependable moments, ended aspirations, and transformed childish trust into hateful suspicion. In later years when George would see himself as little more than Death's lieutenant, he would mourn this day and cherish his innocent youth.

But now was still the early morning of August 9th, George's last few hours of previous life. He still accepted the miseries and luxuries of lessons in his father's Culture Colonies, this latest and final lesson in the "misery" category. So much so that it felt to George like a mental version of a *cilice,* the coarse sackcloth shirt embedded with twigs that he was forced to wear during a lesson in the Medieval Colony.

Like all the rest, he would endure this final challenge because he still envisioned a future on Flowers Island.

What he couldn't imagine, yet, were astonishing worlds hidden behind matter. Worlds Destiny would reveal. Along with darkness, and evil, and the science of massacre. Mysterious forces like *electromagnetic fluid*, another approaching tempest, infused everything but George's awareness.

Still, this day of George's birthday begins like a typical day. With an electric eye on the roof of Flowers Mansion sensing the light of dawn and sending an impulse to the mansion's central computer.

The program responds, the same way it has for the last eighteen years, by playing a melody into the young man's bedroom. A melody so faint, it's softer than George's breathing.

The dawn rises.

The music grows louder in proportion to the light, in barely perceptible measures, until its volume matches the hint of morning creeping into the bedroom.

Outside, sunlight crawls over the eastern coast of Flowers Island, up the rocky cliffs and into the abandoned villages of the Middle Eastern Colony; further to the Medieval Colony, then the Aztec, Asian, Greek, Egyptian and Roman Colonies. Finally, on the far western edge of the island, daylight paints a crimson flush on the grey stone face of Flowers Mansion.

Inside, George sees no light, hears no melody rise with the coming day.

Entranced not in an ordinary dream, but immersed in a waking dreamscape, a nightly vision he has seen a thousand times—a grassy hill overlooking a familiar meadow. Years of training have brought him here and the vision is always the same: Wind caresses George's dream-face. He inhales the fragrance of heliotrope. In clear tones, as real as any in the waking world, a shepherd's pipe charms the air with pentatonic melodies. Echoes bounce off granite cliffs. Below, dancers whirl in a merry circle.

George runs down the hill toward the meadow. A rough, leather tunic chafes his skin. Tall, moist grass slaps against his legs. Breath fills lungs—

His dream-body stops.

He becomes suddenly aware of two realities; the meadow, then back to Flowers Island, the dancers, then back to his bedroom.

The dancers pause, falling like puppets under severed strings, then merge into the scenery.

George awakens to blackness.

He doesn't open his eyes; he's been trained not to.

As always, the melody follows from his dream and fills his bedroom.

As always, George listens to the music grow louder.

When it completes its slow crescendo, he knows the sun has risen.

Snap!

"What the..." Something was outside his window. Above him, on the headboard of his waterbed, a Spectralamp shined a pale orange light.

Tossing back the sheet, George sloshed out of bed and crept to the edge of the railing. Glen, his best friend, is climbing up the mansion's wall on a thick trellis of ivy. "What the hell are you doing?" George called down, not sure whether to be concerned or angry.

Glen had already scaled two stories toward George's third floor bedroom. He moved unsteadily, a roll of cloth draped around his neck. "Damn you, Flowers," Glen muttered through ragged breaths. "Get the hell away!" Glen's footing gave way with a snap, leaving him dangling from the trellis, legs flailing, fighting for purchase.

Instinctively, George reached over the edge, extending a hand, even though Glen was over ten feet away. "Are you trying to kill yourself on your birthday?"

Glen entwined his legs among the thick branches, then looked up. "No George, I thought I'd kill myself on *your* birthday."

They both laughed, knowing Glen was safe.

"So, Glen," George said, with mock innocence, "hope I didn't spoil anything."

Since the two eighteen-year-olds shared the same birthday, each tried to outdo the other by concocting an outlandish birthday surprise.

"Just leave," Glen yelled up, again, this time with a scowl.

"All right, all right," George said, chuckling to himself as he backed away. "Just be careful." He walked to an Edwardian roll top desk and sat before a computer.

As far back as George could remember, he and Glen had played this game on their birthdays. At first, it was silly kid things like leaving "Happy Birthday" notes hidden around the mansion. By their teen years, the game had evolved into serious competition, awarding points for the most ingenious and dramatic *pranks*.

The game had five rules.

One: The surprisor could cause no physical harm to the surprisee.

Two: The surprise had to occur on the birthday, but it need not relate directly to the subject of birthdays.

Three: A total of one hundred points was possible in the competition.

Four: All points would be awarded by an impartial committee of island personal whose decisions were final. And as George and Glen soon discovered, the committee levied heavy "spoiled sport" penalties on any player who complained, or worse, flew into a rage after facing a prank.

Five: Accomplices were allowed, but surprisor forfeited ten points to surprisee for every accomplice used.

The enhanced competition began the following year on their fourteenth birthday. Glen won.

By age fifteen, the milder pranks had vanished. Gone were the days when dressing goats in George's clothing could pass for an acceptable prank, but that and several other surprises won Glen his second victory.

At age sixteen, George filled Glen's showerhead with powdered food coloring and dyed Glen red for his birthday—a ten-point prank. George won that year 89 to 75.

By the following year, their schemes had become even more elaborate.

Snap!

"Shit!" Glen cried.

George winced. The ivy above the desk rustled. Two walls of George's room opened onto long verandas, so George had trained the ivy to crawl across the ceiling, and around lamps and furniture, until the room was decorated with one, giant houseplant. Whenever the wind blew, leaves shivered like fluttering sails.

But there was no wind now. What the hell was Glen doing?

George started to stand, but stopped himself. *I'll find out soon enough*, he thought.

In the upper left corner, the monitor flashed: YOUR CHOICE...YOUR CHOICE, below, a desktop full of icons.

George double-clicked: PLATO'S *REPUBLIC.*

The teachings of Socrates filled the screen.

Flipping quickly to his parts, George glanced through the ancient dialogues one last time. Of course, he had memorized these words months ago. But Jonas Felty, the island's Headmaster, still demanded a pathological amount of repetition, study, and what he called "involvement" in the work. Without fail, Jonas would ask George if he had studied his lines, and now George could honestly say that he had.

"Waste of fuckin' time," he muttered.

For this latest lesson in the Grecian Colony, George had been assigned the role of Thrasymachus, the student who rebels against Socrates' teachings. According to Thrasymachus, justice belonged to the powerful. The duty of the weak was to obey established authority. "Ha," George scoffed, for the hundredth time. He didn't agree with Thrasymachus or even like him. But as with every lesson in any Culture Colony, George played his role with absolute conviction. While acting-out Thrasymachus, George believed every word of Thrasymachus' "might makes right" argument. Regardless of the character he was impersonating, in the reality of the moment, George's concentration was perfect.

Today, after three months of study, Plato's *Republic* would be performed in the Theater of Dionysus before an audience of island dignitaries—the part-time residents of Flowers Island. These were men and women from every region of the United Nation—the former Americas, Europe, Asia, the world; persons of renown in academic, scientific, or artistic fields. Persons allowed by Aaron Flowers, George's father, to participate in the imaginary pasts he had created on his private island.

Precisely at noon, the dignitaries would don the *chitons* of the Ancient Greeks and become (depending on the assignment Aaron Flowers had given them), slaves, citizens, or nobleman; sit on the hard stone benches of the Greek theater and watch Plato's *Republic*. No matter that the *Republic* was never actually performed in Ancient Greece. No matter that the *Republic* wasn't even a play, that Plato never wrote a single dramatic work. No matter. Aaron Flowers wanted George and the other actors to enliven the ancient teachings and bring them to life.

The past and human history were always what Aaron Flowers said they were.

If George played his role convincingly, demonstrated his grasp of Plato's teachings, he would finally graduate from the Culture Colonies. He and Glen could then leave Flowers Island for a one year vacation; visit the United Nation, see in person the lands, oceans, and architecture of what was once Europe, Asia, Australia, Africa, the Americas, and even Antarctica. Tour the cultures he had studied all his life. He and Glen would uncover the mysteries of modern Greece, Rome, Asia, and study the 21st century for the first time in their lives.

But, if George failed today's performance, it would mean another year of "refresher lessons."

George shuddered at the thought. This tedious summer of Greek philosophy had withered all interest in Plato and Ancient Greece. In truth, all the Culture Colonies bored him. He'd had more than enough lessons in bookbinding, blacksmithing, animal husbandry, and for that matter, every aspect of life in the Medieval Colony. In the Egyptian Colony, he'd enjoyed learning about hieroglyphs, had carved them, first, on wooden planks, then later, ground colored rocks to powder, added liquid to make ink, and written on papyrus. Even later lessons in Coptic and Arabic alphabets had fascinated him—at first. But as the years passed, new lessons came and went and training as an Ancient Egyptian scribe stifled his active nature. *Juedixi* gymnastics in the Asian Colony more than complemented his training in the Grecian Colony's *gymnasion*, but no sooner had he mastered a handstand on a tightrope then it was back to the Asian Colony to raise silkworms, an occupation only slightly more appealing than herding pigs and harvesting maize.

Yet, in fairness, George admitted that his father excelled at inventing constructive and valuable life experiences, even though many were difficult and unpleasant. George often overcame challenges in future lessons by exercising skills he had developed during past lessons.

So, sure, the lessons were important. They deserved one's best efforts. But three months of plodding through the minutiae of Plato's *Republic* was way too long. The strain had even malformed George's normally compliant behavior.

Last week, Jonas Felty, playing the part of Socrates, had demanded, again, more "feeling" from George in his portrayal of Thrasymachus.

"I feel it, damn it!" George had burst. "I feel it now. I felt it yesterday. I felt it two months ago!"

Jonas walked calmly to George, his *chiton* billowing in a Grecian Colony breeze. "Calm that restless mind, young Thrasymachus," he said as Socrates. "The light of Truth reflects from a tranquil pond." He tapped George's forehead. "You won't find wisdom in that hurricane."

"Who needs wisdom if it's as boring as you and your fucking pond?" George shot back.

Of course, now, he regretted his actions. He should apologize to Jonas, try harder at his lessons, be patient.

On the other hand...

The performance was scheduled for noon. But George was ditching this morning's final rehearsal because, in his well-thought-out opinion, Glen's birthday surprise was far more important than Thrasymachus nodding at Socrates with profound philosophical concern, saying lines like: "Yes, indeed Socrates, surely that is true." Followed by endless standing around listening, listening, listening, while Socrates outlined, with perfect, often irritating logic, the ideal state of mankind.

Some days George wished he were back milking sheep in the Grecian Colony instead of weaving webs of Socratic logic.

But not today. This morning he had escaped both sheep and Plato—barely.

"No George, absolutely not," Rollins, the island's manager, had said yesterday when George told him he was ditching the final rehearsal and going instead to North Beach to retrieve the Arabian stallion he was giving Glen for his birthday. The horse had arrived two days earlier on the island's weekly supply ship. "Master George, if Jonas wants a final rehearsal, you must need more practice."

George argued that all this rehearsal was really for Jonas' benefit. "I tell you, Rollins, the Headmaster is lost in his role. He demands daily practice to maintain the illusion, to convince himself that he really *is* Socrates."

Rollins closed his eyes as if hoping George would be gone when he opened them again. "I'm sorry, George," he finally said, but without conviction.

In response, George had launched into fifteen minutes of Plato's dialogue, following Rollins around the mansion, reciting everyone's lines: Thrasymachus, Glaucon, Socrates, Ademantus...

Rollins had raised his hands to the heavens. "Good God, George, you're so relentless." Then with the sigh that always preceded capitulation, Rollins said: "Very well, I'll speak with Jonas. You may ride to North Beach and retrieve Glen's horse. But for God's sake be back for the performance."

George had given his most solemn promise.

He would have kept it, too.

But for now, George didn't have to worry about lessons and final performances. The rustling ivy had quieted.

George paused, fingers poised over the keyboard, hoping Glen had left the trellis. "Pranks are fun," George muttered to himself. "But not if they kill you." A second later, the clatter resumed.

*Jesus,* George thought. *What the living hell?*

As Glen cursed, George crept to the edge of the veranda and peeked over the railing. Still precarious, still way too high on the metal trellis, Glen wrestled with a long piece of cloth, fighting to fasten it to the ivy with plastic clothespins.

Concerned, but seeing that Glen was okay, at least for now, George darted back.

Thoughts returned to the Culture Colonies, but this time tinged with regret over his growing disdain. While making the bed, he thought about the pleasant times, the old lessons, years ago, before all this Plato, before Socrates started talking in circles. He recalled the challenge of playing a bronzesmith's apprentice in the Roman Colony; crafting the molds, stoking the furnace, pouring the molten metal, shaping, etching, polishing. The weeks he'd spent in the Egyptian Colony learning the brewmaster's art, the thick, earthy smell of hops and fermented malt. He remembered himself at age eight, playing a knight's page in the Medieval Colony, attending his master, preparing him for the Royal Games.

So many roles, so many possibilities.

As a young scribe in the Middle Eastern Colony, George experienced the origins of writing. Studying in his father's version of ancient Samaria, George used a reed stylus to etch impressions on soft clay tablets. The Asian Colony had its share of pigs and silkworms, but he'd also learned astronomy there, had studied meditation techniques under Master Shang, cast the future with Chinese oracle bones, crafted weapons, bells, idols, and medallions.

So, he wondered: *Why treat Plato in such a dry, academic manner?*

Instead of living for months in the Colony, George, along with his fellow actors, commuted back and forth in the underground tram. The Grecian Colony flourished only during the day. At night, the performers returned to the Mansion Complex, donned 21st century clothing, and went about their everyday activities.

This lesson wasn't real like all the others.

After another quick glance outside, George returned to his desk.

Diary: *Greek hillside dream again, but something disturbing this time. I stood on the same hillside, overlooking the same grassy meadow. As always, the dream was perfectly vivid. I felt the sun on a clear summer morning, the same fresh breeze scented with flowers. Panpipes played and the same group of peasants danced in a wild, swirling circle. But the music....* He paused, remembering, *...was unlike anything I had heard* *before. This tune sounded sinister and dark, as if belonging to a different dream, or more accurately, a nightmare. It shrouded the scene like a dark shadow. But the peasants never noticed! They danced a merry jig while the sad and lonely music foretold a deadly night.* He ended his entry with: *Well, when have dreams ever made sense?* Shutting down his computer and forcing himself to ignore whatever Glen was up to, he left the bedroom.

On the main floor, at the foot of the grand staircase, George paused, amused by a curious juxtaposition of conflicting scents and sounds. Down the left corridor and behind the kitchen's swinging double doors, Miss Ruth, the mansion's cook, spiced, or tortured, a fresh batch of cinnamon rolls with an Irish folk song. Her shrill, exuberant voice screeched like a fiddle bowed with a fipple flute.

At the opposite end of the corridor (and thankfully behind solid oak doors), George's tutor, Jean Francois, sat before the concert grand playing Franz Schubert's, *Scherzo in B-flat major.* That melody drifted on a breeze from the open windows of the Orangery, a conservatory brimming with potted blood orange, tangerine, Persian lime, and Meyer lemon trees. George, poised between bark and blossom, wondered if the dissonance of cinnamon ruined the harmony of citrus, or if each enhanced the other's uniqueness?

He could ask his life the same question.

When he passed today's exam in the Grecian Colony, abandoned his teachers, friends, father, and Flowers Island, and launched his world tour, would he flourish, or fail?

Would twilight on the *Duomo*, or dawn on *Rapa Nui,* outshine this morning's light?

Here, now, splayed before him were beautiful bay windows overlooking a shimmering bay. Behind him, stained glass, and walls adorned with Etruscan frescos; above, Schonbek chandeliers glistening with Swarovski crystals. The frescos were masterful, but not masters, the chandeliers dazzling, but never illuminated. The mansion's monumental fireplace, built with multi-colored stones in swirling patterns that Glen called "mineral milky ways", impressed George as the kind of art van Gogh might create as a stonemason. Striking, scenic, always dressed in kindling, but never dancing with flames, never cuddled for warmth, the hearth sat like a Grecian Pythia, an oracle of possibilities, but barren.

Maids dusted its decorative logs, then the paneled walls—oak, mahogany, maple, the Egyptian armchairs, the buffet cabinets, foyer tables and walnut sideboards—part of a hundred daily tasks in service to a 45,565-sq. ft. mansion.

*Can I really leave all this behind?* George thought.

Forget the luxury. Despite his discontent, he would truly miss the learning and discovery, seeing the world through a thousand different eyes, living adventures, real and fictional, in the island's universe of cloth-bound editions. He had already read every volume in the mansion's three personal libraries. A few hundred thousand more lived in the *Pergamum*, the island's multi-story shrine to books, knowledge, culture, and learning.

He would yearn for those unread books.

But most of all, he would crave his piano. Sure, there were millions of keyboards in the United Nation, some brighter, warmer, richer in tone. Many were masterworks of elegance and design. George's piano, his grand baby, shared the qualities of any fine instrument—a soundboard of White spruce, cut during winter to prevent sap from affecting the wood's stability, a 100-year-old tree, lumber quarter-sawn, kiln-dried and stacked for slow air cure down to a 5% humidity content.

All that matters.

But so does character, the instrument's individual timbre and tenor, how the strings resonate in the player's ears. How its vibrations feed the soul. How eighty-eight notes permeate space and define time.

At least, according to Jean Francois, George's piano teacher.

Always what George called (in private) a "technique freak", Jean Francois worshipped Hanon and his 240 finger exercises, and of course, etudes, from Chopin and all the other great masters. But beyond drills and exercises, he also emphasized "nothingness". Sitting before the keyboard, its eighty-eight possibilities begging for expression, and listening instead, to emptiness. To the vacant pulse preceding creation, that brink of the cliff before gravity defined the future.

"Choose a note," he would say. "A single note from the fertile domain."

What? George would argue. Isn't the entire keyboard a "fertile domain"? A boundless field ripe with sprouts and bursting with creative potential?

"You know what I mean," Jean Francois would scold.

A note, then, from what the conventional world ("sane" world?) would call the lowest register. The ten rarely played bottom notes. Starting with the lowest F-sharp, down to the dark, grumbling A-natural.

Pressing most keys on a piano causes a hammer to strike, not one, but three, and on some notes, two strings. These steel strings are tuned together to the pitch of a given note.

In the "fertile domain", the hammer strikes a single, much longer copper string, wound with other wire to make it thicker, deeper, more resonant.

"Pause, still the mind, attune the ears to silence," Jean Francois would say. "When attention is total and silence is not merely perceived, but realized, press the sustain pedal, strike your note, and listen. Do not hear...listen."

And George would focus, on the note, its pitch, character, reverberation; feel its vibrations, inhale its resonance, listen as a dying chorus of overtones waned, faded, and finally dissolved in time.

For hours after that exercise, intervals, chords, and harmony wounded his ears. Too much sound. Too much clutter. Even the most beautiful melody, chaos, a sequence of carefully crafted pitches designed to smother the true essence of music—silence.

In silence, George listened, and heard, miracles.

Could he find such miracles on the mainland? Would he be lost without his vintage sheet music, stored on this North Atlantic island in air-tight cabinets at 40% humidity, or displayed in vacuum under UV glass? Yes, he would grieve. But mainly for the faded sight of them, their dusty scent, those brief moments when yellowed paper crackled under his fingers. As a practical matter, he had memorized them all. As he had the mansion's collection of classical art, forged them in his mind's eye, as it were. Fitting, because every Grecian goddess and nymph, every Roman nobleman or emperor, every marble, granite, or plaster sculpture lining the corridors of Flowers Mansion were reproductions by talented forgers. Well, not all. A few were *original* works by artists famous for fakery—Han van Meegeran (who forged Johannes Vermeer), and Ely Sakhai (who forged Gauguin).

Yet, all resonated, all inspired, all astonished.

Would, perhaps, the genuine United Nation, the actual mainland, and the real world of daily life seem counterfeit?

The magnetic scent of cinnamon rolls, in triumph over orange and lemon blossoms (perhaps the breeze had shifted), drew George toward the kitchen, to Miss Ruth, still gargling her song and scaring the cats.

He had barely stepped two paces when a voice called out behind him. "George!"

Ferd, Miss Ruth's assistant, looked more hyper than usual with sandals slapping across the marble floor, his stride somewhere between a walk and a run. He bounded up and thrust a bag into George's hands. "Happy birthday, George." Then, as if admitting to grand theft pastry, whispered: "I grabbed this while Miss Ruth wasn't looking. Put the icing on myself."

*I bet you did,* George thought, more than a little suspicious. He wondered why Ferd wasn't in the kitchen helping Miss Ruth right now. Had he been searching for George, or secretly meeting with Glen? Not easy with Glen hanging from the ivy. Never mind, the roll looked and smelled delicious. Warmth screamed: "Right out of the oven!" Still, anything could be a prank. "This is so fresh I should eat it now," George said, studying Ferd's expression for signs of deceit.

Ferd just smiled, the very picture (forged?) of innocence.

"But I think I'll save it for later."

Ferd answered with a buck-toothed grin.

"Yeah," George went on, "this is great. Very thoughtful. Thanks. I'll see you later. Big day in the Grecian Colony."

"Have a great eighteenth, George," Ferd said, pushing through the kitchen's double doors.

As he walked away, George heard Miss Ruth bellow: "Well congratulations, ya found the kitchen. Where ya been lad, I need some..."

George heaved against the mansion's solid oak door and stepped into subtropical sun. Sultry waves of frangipani and gardenia flooded his senses. With eyes closed and face raised to the sky, he wondered how a mere birthday gift could match this moment. Salty breeze fanned the island as the door opened behind him. "Master George," Rollins said, stepping onto the granite porch.

"Good morning, Rollins," George said, thinking: *Don't try to withdraw yesterday's agreement. I'm going to North Beach regardless.*

"Indeed, it is, Master George," Rollins said, in the manner of an impeccable English manservant. "Not to spoil the moment, but your pranks won't distract you from the Grecian Colony?" Rollins' voice was too tender to be offensive, but he had an irritating talent for stating commands as questions." Remember, twelve o'clock sharp. You don't want to disappoint the Headmaster."

*Don't I?*

But said: "Even Socrates couldn't convince me to miss today's lesson." He turned away before Rollins could see the eye roll.

"By the way, Master George, now that I've got you here for what may be the last time today. Happy birthday. Rest assured that your plans for Glen's surprise are still on track."

"I could never doubt you, Rollins."

A smirk furrowed Rollins' already wrinkled face. "Aren't you a little curious about your own birthday present?"

"It hasn't even crossed my mind."

Rollins peered down his nose. "All this Greek philosophy has given you an exaggerated sense of nobility, Master George."

"Not really. I'm just focused on surprising Glen's ass off." A smile cracked a little poise from Rollins' face. George leaned closer and whispered: "Old Flowers hasn't found out about the stallion, right?"

Rollins' expression looked like silence chiseled onto granite. "Of course not. Though you should be studying philosophy, not running after dumb animals."

"One valuable and very smart animal."

"Time is wasted all the same. If your father knew he'd be furious."

"I'm furious at Jonas," George said, trying to sound angrier than he felt. "The surprise has to be on the birthday. Jonas should have scheduled the *Republic* for another day."

"Yes, yes, I know." Rollins removed a handkerchief from his frock coat and blew his nose. "George," he said sniffling. "I wish you weren't so concerned about birthday pranks. Plato is far more important. You're eighteen. A man now. It's time to stop playing games."

*You would love Socrates*, George thought. But he said solemnly: "I appreciate your concern, Rollins. But I know you'll keep our secret."

Rollins snorted. "Even if we both live to regret it." He glanced at his pocket watch. "You have a long ride. *Please* be back in time for your examination."

"I promise."

George walked across the lawn toward the East Wing, eager to see what Glen was up to. He didn't feel all that rushed. As usual, Rollins was over-worrying.

Inside the mansion, Rollins stepped to the front window and watched George disappear around the corner. His watch said: 6:22. Closing the velvet drapes and brushing a fleck of lint from the sleeve of his coat, he walked down a corridor lined with marble statuary to Aaron Flowers' private elevator. After entering a five-digit code, he rode down to his employer's study.

Aaron Flowers looked up from his work when he heard the double doors open. "You spoke with George?" he said, even before Rollins had taken his first step.

"Yes."

"Did you encourage him to study his lessons instead of chasing stallions?"

"Yes."

"And...?"

"He just left for North Beach."

"Good." Aaron Flowers leaned back in his leather chair. "By any chance did he mention last night's dream?"

"Not a word."

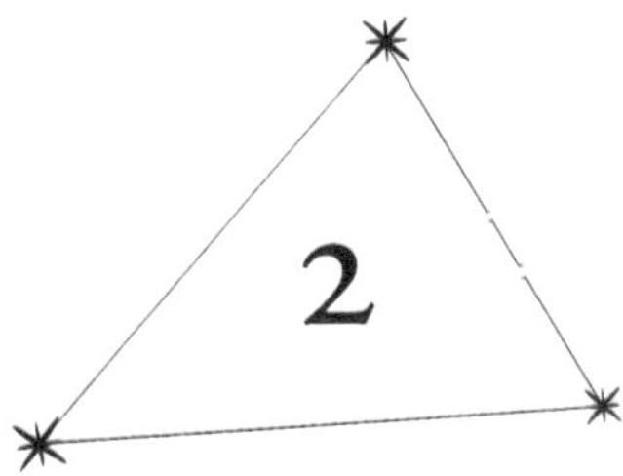

George's bedroom was in the East Wing of Flowers Mansion, a long walk from the front door. To get there, he had to stroll through three acres of manicured hedges, trees, bushes, and flowers; then around a huge garden maze that butted up against the mansion's stone walls.

George chuckled as he approached the maze, remembering one of last year's pranks.

Three days before their seventeenth birthday, George and Glen had cast off from the North Beach marina in their forty-foot sailboat, the *Valdaquez*. It had been an unusually calm August day, hot in the mid-nineties, and the water glistened like green tinted glass. With such perfect visibility, the chances of charting new shipwrecks were excellent.

Using the sailboat's small diesel engine, they chugged around the rocky coast, through calm, nearly flat seas, hoping for a late afternoon breeze. "Screw it," George had cried. "Let's take a quick dive here."

Glen looked over the side. They were on the island's northeastern tip, near a lightly explored stretch of reef. "Didn't find anything last time we were here," Glen said, dropping anchor. "But you never know." George marked the location on their map and grabbed two regulators from the storage locker. He had just fastened a buoyancy control device, his BCD, to a scuba tank when Glen cried: "Georgie, look over there." He pointed to a line of distant cliffs. "Am I seeing things?"

*Took you long enough to notice*, George thought. He shielded his eyes and gazed into the sun, scanning the cliffs in the direction Glen indicated. "What? I don't see anything," he lied.

"Someone is climbing up there." Glen darted below, emerging a moment later with a pair of Bushnell H2o compact binoculars. "George," he said when he had focused the binoculars. It's a girl with super long brown hair. What's she doing in the middle of nowhere?"

"Good question," George said, edging his tone with suspicion. "And how would she get there?" After clipping the low-pressure inflator hose from the regulator to the BCD, George again squinted at the cliffs. "Nice try, Glen," he said. "I see a lot of glare, some craggy rocks, shadows, more rocks. No girl." He scoffed as he opened the tank's main valve. "You think I'm falling for this shit three days before our birthdays?"

"This isn't a prank," Glen said. "She was there."

"Was...?"

"She moved behind the rocks."

"Whatever you say." The pressure gauge read 2900 psi. George aimed his mouthpiece and pushed the purge valve. With a sharp hiss, air whooshed in Glen's face.

"Bite me," Glen said, steadying himself on the gently rocking boat. He kept the binoculars trained on the cliffs. "Je...sus," he said, with a gasp. "She's back. And wearing a blue, G-string teeny. There's a whole lot of nothing covering her ass."

"Uh, huh," George said. "I suppose now she's taking it off."

"Look for yourself." He handed George the binoculars. "Her hair is tied in a braid that reaches her knees. You'll see."

"Right," George said. "That makes her so much more believable." While spending more time than necessary adjusting the focus for his left eye, he muttered: "Glen, there's something wrong with your eyes. I can barely see through your blurred settings."

"Fuck you. Just look."

George scanned the cliffs. "Nice gulls," he said. "A few of those trees are interesting."

"Over there." Glen grabbed George's elbow and nudged his body to the right. "Quick, before we lose her."

George exaggerated the moment, then finally said: "I don't know what you're up to, but I'm here to dive." He offered the binoculars to Glen.

Glen refused. "Look, there, to the right of that tall outcropping. She's climbing the face of that ledge. I can see her with the naked eye."

"You wish," George said. Then: "You are *so* playing me."

"You care to bet on that?"

"Sure."

"Two silver ingots," Glen said.

"Make them gold and we're on."

"Fine."

"Seriously?" George said. "I was kidding." He raised the binoculars. "There must be *something* there. Even you wouldn't risk that much treasure on a prank."

"I have an idea," Glen said, dashing below deck.

As Glen ducked down the companionway, George raised his dive mask to the sun, using the glass to flash a signal toward the cliffs.

Glen banged around, opened and closed footlockers, slammed a few cabinets, and emerged with a pair of Steiner Marine Navigators. "Use some real binoculars," he said, swapping the Bushnells for the Steiners.

George scanned the cliffs and sighed. "You'll thank me for not taking your bet."

"Bullshit. Give me those."

George lifted the cushion, pulled his shorty wetsuit from the stowage locker, and slipped it on. He tried not to smile.

"Goddamn it," Glen said, after several minutes of searching. "She was there. I swear it."

"I believe you," George said.

"You don't believe shit." Glen slumped onto the seat with the Steiners on his lap. "I'm going to find out who she is. And how she got onto Flowers Island without me knowing."

"As if guests have to sign-in with you." George grabbed two pairs of fins. "Do you want the Seawings or the V-flex?"

"Don't care." Glen scanned for his mystery girl one last time.

"Look," George said. "If you saw what you think you saw, she's probably here to play a role in the Roman Colony." He kept his tone matter of fact. "There's a lesson starting next month."

"Next month? Since when do actors arrive this early?"

"You never know," George said, shrugging. "Do you want to explore this reef, or not?"

"And how did she get to the far end of the island? She can't ride the tram and it would take a day to hike this far."

"There's your first lead," George said.

"What?"

"She must have ridden here. Go to the stables and talk to Barry Dee."

"You think this is a joke."

"No. I'm trying to help. If she's not a serious hiker, she rode a horse. You should also talk to Rollins."

"Ah, duh. I'm not a fuckin' moron."

"No. You're just acting like one."

"I can't help it if I'm feeling a connection. Haven't you ever heard of love at first sight?"

"I've read about it," George said. "In third-rate novels."

"That makes you an expert?"

"You fell in love with the first sight of her ass." George snickered. "Let's focus on getting lucky with this reef."

"Very funny." For a moment, Glen stared into the distance. "Sure, why not."

If there had ever been a shipwreck near this section of reef, the sea had swallowed every coral-encrusted timber. They returned to the marina, Glen silent, George stifling a grin.

The game had begun.

The next day, George left the *Pergamum*, the island's sprawling, multi-story research library with, appropriately, a stack of history books. He heard Glen calling. "George, wait up!" Glen's voice had a plaintive quality George had never heard before.

"How's it going, Glen?" George said, his tone as casual as he could make it.

"George, you have to ask Old Flowers who she is."

While on Flowers Island, Aaron Flowers discouraged the deferential treatment normally accorded to billionaires. He liked "Old Flowers" for its familiarity, and accuracy.

"Whom are you talking about?" George asked, to stretch the tension.

"*Whom* the fuck else? The girl on the cliff. According to Barry Dee, no strangers have borrowed horses. No one in the guest lodge knows anything about her, and the cottage complexes are empty until next month's lesson."

Twelve granite steps led down from the library to a network of hard-packed gravel pathways. Gardens of hydrangeas drooped like French courtiers awaiting a beheading. Boxwood hedges, so desperate for trimming they clawed at George's ankles as he walked by; and grapevines, lush green canopies in the stark, sub-tropical sun, now overgrowing neighboring plants and cloaking all signs of fruit.

"I eventually got through to the North Beach Marina," Glen continued, "but that was a dead end. When I mentioned her to Rollins, he freaked."

"Rollins? Mr. Poise? Mr. Calm?"

"He ordered security to sweep the island for intruders."

"Really." George said, shifting the heavy books to his other arm. "I think you're taking this way too seriously. One might say, over-playing it."

Glen looked away. It wasn't until they had passed the cylindrical ruins of a towering stone sugar mill, an ancient remnant of the island's plantation days, now an overgrown lawn ornament covered with climbing roses, that Glen spoke: "I just want to find out who she is."

"No," George said, "you want me to believe you're desperate to find her."

An untidy mass of hibiscus blocked the path. Glen heaved them aside, knocking half a dozen blooms to the ground. "This isn't a prank, George."

"Six months ago, I would have believed you," George said, staring at the fallen flowers. He mourned their shortened life. They only bloomed for a day as it was, but Glen's negligent gardening had pruned their existence to a few hours. "But two days before our birthdays? Sorry. Can't buy it."

"You almost saw her."

"Do you hear yourself?"

"You know what I mean."

"Yeah. That I should blindly trust that you saw some mysterious super-hot babe, naturally half-naked, who just happened to be on a remote corner of the island when we chanced to show up. Do you see my problem with this?" He handed two of the thicker books to Glen. "At least help me carry these cinder-blocks to my room."

"I can see I won't convince you," Glen said, as they veered onto the path that would take them through the sensory garden. Rosemary and jasmine brightened the air and Flowers Mansion loomed ahead.

"Dude, you're practically asking me to hand you this year's win. Whatever scheme you're cooking up may work. But I'm not going to fall into a trap willingly."

"Okay, I'll find her myself."

"Look," George said, "this place can be a madhouse of comings and goings. In that light, I suppose anything's possible. And I'm not saying I believe you. But, on the off chance that you *did* see someone, maybe your dream girl is a stowaway."

"Stowaway? You mean an actress who hid somewhere and never left the island?"

"Unlikely, but a theory. When you mentioned the long, braided hair, I thought of our Middle Kingdom lesson in the Egyptian Colony."

"That was over three months ago."

"Like I said, an unlikely theory. But with enough ingenuity someone could hide out, forage through a deactivated Culture Colony and—"

"Live for months on stored grains," Glen blurted. "Unharvested potatoes, dried fruit. Hell, she could survive on wild edibles for years. George, you're a fucking genius. That's the only explanation."

*Not the only*, George thought.

"I should ride to the Egyptian Colony."

"No," George said, at the mansion's front door. "You should do your job. The grounds are a mess."

"Oh," Glen said.

"As far as I'm concerned, everything can grow wild. But tomorrow, Old Flowers returns from a conference with the Regional Business Alliance. He won't be pleased when he sees these gardens."

"I know, I know. I spend too many hours on the maze. That, and my greenhouse project."

"What greenhouse project?"

"Propagating a new variety of carambola. The fruit will taste amazing. A combination of mango, papaya, lime, and grapefruit."

"Great. We can eat them while we're stumbling over the grapevines."

"Okay, you've made your point," Glen said. "You think I'm chasing a fantasy."

"Not necessarily. But you should chase her in your spare time."

"Can you at least see if Old Flowers knows about her?"

"I suppose I could visit the Dungeon." Their term for Old Flowers' sub-level study. George paused a moment, deliberating. "If Old Flowers is hosting a mystery guest, Leona will know." Leona was Aaron Flowers' personal assistant, confidant, and companion. She lived in that so-called Dungeon, in an elegant suite of rooms adjacent to Aaron's private study. "But, I can't do it now." Of course, he could, but why spoil Glen's torment? "Jean Francois is pressuring me to finish Chopin's *Mazurka in B minor*. He wants a polished performance tonight so he can introduce me to the *Nocturne in F-sharp major*. His personal favorite. I still need hours of practice."

"But you'll visit the Dungeon after?"

"I'll try," George said, twisting the screws a little tighter.

"Then I'll see you later." Glen handed back the books and walked toward the tool shed.

* * *

When, in his fringe vision, George saw Glen walking into the music room, he finished the last phrase of the *Mazurka in B minor* with a staccato crash of chords. Chopin would have cringed. But after playing the piece twenty times in just the last hour, George needed a resounding musical flourish as a way of saying: "Finally! Finished!"

Glen approached the grand piano and wasted no time on preliminaries. "Well?" he said. "Who is she?"

George swiveled on the bench. "According to Leona, Old Flowers isn't hosting any mystery guests. So now I'm even more convinced."

"Good. You believe me."

"Just the opposite. You're not insane. You weren't high on *ayahuasca*, god mushrooms, or devil's trumpet, and you weren't delirious. That brings us back to the stowaway theory. Which I've considered. But with island security, I can't see someone hiding for months in a deactivated Culture Colony." George closed the key cover and stood. At 6' 1", George towered over Glen's slight, 5' 7" frame. "So, I'm sure you've invented this so-called sighting to distract me from whatever birthday surprise you're plotting."

"Looks like you caught me, George," Glen said as he left the study.

George felt a pang of guilt, brief, but sharp. He hated seeing his friend in distress, but that was part of the challenge. If George pulled it off, this would be an epic surprise. Besides, Glen never faltered when it came to dishing out *his* pranks.

Tomorrow, on their birthday, Glen's suffering would end.

At dawn the next morning, George woke up wet. As always, he had drifted to sleep over the waves of his waterbed. But somehow, Glen had snuck into the bedroom and punctured the mattress. The safety-liner had captured most of the water, but the slow seep had soaked the mattress pad, the sheets, and half the bedspread.

*Happy Birthday*, George thought.

Rolling carefully out of the sloshing bed, he crept to the bathroom, alert for hidden dollops of bird shit (Glen's duties in Old Flowers' aviary gave him ample access to guano), checked for exactly that on his toothbrush, found it clean, and then squeezed a foul-smelling goo from his tube of paste. "Limburger cheese," George muttered. "Good one, Glen." He'd score five points on that prank.

Every towel in the bathroom was damp.

Thanks to years of lessons in the Asian Colony with *sensei* Chang, George had mastered the art of profound sleep. In George's opinion, that, coupled with George's lucid dreaming, allowed Glen an unfair advantage.

But, working through handicaps stiffened the competition.

As did a bathroom lacking toilet paper, a tired prank that would barely net him a point. But, Glen knew that mounting annoyances sometimes resulted in "spoiled sport" penalties. Those came in handy during later stages of the contest.

George leaned into the shower, tested for both hot and cold water, and basked in warmth for a full thirty seconds before the hot stopped abruptly. "Bastard!" he muttered, closing the valves. In his haste, he almost slipped on the marble tile. He used yesterday's tee shirt to dry himself.

"Happy Birthday to meee. Happy Birthday to meee," he hummed, holding his temper.

He grabbed the handle of the closet door. It came off in his hand. Another lame prank. Glen must be building to a Grand Finale. *But nothing like mine,* George thought, a second before discovering that the closet was screwed shut. He had no choice but to wear the now damp tee shirt and yesterday's jeans. The jeans lay crumpled on the floor, right where George had thrown them the night before. But now, one of the legs had been cut off. "You'll never win with two-point pranks," George said to the empty bedroom.

Downstairs at breakfast, George discovered no obvious practical jokes. But that didn't stop him from sniffing for sour milk, tasting for 190 proof alcohol in his grapefruit, and poking around in the oatmeal for hot pepper flakes. Everyone at the table chuckled at his absurd one-legged jeans.

Glen usually ate in the mansion's dining room with everyone else. Today, he was nowhere in sight.

*As I would expect*, George thought.

After breakfast, George visited the music room, played *Catch Me* from Robert Schumann's *Scenes of Childhood,* loitered until he was sure no one was around, and then snuck up to the attic where he had fashioned makeshift quarters for his accomplice. After a brief meeting with her, he left to search for Glen.

His friend wasn't in the gardens, or the greenhouse. George called into the maze—heard no response, and finally spotted Glen crouched behind the tool shed, muttering and swearing. When George poked his head around the corner, Glen quickly shut up.

"Hi, George," Glen beamed, covering his irritation. "Happy Birthday!"

"Happy Birthday, Glen."

Knowing that Glen would be (or, at least, should be) trimming oleanders today, George had painted rosin-rubber mineral oil, the ultra-sticky substance used on fly paper, onto the handles of Glen's hedge clippers.

The piney tang of gum turpentine tickled George's nose as Glen splashed it over tacky hands. "Nice try, Georgie Boy," Glen said. "But cheap, vulgar, and crude will only get you three points."

"Four. Rosin-rubber mineral oil is also tasteless."

"That's debatable."

"And the subtext gets me another four."

"Wow, eight points."

"Doesn't matter. I'm mainly trying to slow you down."

"Love the pants," Glen said, changing the subject and wiping the last of the rosin from his fingers.

"Come on. This could be a long day. Maybe we should grab some breakfast." Of course, George had already eaten.

"Sure," Glen said. "I'm starving."

The two walked toward the mansion, both suspicious, wary, searching for a prank that could come from anywhere.

"Holy Shit!" Glen said, his already high voice suddenly shrill. "There she is!" He pointed to a lily pond at the edge of the lawn that sloped away from Flowers Mansion. A woman with long, dark hair waded into the green water. "You bastard. I told you she was real."

Glen sprinted down the lawn with George following.

When they arrived thirty seconds later, Glen paused at the water's edge, confused, or afraid. He had captured his prey, but didn't know what to do next. Scarcely ten feet away, standing waist deep in rippling rings of water, the woman turned, slowly, just as George had instructed.

"No," Glen gasped, as she hurled the wig to shore. Then, "Sara?"

Sara was Glen's older sister, and the confidante and protector who had guided him through years of placement in the Calvary Orphan's Ministry. Rescued by Aaron Flowers when Sara was fourteen and Glen seven, she now lived in El Rincón, a small town in the former state of California.

Surprise!

*Yep,* George thought, with no lack of self-congratulation, *last year I won the game with points to spare, a true Grand Triumph.*

On his way to the East Wing through the gardens of the Mansion Complex, he imagined himself in the Roman Colony driving a four-horse chariot. Before him, wagons brimmed with spoils—gold, jewels, the armor and weapons of his vanquished foes, cages of exotic birds and wild animals—and following the plunder wagons, hundreds of captured enemies, all bent and humbled in chains. Crowds on both sides of *Via Trionfale,* the road leading to Capitoline Hill, deafened the air with cries and salutes. With his face painted red and a purple toga fluttering in the breeze, George raised his arms to nobles and *civitas* alike, welcoming their praise with a humble smile. A public slave, standing beside him in the chariot, leaned to his ear and whispered at regular intervals: "Remember, you are mortal." Loyal cohorts trailed behind, unarmed soldiers dressed in togas and wearing laurel crowns, chanting: "io triumphe!" under clouds of frankincense and downpours of violets and roses. Clappers, cymbals, and drums thumped and clashed as flutes frolicked with strumming *citharas.*

But George's fantasy had not even progressed to the Roman games or the evening's victory banquets before dread seized his imagination.

Laughter, its tone brimming with maniacal delight, was bouncing off the granite walls, echoing down the garden paths, and escaping into the maze.

"Shit," George muttered, his Roman reverie dashed on the shores of whatever Glen was up to.

*This can't be good,* George thought as he turned the corner.

Glen leaned against the Mansion wall, still laughing, his index finger pointing up to George's bedroom. "Happy Eighteenth!" he cried.

Hanging below the railing of his bedroom veranda, a thirty-foot banner announced to the world: GEORGE MADE HASTE ON JENNY'S WAIST in giant red letters on a stark white background.

George dropped the bag containing the cinnamon roll. "Holy Gods," he gasped. The words nearly choked him. His darkest secret was draped across the stone face of Flowers Mansion.

"You Fil-lon-chi slime," George groaned, using one of Glen's own curse words. His fists clenched. He didn't give a damn about losing spoiled sport points.

*Spoiled sport points?!*

He scanned the gardens, saw the unoccupied gazebo, noticed no one rowing on the pond.

So far, he was safe.

But for how long?

Images of Jenny brought him back to Ancient Rome.

She had arrived on Flowers Island nearly a year ago, just after George and Glen's seventeenth birthdays. From the first glance, she became an obsession in George's life, an obsession transformed into humiliation.

They had acted together in the Roman Colony town of *Norba*—she in the role of beautiful Selinia, daughter of a wealthy aristocrat; George playing, Antonius, a slave assigned to the Roman menagerie.

They had noticed each other in the marketplace, and for the rest of the afternoon, George maneuvered himself through the crowd capturing glances of auburn hair, a fragment of profile, a glimpse of smile.

Selinia returned his attentions. The air of aristocratic haughtiness dropped. Her gaze told him she was seeing more than a dirty slave boy, but Roman custom forbade courtship between their classes.

That same day, he followed her to the door of her father's mansion.

That same night, George, as Antonius, snuck over the wall and hid in the branches of a sprawling oak. He watched the house, heard laughter, scolding, commands to the slaves, the barking dogs, the endless cackling of exotic birds. Selinia even passed through the courtyard, right beneath him, but was accompanied by servants.

The next night, he again crept through the courtyard, this time, hiding behind the pedestal of a bronze sundial. Almost invisible crouched in the shadows of the family's hyacinth garden, he barely stirred for almost an hour. Finally, he mustered the courage to throw pebbles through Selinia's window.

The sound alerted the family bodyguard.

George darted to the wall and scaled a lattice of bougainvillea as the guard emerged from the house.

Undeterred, Antonius returned the following night to the relative safety of the oak tree, hoping that Selinia, as smitten as he, would somehow sense his presence and gift him with smiles.

Such were the fruitless dreams on another aching vigil. No amount of staring at her bedroom, or wishing the branches below her window could support his weight, would allow, as Ovid said: *"Two adolescents to explore the booby-trapped world of adult passions and temptations."*

But, George did see her 21st century counterpart, Jenny, when the lesson was over. Even without the romance of the Roman Colony, the attraction remained.

They arranged a meeting in the woods the night before Jenny's return to the mainland. But for George, tension and excitement were too great. The weeks of longing, the fantasies, the anticipation, heightened every second of their first moments together.

The moon was bright, the summer warm and sweet. The vision of Jenny, at last, naked in a scent-drenched meadow, realized.

Kneeling between her legs, savoring her beauty, stroking her budding breasts, arousal overwhelmed all control and...

GEORGE MADE HASTE ON JENNY'S WAIST.

"You traitorous bastard," George growled, grabbing Glen by the collar. "You call that a birthday surprise?"

"It surprised you, didn't it?" Glen said with a snicker, even though George outweighed him by thirty pounds.

George tightened his grip. "I told you about Jenny because I thought you were my friend."

"Come on, Georgie, relax. This is only a game."

"Then I'm finished playing. If you want points, okay, you win. And fuck you for not having the decency to protect my privacy—let alone Jenny's."

"Wait a minute," Glen said, trying to squirm away. "Jesus, George, I didn't think you'd take it so hard. If you'll excuse the pun." He laughed. "Let me explain."

George loosened his grip with a shove.

"Look," Glen said. "I meant this in the spirit of good fun."

"Fun? Hanging my guts on the wall?"

"Come on. Do you really think I'd do anything to hurt you?"

"Then what's that?" George said, pointing to the banner.

"It's like this, Georgie. Your *real* birthday surprise is me climbing up there and taking it *down*." Glen's laughter boomed over the grounds, and was loud enough to attract unwanted attention. "Aren't you surprised I'd do that?"

George stared in pissed silence. But after a moment, even he had to smile. "Fuckin' prick. You'll do anything to score points."

"Almost. But I wouldn't dream of broadcasting your love life all over the island. It's just that it's getting harder and harder to surprise you. Besides, you've won the last two years." He jabbed George's chest with his index finger. "This year, it's my turn."

"I'll concede you twenty points," George said.

"If I showed this to the committee, which I won't, they'd give me thirty points for surprise factor alone."

"The committee would penalize you for sinking so low."

"Okay, twenty-five points and this surprise is between you and me."

"Deal." George glanced over his shoulder. "Can you get rid of that thing before someone walks by?"

"Sure, George, Happy Birthday." Glen climbed the trellis, grabbed the banner, and with a hefty jerk, yanked it away from the ivy. It landed at George's feet.

"Well," Glen said, climbing down. "There went a shit ton of work for a few minutes fun. That banner took me hours to paint. Look at these scratches. Do you think I'd do this if I didn't like you?"

"Never waste a joke on an enemy."

"No hard feelings?"

"Sure, you fucking shithead."

"There's something else you need to know, George."

"What's that?"

"I'm gonna win this year."

"Really?"

"Guaranteed. That scheme last year with my sister? That was a masterpiece. So, this year, be prepared for the ultimate surprise."

George studied Glen's expression. "You look serious."

"I am."

George reached down and grabbed the paper bag. He passed the cinnamon roll to Glen. "Is this your ultimate surprise? Is it filled with mustard or something?"

Glen tore the roll in half. "See? No mustard. I don't play food pranks anymore." He took a bite. "Delicious, as usual. This island would starve without Miss Ruth."

George agreed and ate the other half.

"By the way," George said, gesturing to the banner. "I want that."

"Of course. It only holds deep significance for you."

"Yeah. I'm considering a ceremonial burn in the Roman Temple." He rolled the cloth into a tight bundle and began crossing the lawn.

Glen called after him. "Good luck in the Grecian Colony. I won't be seeing you until tonight. I'm taking the tram over to North Beach."

*Great*, George thought with a scowl. *Glen's the last person I want at North Beach today.* "Why?" George asked, turning back.

"It's my birthday. No gardening. Good time for maintenance on the *Valdaquez*."

"You're going to clean those bilges on your birthday?" George said, immediately suspicious.

"It's my turn, remember?"

"I know, but—"

"And I'm also gonna check the sea strainer, cycle the watermaker, and fill the scuba tanks. I'll be back in plenty of time for tonight's festivities."

"Not a good idea," George said.

"What?"

"Look." George turned away for dramatic effect. "I hate to bring this up. But..."

"Spit it out."

"If you're so in the mood for shitty jobs, you might want to clean the aviary instead."

Glen gaped. "Shit. Did Old Flowers say something?"

"Yes."

"Fuck. What did you tell him?"

"I told him your work in the greenhouse was taking longer than you thought. I told him the African violets looked fantastic. He seemed pleased."

"Thanks. It may seem like a little thing to you, George, but if that's the only birthday present I get this year, it would be enough."

George laughed.

"Seriously. You may have saved my job. I should have cleaned that aviary days ago. It's just that..."

"It's just what?"

"I'm developing a phobia for those rat-assed birds."

"Come on."

"It's true. It takes five hours to clean that overgrown birdcage and I can't stand the place."

"You only do it twice a month."

"That's why I haven't poisoned the birdseed." A longtail landed on one of the hedges a few feet away. Glen's face twisted into a scowl. "George, I hate birds."

"Since when?" George said, his second biggest surprise of the day. He thought he knew every kink in Glen's twisted personality.

"Since always. I just never told you."

"Why the hell not? Spiders make me nauseous. You hate birds. Nobody can love everything. Besides, I don't mind cleaning the aviary. We could trade jobs."

"And have Old Flowers find out I despise his pets? "

"You've got a point."

Glen kicked a chunk of grass out of the lawn. "Shit. I'd like to clean that aviary with a flame thrower."

"Look, maybe we can work something out. Do it today and tomorrow we can both deal with the boat. When we get there, we'll decide whether to dive the *Temperance*, or heal from tonight's party."

"You're right. I better clean the aviary today. Tomorrow, I couldn't go in there without a barf bag."

"So, I'll see you tonight?"

"Of course. By the way, I was serious about the Grecian Colony."

"What do you mean?"

"I mean, good luck. You'll need it."

George laughed. "I could say my lines backwards." He tucked the banner under his arm and turned to leave, then stopped. "But I think I know what you're getting at. Something about this Plato lesson doesn't feel right. It's too easy."

"Yeah."

For a moment, neither spoke. Then Glen said: "Who knows? Maybe you've worked hard enough already. Maybe Old Flowers is going soft. The fact is, the sooner you pass the damn test, the sooner we tour the world." Glen pinched his fingers together. "I can't believe we're this close to getting off Flowers Island. Not that I don't love it here. It's just that the United Nation is so, I don't know, vast. Can you imagine hiking the Andes, checking out *Ollantaytambo*, the Sacred Valley, scaling *Huayna Picchu* and looking down on Inca ruins? Then *Isla de Pascua*, Stonehenge, the Forbidden City, Paris, Prague, the pyramids of Giza?"

"Those places hardly seem real."

"Oh, they are. You'll see. You pass today and a month from now we're out of here. That's when your real lessons begin."

"Yeah," George said, looking away. "I'll see you later."

Glen squeezed George's shoulder. "Really. Good luck."

Glen left to clean the aviary.

*Good luck.*

The words unnerved him. *Focus on the present*, George thought. *Think about North Beach, the excitement Glen will feel when he rides his Arabian stallion. Forget the Grecian Colony.*

But something in Glen's tone, something ominous, worried him.

He turned toward the stables.

*It's only my imagination.*

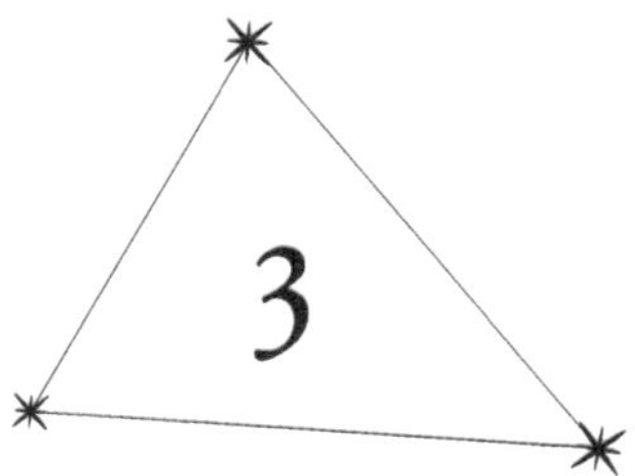

When George arrived at the stables a few minutes later, the island's wrangler, Barry Dee, was brushing down Satin, an aptly named gleaming black mare with a white, diamond-shaped blush on her forehead.

Some stranger, a short, chubby guy about George's age, leaned against one of the horse stalls.

"Morning, Barry," George called, as he entered the stable. He glanced around for a safe place to hide the banner.

"Mornin' George," Barry mumbled over a plug of chew. He hawked a brown wad from the mass deforming his lower lip. "What ya got there?" he said, pointing to the banner.

"Nothing," George lied. "Just a little surprise for Glen," he lied again.

Barry grunted. "This here's Bruce. Davidson's boy."

Michael Davidson was the island's Writer in Residence. He had lived on Flowers Island off and on for years, dividing his time between writing historical novels and tutoring George on the prose styles of Elizabethan authors like Edmund Spencer and Sir Phillip Sidney. George enjoyed Michael's lectures and his writings, but especially thanked Davidson for introducing him to the satirical works of Joseph Hall, Thomas Middleton, and Cyril Tourneur.

George and Bruce shook hands, a gesture that soiled George's palm with some brown and grainy substance. *Good one, Glen,* George thought. He wiped the hand on his jeans and smiled as if nothing had happened. "I'm a great admirer of your father's work," George said. Bruce's fingernails were filthy and he wore a multi-colored, but grubby tee shirt with a "Band X" logo. Below, in a similar font, but barely legible, the words "X-Pand", apparently, the title of something musical. Incredibly, Bruce's sweat overpowered the stable's tang of horse manure. The stink was so strong it reminded George of one of his harsher lessons in the Roman Colony—the crowded barracks he'd shared with fellow slaves. "Your father is an excellent teacher," he said, still wincing at the Roman memory.

"If you say so," Bruce replied, more a derisive grunt. "I never read his versions of history. I prefer my own."

Bruce grinned, but like everyone who met George for the first time, Bruce stared at the scar on the left side of George's neck, the result of an accident in that same Roman Colony. George still hadn't learned to accept the stares. Instead, he deflected them by diverting attention to his piano playing, his fluency in languages; his juggling, a poetry reading, a new painting, some gymnastic stunt. With photographic recall, he would memorize a novel in the time it took to flick the pages, then recite the text verbatim from any page requested. Parlor tricks in the service of temporary distraction.

The permanent fix, cosmetic surgery, wasn't an option. The island's Rule of Separation forbade it.

Bruce continued smiling with his strange, artificial grin; made comical by small, even, too-white teeth that looked like dabs of paint on a puppets face. His hair, both dirty blond and dirty (*no surprise there, Glen*), looked like a wet mop dried in the sun and glued onto a dummy's head. George moved a casual step away—to escape the reeking armpits—and to better appreciate the pleasing scent of horseshit.

"I'm too scientific to get excited about literature," Bruce said. "I'm studying Immunology at Grand Trinity University."

"Really," George said, without much interest. He averted his eyes from Bruce's round, red cheeks for fear of laughing. "So, you're here visiting your father?"

Barry Dee shifted his weight and spit a brown wad over his left shoulder. Bruce Davidson grimaced. "Pretty much," he said, turning back to George. "My father hoped I could get a look at the Culture Colonies."

Barry coughed, and only a snort from the mare and the scuff of the grooming brush disturbed the silence. "Yessir," Barry said, finally, "there's plenty a' culture in them Colonies, ain't there George?"

George got the hint. "I wish I had time to show you around, Bruce," he said. "But today is bad for sightseeing. Besides, the island's Rule of Separation forbids mixing the present with the past. Except for maintenance personnel and certain island residents, no one visits deactivated Colonies. They're not museums."

Barry stopped brushing the mare. "That's the truth, George," he said. "But Bruce's pa weren't talkin' about violatin' the Rule. I suspect he figgered you could show Bruce the Colonies from Madeira Point. It ain't out a yer way."

"I'm only here for one day," Bruce said. "I won't have another chance."

George hesitated. "I have to go to the far end of the island. I don't think I—"

"Well Brucie," Barry blurted, slapping Bruce on the shoulder. "I guess I got ya all excited fer nothin'."

Clearly, Barry had already promised Bruce the tour, and now felt embarrassed that he couldn't deliver.

"As I was about to say," George said, with a glance at Barry. "I don't think I would lose much time if I took you as far as Madeira Point. You could ride back on your own."

Bruce Davidson grinned as Barry Dee darted into the tack room. Moments later, Barry heaved a western saddle onto the mare's back, snugged the front cinch and laced the latigo. When he had secured the rear cinch and breast collar, he said to George: "Zander's all saddled up and waitin' outside in the corral." He led George and Bruce through a wide barn door and into the blinding daylight. "Little warm maybe, but a fine day for a ride," Barry said. He squinted into the sun. "Ya better turn yer tail, Georgie, if ya wanna get that stallion back in time fer today's exam." He hawked a wad to the ground, almost hitting Bruce's shoes, then grunted loudly, as if sorry he'd missed. "Oh, why I 'bout forgot. Happy birthday, George. Yer gettin' to be near a full man."

George smiled. "I'm working on it."

"Come on, Brucie, let's get you acquainted with Satin here. She's a gentle soul, but yer gonna wanna..."

While Barry was dealing with Bruce, George turned the corner and unlatched the metal gate to the corral. His horse, Zander, grazed on a pile of hay at the far end. *That will do for now*, he thought, noticing an old milk canister sitting below a pair of open shutters. He crept along the outside of the stable, then crouched below the shutters. Carefully, and as quietly as possible, he removed the rusty lid and stuffed the banner into the canister. Barry's hoarse whisper, amplified by the concave ceiling of the open barn, drifted through the opening.

"I give yer credit for lookin' ignorant as hell, Brucie—if that's yer real name." Barry sniffed. "It's gonna get pretty obvious if they keep sendin' creatures like you in here." A moment of silence, then: "This is serious business, don't they know that?" George pressed against the wall, his hearing acute. "Tell me, Brucie," Barry went on, "do yer ride a horse like the lame goose yer look?" Then a deep, jagged laugh.

"I can probably ride better than you," Bruce said, his tone flat. "And you can shut your phony bumpkin yap." He hadn't a trace of anger in his voice. "I don't see why I can't have a little fun with this. I won't give anything away. You watch *your* ass."

*Ah, ha,* George thought. *Glen's got* two *accomplices for his "ultimate surprise". That will cost him points.*

Barry Dee grumbled. "Relax, sonny, you'll have yer fun. But it's a long way to the mainland if George gets hurt."

*Hurt?*

George scuttled along the wall and retrieved his horse.

Barry launched into an uproarious laugh when George led Zander out of the corral.

"What's so funny?" George asked, hiding his discomfort with a smile.

Barry offered up a chew-dripping grin. "Oh, I was just learnin' from Bruce about this Immuno...oh, whatever it is, that germ shit he's studyin'. He's tellin' me them future germs is gonna make my life better. Screw that. I like the germs I already got."

George forced a chuckle and mounted his horse. Bruce followed. "We'd better leave before Barry starts telling germ jokes," George said.

Barry scoffed, turned away, and without a word, pointed to an old Mercedes Benz hubcap nailed onto a post about ten feet away. "You wait up, Georgie!" Barry cried. "I think I smell bullshit!"

*Here he goes,* George thought.

Barry spread his arms like two wings, and with a grace you wouldn't expect from his old body, swayed back and forth building up momentum.

And one, and two, and...

He sucked in a violent breath—then thwack—blasted a hideous brown slime dead center into the Mercedes triangle.

"Eee, yessir!" Barry screamed, slapping his knee. "I can puke cannonballs when I see enough bullshit." He glared at Bruce. "George, don't go steppin' in no science, today, ya hear?"

"I'll do my best," George called back as he nudged Zander toward the trail.

When they entered the woods, George turned in his saddle. "What'd you say to piss him off?"

"Nothing," Bruce said. "The old bastard just needed to shoot his mouth."

Only one horse trail, twenty-two miles long, cut through the middle of Flowers Island, linking the North Beach marina with the Mansion Complex; one trail, with no appendages branching off to the Culture Colonies. As Aaron Flowers intended, travel to and from the Colonies was via an underground tram built into the vast network of caverns that honeycombed the island. When a lesson was underway, the island's employees, along with the actors and historians chosen for their knowledge of the past, all rode the tram at one-quarter speed, in total darkness, emerging later into the light of another century. Between Colony lessons, only George and anyone invited to accompany him, had permission to wander freely on the surface. Others required special passes authorized by Aaron Flowers and issued by Rollins.

George glanced over his shoulder. Bruce's painted smile glared against a backdrop of dark junipers and cedars, his little white grin a perfect vision of insincerity.

When the terrain allowed, George urged Zander into a brisk trot, keeping a shout's distance ahead of Bruce. No time to dawdle, no time to talk, he told himself. North Beach is still two hours away.

But time wasn't the real reason for silence.

The conversation he had overheard at the stable formed a Mobius loop in his mind. Why had Barry called Bruce a "creature?" What did he mean by: "... it's a long way to the mainland if George gets hurt?" And would Glen enlist this "creature", a stranger to George (he didn't believe for a second that Bruce was Michael Davidson's son), in a birthday surprise that might be dangerous?

The trail carved deeper into the thicket, rose gradually for another mile, then widened into a grassy meadow. A sudden memory of last night's dream—peasants dancing, leather, cypress, sun searing his face—whirled in George's mind for a snap of a second, then faded as he felt his body swaying in the saddle.

Bruce used the improved condition of the trail to narrow the gap. "George, wait up!" he cried.

*No way,* George thought. *Whatever Glen's game, I won't trap easily.* "We're almost there," George yelled back. "Come on!" He prodded Zander into a gallop; dashing up a gradual incline toward the small plateau Old Flowers had named Madeira Point. At the top, he pulled hard on the reins.

"You're a born equestrian," George said, when Bruce thundered to a halt beside him.

"I've ridden a time or two," he said, either modest or a liar.

"Really," George said.

"Yeah, back in summer camp." A gust blew swirls of dust across the plateau, causing Satin to jitter. "Whoa, there!" Bruce said, calming the mare with authority.

George swept his arm across the horizon. *I can play Glen's game,* he thought. *My way.*

"This is Madeira Point," he said. "It's the only spot on the island that gives a view of all the Colonies. Of course, the Egyptian and Medieval Colonies are too far away to offer much detail, but if you look closely to the east, you can make out the spires and domes of Byzantion, a small city in the Middle Eastern Colony. And there..." George pointed to the southeast. "That's the Aztec Temple of *Ehecatl.* It sits on an island just off the northern shore of Lake Sisyphus."

Sliding off his saddle, Bruce walked a few yards to the edge of the plateau. "Unbelievable," he said, followed by a gasp. "Such a bogus crock of shit."

"What?" George said.

"How can you have an Aztec Colony in a Grecian lake?"

"Well, Sisyphus is just a name we—"

"And those spires and domes in your city of Byzantion? First off, Byzantion was a trading city on the coast of the Black Sea. It wasn't in the middle of the woods. And second, that style of dome never existed in the ancient city of Byzantion. It's from a much later period. From this distance, I'd guess around 600 A.D., not B.C."

"All the Colonies function as templates for lessons from various periods of history," George said. "They're not always one hundred percent historically accurate."

"Don't kid yourself, George. They're not historically accurate *at all.* Real history, true history, is layer upon jumbled layer of so-called civilizations rising from ruined societies that themselves rose from prior ruins. These Culture Colonies are nothing more than your father's personal *version* of history. In other words, historical fantasies no better than my father's silly novels."

"Even if that were true," George said, his grip tightening on the saddle's pommel. "They can still teach a lot about human culture."

"Again," Bruce said, "your father's perspective of human culture." He turned to face George. "Look. I'm not saying these Colonies aren't magnificent. If nothing else, I'm in awe of the logistical accomplishment—the engineering, the material transport, marshalling the labor, all of it." Grabbing Satin's reins, Bruce led the mare a hundred feet to the far western edge of the plateau. Of course, Bruce would never make the connection, but from that spot on Madeira Point one could see in the distance a branch of the Egyptian Colony's Fayum River feeding a section of Roman Colony aqueducts. A juxtaposition of historical periods that George had never pondered before. For a moment, he considered this cultural mingling in the context of Bruce's critiques, then quashed any notions of their validity. Glen knew George better than anyone. He had clearly coached Bruce in the best way to get under George's skin. Reacting angrily to Bruce's insults of the Culture Colonies, to George's upbringing, or to questions of Old Flowers' motivations would only result in "spoiled sport" points that George could ill afford to lose. "How many years did it take to build all this?" Bruce was asking. "And how much money?"

"What?" George said, emerging from deep reverie.

"How many years—"

"I heard you," George snapped, irritation defeating reason after all and paving the way for spoiled sport points. He inhaled a deep, calming breath. The action reinforced the patience and hospitality that Bruce's arrogance had frayed. "My father built the first Colony in 1960," George said with an even tone. "The last was finished thirty-eight years later, one year before I was born. I have no idea how much it all cost."

"I guess I can believe that," Bruce said. "But do you know what it all means?"

George narrowed his gaze and studied Bruce's silly puppet cheeks, his too-white painted grin. "I don't understand your question."

"The point. The purpose."

"Isn't it obvious?" George said. "Education."

"Maybe on the surface. But I'm referring to the real purpose. You said your old man didn't build museums. What do you *really* do here?"

*Where did Glen find this guy?* George thought. He wanted to slap Bruce's smirk all the way to the Egyptian Colony. But he said in a clear, almost academic voice: "Is it so hard to imagine that my father worships art and culture? Is it inconceivable that he should re-create the past as a way of teaching about the present?" George pointed to the Aztec Colony. "For example, we don't just study *quipus*, the so-called 'talking knots', we use the type of wool, its color, and the shape of the knots to send messages, record lunar cycles, register tax obligations, compile census records, and tell stories. We utilize the tools of ancient cultures, farm similar crops, build with native materials, worship esteemed gods, follow local customs, and live with ancient artifacts. That gives us a true appreciation of human history."

"Bullshit," Bruce said, with a dismissive wave. "You could pillage every museum on Earth without finding enough artifacts to stock your Colonies."

"Of course, they're reproductions."

"More fakery."

"Call it what you like," George said, eager to be done with this charade. "I'm going to North Beach." He pointed to the trail behind them. "The stables are that way. You can't get lost if you stay on the path."

"Must be hard to find people willing to milk goats, or plow fields with sharpened sticks," Bruce said, making no attempt to mount his horse.

"On the contrary. Thousands apply every year."

"Desperate actors looking for a gig?"

*Sure,* George thought, *actors like you. But a lot more convincing.* "Colony lessons are open to *anyone* who can pass the audition," George answered, his words aimed at Bruce. "But most applicants are at least semi-professional, either in theater, or films. My father hires people who can sustain their parts for long periods. They're also well versed in the chosen culture, the lesson's era, and they pass a series of difficult examinations. Ideally, they look, act, and even think their roles."

"So, you live in this phony past and try to act like you've never seen a television, a movie theater, or a rock concert?" Qualms and feelings fused with loss, failure, and exclusion—even banishment. George had experienced television, movie theaters, and rock concerts, but only in books. "What do you and your actors do if a plane flies over?"

"Planes?" George said.

"Yeah. What if a jet flies over during a lesson?"

"I don't know. I guess whatever the Ancient Greeks, or the Egyptians, or the Romans would do."

"You mean freak out."

"Probably. Though I've never seen planes during a Colony lesson."

"Your old man has connections."

"No. It's the magnetic fields. In this part of the Atlantic, instruments tend to malfunction. Air lanes don't cross over Flowers Island."

"Very convenient for the Ancient Greeks, I'm sure. And how long do you play these culture games? Days, weeks?"

"Depends on the lesson."

"And outside the Colonies. Does everybody dress up like Ancient Egyptians on Egyptian holidays?"

"No. My life outside the Colonies is normal."

"Normal?" Bruce laughed. "That's a good one."

"It is normal," George said, his claim as vacant as the Roman Coliseum. Temper growled behind a forced calm. "Aside from my lessons in the Colonies, my life is no different than anyone else's."

"Sure, George, anything you say."

"All right, what's so different about it?"

"I could give you a list. And I've only been here since last night."

"I'm listening," George said.

"Okay. There's no internet, for one thing, no cell service, no alcohol, not even beer, and nobody smoke cigarettes, let alone anything good. The library is crammed with literary garbage and enough boring history to choke a mastodon.

The food reminds me of that guru shit I once gagged down in San Francisco, and worst of all, there's no flat screen with a satellite connection. You'd think there would be, at the very least, a television with a few DVDs."

George stared into the woods. "Television is forbidden," he said.

While Satin nibbled on patches of grass, Bruce strolled along the edge of the plateau, still fascinated by the Colonies. "On the other hand," he said, "you've got your own private Disney World. That's pretty cool." He called back to George. "I suppose you always play Prince Flowers, the royal student of culture."

Despite the twitch in his jaw, the result of teeth-clenching exasperation, George granted Glen a grudging respect. He had prepped Bruce with sadistic ingenuity. Exploited George's frustration with life on Flowers Island, the relentless study, the exercises, the doubts about the meaning of it all. To say nothing of George's questions about his true place in the world, the greater world, the world beyond wealth and privilege, the world shared by the majority, the world of the common man. The urge to discover that world burned in both George and Glen, more so as they approached their eighteenth birthdays. But soon, they'd be free to leave Flowers Island and taste real life, liberated from schedules, lessons, and training. They would revel in that moment.

"I've played the part of royalty once or twice," George said, still annoyed, but now absorbed enough in Glen's game to want to play it out. This was, after all, leading to Glen's "ultimate surprise". "But during most of my Colony lessons, I live like anybody else. I get no special treatment."

"Sure," Bruce said, with well-lathered sarcasm.

*Goddamn bastard!* George thought. Even though he knew this was an act, something about Bruce's snotty little grin still infuriated. This role of haughty prick seemed too natural, too effortless. His tousled hair and stinking pits mocked hygiene in the same way his grubby mind ridiculed Colonies.

*Prince Flowers, indeed,* George thought. He remembered one of his earliest and most bitter lessons. He had been the farthest thing from a prince in that Colony.

As Bruce paced from one end of the plateau to the other, George felt a sudden urge to violate the Rule of Separation, reveal how frightening and strenuous the Colonies could be. *You want the truth,* George thought. *I'll shove it down your annoying face.*

"I shouldn't be telling you this," George said.

This piqued Bruce's interest. He stopped, giving George his full attention.

"But, since you're Michael Davidson's son." *In your dreams*, George thought. "It probably won't hurt."

"I'm listening," Bruce said, smug, stifling a yawn.

George leaned forward in the saddle and pointed toward the Roman Colony. "Many years ago, I was sent to the town of *Helvia Recina*, a small *municipium*, or town, and without a part to play. I wasn't sure what to do, but everyone else was. They treated me like an outcast, a common urchin. Sometimes I worked in the stables, or the granary. At one point, I was lucky and found a potter who offered me gruel and bread in exchange for a day of mixing grout. But even that didn't last long. I was cast away for no reason and ended up hoeing the fields. Later, I begged when I couldn't find work.

"For weeks, I lived in the streets with runaway slaves and drunken war veterans. At night, I hid in alleys to avoid stampeding horses and screaming chariot drivers. I barely slept thanks to the constant din of the city. Soldiers patrolled the streets, trying to keep order, but even wealthy citizens with armed bodyguards were beaten and robbed." George turned his attention back to Bruce. "And every night I witnessed the *plebeian's* favorite sport."

With a sneer, Bruce asked: "And what was that, pray tell?"

"It didn't have a name. But they loved throwing objects from windows; bricks, clay pots, sharp objects, each other. I was lucky. They never hit me with anything but garbage and shit."

Bruce guffawed. Delight in the image of Aaron Flowers' son, covered in garbage, gleamed in his eyes. "And you expect me to believe that?" Bruce said, when he stopped snickering.

"You can believe anything you want," George snapped, so annoyed with Bruce, and so weary of this farce, he was ready to admit that Glen had earned a dramatic victory—by default—through the sheer quantity of spoiled sport points.

George closed his eyes. He wanted to end the questions, the probing, and the penetrating analysis of his life and all its whys and wherefores.

"Don't get pissed," Bruce said. "This is what scientists do. We look for truth."

"You're looking at it now," George said, pulling up on Zander's reins. "You should learn to recognize it."

"Relax." Bruce's smile taunted back. "It's not my fault you live in a dream world." A look, quizzical, but false and exaggerated, crossed Bruce's face. "That's funny," he said. "I just had a déjà vu. I remember a dream about being here before."

"And I'm the one living in a dream world?" George said, relishing the barb.

Bruce stared. "What's down there?" He pointed to a spot over George's right shoulder."

In the distance, about half a mile away, the outline of a hut. Grey stone gleamed in the mid-morning sun, in stark relief against the green background of the forest. "Nothing. An abandoned shack," George said. "I played there as a kid."

Bruce guided the reins over his horse's neck and heaved onto the saddle. "I remember that hut," he blurted, wide-eyed. "It's inside."

*Here we go*, George thought. *The prelude is over. Time for Glen's "ultimate surprise".* "What's inside?" he said, not sure why he was still playing along.

"You'll find out." Bruce leaned forward and heeled the mare's flanks. The horse lurched down the meadow toward the hut.

George watched them shrink slowly down the hill. But instead of following, he focused on the horizon, on the view from Madeira Point, trying to see all the Colonies at once. His vision blurred and transformed the Colonies into masses of brilliant color blotched over a green landscape; two dimensional, unreal, a trick.

Just like Bruce.

With a gentle nudge, George urged Zander down the hill, arriving at the hut several minutes later. He had played along in the spirit of good birthday fun, and lost. Now, he had to get this over with. He was still certain, well, fairly certain, that Glen knew nothing about the stallion. If he could stomach playing along with Bruce, just a bit longer, pretend he had no idea a bunch of friends were hiding in the shadows, ready to scream "Happy Birthday" when George stepped into the hut, he could still get to North Beach and retrieve the horse.

*Nice try, Glen,* he thought. *But I doubt the judges would consider a surprise party in an old hut all that "ultimate".*

He tied Zander to the branch of a blown-down juniper. Satin grazed a few feet away, untethered.

Glancing around, feigning casualness, he looked for any signs of activity. Nothing but age and decay. He remembered digging secret underground forts here, and building a crude treehouse. A shallow pit was all that remained of the fort, and climbing vines had swallowed the treehouse. As far as George knew, no one had ever even lived here. But some worker from the island's army of maintenance personnel had once tended beds of begonia and heliotrope. A few flowers still survived among the weeds that bordered the cottage. The vegetable garden (its sole produce now a few fluffy stalks of pampas grass), the grapevines, and the cedar fence had long ago disappeared under thorny brambles.

The earth felt marshy from the drench of summer storms, but as George picked his way through the brambles, only Bruce's tracks were visible. The others knew how to play the game. They had arrived stealthily.

He approached the front door, saddened to see a rotting slab of termite-infested oak hanging from one hinge. As he leaned over the threshold, dust prickled his nostrils, then mold, then damp. A single chair under a rough-hewn table, a fireplace half-filled with blackened logs, and a window on the far wall, boarded up, like two others he had seen outside emerged from the gloom when he stepped into the hut. "Bruce!" he called out.

"Back here!" Bruce cried from the next room. "What took you?"

*Act surprised*, George told himself as he crossed the room to what he remembered was the bedroom. The wide plank floor squeaked under his feet.

"It's about time," Bruce said. He stood ten feet away beside a rat-eaten mattress with a lighted match at eye level. His wooden grin stared through the flame and his right arm was behind his back, as if shielding something from view. He was alone.

"I considered not coming at all," George lied. It further irritated him to be wrong about the surprise party. "What the hell is going on here? I've got two hours to get to North Beach. Then, if I'm lucky, I might get to the Grecian Colony in time for my exam." He clenched his fists. "Whatever you're up to isn't making things easier."

"Relax, Prince Flowers," Bruce said. "I told you I had a vision, a déjà vu, and I remember being here before. Doesn't that amaze you?"

"Your capacity for bullshit amazes me."

The match burned too close to Bruce's fingers. He shook it out and spoke through the blackness. "Call it bullshit if you like, but I knew it would be here. I found it. And I'm keeping it."

"Keeping what?"

A light thud as Bruce placed something on the floor, then a moment of fumbling with the matches. A second later, orange light flared over his face. He reached down and picked up the object he'd been hiding behind his back. "Somebody hid this under the floorboards next to the bed." He held the object next to the flame and George gasped. Bruce laughed. "Incredible, isn't it?"

Even under the light of a single match, the stunning golden chalice radiated a familiar, deep yellow glow. Somehow, the priceless ritual chalice from the temple of the Grecian Colony, the Chalice of Dionysus, had ended up in this abandoned hut. *Impossible*, George thought. Glen would never violate the Rule of Separation like this, would never steal the Chalice of Dionysus, would under no circumstances risk his job and life on Flowers Island for the sake of a birthday surprise.

Though George had to admit, he *was* surprised.

But was there another explanation?

"Who are you?" George said. "Please don't tell me Glen put you up to this?"

"Who the fuck is Glen? Ouch! Goddamn it!" The room blackened again.

Another thump as the chalice landed on the mattress. A match flared. "My old man told me about this island," Bruce said, greed swelling his voice. "I know about the pirates. I know about the caverns and the loot hidden everywhere." He tittered. "If this isn't one of your phony artifacts, it's going to buy my freedom."

"It's not a fake," George said. "And there's no way in hell you're keeping it. It's going back to the Grecian Colony before somebody tells Old Flowers it's missing."

"Then I guess we have a problem," Bruce said. "I *am* keeping it."

Avarice shone in the dark, puppet eyes. The resolve in his stiff, grim expression gave him the aspect of a much better actor. Was this his great moment of inspiration?

"Fine," George said. "I officially concede the contest. Bravo Glen wins. Happy Birthday to all."

"What the hell are you talking about?" Bruce said.

The throbs in George's temples were beating their way to a migraine. *How totally absurd*, he thought. *The worst part was the time consumed by this fiasco.* "Look," George said. "I'm sure we can work this out." He took a cautious step forward. "Rollins must know about this. He'll confirm that your chalice isn't some lost pirate treasure." George moved closer. Bruce pressed the chalice to his body. "I can't explain how it got here, but believe me, stealing that chalice will swirl you in a serious shit storm." George stepped again, ready to lunge at Bruce and wrestle him to the floor. "I can prove it. There's an engraving on the bottom. The artist etched his—"

"Ahhh!" George cried as the floor buckled, caved to one side, and swallowed him in a swirl of splintered wood.

Then a weightless fall that suspended time and grew under him like a grave digging itself deeper.

"Uuhh!" George gasped when he landed on a hard surface. The impact bashed his hip and air whooshed from his lungs. But an inclined plane had lessened the shock. It slid him spinning down a ramp, cold and slippery, down, down, fast at first, then slower by degrees until he skidded across a slick, level surface.

He slammed head first against a solid wall.

Bruce stood in the dark.

The panic in George's voice, and his scream, lingered in the room like a jagged echo. Both dampened Bruce's glee. He had played his part and achieved the goal, but somehow, he'd imagined more adventure and a little less tragedy. For the space of a few adrenalin charged breaths, he even felt sorry for George. The money, the possibilities, the Flowers name—too much privilege had encumbered sympathy. But now, Bruce saw something familiar in George's pain.

He lit another match and carefully retraced his steps.

The original instructions warned him to follow the perimeter, away from the trap set for George. With his back close to the wall, he inched his way to the threshold of the bedroom. A low mechanical hum, and vibrations, resonances that reminded him of a rolling metal gate, or the closing of an aircraft hangar, echoed from somewhere below.

As instructed, he threw the matches into the opening and turned to leave, but stopped. Rays of dusty light leaked through gaps in the rotting front door and cast Bruce's shadow over the splintered boards. He knelt and called into the darkness: "I'm going to *get help*, George."

*Nice touch*, he thought.

Outside, the sun seemed unusually warm, the breeze humid and smelling of rain. He gathered both horses without hurrying, then stuffed the chalice into his saddlebag. He glanced back at the hut and couldn't restrain a deep, satisfied laugh; a pat on his own back for a job well done.

"Sorry I had to lie to you, George," he said to the wind, the trees, and to this satisfying moment.

He felt like riding off into a sunset.

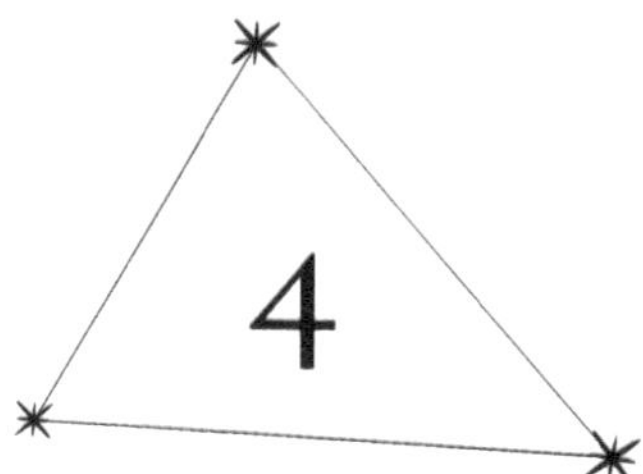

# 4

Captain John Hanagan aimed at the setting sun and leveled the Turbohawk XT at 41,000 feet. He glanced across the cockpit at Cerissa. "Are you ready to stop the sun?" he asked.

Sixteen-year-old Cerissa Maxwell smiled, then checked on her mother, Kathryn, seated in the main cabin. As usual, *La Corporada*, a mocking, but nevertheless useful title that Kathryn relished for its connotations of dedication and ruthless efficiency, was entranced—by her laptop, by corporate memos, research projects, legal correspondence, and currently, by planning, organizing, and scheduling the minute by minute details of this vacation.

"I'm ready," Cerissa said to the captain.

"Here we go." The captain eased the throttle forward, revving the turbofan engines to a screaming 7000 pounds of thrust. The little jet hurled toward the sound barrier. "Have you decided *where* you want the sun to stop?" the captain said.

Using a technique she had learned as a child, Cerissa attuned to the resonance of Captain Hanagan's thoughts. She knew exactly how to answer. "Let's leave the sun peeking slightly above the horizon."

"Good idea," the captain said. "I was just thinking the same thing. Now, promise you won't stare directly at it."

"I promise."

For several minutes, the captain maintained a steady 490 knots. As the sun gradually set, he just as slowly increased the air speed. "You always have to remember your latitude, Cissy."

That name again; it followed her like a second shadow and was just as clinging. She hated the sound of it, along with its undertones of timidity and weakness. Though, in truth, not when Captain Hanagan used it. From his voice, "Cissy" brimmed with warmth and genuine affection. Unlike her own father. That man rationed feelings as if doling out hardtack to starving sailors.

"When we left Heathrow," the captain continued, "we were at 52 degrees north. So right now, the sun's moving at 550 knots. When it sinks down to where you want it, we'd better be going 550 or we'll lose it."

"What happens when we drop to a lower latitude?" Cerissa asked.

Captain Hanagan cocked his head. "That's an excellent question. You say you've never done this before?"

"No, never," Cerissa said.

"You must be a born physicist." He chuckled. "Of course, a physicist like yourself, along with every third grader in the world, knows that the earth isn't flat. So, we're not really flying due West. More like a kind of semi-circle, following the curve of the earth. Now, if we were at the equator, the sun would be sinking at 1000 knots an hour. No way this little bird could catch it. But Bermuda is 32 degrees north."

"Can we have a sunset all the way to the islands?"

Captain Hanagan cleared his throat. "Not exactly. You see, we're sub-sonic. Top speed around 650 knots, just below the sound barrier. Factor in the 100 mile-an-hour head winds and..." The captain shrugged. "Let's try for an extra-long sunset." He pointed to the horizon. "Is that about where you wanted it?"

"Perfect," Cerissa said. "Isn't it beautiful?"

"That it is, Cissy," the captain said. "That it is."

The sun froze, a tiny explosion of orange bobbing on a billowy sea. But for the hum of the turbines, the purples gently morphing into magentas, and Captain Hanagan's Omega Speedmaster faithfully recording the seconds, time stopped like a breath held in silent awe.

"It feels so strange," Cerissa said, breaking the spell. "Like putting the world on pause."

Captain Hanagan gazed out the cockpit window, his mind adrift.

After a moment, Cerissa said: "I bet you've seen some wonderful things up here."

The captain grinned. "I bet you're right," he said, with a wink and a quick scan of the Primary Flight Display. "And it's funny you should say that, Cissy, because I was just thinking about the first time I got my hands on a real jet. Back in the 82nd Flying Training Wing when the T-38 was the hottest bird in the sky." With an odd half-smile, he shook his head, recalling a wistful memory. "That's a lot of years," he said, coming back. "But when I was a few years older than you are now, I flew out of Williams Air Force Base, near Phoenix. Of course, that base is closed now. But back then, we had forty crews, some of the greatest guys..." He peered across at Cerissa. "Funny, how it comes back so vividly." He removed his headset, gently massaged his ears, and then snugged the ear cushions back around his head. "Anyway, with forty crews you've got eighty guys fighting for air time. With luck, you're talking maybe two missions a week to squeeze in combat training, photo recon, scramble and search, all of it."

"What's that?"

"Scramble and search?"

"Yes."

"Well," the captain said, "it's like a game of hide and seek at fifty thousand feet." He leaned on the arm rest and peered over the rim of his glasses. "You always get me talkin', don't you?" Cerissa teased him with a "who me?" grimace, and smiled. The captain shook his head. "Well, the point is, Cissy, with limited flight time, a guy had to get his fun all at once." He pressed the microphone to his lips, leaned closer, and whispered: "Should I tell you about the most fun I ever had in the T-38?"

Cerissa nodded.

"Strictly against regulations, of course. But you won't tell anyone." Cerissa shook her head. "Good. Because the most fun I ever had in the T-38 wasn't at fifty *thousand* feet. It was at *fifty* feet."

He settled back. "Hard to describe the feeling, to be honest. A kind of bliss, I guess." Twilight colors tinted the cockpit. "But imagine flying through the air at 800-miles per-hour—fifty feet above the Arizona desert. The world disappears. Everything's a blur. You're overwhelmed by pure power, pure speed. The G-force clamps you to your seat, but you keep pressing the throttle—550, 600, 700 miles an hour—faster, then faster still. You merge with the speed. Nothing matters but you and your bird hurling through a blinding tunnel of color!"

He paused, breathless though he'd barely moved a muscle. Veins pulsed in his temples, hands clenched the yoke. Tangible excitement charged the cockpit.

But a second later, the captain heaved a breath. "Whew," he said. He loosened his grip and flexed his fingers. "Haven't thought back to those days in a while." He chuckled. "And I guess I fudged a little."

"Fudged?" Cerissa said.

"Yeah. When you're fifty feet off the ground at 800 miles an hour, *almost* everything disappears." He pinched his thumb and index finger together. "There's still one, teeny tiny point of clear horizon. But it looks a million miles away." He bellowed a loud, hoarse laugh. "Yes sir, that's the most fun I ever had. Makes me feel young just thinking about it."

"Sounds wonderful. I'd like to try it someday."

"Someday," he said, returning the high-five she offered.

Cerissa giggled, playing the little girl with a handsome, older man.

"I wish I could promise you a sunset all the way to Bermuda," the captain said. "But I can't outrun the laws of physics. Should be twilight when we touch down at St. George's."

"Thank you, John." Cerissa said. "But I won't be allowed to sit here much longer anyway."

At that instant, the steward, Fernando, tapped on the captain's shoulder. He leaned in.

"Yes Nando," the captain said, pulling the ear cushion away.

"*Señora* Maxwell...want see Cerissa," Fernando said in a loud voice. He offered Cerissa a furtive eye roll he knew she'd appreciate.

Though everyone on board spoke fluent Spanish, Kathryn Maxwell insisted on English while traveling beyond the borders of their current residence: the former Costa Rica. As a prominent World Citizen, she felt honor bound to advance the United Nation's "official" language.

"I'll be right there!" Cerissa called to her mother with unnecessary volume and vigor. Then to Fernando in a voice only he could hear: "Why send you? She can't get up herself?"

Fernando shrugged, confused by *La Señora's* motives, or more likely, puzzling over the meaning of "get up", yet another "up" construction that made English grammar so frustrating. How exactly does someone "get" an "up"? he wondered. He had only recently figured out how to "shut" an "up", (*cállate*) and was still wondering how *novios* could "make up" (*hacen las paces*) just before the wedding after fighting about how much "make up" (*maquillaje*) the bride was wearing.

Of course, Cerissa always sympathized and often secretly conversed with him in his native tongue, trying to give him a heads up (*el aviso*) on the many English idioms that come up (*de ofrecer*) and don't add up (*no tienen sentido*) to non-native speakers. She had even taken the time to type up (*podia teclear*) many of the most common and useful idioms so he could brush up on (*estudiar mas*) his language skills, keep up to date (*mantenerse al dia*), and avoid translation mix ups (*confusiones*). Like any good language instructor, she advised Fernando to listen up (*hacer caso de*) as a child would, and anchor the language by associating the words with real-world situations instead of looking up (*buscando*) the words on a search engine. It's natural to fuck up (*cagarla*), Cerissa had said, especially at first. So, smile, keep up (*mantiene*) with your lessons, put up with (*aguantar*) mistakes and misunderstandings, and you'll be up to speed (*suficientemente preparado*) in no time.

Exhausting as it was, Fernando recognized good advice when he heard it.

But then *Señora* Maxwell asked him to "beef up" the galley's stock of *Maracuyá* and coconut crème for her favorite cocktail, the Jaguar Colada. Because, after all, they'd be "cooped up" in this jet for many long hours over the course of their months long vacation.

At the time, Fernando didn't think *pastilla de caldo* (the closest translation for liquid beef he could find on Google) would taste good in a coconut crème-based cocktail. But after finding beef bouillon in convenient cubes and adding extra *guaro* and *Maracuyá* to the cocktail, Fernando admitted that *La Señora's* tastes were not only *muy ecléctica*, but also refreshingly *original*.

He couldn't wait to serve her this new "beefed-up" cocktail.

"I'll be going now, Captain," Cerissa said. "Larry can come back to his seat."

"But you're so much prettier than Larry. I think I'll make you the new co-pilot."

Cerissa giggled. "Good idea. Maybe we'll leave Larry in Bermuda." She leaned closer and whispered: "With my mother."

Captain Hanagan smiled as Cerissa turned to leave.

The Turbohawk XT is normally configured to seat eight passengers. But Kathryn Maxwell hated cramped spaces. "I want four seats facing each other, and a plain mahogany worktable between them." She ordered common polyester curtains for the windows—no extravagant bar, special lighting, fancy sound system, or custom wood paneling—then sat back and enjoyed the beautiful Spartan interior. Thanks to avoiding unnecessary frills, Kathryn's Turbohawk XT had cost the Flowers Corporation only twenty-seven million dollars.

"Wouldn't it be fun to follow a sunset around the world?" Cerissa asked, taking a seat opposite her mother. She waved to Larry as he entered the cockpit.

Kathryn Maxwell added a flurry of keystrokes before looking up. "I'm sorry, dear, what were you saying?"

"Nothing," Cerissa said, frowning, the wonder she had felt while in the cockpit already fading with the sun. Scarlet inflamed the clouds outside her window. Another glorious distraction from this sham vacation.

Kathryn closed the laptop. Her lips pursed in what Cerissa recognized as well-practiced tolerance for her daughter's petulance. "Wait a few years," she said, her tone pleasant and equally well-practiced. "Chasing the sun is bound to become the fashionable sport of your generation."

*I'm sorry, dear, what were you saying?* In her mind, Cerissa echoed her mother's words, but with a sarcastic lilt. *You heard my question,* she thought, while peering into Kathryn's guarded brown eyes. *"But, of course, you have to control every conversation and situation.*

"Fasten your seatbelt, dear," Kathryn said, proving the point.

Once again, Cerissa wondered if nurses had handed Kathryn the wrong infant. She marveled that a woman of such dark, scenic beauty—a Lady of Mali carved by the gods from a granite cliff—could spawn a green-eyed blond with features Cerissa could barely call pretty.

"You mean the fashionable sport for the *rich* members of my generation," Cerissa said.

Kathryn nodded. "Don't worry. You'll always be one of them."

"I hope not."

Kathryn sighed. "Let's not argue. As I've said, I appreciate your idealism. But you should accept reality. Not everyone can be as lucky as you."

Cerissa closed her eyes, fighting swirls of thoughts, tremors of feelings.

"What's the matter, *cariña*?" Kathryn asked, her endearment lathered with motherly concern. "What are you thinking?"

Cerissa hated that question above all others. "Nothing."

"You're thinking about home."

"Yes."

"Things won't be the same when we get back," Kathryn said. "You need to accept that reality, too."

"I won't argue about Conrad again. I've made up my mind."

"So have I. Let him find someone his own age."

The sky darkened, the sun finally setting, Cerissa's reflection in the window as nebulous as her future.

"You enjoyed Paris, didn't you?" Kathryn said, trying to lighten the mood. She beamed and closed her eyes, breathing in the memory as if inhaling a bouquet of fresh-cut *muguet*. Cerissa squirmed at her mother's feigned enthusiasm, but agreed with what Cedric, her wayward father, had once said about his ex-wife: "Her wily smile redeems her mean demeanor."

True. But even genuine smiles would never give Cerissa a loving relationship with her mother. That possibility had strangled like any desire grasped too tightly. Especially after Kathryn embraced *her* new reality—thanks to Fabiana, Cerissa's nanny and teacher, Kathryn would always, on some level, fear and mistrust her own daughter.

And all these years later, Kathryn still suffered the loss, still seethed at betrayal. Overwhelmed by anger, in need of retaliation, she had punished Fabiana, in the eyes of polite society merely dismissing her. But within the brutal corporate underworld, Kathryn had balanced the account by ordering Security to "disappear the vile *bruja*".

Too late. The damage was done. The mutilation, as Kathryn called it, had already warped Cerissa's mind.

At times, even Cerissa agreed.

When Fabiana first introduced *los juegos*, the games, Cerissa was barely two. Fabiana's children were only slightly older, but already able to read each other's minds. When by age four Cerissa and her playmates all conversed mentally in both Spanish and English, with or without Fabiana and her strange magnetic *brujería*, reading thoughts seemed as natural as chasing geckos through the garden.

But, as Cerissa matured and explored life away from gated estates, monogrammed shirts, doormen, chefs, and false empathy; stepped beyond Kathryn's friends, associates, and their diazepamed anxieties and into communities of hunger and adversity, she discovered locals crammed into desperate cities. The homeless, the wretched, the diseased, as scabrous as their impoverished villages—all revealed the casual reality of daily existence and battered her mind with grief, misery, and despair. After years of privilege, she had glimpsed truth, and its companion, suffering.

Drowning in heartache, she recognized that most minds roiled in babbling, disjointed thoughts. Many snarled in twisted desires. Spite and menace lived with joy and elation while love battled doubt and obsession.

Even Kathryn's moment of realization had wounded Cerissa. That sudden insight, the improbable, but undeniable recognition that her eleven-year-old daughter's uncanny hunches, mysterious intuitions, and empathetic rapport had, all this time, emanated from the ultimate violation of privacy.

Trust vanished, replaced by fear and shame. In the distraught weeks that followed, Kathryn recognized that Fabiana, the malevolent *bruja*, had forever maimed her Cerissa, had shredded their bond.

I love you," Kathryn had said, "but I can't live with you always in my mind." She demanded a defense, a way to create a mental citadel and regain her privacy. "I can barely abide my own thoughts," she confessed. "Let alone share them with others, even my own daughter."

Cerissa offered that shield.

Ironically, the technique came from the vanished Fabiana, and had, from the beginning, been part of the *juego*. "*No hay ganancia en entrar furtivamente en la mente, si otros pueden hacer lo mismo,"* she had told the children. *No gain in sneaking into the mind, if others can do the same.*

She had taught her charges, what she called, *La Función de la Cortina*. Literally, the Performance of the Curtain, but what Cerissa called, the Curtain Technique.

It involved the mental practice of envisioning a curtain, or a wall, or a drawbridge, a chasm, or an impenetrable door or barricade, in truth, whatever in the user's mind evoked a sense of obstruction, blockage, or obstacle. Over time, and with focus, visualization, repetition, and belief, the apprentice harnessed the powers of the unconscious mind and developed, what Fabiana called: *"La víbora que se traga"*. The viper that swallows itself.

Cerissa later realized that Fabiana's "viper" was really a kind of subconscious feedback loop that continuously reinforced the imagery used for the chosen barricade. Enough practice with *"la víbora"* empowered the novice to subvert the most skilled mind reader.

For Kathryn, curtains seemed too flimsy, as insubstantial as the images she was trying to cultivate. She chose instead the image of a bank vault, specifically, the massive vault of the *Banco Nacional de Costa Rica*. In her imagination, she saw herself shielding thoughts behind an impenetrable steel door, its ten-meter thick, million-ton titanium barrier (Cerissa encouraged exaggeration because evoking emotional response was part of the exercise), impervious to intrusion.

After weeks of determined repetition, the image of the vault and the smooth texture of the steel door combined with the smell of dust, and paper, and the empty press of silence, to anchor the imagery in Kathryn's mind.

Cerissa was delighted. She could no longer hear her mother's thoughts or distinguish Kathryn's daydreams from her own. This season of suspicion could end. Rejection, abandonment, and divorce had already cost her one parent. She could ill afford to lose another.

If only her mother would truly believe, fully trust the effectiveness of this new ability.

If only.

Two simple words that only heightened Cerissa's guilt. Because Kathryn, the executive, having suffered profound vulnerability, not only employed her new mental defenses, but also seasoned every normal conversation, deed, and gesture with extravagant caution.

"Of course, Paris was beautiful," Cerissa answered.

"And the former Greece, Italy, Egypt?" Kathryn persisted. "How many sixteen-year-olds spend the summer touring the former Old World?"

"Too few can afford it."

"Oh, don't be so solemn," Kathryn said with impatience. Followed by a shake of the head, a sigh, and the hurried movements of familiar exasperation as Kathryn reached into a leather tote and removed two objects.

The first was a hardcover book so perused and earmarked its spine creaked when Kathryn handed it to Cerissa. Binding loose, cloth frayed along the edges, heavy enough to prop open a barn door—the volume smelled of dust and age and even a hint of mold. Cerissa crinkled her nose as she ran her fingers over its slightly stippled surface.

"I haven't seen a real book since you got us into the *Bibloteca Nazionale Centrale di Roma,"* Cerissa said, her mood suddenly brightening. "Where did you find this?"

"I have my ways," Kathryn said with her wiliest smile.

The second object, a four-inch square velvet jewelry case, she pushed aside.

"What's that?"

"Just a trinket," Kathryn said, a mysterious, but calculated glint in her eye. "Something I picked up in a curio shop near the Old Fort of Zanzibar. I thought you might like it as a memento of our trip."

"Mother, that's so sweet," Cerissa said, reaching for the case.

"Ah, ah," Kathryn said, covering the case before Cerissa could touch it. "Culture before frivolity."

"Twelve weeks of culture isn't enough?"

"You might change your mind after reading this book."

Cerissa forced a smile. "Maybe."

"Look on page 353, after the section on Bermuda."

Cerissa flipped through the pages, found page 353 and begin reading the first paragraph of Chapter 11. "Oh...," she said.

"This is the only published history I could find," Kathryn said. "On or offline."

With the flick of pages and the texture of real paper fluttering under her fingers, the vacation became more than Kathryn's tactic to separate Cerissa from Conrad. "Are we really going to Uncle Aaron's island?"

Kathryn Maxwell nodded, saving her look of triumph for later.

"I can't believe it!"

Cerissa knew "uncle" Aaron Flowers only acted the role, but she encouraged him and always played along. Mainly because he was the most wonderful, generous, and fascinating man she had ever known. Always arriving unexpectedly, he would enthrall her for days with tales of ancient civilizations, space aliens and their visits to Earth, and parallel worlds coexisting with our own. Often, he challenged her at *mehen*, an Ancient Egyptian board game played on a circular stone in the shape of a coiled snake. Marbles, made of actual marble, were chased around the serpent's tail by a small, sphinxlike lion carved from soapstone. Ancient versions of dice, some as simple as painted stones, others fashioned from knuckle bones, or shells, and often ivory, drove movement around the board. The lion was said to symbolize Destiny, the marbles, mankind's attempt to outrun it.

Then, as was his way, Uncle Aaron would leave the ancient realms and present entertainments from the modern world—laser fog lights, plasma balls, stick figure acrobats that twirled for days before stopping—then delight Cerissa with electronic keyboards that not only imitated other musical instruments, but mimicked waves, and thunder, bird calls and rustling leaves, and even created oscillations that tickled the skin, relieved headaches, and lulled listeners into soothing trance.

But, most intriguing of all, Uncle Aaron hinted at an upcoming adventure, a visit, someday, to a mysterious island.

"This is better than a dozen summers in the Old World," Cerissa cried. "I've dreamt of this moment."

"You've earned it. Just remember, it's okay for you to know the things in this book, but don't discuss them while we're on Flowers Island."

"Why not?"

"It upsets your uncle. He likes to believe the island had no history before he created it. You'll understand when you see his Culture Colonies."

"Mother, listen to this." She read the text: "'The logbooks of 17$^{th}$ century Spanish explorer Guillermo Valdaquez were uncovered, along with thousands of others, in the archives of the *Museo Marítimo de Barcelona* as part of a research project cross-referencing climate data from past centuries with modern meteorological records. According to the logs, Valdaquez, captain of the brigantine, *Madeira*, came upon an island ninety-seven miles northwest of Bermuda in the year 1632. He christened the island: *Isla de las Flores.*

"'Arriving in August in the middle of the storm season, Valdaquez, a man inflamed by greed and the quest for glory, ordered eight men to explore the island. High seas and the barrier reef splintered their boats and all eight drown."' Cerissa stared at her mother.

"It gets worse," Kathryn said.

"'After anchoring beyond the reef for three days, winds shrieking, grief and fear inciting the crew to mutiny, Valdaquez hanged a traitorous sailor from the mainsail. The whispers stopped."'

"That's horrible," Cerissa said.

"In those days, captains were ruthless. As often as I've felt like hanging someone from the mainsail, I've also had to consider the Labor Board."

"That's not funny, Mother. It must have been terrible."

"It's colorful."

"And here we are, visiting in August. Are we going to crash on the reef?"

Kathryn shuddered. "God, I hope not. You know me and boats. But the fact is, there's only one strip of beach on the whole island."

"One beach?"

"Yes, beautiful pink sand for almost two miles. It's on the northern coast."

"Why only one?"

"You should study the geology of islands and find out."

"Mother..."

"I don't really know the answer. But I think Flowers Island is a newly extinct volcano."

"How new? And are they sure it's extinct."

"Hard to say. Baby extinctions are only ten million years old."

"Very funny."

"All I know is, jagged cliffs form a perimeter around the island, inaccessible to ships. Beyond the cliffs, the land slopes into a huge valley covered with dense woods. I suppose the valley is the ancient crater."

"If it's all cliffs, why would Valdaquez name the island, *Isla de las Flores?* Where are the flowers?"

"Good point." Kathryn reached for the book and flipped to page 355. She pointed to the quarter-page map of *Isla de las Flores*. "See that little dot?" She indicated a speck on the map, a tiny island off the northern coastline. "Uncle Aaron named that Little Flower. It's an atoll about a mile off shore. Somebody built an old radio shack, but nobody lives there. The whole atoll is little more than a steep, volcanic rock jutting up a few hundred feet above sea level. A person can stroll the perimeter in twenty minutes. But unlike Flowers Island, Little Flower is surrounded by beaches and a beautiful lagoon. There are large breaks in the coral reef. No doubt Valdaquez landed there and climbed to the highest point. That's when he saw the fabulous colors on the main island."

"But he couldn't sail to North Beach?"

"No. Even today there's only one passage through a narrow section of reef. You'll find out why a little further in your story."

"Flowers Island doesn't sound as romantic as I'd imagined."

"Don't get disappointed yet. Read some more." But when Cerissa ignored her and read silently for several long moments, Kathryn asked: "Are you going to share the story with me?"

"I thought you knew it."

"I do. But I like hearing you read aloud."

"Why?"

"To hear the excitement in your voice. That's been a rare experience on this trip."

"Trust me, Mother. This part isn't very exciting. The book goes into long descriptions about the insects that built the reef from their waste products. I'm scanning for the good parts."

"No sense wasting time on biology."

"I'm interested in the story, that's all. It basically says that, thanks to the currents and the deadly reef, *Isla de las Flores* became the most feared island in the Atlantic. But I'll read aloud if you like." She took a sip from the water bottle Fernando had left on the table. "'A century after Valdaquez discovered the island, a group of "privateers", common pirates fleeing from the British, ran aground on the barrier reef. Survivors inhabited the island for almost a decade. The soil was fertile, the sub-tropical fruits edible, fish, both fresh water and ocean varieties, plentiful. A vast honeycomb of caverns provided shelter during the hurricane season.

"'The pirates' lives were more than comfortable. When the currents thrashed merchant vessels onto the reef, clothing, food, furniture, sometimes live animals, washed ashore. Life brimmed with plunder, but without the dangers—until the earthquake of 1755.'" Cerissa looked up.

"There haven't been earthquakes since Uncle Aaron's owned the island," Kathryn said.

"I'm glad to hear it," Cerissa said, returning to the book. "'According to scraps of correspondence and the folklore of the time, the earth heaved, swallowed hill-sides, toppled forests, and severed faces from cliffs. Most of the pirates perished.'"

Again, Cerissa slumped into silence.

Kathryn shrugged and busied herself with whatever matters beckoned from her laptop.

Until Cerissa blurted: "Mother, this island is cursed!"

"I don't know if I'd go that—"

"But it's all disasters," Cerissa said. "Scientists found evidence of tidal waves. Then, a hundred years after the earthquake, some British settlers were caught in a tempest that nearly destroyed their ship. They drifted for weeks before landing on *Isla de las Flores*. The earthquake had shattered a section of the reef and opened a navigable passage." Cerissa looked up. "I see why boats can get to the island now. Anyway, the settlers traded with West Indies merchant vessels, and for a while, thrived. But within two years, most had died from malaria and yellow fever. Mother, listen to this: "'Word of the plague spread faster than the disease. Ships stopped trading with the island. *Isla de las Flores* perished, slowly, first from fever, later from neglect. By the 1840s, rats were the only survivors.'" Cerissa stared at the dismal words, the island's romance defeated by history. "This is horrible. Not what I imagined."

"Perhaps," Kathryn said. "But it's reality. The past is more than Sistine Chapels and Parthenons. Ugliness and pain are necessary. How else to appreciate the good and beautiful? Go on."

Cerissa carefully turned another yellowed page, and sighed. "'In 1952, the United States purchased the small, uninhabited island from the Spanish government. As one of many outposts in the Coast Guard's Hurricane Warning Display Program, *Isla de las Flores* enjoyed a small airstrip, barracks, and a modern weather station. But the base was abandoned eighteen months later.

"'While no official explanation was ever given for the station's closing (probably to avoid the growing Bermuda Triangle debate) sources familiar with the Hurricane Warning Display Program claim that an investigation revealed unusual outbursts of electromagnetic energy, caused by, or in combination with, a phenomenon called "hexagonal clouds". These clouds, formed by localized columns of sinking air called micro-bursts, blast down from the bottom of a storm system, hit the ocean, and create waves up to fifty feet high. Wind speeds can reach 170 MPH over a forty-mile radius. Beyond endangering the lives of station personnel, these disturbances damaged infrastructure, forced constant calibration of delicate instruments, and generated unreliable or erroneous weather data. Radio signals were often reduced to useless garble for days at a time.

"'Lacking a calm harbor, offering a single passage through a treacherous reef, located in the hurricane zone, *Isla de las Flores* became a beautiful, useless, curiosity. Tourism avoided an island fraught with so many dangers. Especially when Bermuda, less than a hundred miles southeast, offered easy access to paradise. Today, *Isla de las Flores* is uninhabited."'

Cerissa turned the page. "That's all?"

"I'm afraid so. In the annals of North Atlantic history, Uncle Aaron's island is little more than a footnote. Of course, that's how he likes it." Kathryn Maxwell leaned forward, resting her elbows on the table. She studied her long, polished nails. "So, what do you think?" Kathryn's eyes glowed with a familiar, strategic glint.

"I think the explorer, Valdaquez, was actually a psychic. He named the island several hundred years before Uncle Aaron was born."

Again, the cunning smile. "Exactly," Kathryn said. "And you know how superstitious Aaron is. Can you imagine him finding an island named Flowers? With an omen like that, he'd turn a desert into paradise."

"How did Uncle Aaron find it?"

"That may be the strangest part of the story." Kathryn gave Cerissa her 'I hope you're mature enough to understand this' look. Cerissa restrained a smirk.

"I hadn't planned on telling you this, but maybe now is the time." She paused, a move Cerissa would normally chalk up to dramatic effect. But in this instance, something in her mother's eyes, an almost haunted look, combined with the firm set of her jaw, told Cerissa that Kathryn was about to say something genuinely disturbing. "Remember the cliffs surrounding the island?"

"Of course."

"Years ago, when Uncle Aaron first discovered *Isla de las Flores*, he crashed his plane."

"Into the cliffs?"

"Yes."

"Oh, my god! Is that why he limps?"

"Yes."

"He never mentioned that accident."

"He never will," Kathryn said. "Because he crashed his plane deliberately."

"What?" Cerissa cried, her vision of Uncle Aaron suddenly, somehow, blemished. "But why?"

"Why else?"

"I can't believe he wanted to kill himself."

Kathryn shrugged. "Life isn't simple, Cerissa. Aaron had endured a period of horrible grief. He was overwhelmed, despondent. Crushed by a terrible family tragedy. He was also young, only twenty-six, unprepared to deal with the responsibilities of running a multi-national corporation. The wealth, the questions, the scrutiny, the pressures, the thousands of people now relying on him; it was too much. With his superstitious nature, he believed fate had killed his father as punishment for a horrible crime."

"What crime?"

Kathryn lowered her eyes. "Maybe someday Uncle Aaron will tell you."

"But he's still alive," Cerissa said, incredulous, still not fully embracing her mother's words.

"He told me something compelled him to veer off at the last second. The trees lessened the impact, but he crashed and spent several days trapped in the wreckage, barely alive, his hip broken, ribs shattered. Luckily, he had water and a little food, but it took days to make radio contact. Searchers found him a week after the accident."

"Why so long?"

"The book told you," Kathryn said. "Remember the weather station? The radio interference? And he didn't file a flight plan for a suicide mission."

Cerissa reached for her mother's arm and clutched it. Kathryn lightly stroked the back of her daughter's hand.

"Excuse me, *Señora*," the steward said. "*Señor* Hanagan...er, pilot gave message."

"Yes, what is it, Fernando?"

"The boat to drive to *la isla*...no it go. Sea *capitán* very...*enfermo*."

"Sick," Kathryn corrected.

"Sí, sick."

Cerissa chuckled at Fernando's inadvertent play on words. "Shhh," scolded Kathryn, "he's trying. How long, Fernando?"

"They look new captain. Find him *mañana*."

"Thank you, Fernando. Radio the Sonesta Beach Hotel for reservations."

"*Por supuesto, desea quedarse en...*" He stopped the instant he saw her raised finger. "I am sorry, *Señora*. You like I should order *Suite Executive*?"

"No. A single room with twin beds will be fine."

When Fernando stared with a blank expression, Kathrine said: "*Habitación individual con dos camas*." Improving Fernando's English was secondary to getting the precise room she wanted.

"There is more?" Fernando asked.

"How long before we land in Bermuda?" Kathryn said.

"Twenty minute." He bowed and returned to his station.

When Fernando had moved beyond earshot, Cerissa said: "You're torturing him, Mother. I'm not going to forget how to speak English."

"I wonder sometimes. You should hear yourself after a few months with your *ticas*. You sound like a barrio girl."

"What's wrong with that?"

"It gives your English a shabby accent. Besides, Fernando needs the practice. Do it for him."

"Whatever," Cerissa said. She closed the book. "Even after all this." She rested her palm on the cover. "I'm still glad we're visiting Uncle Aaron's island." She glanced at the jewelry case, then at her mother.

"Oh," Kathryn said. "I almost forgot. I hope you like it." She slid the case across the table.

The brass hinge creaked when Cerissa opened the case. "Oh, my," she said. "This is beautiful." And it was sincere delight, her appreciation enhanced by the gift's unspoken, but powerful subtext. With the tip of her finger, she stroked the polished silver, the symbolic *víbora*. In her customary, and in this case, loving way, Kathryn had found the perfect souvenir. Expertly crafted in the shape of a serpent swallowing its tail, to Cerissa, the bracelet embodied a new acceptance of, and perhaps even a fresh beginning in, their relationship. The viper's tiny ruby eyes glowed under the soft cabin lights. "I adore it," Cerissa said. She leaned across the table and kissed her mother's cheek.

"You may want to store it in the case until we return home."

"No," Cerissa said. "I want to wear it always." With some difficulty, she squeezed her hand through the bracelet and admired how it looked on her left wrist.

"Lovely," Kathryn said, smiling.

The last rays of the dying sun shone through the window. "I can see lights," Cerissa said.

"St. George's." Kathryn leaned back, and as sudden as a smile, her expression soured. "I hate that Aaron destroyed the Coast Guard's airstrip," she said, followed by a shudder. "The company boat is bad enough, but god knows what they'll give us when we charter. I can almost guarantee another nauseating experience."

"It's under a hundred miles," Cerissa said. "Maybe the waves won't be bad." But after reading about Flowers Island, the frightful seas, the reef, the winds; her words offered little comfort.

"Well," Kathryn said, sounding resigned, but in truth, far from it. "One way or another, we'll be on Flowers Island by tomorrow night." She removed a tube of lip gloss from her purse and dabbed the wand on her lower lip. "By the way," Kathryn said after a moment. "Uncle Aaron has some things to tell you about his son, George."

"What?" Cerissa said, attention drawn from the bracelet. "Uncle Aaron has a son?"

"Uncle Aaron is full of surprises."

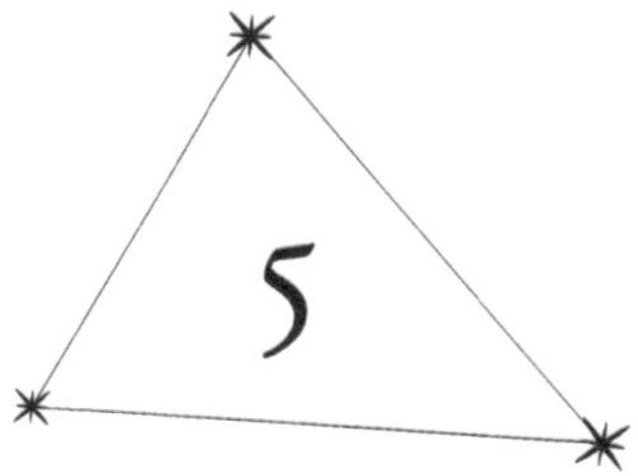

George awoke on a hard surface in utter blackness. Cold chilled the left side of his body. His left arm, wedged between his torso and the wall, tingled with prickly numbness. "Ahhh," he groaned, shifting to a seated position. The wall drained heat from his back, but the movement returned feeling to his arm.

He blinked, twice, three times, searching for the slightest hint of light in the oppressive gloom. Empty blackness. He covered his nose against the air, heavy and dank, like the catacombs of the Medieval Colony, but foul. Sickened by the moldy stench of tubers rotting in a root cellar, he swallowed to stifle the urge to vomit.

"Bruce!" he called, and cringed when pain stabbed his chest. Touching the tender ribs brought memories of the splintered floor, the fall, the fear, the thud as air whooshed from lungs. "Ouch," he whispered, pressing an aching spot on his hip. He would smart for a while. But compared to the *tlachtli*, the ball court in the Aztec Colony where playing with a nine-pound solid rubber ball cracked ribs, tore muscles, and left both teams limping for days with purple bruises, this was nothing.

Even so, his fingers explored the swelling above the left eye, and the slick of blood already starting to crust. With both hands, he confirmed what he suspected.

No bones broken, no deep wounds.

And though everything about this predicament was stupid, even absurd, at least there was a simple way out. "Bruce!" he called again. Of course, no answer. *Probably ran off with his treasure.* "You won't get far, you stupid shit," he said aloud. The words bounced off the walls of—what exactly? An old cellar, a utility vault, a crypt?

*Just find the ramp.*

Feeling along the wall as he stood, George paused to ward off a swirl of dizziness, carelessly touching that swollen spot on his forehead. "Still there," he said, with a cringe.

*But this*, he thought, returning his attention to the wall and walking slowly along its face, *is odd.* His fingers traced the length of a surface that felt too smooth for poured concrete.

*Polished granite, maybe marble?*

Blocks, but so perfectly laid his fingers could barely distinguish between them. With no cracks or mortar, and stacked with the precision of an Incan wall, this wasn't a utility vault or an ancient basement.

*A remnant from an early Culture Colony?*

Not likely. The Middle Eastern Colony was close, but still miles away, the Roman Colony even further. More importantly, the Rule of Separation forbade lessons outside *any* Colony.

His fingers butted into a corner. "Shit," he said, out loud. "I'm not thinking straight. I should have crawled across the floor to the opening." Though spoken words offered frail comfort, they barely challenged the dread inching toward panic. The wound on his forehead could be more serious than he thought. It pulsed along with a surging heart.

*Stay calm*, he thought. *Find the ramp. Count the steps.* Then as suddenly: *Why?*

He groaned, and tried to banish a surge of images—Black Widows, snakes, rats, cockroaches—creatures of the dank and dark that might lurk anywhere.

"Stop!" he cried, and moved systematically along the adjacent wall. For no reason beyond just doing so, he counted his steps. "One, two, three, four..." Nine paces to the next corner.

"Okay." Logically, he must be steps away from the opening in the front wall. But by step number six, dread had engulfed logic.

"Goddamn Fil-lon-chi!" he screamed, when he found the corner at the ninth step.

To confirm his theory, he paced another nine steps, found the fourth corner, and knew he was again at the back wall.

A chamber, nine paces square. No opening. No ramp.

"Fuck!" he said, slumping again to the floor.

This made no sense. Glen could never engineer a prank like this. Old Flowers would die before violating the Rule of Separation. And Bruce was...

*Bruce...Bruce...Bruce.* The name battered George's mind along with images of that silly puppet face, memories of the lies, the artifice, the Chalice of Dionysus. Nothing about Bruce and his ridiculous dejá vu made sense.

With a groan, George stood and retraced his steps, counting aloud, "One, two, three, four, five..." around the chamber, palms sweeping up and down the polished surface, a thin film of damp wetting his fingers.

After three full circuits, he stopped. Even in the chill air, sweat trickled down his temples. Every angry breath was a stab with an icepick, his chest tight, restrained, his own body feeling like a straitjacket binding him to himself. And all the while, his mind played along with just such ludicrous images as if they made sense amidst thoughts of slow death, alone, in a cold, black pit.

Something was very wrong, way beyond a body trapped in the dark, way beyond terror and panic. Perceptions, already reduced to putrid air, hard echoes, and numbing cold were numbing further still. Thoughts, though muddled, and until now fueled by adrenalin, drifted toward a leaden, senseless void.

"No!" George screamed, seeking focus, conjuring an image of Master Chang. The Asian Colony. His lessons and training and the Victorious Breath, *ujjayi*, filling the lungs, contracting the throat, breathing calmly through the nose.

Minutes of this long-practiced exercise invoked something resembling clarity. Enough to form an idea.

*Maybe there isn't a ceiling.*

Could he leap to the top of the wall and crawl out?

Struggling to his feet, but feeling no sensation in his legs, he leaped as high as he could, once, twice, and a third time before crumpling back to the floor, hands tingling, skin itching with a familiar, poison ivy burn. His hard-fought clarity smothered in swirls of murky thoughts.

Then slowly, one labored breath at a time, sensation faded. His groans sounded to his deadened hearing like a gasp lost in the wind.

Terrified, but too numb to protest.

*I must...breathing... still...still.*

No sensation of expanding chest. No whistle of air. No feeling in fingers. The musty stench vanished, replaced by a vague, hazy image.

A body, lost on a black glacier, heat and life flowing into darkness.

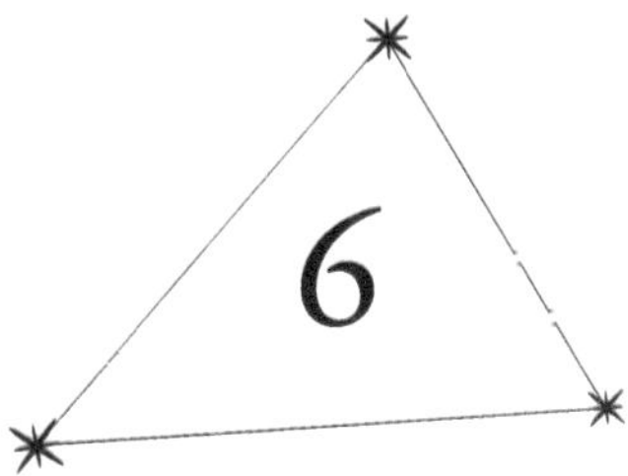

The iron weights dropped with a crash. "Uhhh...," Aaron Flowers groaned. Leona Franklin, Aaron's personal assistant, leaned into the exercise room from the threshold of the study. "Aaron...? Are you all right?"

Old Flowers stared at the ceiling, hands still clasping the foam grips. "Never better," he said. "Maybe a little dizzy."

"Dr. Feldman cautioned you about over-exerting," Leona said, a calm statement of fact. "At your age—"

"Hands can slip at any age," Aaron snapped while heaving to a seated position. He reached for a towel.

"You said you were dizzy."

"I am. From all this unnecessary concern." With the aid of his cane, he stood, angled to face her directly, and wiped sweat from his forehead. "I came close to pressing 130 lbs.," he said, with a glance at the weight machine. "By next month, I should hit 135. If Feldman doesn't like it, I'll shoot for 140."

"Don't catch a chill, sir," Leona said, handing him a thick cotton robe.

"Have you heard from Rollins? I expected news by now." He exchanged the towel for the robe, but smirked at mortality before slipping the robe over his gym shorts. Conventional theory would have long ago doomed his seventy-year-old body to paunch and sagging pecs. But Aaron's physique, though as distant from perfect as wilt from bloom, still crunched 2,000 abdominals a week, and even when scrutinized in a full-length mirror, reminded him that grit polished the hardest stone. In Aaron's estimation, a thirty-year-old mind still dwelled in this ancient body, and the battle would rage until Nature stole his final breath.

"I'll check the computer," Leona said. "Maybe Rollins has logged in."

"You do that. I'll be with the birds."

The cliffs of Flowers Island had fractured Aaron's tibia in four places, and worse, had splintered the knee. In subsequent years, post-traumatic arthritis had developed in both hip and ankle joints. Regular strenuous exercise somewhat eased Aaron's misery, along with a range of treatments—a diet rich in turmeric, various forms of physical therapy, massage with tincture of camphor; yoga, meditation, bee venom, and most effective of all, daily applications of nutgrass, yeast, and valerian poultices. And because he scorned modern pharmaceuticals, fearing their compound and mutually reinforcing side effects, the result was a life of chronic pain, accentuated by a right leg almost a centimeter shorter than the left, and a limp that orthopedics could aid, but not cure.

Sliding metal doors opened to the tunnel leading to Aaron's aviary. But this was no mere tunnel of native stone or golden *Botticino* marble. Color, and light, in every hue and permutation was central to Aaron's experience of the world, indeed, it shaped his view of reality itself. So, lasers shimmered in this tunnel. When Aaron, with his odd waddle, strolled to the aviary, he bathed his body in a brilliant luminarium of aqua marines that flowed over Ferragamo sandals, surged up walls of gingerly melded gold and intoxicated burgundies, and illuminated a ceiling of enlightened indigos.

At the end of the light tunnel, a second set of doors. They opened with a soft whoosh as Aaron stepped into a clamor of cheeps and twitters, nature's symphony to his ears, dissonant shrill to Glen's, and assertion, threat, or seduction to cockatoos, macaws, African greys, and Eclectus parrots. Cedar, harvested by Glen from the forest floor and fed through a massive chipper, covered the floor and scented the air. "Bernie Boy...?" Aaron called to his favorite cockatoo, always with the same tone and inflection. He brushed aside a broad Monstera leaf, still damp from last night's rain, and walked to the edge of a pool tiled with Cobalt Blue fire glass. "Where is my little rascal?"

From the mansion's sub-basement, the aviary rose two flights to just above ground level. A small service lift, hidden behind a decorative wall of volcanic rock cladding, connected the aviary to the outside. The size of a small theater, but circular, with a domed ceiling of fine bronze mesh, the enclosure housed over two dozen sprawling rubber trees, Java Glory vines that curled red flowers over purple over yellow; banana trees, taros, Angel's trumpets, a mealworm farm to delight the birds, and of course, a sitting area on a raised wooden floor, comfortably furnished under a canopy of palm thatch woven into ribs of bamboo.

On sultry afternoons, Aaron dragged the wicker couch to the edge of the pool, close to the artificial waterfall, and dozed in the mist as sixty-three exuberant birds soothed his pain.

Bernie flew down from a perch near the ceiling just as Rollins entered the aviary. "There's my good man," Aaron cooed, referring to the bird, but as easily to Rollins. "Are we hungry?" He fed Bernie an unpeeled tangerine and watched the bird mangle his way to the fruit. "Well?" Aaron muttered to Rollins while smiling at the bird's antics.

"Bruce returned a few minutes ago."

Aaron limped to the sitting area and plopped onto a wicker chair. He rested his cane on the glass coffee table. Then, grabbing the deck of cards that always seemed within easy reach, he fluttered into a simple riffle shuffle. "Excellent," he said, without looking up. "How did everything go?"

"As planned," Rollins said. He sat in the chair opposite Aaron, though not comfortably. With a frock coat buttoned at the waist, silk vest, and impeccably pressed Callahan trousers, ease and relaxation ranked well below historical accuracy. "You seem surprisingly calm," he said, his own tenor noticeably unsettled.

Aaron strip-shuffled while meeting Rollins' gaze. "You said everything went as planned."

Rollins frowned when a droplet from the moist canopy landed on his cheek. He wiped it away with a flick and scooted the chair to the left. "This time there's a stranger involved," he said, more exasperated than usual. "And with the risk—"

"Risk?" Aaron said.

"You know what I mean."

"More risk than climbing a ladder, or riding a horse?" He cut the cards. "Don't worry. My calculations are precise." He dealt the cards into a pile, face up, every fifth card revealing an ace, and all four expertly drawn from the bottom of the deck. He settled back, eyes fixed on Bernie and the slaughtered tangerine. "Such a good *Bernie Boy*," he said. The cockatoo responded to the cue and flew to his habitual perch on Aaron's shoulder.

Leona leaned into the aviary from the luminarium. "Sir," she said. "I thought you should know that Kathryn and Cerissa are delayed on Little Flower."

"What?" Rollins said, surprised. "Why wasn't I told?"

"It's nothing serious," she said, addressing her reply to Aaron. "A minor hindrance."

"That doesn't answer my question."

"I just now found out," she said, with a shrug.

"I mean told about their *visit*," Rollins persisted. "When was this planned?"

"Long ago," Aaron said, as he gathered the cards, flowed into an elegant Sybil cut, and finished with a one-handed shuffle. Then, removing the top card, he held it face down in his palm, bobbing it up and down as if gauging the card's weight. After a deliberate moment, he placed the card on the table. As they had many times, Rollins and Leona watched as Aaron repeated the move with the remaining deck, the demonstration ending with two piles—a small pile on the left, a much taller one on the right. "Care to wager?" Aaron asked.

"Yes!" they both blurted.

"You counted," Aaron said, wagging his finger.

"Of course," Leona said. "There are thirteen cards in the small pile. There should only be twelve."

"Let's see where I went wrong," Aaron said, flipping the small pile face up and splaying the deck's kings, queens, jacks, and aces. "Ah, ha! The ten of spades ended up with the face cards. Must be the weight of the pigment." He held the ten of spades in his left hand, the jack of hearts in the right. "The dark ink of the ten of spades weighs almost as much as the greater amount of red ink on the jack of hearts. Somehow, it varies just enough from deck to deck to throw me off."

Rollins smiled. "Do you think an audience will believe that?"

"Of course. When I convince them that I'm feeling the weight of the heavier face cards with nothing but my keen sensibilities."

"And that you're not using a marked deck."

"All in the presentation," Aaron said.

"Much like George's final lesson," Rollins said. "Which, I see, now involves Cerissa."

"My apologies, Rollins. But some things require the utmost discretion."

Rollins started to speak, thought better of it, and turned with a glower to an innocent pair of Eclectus roosting on a hanging branch.

Aaron sighed with a long, deep grumble. "Okay, let's have it," he said, leaning slowly forward to avoid startling the cockatoo. He propped his elbows on his knees. "Though I already know."

Rollins faced his employer as a friend. "Aaron," he said, grave, deliberate. "This lesson is extreme."

"Yes, yes, and the staff is grumbling again." He straightened and settled back. "Don't tell me. Dr. Feldman and Headmaster Felty are disturbed."

"In this case, I share their concerns. Especially with this new development."

"Ease your mind. Cerissa is well prepared."

"Does *she* know that?" Rollins inquired.

With a scoff, Aaron grabbed the cane and leveraged his wiry body to a standing posture. "Jonas Felty thinks George should revolve around Socrates. Dr.

Feldman would apply tourniquets to a blood blister. I'm weary of their doubts." With a loud thump, he hammered the floor with the tip of his cane. The motion startled Bernie and sent him flying into the foliage. "Damn them," Aaron said, followed by an amused scoff. "They've upset my birds. And for that, they'll pay."

"Aaron," Rollins said.

"Yes. I'll construct a Hades Colony. A fiery inferno for the doctor, his Socratic conspirator, and anyone else not committed to my methods."

"Aaron," Rollins repeated. "We're all working toward the same goal."

"Ha!" Aaron said, limping to the edge of the pool. He faced the waterfall and raised his voice to be heard above the splattering spray. "I'm following historical precedents here. I've researched everything. Everything!"

"If I may, sir," Leona said, turning to leave.

"Of course," he said with a wave. "Keep me apprised." Then turning to Rollins: "I'm not obliged to share *every* detail of *every* lesson. And I don't need anyone's approval."

"True. But maybe you tell us too little. Rumors travel when an outsider is brought in."

"Rumors travel regardless. I won't risk years of planning on a few wagging tongues."

"Understood. But when your own people aren't involved, they can't protect George. They fear another Roman Colony incident."

Though anger roiled toward outburst, Aaron softened his tone, not for Rollins, but for the birds. "Must they remind me of my one failure?"

"They're edgy. Until now, you've never broken the Rule of Separation. You tricked George and they don't like it."

"Anything else?"

Rollins shrugged.

For the next fifteen minutes, Aaron puttered away his annoyance in the forest of taro plants, trimmed the dead or dying elephant ear leaves, snipped off withered strands of bamboo, and heaped fronds into neat piles. At some point, always in Aaron's estimation later rather than sooner, Glen would saunter in and half-heartedly drag the debris to the compost pile.

"You're doing Glen's work again," Rollins said, not for the first time.

"Probably until I drop," Aaron said.

"The floor is getting a little thick. Wouldn't you say? I'll speak to Glen."

"Positively ripe," Aaron said. "But don't bother. Glen was here this morning. I sent him away."

"What? Why?"

"Because that's the result of two hours of listless shoveling." He pointed to a wheelbarrow half-filled with soiled cedar chips. "When he wasn't staring into the pool, he was muttering to himself about god knows what. Probably the latest birthday prank." When Rollins narrowed his eyes, and frowned, Aaron added: "Don't worry. When George is back, in perfect health, the rebels will quiet down."

"I wish I shared your confidence. George is strong, and healthy. But how can he endure this lesson on half a cinnamon roll?"

"What?" Aaron said.

"According to our spotters, George was so focused on getting to North Beach, he skipped breakfast."

"That's all? Half a roll?"

"Do you see why we're concerned? George is trapped in a challenging lesson without so much as a full stomach. Or even water. A lesson like this could last for days."

"Hmmm," Aaron said, while limping back to the sitting area. Gathering his cards, he splayed them across the table in a ribbon spread, flipped them face up, then back down, regrouped them into a tight deck, flowed effortlessly from a simple overhand shuffle to a complex two-handed swivel cut, then to a plain Hindu shuffle, followed by an elementary dribble that grew from a tumbling cascade into a towering anaconda. All the while, he pondered George's dilemma. "You're right," he said to Rollins when the falling cards had coiled into his left hand. "It would be prudent to modify this lesson. I'll make the necessary arrangements."

"Wise decision," Rollins said, without turning to leave.

"Anything else?"

"No, sir. I'll look into Kathryn's transportation issues."

"You do that," Aaron said, his hands again a frolic of motion.

Rollins' departure—beams casting into the aviary from the luminarium, the swish of closing doors—scarcely entered Aaron's consciousness. He was focused, instead, on the cards, his hands, and their instinctive display of the Zarrow shuffle. A slight of hand that appears like a normal riffle shuffle, but in fact, leaves the cards in the exact same order.

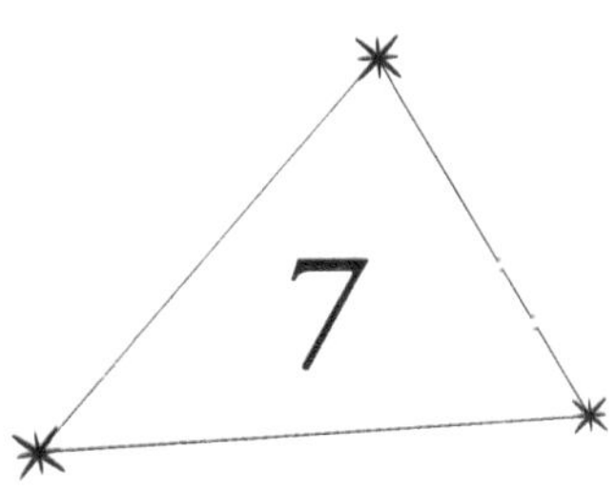

# 7

Cerissa and Reggie were paddling the inflatable boat toward Little Flower's sandy beach when Cerissa glanced over her left shoulder. "That doesn't look good!" she cried, pointing to a giant swell building in the distance.

"A-kaw!" Reggie bellowed, smiling as he gauged the wave and heaved hard on the paddle. "Get ready, ladies!"

Kathryn gripped the safety loops and leaned forward, too sick to open her eyes.

Cerissa, in the stern of the Zodiac Cadet and ready for any adventure, matched, as best she could, Reggie's strokes.

"Pump it!" he screamed. "She's gonna break just right!"

"What do you mean?" Kathryn cried.

Ignoring her, Reggie flung the paddle to the bottom of the boat and scrambled to the bow, oblivious to his generous ass inches from Kathryn's face. "Hang on!" he said, grabbing the bow line. "I'm takin' her in."

Cerissa lurched to the rowing seat and gripped the nearest strap, thankful for a beach only yards away.

The sea swept up behind them. "Eee-yahh!" Reggie screamed.

The Zodiac heaved skyward, plummeted down the face of the wave with a wall of water towering behind, caught an edge as it dived into the surf, flipped its tail like a startled dolphin, and hurled bodies into raging froth.

Cerissa surfaced first. "Mother!" she gasped, struggling to stand in the powerful ebb. The Zodiac had beached twenty feet away, upside down, and behind her, a mass of hair and seaweed breached the surface.

*"Hijo de puta!"* Kathryn cursed, as a second wave knocked her to the sand. Coughing, she crawled through the swirling foam.

"I've got you," Cerissa said, hugging Kathryn's waist and helping her to the beach. They plopped onto dry sand. "Whew! That was exciting!" She surveyed the beach. "Where's Reggie?"

"Drowning, I hope," Kathryn said, brushing her arms and scowling with equal vigor.

Cerissa plucked kelp from Kathryn's matted hair. "Mother. I'm serious."

"So am I. That cocky bastard almost killed us." Her once baggy shirt clung like a second skin.

Cerissa laughed. "Killed? Try churning the surf at *Dominical* sometime." She scanned the seas, hoping for a glimpse of Reggie. "This is not good." She leaped up and waved to Coz, the co-owner of the *Sea Maid*. "Reggie could be pinned under the reef."

From the *Sea Maid*, one prolonged blast from the boat's dual trumpet horn.

"That means he's not—"

"That's right," Kathryn said. "He's leaving."

"No way. Coz wouldn't leave his partner behind."

"Jesus jumpin' Christ," a muffled voice said as the Zodiac rose and flipped over. "I really thought I had her." Teetering and waterlogged, but unharmed, Reggie pounded his head to clear his ears. A Tampa Bay ball cap faded to the reddish brown of blooming algae, skewed to one side of his balding head.

"Mystery solved," Kathryn said, snuffling salt water from her nose.

With the poise of a dockside drunkard, Reggie ambled over. "That was some bitch ass, over the falls, surfin'," he said, beaming. The yellow-toothed grin, the patchy stubble, grey over tan, the brinish squint—all perfected his proud-pirate pretentions. "We *lucked* on that wave, ladies, let me tell you."

That got a friendly nod from Cerissa, and a spike from Kathryn's brows. "Do you mind telling me why the *Sea Maid* is leaving?" She pointed to the departing boat.

"Goddamn you, Coz," Reggie muttered through a glower aimed at the open water.

"You were hired to land us on Little Flower, and *leave*."

"That's what I..." He glanced at the Zodiac as if considering a quick escape, but instead, faced Kathryn and shrugged.

"What's going on?" Kathryn asked.

"Not sure," Reggie said, looking away. "Maybe he's runnin' from them freak waves. They come in threes, ya know."

"Don't be absurd."

"I ain't. And I don't remember *leavin'* as part of the contract."

"You'll remember the lawsuit if photos of Aaron's Colonies show up on Facebook."

"Oh, yeah," Reggie said, tacking to defiance. "Since when does Aaron Flowers own the ocean?" But cheek wobbled under flabby jowls as soon as Reggie met Kathryn's glare. "Well, that is, I mean, sure, Mr. Flowers owns this part of the ocean. But Coz owns half our boat. I can't stop him doin'..."

"Doing what?" Kathryn said with scorn.

"Whatever."

"Mother," Cerissa said, sensing the coil before the strike. "The marina on Flowers Island must be heavily guarded. Along with that two-mile beach of pink sand you mentioned. That means Coz would have to anchor the *Sea Maid*, swim to land, scale the cliffs, and hike to the Colonies. I doubt he's that reckless, or ambitious."

"He is, goddamn it," Reggie blurted.

"What?" Kathryn said.

"Nothin'."

"Don't give me that," Kathryn hissed, *La Corporada* upright, posture intimidating. With brows like gleaming scalpels, she leaned toward Reggie. "If your partner trespasses on that island, we'll seize every asset from your wretched life—your boat, your savings, whatever shack you live in. We'll strip you down to your underwear."

"Me? It wasn't my idea!" Reggie cried. "I told him no fuckin' way. Look." He pointed to the cabin cruiser, about to round an outcropping of rock. "That's Coz goin' rogue. I'm here doin' my job."

"You'll pay all the same," Kathryn said.

"But it's not my fault."

"You knew what he was up to."

"Mother," Cerissa said. "Can't we just let it go and enjoy our trip to Flowers Island?"

"That's right," Reggie said. "Relax. Your copter won't be here for another few minutes. Catch a little sun. Might make you feel better." He was referring not only to their recent adventure, but also to the fact that Kathryn had remained below deck; fighting seasickness for the whole twelve-hour cruise to Flowers Island.

Kathryn forced a smile. "Where we come from, Reggie, people avoid the sun." She glanced at Cerissa. "Most people."

"I never do," said Cerissa, cheerily. Her soggy beach towel had just washed ashore. "I like the sun over every inch of my body." She grinned at Reggie.

Reggie shifted his weight. "Well, darlin', don't worry about being shy around me. I—"

"Reggie," Kathryn interrupted, "collect our luggage."

"Er...a, yes ma'am. Thank you, ma'am. When Coz comes back, no way I'll let him sell photos to the tabloids."

When he sauntered back with three suitcases, all leaking, he frowned; no doubt disappointed that Cerissa had only stripped to a bikini.

"You'll get wrin...kles," Kathryn sing-songed as she passed her daughter and sat in the meager shade of a Chinese Fan Palm.

"Beautiful, bronze wrinkles," Cerissa said.

Reggie pulled a smoke from the waterproof pack he carried in his back pocket. He lit up, but even before the match littered the beach, Kathryn said: "So much for quitting."

"I meant it. This is my last pack."

"I'm sure."

Reggie sniffed, took a deep, defiant inhale, then spotted a trail leading into the underbrush. "I'll go in there if it bothers you," he said, shuffling off. He and his cigarette disappeared into the woods.

Kathryn relaxed in the shade while Cerissa tanned on the beach. Reggie emerged swatting mosquitos a few minutes later.

For another thirty minutes, the three sat, waiting.

"Your people are none too fast with that chopper," Reggie said, lighting his fourth cigarette. Before leaving the *Sea Maid*, he had radioed the Flowers Island Marina. They told him to expect helicopter transport within fifteen minutes.

"This is unusual," Kathryn said.

Normally, when notable guests visited Flowers Island, they were dropped off at Little Flower. A mile off shore with easy access to safe anchorage, it made an ideal way station. Even though, on a reasonably calm day, a ship could safely navigate the channel the earthquake of 1755 had opened through the reef of Flowers Island, the crossing could only be made during high tide by a sailor familiar with the channel.

"Something is wrong," Kathryn said after another ten minutes. "I'm going to radio the marina."

Reggie snuffed the cigarette and conspicuously placed the butt into the front pocket of his shorts. "Not to bring up a sore subject, Mrs. Maxwell, but I'm guessing Coz won't be back anytime soon."

Kathryn stood and brushed sand from her bottom while saying: “I wasn’t referring to your ship’s radio. There’s one here, on Little Flower.”

“Really?” Cerissa said. “Maybe we’ll have time for a climb to the summit.”

“Let’s find out.”

Both followed Kathryn into the woods. “I’m warning you,” Reggie called ahead. “There’s four million mosquitoes in here.”

After a short walk, the trail led to a bamboo hut, built on stilts, and so swallowed by foliage it looked like a bulbous mass of undergrowth. A sagging porch with missing sections of hand railing surrounded the hut. “Down there,” Kathryn said, pointing to feeble-looking wooden stairs. “There’s a generator in that tool shed. See if you can get it started. We’ll need electricity to run the radio.”

Reggie, eager to gain favor with Mrs. Maxwell, said: “I’ll have her runnin’ in a flash.”

“I’ll help,” Cerissa said.

“Be careful. If the wiring is anything like this cottage.”

The door to the tool shed squealed when Reggie forced it open. Sandals sank into the muddy floor. “Shit!” Reggie muttered. A section of roof had blown away, exposing half the shed to the elements. “God knows how long it’s been since anybody’s used this generator.” His confident tone suggested that, nevertheless, someone with his expertise could overcome any obstacle. “Here, this should do it.” The switch broke away from the rusty housing when he turned the key. “Friggin’ salt,” he said, brushing away flakes of oxidized metal. “The terminals are corroded to hell.” Twisting a stainless-steel lever, he raised the access panel and propped it open with a short rod. “This battery might be long dead. The windings in that motor could be shot, the—”

“Can you bypass the switch?” Cerissa said.

Reggie squinted, no doubt surprised that she knew enough about generators to ask the question. “You must be reading my mind, little lady.” He laughed. “That’s just what I was fixin’ to do.” Searching the contents of a plastic toolbox, he removed a flat blade screwdriver. “If I were you, darlin’, I’d stand back. Might be some sparks.” With his left hand securing the body of the switch with insulated pliers, he bridged the terminals with the blade of the screwdriver.

The generator cranked with a screeching, almost desperate, whine, then grumbled to life.

“All right!” Reggie screamed over the roar. “Let’s see what in hell’s holdin’ up that chopper.”

They walked up the stairs, Cerissa in the lead, Reggie’s thoughts so blatant and comical, she couldn’t resist listening in.

*I need a few more clients like this,* he thought. *I'm so fuckin' sick of hiring out to drunken accountants and their droopy wives and their wives' droopy girlfriends who bring along drunken accountant husbands. God.* "Watch your step, Miss Cerissa," Reggie said. "These planks are none too sturdy." Then: *What do people expect for a lousy 500 credits a day? They may not catch a fish, but at the very least they'll catch a buzz.* "After you," Reggie said, holding the door for Cerissa. *Man, this pair is different. The older one's stiff as a fish board, but this little sweetie...I'd boogie her bunny."*

The hut contained the bare amenities of a functional base camp; two folding chairs, an unsteady wooden table, a footlocker, four ancient, olive drab cots. A single bulb dangled on a cord over a dusty heap of antiquated radio equipment.

"Aaron was never interested in upgrading the Coast Guard's old equipment," Kathryn said. "Not even on the main island. I hope the radio still works."

"Christ, it stinks like monkey piss in here," Reggie said.

"It's a jungle," Kathryn said. "You obviously found the generator."

"It's running for the moment. I gotta open a window."

"I've already tried. They're swollen shut."

Disregarding her, Reggie strutted to one of the two windows, head high, gut sucked in, tan bulging through his muscle shirt. He pressed his palms against the wooden frame and pushed upward. Hard. He strained with a series of shoves and grunts until sweat broke out on his forehead. "Bastard," he muttered stepping back to catch his breath.

"Never mind," Kathryn said. "We'll only be here a few minutes."

But the window was a beatable adversary. "I gotta have some fresh air," Reggie said, annoyance blending with petulance to express the perfect whine. "I felt it budge." A lie as obvious as his true motivation and fuel for another onslaught. "Come on, you son of a bitch," he groaned while bracing his feet and heaving with such force the decaying wood cracked away from the glass. "Ahhh!" he screamed.

But his hand fixed to the window.

"Oh, my god!" Cerissa cried, pushing past Kathryn as her mother leaped from the chair.

A wide, six-inch sliver had speared Reggie's palm, burrowed under the flesh, and emerged as a ragged splinter. "Slug...sucking... bastard, "Reggie said, more as a statement than a curse. Chastened by shock and as calm as a puddle, he stared at the bleeding gash, red oozing around white, trickles dripping off a trembling wrist and pooling on the floor. "That was really fuckin' stupid."

"I'll say," Kathryn said.

"Mother!" Cerissa cried. She rested a hand on Reggie's shoulder. "Can you pull it away without making it worse?"

"I can try." But after tugging lightly, he winced and gave up.

"Maybe it's better to leave it in," Cerissa said. "We need to break it away from the frame and get you to a doctor."

Kathryn agreed. "Cerissa, see if you can find a first aid kit."

"Jesus damn, that's startin' to hurt," Reggie said, his tone still surprising, so matter of fact.

Kathryn took Cerissa's place. But instead of offering a comforting hand, she gripped Reggie's in both of hers and counted: "One...two..."

A sharp jerk broke the splinter away from the window frame.

Reggie flinched, but still didn't scream. His hand might be lost, but there was still hope for his face. "I didn't want that window opened anyway," he said, as Cerissa found the footlocker, shoved blankets to one side, poked through various hand tools, a mess kit, some ancient paperbacks, playing cards, binoculars, a dive mask and snorkel, and finally found a first aid kit under a pair of fins.

"This should ward off infection until we can get you to Dr. Feldman," Kathryn said. She poured hydrogen peroxide over the wound, wrapped gauze as tightly as she dared where the huge sliver had torn through skin, and ordered Reggie to apply pressure with his uninjured hand. She cocked her head. "I really don't like the sound of that generator. It's fading in and out."

"Oh, yeah," Reggie said, slouching on the cot farthest from Kathryn. "Somebody plumbed the generator for propane, but the gauge was in the red."

"Wonderful," Kathryn said, with more restraint than Cerissa expected. "Do you remember the frequency the marina gave you?"

"Of course."

"Can I *have* it?"

"Sure," Reggie said. Then, to Cerissa: "Are there any drugs in that footlocker?"

"No."

"Figures. I only have 'em when I don't need 'em." He settled back. "The frequency is—

An explosion sounded in the distance.

"Jesus!" Reggie cried, bolting upright.

"Now what?" Kathryn said. Her expression went from wary to worried. "Cerissa, stay with Reggie." She snatched the binoculars from the footlocker and opened the door. "I'm going to find out what happened."

"I'm not sittin' here like a beached whale," Reggie said, though he cringed with the slightest movement.

"You're in no condition to—"

"I ain't doin' it," Reggie said, on his feet and pushing past Kathryn.

Cerissa followed. "You told me to stay with Reggie." She grinned on the way by.

The light dimmed and the generator stopped.

On the beach, their view of Flowers Island was hampered by a rocky spit of land, but above the trees, dark plumes curled in the turbulent air.

"How do we get to the Valdaquez lookout?" Cerissa asked her mother.

"The first branch off the main trail. It's a ten-minute climb."

"What are we waiting for?" Reggie said. Blood oozed into the gauze and dripped onto the sand. The sliver with its jagged red point looked like a grisly *puñal* clutched by a dying street fighter. Cerissa banished the image and led Reggie up the path.

Minutes later, when her mother and Reggie arrived at the barren knoll, Cerissa grabbed the binoculars. Reggie flopped against a boulder, panting out the last of his enthusiasm in labored, wheezing breaths. "Too many cigarettes, too many beers," he said.

"Oh my," Cerissa said.

"What is it?" Reggie and Kathryn cried simultaneously.

"Some guy is riding a horse and shooting a flare gun." She passed the binoculars to her mother.

"This I gotta see," Reggie said, struggling to his feet.

But Kathryn hadn't finish *her* turn with the field glasses. "Looks like someone escaped from the Lunatic Colony," she said to Cerissa. But behind her mother's smirk, genuine dismay. True to its history, Flowers Island had staged another tragedy.

"Can I see those now?" Reggie said. He somehow managed the binoculars, and the bleeding splinter. "Holy shit and I'll be goddamned. There's a yacht burnin' in the harbor." Still winded from the steep climb and grimacing with every breath, he swayed with the effort of balancing the binoculars. "Real shame," he said, turning from the eyepiece to stare at the sliver, the aching flesh on the fringe of the gauze, the bloated, purple fingers. "But I gotta rest."

"I'll take those," Cerissa said, snatching the binoculars before he let them drop. She led him to a wedge of shade between two large boulders, eased him to a comfortable position, and returned to the lookout. "It's hard to see through all the smoke." Burning diesel tinged the air. "But it looks like..." A long pause, followed by a quick scramble to a higher vantage. "The dock crew cornered the guy on the horse. They're dragging him away."

"What about the helicopter?" Kathryn asked.

"The yacht is listing hard to port, but the copter looks okay."

"Thank god," Kathryn said. Then, unable to resist a jab, she called to Reggie: "Hang ten, brau, we should have you to Dr. Feldman within the hour."

Reggie answered with silence.

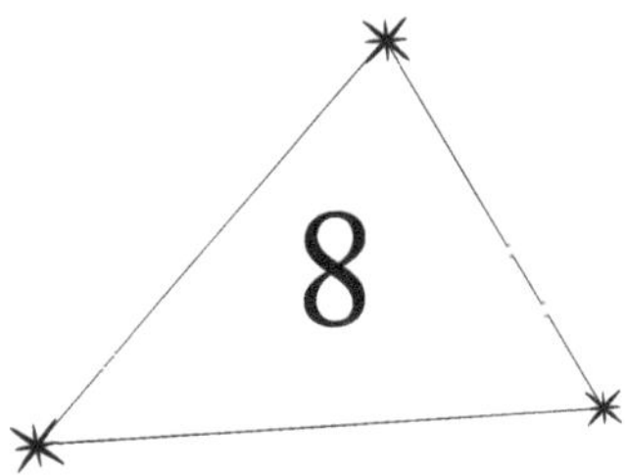

# 8

As time passed and darkness pressed, George ached for the delight of pain. He could endure isolation and tolerate this mysterious new lesson if the sting of his wounded forehead anchored him to the physical world. But now, the chamber's cold had vanished. Sensation—back leaning against the granite wall, fingertips touching his face, awareness of lungs filling with air—all had faded. Paralysis locked his body. Wide eyes saw only darkness. The chamber's stench flattened to stale, and taste died on a tongue so thick, speech garbled on swollen lips.

With sound reduced to barely audible groans, and breath entrusted to reflex, George floated in random memories—dream fragments, images of Culture Colonies, his youth, daily life on Flowers Island. He thought about Old Flowers and the mother he had never known.

*Concussion,* he thought, not for the first time.

*But I'm not dead. Not yet.*

The hieroglyphics of the *sebayt,* the sacred teachings from the Egyptian Colony, declared: *"Man remains over after death, and his deeds are placed beside him in heaps."*

There were no heaps of deeds here.

Only time, and blackness, and a frightening hunger to feel, anything.

*Spinal damage*, George thought, as terrible possibilities flooded his mind. *That can't be! Only minutes, or hours ago, I ran around this chamber. I jumped.*

Then a memory, a conversation with Dr. Feldman. Concerned about the brutal games played on the Aztec *Tlachti,* Feldman had warned George about traumatic brain injury. Dizziness, lack of equilibrium, lightheadedness, numbness, all these symptoms had followed his fall into the chamber.

*My brain is swelling!*

He imagined his skull and pieces of bone rupturing blood vessels.

*If I don't escape soon, I* might *find my deeds.*

Desperate to feel something, he willed his body to move, felt no response, and focused attention on his chest. He believed his lungs were filling with air, exhaling, filling and exhaling. Yet, absent the sensation of rising ribs, without hearing and feeling the rush of breath, how could he be sure this wasn't death and the first step along that journey?

*No. I am not dead.*

Or was denial the first step?

Time passed.

Adrift in emptiness, moments detached from minutes, hours from days. Starved of physical hunger, craving thirst but denied the impulse, George sheltered in imagination. Memories, images, even nightmares sustained him. Remembering famine and the primal aliveness of need spawned visions—weeks in the Grecian Colony enduring the Spartan *agōgē* instructions. As a child of eight, he scavenged for roots and berries, stripped bark from trees, dug for grubs and ants. Competing against the boys in his *agélai,* he learned to tolerate hunger so profound that weight loss, fatigue, and fainting barely mattered.

Did it matter now, in this dark pit of murky memories? Struggling to form even the simplest thoughts, his fantasies fused with hallucinations and delirium diluted by dreams. Consciousness, one moment floating to inner worlds; the next, ebbing back to reality's chamber, finally landed on the Greek hillside of his nightly dream. His body running, feeling the chafe of leather against skin, he breathed in the scent of heliotrope. Below, dancers, tassels whipping and arms flailing, whirled in a circle-dance. The sun, the antidote to blackness, burned his skin.

The sun?

A voice, as distinct from his as shout from silence, called from the dream: *"There is light in this chamber."*

*What?* George thought.

Again, with a soft, almost musical tone: *"There is light in this chamber."*

George sat, wondering. *How had light ever entered this sunless pit?*

With no concept of time or its passing, an itch answered him. Then sometime later, the lost sensation of warmth. Soon, he could feel movement, his lower jaw, and prickles in his fingers and toes. Clenching fists and feeling the pleasure of fingernails biting into palms, he sighed and relished the pain. Breathing awakened his sense of smell, the stink of must and damp as lavish as lilac. Stretching revived muscles. The skin on his forehead was tender, but time had eased the swelling.

Slowly, he rolled onto hands and knees and paused as a steady, painful pulse throbbed in his temples. In a sluggish crawl, he searched the marble floor, guided by impulse. With arms sweeping left to right in a wide arc, he explored variations in texture, every chip, every crack.

*There is light in this chamber!*

His hand slapped something light. It hissed across the floor and struck the wall.

*Matches?*

Groping toward the sound with fingers outstretched, he grabbed the matches and whispered: "There *is* light in this chamber." But the hoarse, barely recognizable voice drained joy from the words. His tongue felt leathery, thick, his throat so dry he could barely swallow.

"I can do this," he mumbled, and the walls echoed as he counted four matches.

Fumbling, he struck once, twice, three times before fire illuminated the chamber.

"Jesus!" George cried, his unearthly voice adding eerie to disgust. "What is this?"

The wavering light revealed thousands of gleaming tiles, some as tiny as a baby's fingernail, others the size of Roman imperial coins.

Struggling to his feet, fighting a dizzy swoon, the flickering light fading in the breeze of his motion, he approached the nearest wall. Such complexity, such dream-like images, as baffling as his predicament.

"Ouch!" The fire nipped his fingers.

Striking a second match, George held the flame higher.

Reminiscent in style of Hieronymus Bosch and his *Garden of Earthly Delights*, the mosaic portrayed a festival of horror populated by frightening mythological creatures—*Kishi*, the two-faced African demon, human forward, hyena behind, *olgoi-khorkhoi*, the Mongolian Death Worm, *Tsuchigumo*, the giant spider that had haunted George's nightmares as a child, and most common of all, satyrs. Half man, half goat, they celebrated their earthly delight by raping women and men with huge, club-like phalluses, or hunching like starving wolves over their victims. Many tore entrails from slashed bodies. Some victims, peasants wearing remnants of Medieval clothing, cowered in terror with arms raised. But most were naked, splayed over burning pits, tied to trees, or piled in bloody heaps.

"No," George cried, as the second match singed his fingers. "I'm not seeing this."

But the images returned with the third match.

"Why?" George said, dizzy, confused, crouching slowly to the floor. Then: "I know why."

As twisted and painful as this was, it had to be his true, final lesson. Thrasymachus, Plato's *Republic*, Old Flower's so-called Rule of Separation—all lies, distractions to trick him into this last challenge. Passing this test meant escape.

Somehow, there was a way out of the chamber.

Standing, he swept the match over horrible scenes of babies impaled on sticks and hung over campfires. The remains of those who had gone before; bones, skulls, appendages torn from bloody sockets, littered the festival of massacre. The mosaic's vulgarity seared George's imagination. "Ouch!" As palpably as the match burned his fingers.

What sickness had possessed this artist? What evil? And how could Old Flowers commission such a scene?

Then a sudden surge of images—last night's dream—the Greek hillside, the dancers, the sun, the clue that had led him to the matches. "The dancers," George said, words mangled by a grimace. "Find the dancers."

Striking the final match, squinting through pain and sweat, he wiped his forehead and raised the feeble flame.

The match wavered and dimmed.

With the last remnant of flame, he ignited the empty matchbook, the sudden blaze illuminating a dark corner and a solitary spectacle of joy. Here, instead of suffering, peasants danced. Their arms embraced in a merry circle, and oddly, the tiles seemed slightly out of alignment.

With a final gutter, the fire died. But the peasants lingered in George's mind.

Probing along the wall to the corner, he crouched. Pressed his palms against the cold stone, first near the floor, then higher. No movement. On his knees, he leaned his shoulder into the wall. When this failed, he thumped it hard with the left side of his body, again, and again, and again...

A gritty, scraping sound.

Exploring the surface, he detected a faint ridge and followed its outline. A rectangle, a narrow block. It seemed wider than his head, but not by much. He slammed harder. "Move!" he screamed with each thrust. "Move!"

Something stirred behind him.

Echoes?

With hearing focused, George listened for the span of many breaths.

Silence.

*Those goddamn satyrs are creeping me out*, he thought, turning back to the ridge. By tracing the contours with his fingers, he aimed his shoves with more precision, more force.

Another scrape, slight, but distinct.

Sitting back and bracing his body with his arms, he gritted his teeth and kicked the wall with the heels of his tennis shoes. The pounding shuddered up his body and jarred his head with such force, sparks floated behind his eyelids. Still, he kicked. In a rage, he screamed: "Move, goddamn you!" Each shift of the block spurring him on. The pit would not defeat him, nor would fear, injury, or pain. He kicked and kicked until a final determined strike dislodged the block and rammed it through the wall.

"Yes!" he screamed as drafts flowed into the chamber. Stale air, tainted with a tomb's musty reek, but thrilling.

George laughed, and the hard walls laughed back.

Then a hiss.

Air whispering through the opening?

No. This came from across the room.

Turning, he faced the opposite wall and sensed movement. Images invaded his mind. The satyrs. The spider *Tsuchigumo.* The screaming peasants.

*Am I hearing whispers?*

"Who's there?" George called, when he heard a shuffle.

Silence.

He stared into the blackness, convinced that Old Flowers was up to his tricks and beginning phase three, or four, or five of this lesson.

Or was this a trick of the mind?

*You won't defeat me with fear,* he thought. *And I won't defeat myself.*

But a low growl froze him.

Panic, unmoved by logic or mental assurances, halted his breath. In the stillness of that pause, another's breath. Soft, steady, interrupted by barely perceptible snorts.

*Something* is *inside the chamber!*

An actor? A speaker embedded in the wall?

Or a brain adrift in delirium.

Frantic, wary of turning his back on the presence, but also desperate to escape, he felt for the opening and thrust his arms through the hole. With head squinched between them, he writhed in the crush of the tight space, squirming, thrashing, kicking. His shoes gripped, then slipped on the damp floor.

"George..." a voice hissed.

Reaching toward another blackness, shoulders compressed, lungs suffocating in an ever-tightening vise, he thrust, twisted, inch by straining inch.

*This space is too small!*

Jammed in the opening and grabbing for anything solid, he clawed into the moist soil and pulled.

"George..."

*I'm wedged!* he thought, remembering in a flash the terror of a near drowning. Sixty feet below the waves, mask and regulator ripped from his face by a sudden turn in a narrow tunnel of reef, he groped for an air hose lost in the tight crush of coral.

Training and calm had saved him. But the incident haunted him for days.

Now, he was drowning in a sea of air with lungs too compressed to gasp it.

He needed that same calm, and gained it by expelling the last of his breath.

Using his left foot, he pressed on the heel of his right and kicked off the shoe. Then, with the traction of a bare foot, he thrust against the floor while scrabbling into the bare ground beyond the chamber.

He pushed, pulled, jammed his legs against the floor and shoved forward.

"Ahhhh!" he cried, when his chest cleared the opening and air filled his lungs.

Panting, torso beyond the wall, legs slumping inside, half laughing, half sobbing, George had barely savored his escape when hands grabbed his feet.

"No!" he screamed, a reflexive lurch kicking something solid.

The grip loosened as George twisted, yanked with all his strength, and slithered through the opening.

Headlong, he scrambled on hands and knees into darkness, as far from the chamber as his strength could take him. Too tired to stand and savoring the return of sensation, he thrilled as earth ground under his palms. Muscles flexed. Lungs heaved. Hearing the scuttle of a living, panting body drove him through the stink and dank of this new unknown.

Time vanished in hypnotic forward motion until cold dirt transitioned to smooth concrete.

*A utility tunnel*, he realized, slumping to the floor, laughing through exhaustion. *I'm free! Somewhere near the underground tram.*

Safe now, far from the cruel, difficult lesson, and so tired he could barely form a coherent thought, he wanted nothing but sleep. Even a new sound, hollow, as if from a long tunnel and approaching, barely aroused interest.

"What the hell?" he moaned, forcing his gaze into the gloom and squinting at a hint of light.

The clomp, clomp, clomp echoing down the tunnel sounded like cloven hooves.

*No more satyrs,* George thought as anger stifled a brief shudder of fear.

"Fuck you all!" he yelled down the tunnel. "I'm in no mood for Glen in a satyr suit."

He laughed while rolling onto his back, closed his eyes, and collapsed into sleep.

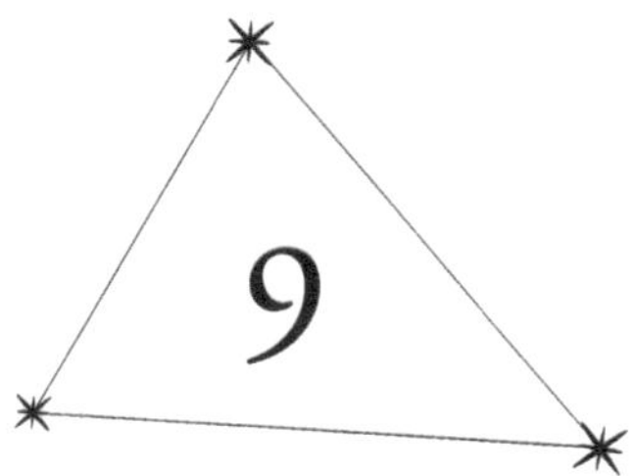

"Greet the morning behind closed eyes," Jonas always instructed. "Lest inner vision be blinded by light."

*More like blinded by pain*, George thought, as he recalled his headmaster's words.

Beginning at a swollen forehead, misery branched out, sent shoots across temples too tender to touch, cored into a muddled brain, and throbbed his inner ear. Vertebrae cracked when he shifted his head, and for the first time, George truly appreciated the wisdom of "greeting the morning behind closed eyes." If his head felt like the anvil under a hammer now, what chance did inner vision have in blinding light?

At least he wasn't lying on hard concrete. A pillow cradled his aching head. Melodies of trickling water splashed nearby. Familiar sensations like pressure, temperature, hunger, thirst, and of course, pain, grounded him. Even the shudder from recalling the chamber reinforced his return to the physical world.

Rolling onto his back, he squinted up at a domed roof of frosted glass. Dazzling sunlight poured over stone walls and into a furnished room built inside a cavern.

"Odd," he said. He thought he knew every inch of Flowers Island. But this room surprised him, in its way, as much as the chamber.

An itch drew his attention to a wad of cotton taped across the crook of his arm. Removing it revealed a tiny crust of dried blood where a needle had punctured his vein.

*Someone has injected me with something!*

Leaping to his feet, too quickly, he bent forward and gripped his knees until the swoon passed. But even with a clear head, he froze in disbelief.

His body towered over tables, lamps, the chairs; he was a giant standing in the cave of a dwarf.

Couches sat legless on the floor. Classical paintings hung on the cavern walls, level with his waist. A grand piano, though not inlaid with mother of pearl filigree like the instrument in the Mansion's Music Room, still flaunted elegant, Brazilian mahogany lines and magnificent, hand-carved legs.

But those legs were so short the keyboard almost touched the floor.

"I'm Alice," George said in a booming voice, his words lathered in sarcasm. "In Wonderland. And I'm done playing games." This wasn't culture, or studying civilization through live reenactments. Philosophy and higher learning doesn't flourish in dark chambers. Scenes of murder and torture don't bestow wisdom. "I won't be tricked into another chamber," he called into the room. A room with walls of jagged stone, full of small, shadowy crevices and perfect for hiding cameras and peepholes. "I'm done with this lesson," he said through gritted teeth. His rage was amplified by hunger, throbbing temples, and a mouth as parched as the Atacama Desert.

But clearly, the lesson wasn't done with him. On a tall bookshelf that spanned the length of the room, a single, leather bound volume jutted out from the rest. George recognized the author and text even from ten feet away, but approached the shelf to confirm his suspicions. *Of course*, he thought. *What else?* With more contempt than Plato deserved, George slammed the *Republic* back into place. "Could you be more obvious?" he said to the cowards lurking behind spyholes.

But at least moving eased the pain. So did kneeling before a stunted sink and quenching his thirst with long draughts of cool water. Warm, invigorating sunshine flooded down from the skylights. His clothes were still filthy, but oddly, he was wearing a clean pair of tennis shoes.

*More mystery,* he thought, as he strolled around the room. *But they'll give up eventually. I'm not playing along.*

A beveled-glass cabinet caught his eye, inside, small, hand-carved *Qing-Tian Tang* horses in reddish-purple jade, zodiac cougars in yellow jade, a stunning mountain village scene carved in white jade, and numerous layered balls, dragons, and vases in the typical rich green. "This dwarf has good taste," George said with a scoff. Massive silk tapestries covered an entire cavern wall. From stone alcoves, life-sized mahogany statues glared out from the shadows; jungle cats, native hunters, monkeys hanging from vines and staring with simian confusion. Behind the carvings, a delicate artificial waterfall splashed into an oval pool.

Obviously, Old Flowers had spared no expense on this lesson. But why furnish a room with legless furniture?

Italian marble floors led to three tunnels branching off the main room, and from the right branch, a faint, but familiar, slowly emerging sound. Rhythmic and hollow, and at the pace of clomping hooves, the sound prickled his flesh and reawakened memories of the chamber. "This isn't real," he said, though words calmed less than whistles over tombstones.

Focused on the tunnel, short, tight breaths edging toward panic, George listened as the clomping grew louder, more distinct.

With as much resolve as he could muster, he stood his ground, all the while telling himself that this lesson was stupid, pointless, and overly theatrical.

But sickness churned a queasy stomach, satyrs an unsettled mind. Memories—of murder, disemboweled peasants, darkness, dread, senses dying in a bottomless void—silent, but seeping from his pores in cold sweat.

Grabbing a spear from one of the wooden natives, he faced the tunnel, knowing how absurd he must look to the hidden watchers. Yet, Old Flowers and his chamber had redefined danger. Splintered floors, hard ramps, and dark pits suggested new, more painful lessons.

*Okay,* George thought. *Send him in.* If some actor was going to attack him, test his courage, or teach him to endure another level of pain, he was ready.

The hoof beats grew louder. The spear's steel tip glistened in the light.

Or maybe this wasn't an actor. What if a wild animal had escaped from the Roman Colony? The menagerie was full of hoofed creatures, many with deadly horns.

George crouched, ready to lunge. He imagined plunging the spear into a crazed bison. The heart! Go for the sure kill.

Sweat burned his eyes.

The hooves thundered now, louder, louder, following their own echo and clearly not a bison. The pace was two-legged.

A figure emerged from the tunnel.

George stepped back.

"Feeling better now?"

*This* was the mysterious dwarf?

A man perhaps a few years older than Old Flowers stepped, or rather, clomped across the marble floor. He stopped a few feet from George. A double amputee severed a few inches below the hip and wearing a white collared shirt and beige cargo shorts, he displayed his stumps openly, without prosthetic socks. Deep lines etched the man's face when he smiled at George's weapon. "Hunting something?" he said, using his arms as legs and swiveling away with a graceful motion.

George lowered the spear, embarrassed as he watched his "satyr" clomp over to a small kitchenette. The wooden blocks in each hand did sound a lot like hooves.

"You should have Dr. Feldman take another look at that forehead," the old man said from across the room.

*Another?*

"Any dizziness or blurred vision?"

"I'm fine," George lied. The swelling had enflamed from throb to burn. His ear shrieked at the slightest movement.

"Uh-huh," the old man said. "Then how about something to eat? A good meal will help bring you around."

*Bring me around?*

The old man opened a low (of course) freezer and stared inside as mist spilled into the humid air. While rummaging, he chatted with the friendly air of someone unfazed by strangers with sharp spears. "You have your mother's green eyes, but not her auburn hair. You're dark like Aaron." He smiled over his right shoulder, removed a plastic-wrapped package, and placed it into a microwave sitting on a floor-level counter. "Thank god you were spared Aaron's nose," he said, with a laugh that sounded like a scraping rasp. He programmed the oven with a few beeps, pivoted on one block in a sort of leaping motion, and clomped to a legless armchair. "I'll let you serve yourself when the timer dings." With a faint groan, he seated himself, again gazing at George with wide, gray eyes. "He'll never admit it, but it amuses your father to see Eloise in your features." Another rasp-laugh. "And that, my friend, exhausts my supply of small talk. Your turn." But before George could respond, he added: "Don't hate your father, George. He's kind in his way, but hard."

*Even cruel*, George thought, still infused with the chamber's darkness. But self-pity felt absurd in the face of the old man's deformity. "You obviously know who I am," George said. "How is it that we've never met?"

"A failing on my part. Don't take it personally. My work..." The old man reached for a pipe and stuffed it with a small, dried cannabis flower. He shrugged. "I'm happiest alone with my projects. But I'm delighted to meet you now. My name is Jonathan."

"Pleased to meet you, Jonathan," George said, returning a sturdy handshake and feeling the chafe of a calloused hand. "And for the record, I don't hate my father."

"Not even after your latest lesson?" Despite his handicap, Jonathan looked formidable. His biceps were huge, his broad shoulders powerful. Unlike the many *monstrums* George had befriended in the Roman Colony—hunchbacks, dwarves, slaves maimed on purpose and kept as sexual pets by demented masters—Jonathan wasn't bloated by excess or humbled by life on the margins of society. Strong and lithe as an acrobat, he "walked" with graceful ease, stumps forward, on the blocks fitted with hand grips. He spoke confidently and clearly, an educated man, with, not exactly a drawl, but a soothing southern cadence. All the while, he flustered George with a thoughtful, penetrating gaze.

"No. I can't hate my father," George answered. "But I'm angry that he violated the Rule of Separation."

"And the drug?"

George stared down silently, suspicious.

"You were passed out when I got to you," Jonathan said. "Before that, I heard delirious rantings about satyrs. Do you remember?"

"Barely."

"I'm not surprised."

"With all due respect, Jonathan," George said, "I don't believe you. I was injured, exhausted, frightened. But drugs?"

Jonathan exhaled a billow of smoke. "Tell me about the chamber."

George shuddered and turned away. Water splashing into the oval pond drew him toward its comforting trickle. But he stopped halfway and stood before the ornaments of Chinese jade. "It was horrible," he said.

"Can you be more specific?"

"About what? The pain, losing sensation, feeling abandoned in a dark tomb?" He faced Jonathan, but stared beyond him at the far wall and the brilliant colors of the silk tapestries. "Or do you want me to describe the mosaic, the scenes of satyrs raping dead babies, blood, murder, the feast of guts and gore, Hieronymus Bosch, but a thousand times worse? It was a glimpse into hell that even art couldn't justify. It sickened me."

George closed his eyes, trying to shake off the memory. When he opened them, Jonathan was smiling. "Don't be so hard on yourself, George."

"What do you mean?"

"There's nothing on those walls but plain, white, Carrara marble."

"Not true. I know what I saw. I'll never forget it."

"Please don't."

*Christ*, George thought, *this is Bruce all over again. Another lure, another pit.* "I couldn't have been drugged," he said in a tone oozing defiance. "I haven't eaten since..."

With a small pocket knife, Jonathan scraped the charred herb into an ashtray and placed the pipe on the end table. "Since last night?" he asked.

"Yes, except for..." the words barely audible, "...half a cinnamon roll."

Jonathan sighed and leaned forward. "I'm sorry about all this, George. I wish Aaron wasn't so, how should I say, fixated on the ancients and their methods. Especially when their techniques are dangerous and based on ludicrous religious dogmas."

"What are you talking about?"

"George, when I got you to my quarters, I called Doctor Feldman. After an infusion of saline to rehydrate you, he took a blood sample. That will be my proof." George rubbed the puncture in the crook of his arm. "Feldman, Jonas Felty, and many others are concerned about you. They—" A long, piercing beep from the microwave. "There's your meal. It's very important that you eat."

"First tell me why Plato's *Republic* was jutting out of your bookcase."

"George, please. You've been starved. You need to build up your strength."

"What for? My next lesson?"

"Of course not."

"Admit it. You're here to trick me, to test me. This could be the first step toward a torture session in the Medieval Colony."

"Oh, my!" Jonathan said, bursting into laughter and clapping his hands. "Forgive me, George, but now I'm thoroughly convinced that your training has gone too far. The Colonies, emersion in the past, your endless psychological exercises, all are more real to you than ordinary life." He rubbed the back of his neck and sighed. "George, it's time for you to *get away* from the Colonies."

For a long moment, neither looked at the other. Jonathan stared at beams of light streaming from the skylight, George, at one of the wooden natives crouched in the grotto. The spear in the native's hands, the one he had used to "defend" himself against poor, crippled Jonathan, rekindled feelings of shame. The statue's eyes, buried in deep shadows, stared out from the grotto. Its features blurred, and for a moment, transformed into a leering satyr.

George stiffened, glared back at Jonathan, studied his profile, the sharp goat-like features, the powerful torso—

"Are you all right?" Jonathan said, the words shattering George's fantasy. Jonathan chuckled. "You're every bit your father's dreamer, aren't you? Now, about that food. If you will, sir," he said with exaggerated formality, "please follow me to the dining area."

Hoisting himself off the chair, Jonathan clomped across the marble tiles and down a short corridor, waddling like an unbalanced mechanical device. George followed with his plate of food, wondering why Jonathan didn't use a wheeled platform to slide across the floor.

When they arrived, Jonathan indicated a *tatami* mat before a low *horigotatsu* table, an obvious choice for a legless hermit, but lacking the convenient recessed floor. George didn't care, preferring to sit cross-legged anyway.

Once George had settled, Jonathan waddled to a closet, reached in, and removed a small, wheeled platform much like George had just imagined. "This frees my arms," he said. "I use it when I have to carry something."

"Can I help you?"

"Of course not. Didn't you learn anything from the freaks in the Roman Colony?"

George flushed.

Jonathan then rolled to a wooden cabinet furred out from the cavern wall. Removing a cloth napkin embroidered with the letters JEF, a placemat, a pottery cup decorated with barbotine patterns, and a silver knife and fork, he set the table with the refinement of an English butler. "Don't worry about drugs in your food," he said. "Miss Ruth makes these dinners for me. She's worried sick about you, by the way, and furious with Aaron." With an expert scoot to another floor level sink, he filled a glazed flagon with water and placed it in front of George. "Water is very important. Flushes toxins from the system."

George filled the cup, drank it down, then forced himself to drink another. "I'm sorry if I seem ungrateful," he said, as Jonathan glided across the floor; stopping, turning, balancing a bowl of fruit in one hand, propelling himself with the other. After cutting a slice of dark rye, he brought cheese, poured wine for himself into a crystal goblet, and slid from the wheeled platform onto a cushion opposite George. "Not too long ago I was hurting," George said between mouthfuls. "That much I know. I appreciate your kindness and hospitality. But all this..." He swept his hand over the room. "I fell for Bruce's lies and it got me into, what would you call it, the Edgar Allen Poe Lesson?" He drank another swallow and couldn't remember the last time he'd felt so parched, so hungry. Aches and throbs eased with every bite. "I escaped, so maybe I passed that lesson. But as far as I'm concerned, the Rule of Separation is dead. It's only logical to assume that this is part of some other lesson. Maybe a test of loyalty. You trying to convince me that my father drugged me. Well, I say he wouldn't do that and none of this is real."

Jonathan smiled. "Miss Ruth's Eggplant el Greco is real. Delicious, isn't it? Did you know your father lured her away from Zabar's?"

"Yes."

"George, I'm going to say it again. Try to hear me. This isn't a lesson. It isn't a game. I wish it were. My first move would be to tell you how the Colonies blur the past with the present. How they condition the mind to believe the impossible. Please, for your own good, consider those implications."

"Things will be plenty real once I get out of *here*."

Jonathan sighed. "Very well. Then I suggest you leave before Aaron suspects we've talked. But before you go, I've got something to show you. Take your time." He indicated the half-finished slice of bread and the last few forkfuls of Eggplant el Greco. "Follow when you're done. You can walk faster than I."

Jonathan scooted across the floor to his blocks, and clomped out of the room.

A minute later, George folded the napkin, knelt before the sink to wash his dishes, and followed Jonathan back to the main room.

Hollow echoes sounded from the tunnel where they first met, so George skirted around the dwarfed piano and sprinted down the now well-lighted passageway. He caught up with Jonathan a few paces beyond a wide bend and slid to a stop before an electric golf cart. The sight shattered an important assumption. George was suspicious of Jonathan partly because he knew a legless old man could never have transported him from the chamber. Now he wasn't so sure. The powerful stride of the clomping figure reinforced a definite: *Maybe?*

"My work is a good distance from the living quarters," Jonathan said. "Gives me a chance to walk." Despite his earlier assertion, he maintained a pace with his arms equal to George's normal walking gait.

A good fifteen minutes passed before they entered another chamber, a vast room with towering ceilings that shared the grandeur of the Stadium of *Philippopolis*, but was a third the size. "My development room," Jonathan said.

George stared, amazed.

Another series of skylights illuminated a huge wooden platform, upon which was built a miniature replica of Flowers Island. "I'm still building the Aztec Colony," Jonathan said. "I may even live to finish it."

A shoreline of blue ringed the knee-high platform, then merged into jagged *papier-mâché* cliffs. Within the woods, Jonathan had built detailed scale models of each Culture Colony, down to every building, field, garden, statue, fountain, and tree. Wide aisles separated individual Colonies, and walkways within each, broad enough to allow easy access, wove through his miniature world. Human figures, horses, and every domestic animal imaginable, froze in the act of walking, riding, scampering, playing, dancing and living Medieval, Asian, Egyptian, Grecian, Middle Eastern, Aztec, and Roman lives.

"Our domain," Jonathan said, with a sweeping wave of a wooden block. The twin spires of the Medieval Colony stood watch over the island. George marveled at the craftsmanship and intricacy.

Only after strolling the length the room, past replicas of Egyptian deserts and Asian temples, could he dare ask: "How long did it take to build all this?" He cringed when he realized that Bruce had gazed over the real Colonies and asked the same question.

"Please. Don't make me remember that far back," Jonathan said, smiling. "I started, I don't know, a few months after you were born. The Culture Colonies were finished. The doctors had just found cancer in my spleen. Perfect timing, wouldn't you say?" He grumbled his scratchy laugh. "My life's work was done." He gazed a moment over the miniature landscape. "I was tired, eager to join the crumbling bones of Guillermo Valdaquez. But Aaron wouldn't let me." His shoulders heaved. He sighed. "Your father. With whom but Aaron could I build monuments, and tombs?"

As he spoke, clouds passed over the skylights, dimming the room, casting shadows over the replica. Jonathan pointed to the ceiling. "Look! I speak of your father and clouds appear. Did you learn about omens in one of your Colonies?"

George laughed. "This is the hurricane season. It would be an omen if there wasn't a storm brewing." He walked under a skylight and peered up at the dark clouds. "My father and I used to play a game," he said. "During the first storm of the hurricane season, we'd go to the main floor library and re-set the grandfather clock. It didn't matter if the storm hit at four in the afternoon, or eight at night, we'd set the hands at twelve noon. Then every day when the twelve chimes rang, we'd note whether a storm was brewing. It was amazing. Within thirty minutes on either side of the chimes a storm would hit. Later, Old Flowers told me that, back in the 1950's, the Coast Guard's weather station had discovered the same phenomenon. It's common to many parts of the world."

"I should look for a better omen," Jonathan said, clomping over to the partially completed Aztec Colony. "I've played games with your father, too, life and death games. He told me he could cure my cancer. "'Try this diet,'" he said. "'Practice these exercises. I'll show you how to use this blue light. Sleep under a blanket of steel wool. Focus your mind. Use this herb. Meditate. Find your balance.'" Ha! Part of me wanted to die just to prove him wrong. But something in his bag of experiments worked. Total remission."

George's mind whirled. Compared to Bruce, Jonathan was an Oscar winner.

"Look at this," Jonathan said, his tone brightening with the reappearance of the sun. Clomping to the far end of the platform, he reached under and retracted one of several low, wide cabinets, all on rollers. Opening the first, he revealed stacks of blueprints. "Here lies the soul of the model, and of Flowers Island. The inner workings of the Colonies, the designs, drawings, and schematics."

"You carved these tiny figures, built this model, *and* designed the Culture Colonies?

Jonathan shrugged. "At one time, they called me a world-renowned architect. But then..." He stared down at his stumps and scoffed. "Destiny had other ideas. It took me years to realize it, but when Fate severed my body, it also expanded my world. Artists, engineers, historians, builders, agrarians; craftspeople from potters to weavers to luthiers joined me to fabricate a new, ancient world. Looking back at my early work, I see vacuous skyscrapers and towering insignificance."

"But your life's work is hidden. Very few will ever see and appreciate it."

"What do I care for appreciation? Creation is the goal—the struggles, the quest, the accomplishment. What adulation could equal such joy?"

"And you're still creating."

"If I stop, Time tortures a man like me. With the Colonies completed, there was nothing I wanted more than to build them again." He gestured to the half-finished Aztec Colony. "Considering my age and circumstances, I'm happiest at this scale."

George stared down at the giant in the severed body. An actor? That possibility seemed less and less probable. And the Colonies? Because the Rule of Separation demanded silence, Old Flowers had always refused any account of their construction. George smiled at the wonder of it all. Finally, an intriguing mystery had been solved.

"Pay close attention to your dreams when you leave this island," Jonathan said.

Startled, George said: "What?"

"I mean *really* pay attention. You may be in for a few surprises." He rolled the blueprints under the table.

"I doubt a dream could surprise me more than the chamber."

"If you had any idea how..." Jonathan closed his eyes. He rubbed his temples as if warding off a headache. "Never mind. Words are useless." He sighed, looking for the first time worn and shrunken, a man faded by age. But as quickly, his lively demeanor returned. "Do you remember the quarry, one of your childhood playgrounds?"

"Sure."

"Then you know the trail below the boulders. It's overgrown, but you should be able to follow it north to the Roman Colony."

"But if we're near the quarry, the mansion is four miles *south* of here."

"Exactly. Stay away from the mansion. Let the searchers find you somewhere near the Roman Colony. That way you can tell them you escaped from the chamber and found your way to the surface through the *Cloaca Maxima*, or some ventilation shaft."

"But why?"

"Because if Aaron discovers we've talked, you'll be more closely watched than usual and have no chance of escaping from the Flowers Corporation."

"I don't see what's so bad—"

"Enough talk!" Jonathan said, patience exhausted. "If you want to get to the surface, follow me."

He hopped to his right and clomped toward a different, but identical-looking tunnel. After several minutes of silent walking, they arrived at a solid metal door. Jonathan stared up. "Good luck, lad. Don't fall into any holes."

He reached into a small cavity about a foot above floor level. A click, then a mechanical hum as the door slowly yawned open. Behind it, a passageway.

"There's no lighting beyond this point. Use this." From his shirt pocket, he retrieved a penlight. "You'll find a ladder at the end of this tunnel. Be careful. It's a thirty-foot climb without a safety cage. At the top, there's a ledge and another metal door. Locked, of course, but the code is 1-9-4-5." He laughed. "My little joke. I wouldn't expect you to see the humor." He squinted. "You look strange. Is there something on your mind?"

"Yes. Why was Plato's *Republic* jutting out of your bookshelf?"

"Such a suspicious young man," Jonathan said shaking his head. "The reason is hardly ominous, George. You saw my library. It's extensive. With too much to read, it's easy to neglect one lonely volume. And the *Republic* is so special, so glorious. Its wisdom sparkles after more than two thousand years. Why? Because it offers no answers, only questions. I leave it jutting out of my bookcase to remind me that uncertainty is life's fundamental truth."

George swirled in his own doubts and questions—about Jonathan, the true purpose of Flowers Island, his father, his very existence. "Thank you," he said and aimed the light into the darkness.

"Your destiny is written," Jonathan called out behind him.

His voice echoed, as if to repeat a fundamental truth.

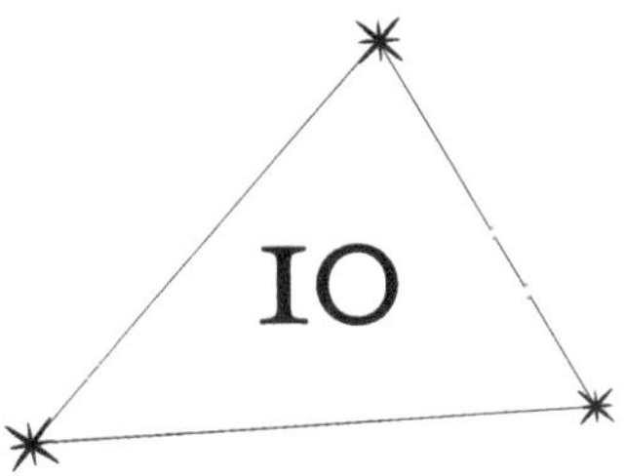

# IO

As Jonathan had promised, George emerged from the island's subterranean world near the quarry. The long walk down the corridor, with the dimming penlight, had given George a chance to arrive at a very important conclusion—don't arrive at any conclusions. It was all too absurd. Bruce was crazy, phony, lying, or all three. Old Flowers had violated the island's cardinal Rule of Separation, it seemed. And Jonathan?

*Flowers' Asylum*, George thought. It had a nice, yet disturbing, ring to it.

George climbed the boulders above the quarry, found a precipice near the top giving him a sweeping view of the valley below; saw Lake Sisyphus to the south, the Mansion Complex beyond it, the green *Vale of Tempe* to the west. The Grecian Colony was one hill further. The Medieval spires, like two shafts of grey light, peaked above the hills to the north.

Breathing seemed like a new sensation. The fresh air, the summer, green Maidenhair ferns drenched in yellow Milkberries, all filled him with the first sense of wellbeing he had known in almost two days.

But the feeling felt elusive, as if at any moment, a breeze would whip by and blow it away.

A pounding, mechanical thunder grew in the distance. Darting under a rock ledge, George watched the helicopter pass overhead. The sight added an ominous dimension to Jonathan's words: *"If Aaron discovers we've talked... closely watched... escape from the Flowers Corporation."*

But why?

The copter flew south to the Mansion Complex.

Jonathan, the hermit genius, living alone and content in his stunted world. Or another actor weaving illusions?

Too many words, riddles, warnings.

George banished conflicting thoughts and climbed down the mountain. At the bottom, he traveled north, as Jonathan had suggested, along the overgrown road that led to the Roman Colony, away from Flowers Mansion. "I'm not going back to the mansion without that stallion," he said aloud.

But an inner voice told him the horse wouldn't be there when he arrived.

Something rustled behind.

George whirled around and scared a deer.

*Goddamn chamber.*

First a fox, then a rabbit, now this fearsome deer had jabbed his prickly nerves.

*I've never felt this jittery before*, he thought, as imagination transformed branches into gnarled appendages; wooden arms and twig fingers grasping toward him like some childhood fairy tale. "Stop!" he screamed to the forest. But something had changed, in his mind, in his life. Trauma had followed him from the chamber.

Trees rustled in the breeze, normally a pleasing melody, now a dissonant clatter.

He leaned against a lightning-charred stump and rubbed his eyes. Again, Jonathan's voice: *"Don't be so hard on yourself. There's nothing on those walls but plain, white, Carrara marble."*

*Bullshit.* He knew there were satyrs on those walls.

Sunlight filtered through branches in misty blotches. August. Storm season. Four weeks of clockwork thunderheads rolling over the island. It was too early in the day for a serious storm, but by evening the grandfather clock would chime its alarm.

"Let's get out of here," he heard himself saying.

*Let's? Why did I say that? I'm alone.*

He turned in a full circle, just to make sure, then quickened his pace, knowing that this wild slash of trail ended at the Roman Colony. Beyond that, he would follow a creek that emptied into the Fayum River, near the Egyptian Colony. From there, the horse trail would lead to North Beach.

The sun dipped closer to the horizon.

Dense underbrush swallowed the path for long stretches. Nothing looked familiar. Odd for a trail George had traveled many times as a child. But maybe not. His wits still felt deadened, his thinking muddled. Jonathan's words haunted his mind. *...I called Doctor Feldman...That will be my proof...*

*Proof that Old Flowers drugged me,* George thought. Yesterday, that notion would have seemed outlandish. Just like the chamber.

Crossing through fields offered rare glimpses of sun, but also exposure and feelings of vulnerability.

Back under the canopy of bristly casuarina trees, buried from the knees down in asparagus ferns, shadows became hiding places for *numina*, the forest spirits of the Roman Colony. *"Be wise, Antonius,"* his *paterfamilias* had said. *"Don't let the* numina *trick you. They are Gods, living in the God's world with no natural love of man. Beware! They sport in robbing a man of confidence and trapping him in circles. Never travel at night. Never leave the road."*

*What road?* George thought, returning to the present. The meager trail dipped into a ravine and vanished, leaving George uncertain, following instinct, and surrounded by dark thoughts.

Thirty minutes later, the trail reappeared and led him to a spot he had passed an hour before. "Fuck you bastards!" George muttered, cursing the *numina*. The Roman Colony felt like an outpost at the edge of the world, North Beach like a mystical land of dreams. He primed himself for a night on hard ground. Still, the air brimmed with jasmine, prickled with wild rose. The sighs of mourning doves soothed the afternoon. Sweat, exertion, a full stomach, and stabs of light through a thousand shades of green buried memories of the chamber.

Laughter.

Crouching, George focused on the sound, waited, and heard it again. Then banter and the whinny of a horse.

Slowly, he crept through the undergrowth, crawled up a small rise, and peered down at a clearing where four men dressed in the leather garb of Roman cavalrymen, their horses grazing nearby, slouched in conversation. Each carried a *loculus*, an Ancient Roman satchel. Lunching on bread and grapes, they used a *pugio* to cut "Phrygian", a she-ass cheese curdled with fig juice, obvious by its square, or *quadrate*, shape. Both food and conversation were seasoned with *massilitanum*, swallowed from a bloated wineskin. George cringed. He hated the taste of *massilitanum*. But his throat was so dry he craved liquid, any liquid, even the heavy, acrid wine that the poet Marcus Martialis considered "poisonous". For a weak moment, George even considered allowing the cavalrymen to "find" him. But he banished the notion. *I won't give Old Flowers the satisfaction.*

Instead, he settled into the underbrush and rested, trying to breathe clarity into his thinking. He knew that, eventually, his nerves would settle, tension in his hands would loosen, breathing would feel less constricted. Trauma and memories of the chamber would fade. The painful swelling on his throbbing forehead would stop clouding his vision.

But peace and comfort eluded him. After a few restless minutes, the nagging urge to get to North Beach drove him back to the crest of the knoll. Laughter, sluggish movements, and bursts of raucous speech suggested minimum interest in finding George, but great dedication to *numina*, especially *Bacchus*.

*Fine. I'll leave the trail and go around them.*

Back in the thick of the woods and giving a wide berth to the legionnaires, George hiked for another hour over hills matted with olivewood. Vineyards bordered the Roman Colony, so he avoided them, along with the *villa rusticas*, some stylish and decorated with frescos and marble columns, most plain mud and wood structures with thatched roofs. Of course, everything was tranquil and museum-like—static, artificial, lacking the animation of Old Flowers' legions of actors. Yet, year-round gardeners sustained, among many others, crops of olive trees, figs, garlic, artichokes, vast gardens of produce and culinary herbs, and all the fruits of an active Colony. Horticulturists traveled between all seven Colonies, but in Rome, propagated wheat, emmer, spelt, and barley. Maintenance personnel trimmed hedges, repaired latrines, hauled stone, dug trenches, and paved Ancient Roman streets. They preserved elegant *domus* for the wealthy, and the stacked, cramped *insulae* apartments for everyone else.

Today, a sultry sun called forth the goddess *Flora*. She scented the breeze with rarities like lemon blossoms and citron. Then just as impressively, mingled her perfume with the tang of chicken shit.

Suddenly, the awareness of running water. Out of sight, but nearby, the brook feeding into the Fayum River. Finally, cool water, and a stream that would lead him to the Egyptian Colony, and from there, to the horse trail and North Beach.

Relief energized him. But just as quickly, voices froze him at the water's edge. People, and horses. This time coming from ahead and just around the bend.

"Whoa...", said Barry Dee, his voice so close it was unmistakable.

With a lurch fueled by panic, George dashed back to a wide oak he remembered passing a moment earlier. Each step crunched dry leaves and branches that, to George, sounded like elephants fleeing into the underbrush. Patches of soft earth revealed easily tracked footprints.

Darting behind the oak, he crouched low and peeked through a thicket of ferns as Barry crossed the brook. He was riding Lucy, his grey mare. Once on dry ground, Barry halted the mare and waited for his companions, riders still hidden by thick foliage, but close enough to hear over the running water.

"Never seen any dangerous ones," Barry Dee called out in response to some question. "Least not one's that warn't more scared a you then you a them." A deep guffaw, then a brief silence George hadn't expected. No explosion of chew hurled behind the words.

George ducked further below the ferns and listened.

"I suppose you would know better than I," said an even more surprising voice, female, and mature, no one George recognized.

"He's right, ma'am," said a third voice, Glen's. "We've only had one snake bite on Flowers Island since I've been here. That's almost sixteen years."

"What about the one that bit you yesterday?" Barry scoffed.

"Would you get off my back about yesterday? I wasn't responsible for my actions."

*Yesterday? I wasn't responsible for my actions?*

George remembered Glen eating half of his cinnamon roll—a drugged cinnamon roll?

"So, you've only had that one bite?" the woman persisted.

"Yes, ma'am," Glen answered.

Curiosity eclipsed caution. Glancing over the ferns, George almost cursed when he saw his friend cross the brook on a black Arabian stallion.

*Goddamn it!* he thought in a roil of anger. *So much for the birthday surprise.*

Forget about North Beach. Nothing to do now but accept defeat and return to Flowers Mansion.

He rolled onto the mossy earth and stared up through the oak's towering canopy. But, damn it, he wouldn't submit to their "rescue". He rejected this lesson, renounced Flowers Island, the Colonies, and Old Flowers' manipulations. He disowned Plato and his wretched *Republic*, scorned Jonas Felty, the actors, the teachers, Jonathan, and whatever version of his life these lessons were designed to shape.

*Fuck you all!* his thoughts screamed. *I'm not your project! I can't be fashioned from a set of blueprints! I'll return to the mansion, but on* my *terms.*

"In the former Costa Rica," the woman continued, "there are stories of snakes coming out of the jungle and into people's houses. Monsters the size of trees. They even look like trees."

Silence followed, and George grumbled a muffled scoff. Never had Barry Dee suffered a loss of words.

The three pursuers weaved through the trees, coming to within ten feet of George, but like the Roman cavalrymen, seemed too nonchalant for a serious search.

"You're absolutely certain Flowers Island has no poisonous snakes?" the woman asked again.

"Trust me," Barry said, "the only snakes on Flowers Island is workin' fer Ol' Flowers!" He laughed. So did Glen. The woman didn't.

She replied stonily: "That was my second concern."

Her words dropped an anvil over further conversation, crows squawked louder than squeaking saddles, hooves faded under the sound of running water, and George devised a new plan.

The sun sank to within a hand span above the trees. He remembered the moon on the night before he crashed into the chamber—little more than an orange sliver. Now, only two nights larger, its light would barely filter through the trees.

No problem. He still had time.

Ancient Roman warnings swirled through his mind, but he banished them. More needless clutter in a brain that needed rest, and peace, and the soothing balm of nature. Every muscle ached in a body that felt somewhere between exhaustion and nausea. A bitter aftertaste reminded him of the chamber's stinking decay. The lump on his forehead hammered.

Climbing a large boulder in search of shade and a refuge from rescue patrols, he stopped. The terrain looked familiar. To his left, a field of monolithic stone. On the right, the brook followed the woods along the rim of a canyon. He'd been here before, years ago as a child. Old Flowers had guided he and Glen to a swimming hole below a waterfall.

*Perfect,* George thought, though he remembered the area as exposed, slabs of rock bordered by towering cedars. The falls would muffle the sound of approaching searchers, but he needed water and it was worth the risk.

He wiped his forehead; felt the grime, saw mud-caked hands, smears and scrapes on filthy arms. *I need this,* he told himself. *The water will revive my spirit and renew my strength.*

And at that moment, last night's dream flashed into his mind. The sun, the Greek hillside, the dancers. This brook and the waterfall beyond were never in the dream, but somehow the two felt connected.

After drinking his fill, George worked his way slowly, warily, to the crest of the falls. Below, slabs of sandstone surrounded the pool. Yellow primroses opened to the late afternoon. A horse grazed on the greenery creeping down the canyon walls.

And resting face up on a section of rock, a young woman, as naked as the flowers.

*This is a trap,* was George's immediate thought. Followed by the mental voice of Headmaster Felty, speaking as Socrates:

*...so must we take our youth amid terrors of some kind, and again pass them into pleasures, and prove them more thoroughly than gold is proved in the furnace, that we may discover whether they are armed against all enchantments....*

So, there it was. Straight from the text of Plato's *Republic*, the ancient philosophy that had excited him at first; infuriated, bored, and annoyed him mostly, and now enlightened this moment.

And could Old Flowers be more obvious?

The dark chamber had surely been his father's version of taking *"our youth amid terrors"*, and this beautiful, naked girl his way of passing George *"into pleasures"* as a method of testing him *"more thoroughly than gold is proved in the furnace"* so that George may be *"armed against all enchantments"*.

Carefully, compelled by curiosity, George climbed down the cliffs toward the naked girl, the sound of his movement masked by the falling water.

At the edge of the woods, he stopped. *What the hell am I doing?* He felt dizzy and slightly nauseous. Had he been more dehydrated than he thought? Maybe too much water too quickly?

He was still ten feet away, hidden by brambles, peering through the branches. *Enchantments,* he thought again, as the young woman stirred. She sighed. Her voice, like a cool mist, drifted over the splashing water. *Stop this!* he thought. *I can't play this game.* Yet, he marveled at his father's ability to cast players for Colony lessons. This sleek, fair-haired beauty was certainly enchanting, but also a trick, another lesson, party to Old Flowers' version of George's life.

*I have a new plan now,* he thought.

He would make his way to the caverns near the Egyptian Colony, hide for a few days, forage for figs, melons, beans and berries, and try to make sense of the chamber, Jonathan's words, and why Old Flowers had violated the Rule of Separation.

*This actress plays no roll.*

So why couldn't he stop staring?

It wasn't her nakedness. Public nudity was unexceptional, even customary, during numerous lessons in the Culture Colonies. And sure, she was his "type". But, he reminded himself, he had often pursued more than physical beauty. Depth and intelligence placed high on his list of desirable qualities, as did interest in music and appreciation of culture and language. If a woman excelled in sports, not necessarily a gymnast like himself, but proved to be healthy, vigorous, and adventurous with a nimble mind and a keen fervor for life, he ignored her size, shape, or hair color.

But then he remembered various past adventures. Choices he had made with no regard for lofty virtues. When fetching buttocks and eager nipples defined cultural appreciation.

*And whose fault is that*, George thought, blaming Old Flowers for the skirmish of contradictions attacking his thoughts. Was George the boy who lives in the mansion, or the George of the Culture Colonies? Should he believe in the romantic love of Ancient Egypt, or arranged courtships like the Middle Eastern Colony? Wedding night deceptions like fish bladders filled with chicken blood were common for non-virgins in the Asian Colony. Should marriage be a charade? The Aztecs thought so. Masks and disguises filled vital roles in Ancient Aztec courtship rituals, along with familial manipulation. In the Grecian Colony, marriage partners were chosen for compatibility between the *kyrios*, the head of the household, and the size of the dowry. An Ancient Roman custom used kissing, not for affection, but to determine the state of drunkenness.

*And why the hell am I thinking about marriage?!*

Was it because this young woman, lovely on the surface, was in truth an actress, *deception,* wearing nakedness to *disguise* some form of *manipulation?*

Was she the essence of this lesson? Had Old Flowers chosen George's wife, mate, consort?

*No!* George thought. *I make my own choices.*

But there she rested, open, vulnerable, and so compelling.

Younger than George by at least a year, her breezy blond hair landed in delicate wisps on velvety shoulders. Golden skin on naked breasts glowed like the sweet flesh of a New Zealand pear, and with that image came tingles of shame and awkwardness. Anger at Old Flowers, this lesson, and her role in this deception had blinded him to his own naked boorishness. *Who am I to crouch here and stare?* he thought. *Dress her with suspicions and assumptions, steal her privacy?*

He forced his gaze to her left wrist and the silver bracelet, the snake eating its tail, the *Ouroboros*, an ancient icon representing the beginning and end of time. George had first seen the symbol on an Egyptian Colony sarcophagus, then later in the magical traditions of the Grecian Colony; later still in Medieval alchemy.

This person, even naked, dressed in sumptuous symbolism.

But there was nothing symbolic about her allure.

*Leave,* he thought, *now. Turn away and walk, no run, to the Egyptian Colony, to the caverns.*

Yet, he remained transfixed.

Proximity evoked feelings of recognition, and familiarity. George saw, or thought he saw, ripples of heat distorting the air around her body. *It's the warm stone*, he told himself. But the stone lay mostly in the shade, and cool mist dampened its surface.

Slowly, fascinated by her radiant waves, and beauty, George crept closer. He held his palms inches from her skin, felt the heat, and shuddered as mild electrical shivers pulsed over his fingers. *Aftereffects from the drug,* he thought. Pain, jitters, twitches; all had followed him from the chamber. Fear and adrenalin muddled his mind and jumbled his senses.

The young woman stirred.

The movement re-awakened guilt. *What am I doing? I should be fleeing.*

An inner voice screamed: *"You're staring like a pervert!"*

The girl sighed, shifted her head, and faced him directly for the first time.

George gasped. He blinked and focused on a single blemish—a thin, hair-like scar running down the length of her neck, much like George's scar, but below her *right* ear.

George touched the left side of his neck, "No...", he groaned.

The young woman awakened, saw the mud-caked stranger looming over her, and shrieked.

George sprang up, lost his balance, tripped on a rock, and landed on her pile of clothes.

They were six feet apart, George leaning back on his elbows, ashamed, but wary.

The actress sat up and stared; silent, curious, as if studying a rare, exotic organism. With crossed legs, hair flowing down a straight back, hands resting palms up in her lap, (and of course, breasts as pleasing as lotus buds), she embodied a familiar fantasy—every yoga instructor George had ever imagined naked.

The young woman chuckled.

George flushed, again, sat up and pulled her clothes out from under him. She was so lovely he wanted to see every artful inch of her, but instead, forced his gaze to her guileless green eyes, and that pretty half-smile, poised and innocent. He reminded himself that, as his father's agent, she would have to report everything. "Sorry I startled you," he said, tone flat and detached. But even to his own ears failing at feigned indifference. She noted the deception with a tilt of her head, and an ever so slight upward glance, not quite an eye roll, but a delicate mockery of fake apathy.

*I deserved that*, George thought. He wondered if the pounding in his ears was audible, if the mud on his face would absorb the cold sweat. He held out her lime green tee shirt, beige shorts, and beige (also called "nude" he would later find out) panties.

But she made no move to take them.

Should he care?

Did he have a choice?

"I'm on my way to the Roman Colony," he lied with instant regret. "I mean, I was just passing by." Truth feeling so much better. "But I started out for North Beach yesterday...on my horse Zander...not sure where she is now, but I assume Bruce took her back to the stables. Anyway, we became separated, but I decided to continue without her, and in the meantime, got kind of filthy..."

Silence.

And those eyes, both intriguing and intrigued.

If the essence of acting is subtle projected emotion, this girl could animate marble. She even resembled a statue—beautiful, sculpted, tranquil—yet her slightest expression electrified. A glance felt like a flint blade piercing the heart on its way to the soul.

Finally, after what seemed like a thousand peeps from a single sparrow, and a *culeus* of water over the falls, George squirmed like a *criminalis* sewn into a leather sack. "Are you going to say something?" he blurted, frustration thwarting courtesy.

"You're so naked," she said, with an ironic smile and a shake of the head. The flint blade thrust a little deeper. "Yours is the most exposed mind I've ever known. It's fascinating."

"What?"

"The images in your mind are fantastically distinct. Very unlike ordinary people. More like those gigapixel digiboards you see in the *Mercado Central*."

*You think you're reading my mind*?! George thought. But he said: "What's a digiboard?"

She laughed, amusement, not ridicule. "You'll find out soon enough."

*Are you referring to digiboards?*

Her smile became suddenly wistful. For a moment, she stared at the waterfall, its mist cooling the air around them. "I envy the luxury of an uncluttered mind." Then facing him with a look as grim as cemetery statuary, she said: "Uncle Aaron and my mother are planning *something*. Whatever it is, I won't play along."

"Uncle Aaron?"

"And I already feel guilty about skulking around in your thoughts. Close a mental curtain and I won't be able to see beyond it."

Still not believing, but alarmed by the slightest possibility, George envisioned the Medieval Colony and the iron gate at Tintagel Castle. For good measure, he imagined a raised drawbridge—even though the castle lacked a moat.

"A drawbridge will work," she said, saying *drawbritch* with a pleasant, Latin American accent.

"You saw that?"

"George, despite what you're thinking, this isn't a lesson."

"Who is your mother?"

"Kathryn Maxwell."

"Oh," George said.

Kathryn Maxwell. George had met her a few times, but only briefly. Next to Aaron Flowers, she was the most powerful officer in the Flowers Corporation. She managed the corporation's holdings in Central America and protected them from all manner of rebels, guerillas, rightists, leftists, "overtists" and "covertists". In the process, she became the corporation's most feared executive. Aaron Flowers praised her constantly. But even he had once commented on the "grimness of her personality", and had likened her to a "warlord trapped in a beautiful body."

"My name is Cerissa. Mother and I were returning to the former Costa Rica when she surprised me with this visit." She paused and ran her fingers lightly across the surface of the smooth rock. Her eyes narrowed. A bitter scowl pinched her beautiful features. "It was the excitement."

"I don't understand."

"I know better than to trust her motives, but I was so thrilled to come here."

"I've met your mother. She's..."

"Go ahead and say it. I don't have to read your mind to know what you're thinking."

"I was going to say a bit cold, or something."

"More like a frozen lizard when she's in work mode. Which is most of the time."

"You called my father 'Uncle Aaron'. Are you and I somehow related?"

After a smile moist with flirtation, she said: "I hope not."

*Me too*, George thought behind his Medieval drawbridge.

"I call him 'Uncle Aaron' in the Central American sense, as in *Tío Aaron*, a form of endearment."

"I see," George said.

"He's the closest thing I've ever had to a father. I don't see him much, but I see my real father less." She pointed to her shorts and tee shirt. "I'll take those now."

After handing her the clothes, George stood and walked a few paces to the brook. He focused on the water cascading down tiers of cliffs, wishing all the while that he could focus on her instead. Not for the sake of lust, not exactly, though longing played its part, but for the simple pleasure of seeing her. The way she moved, her body's grace, or awkwardness. And the light; the way it sheened her hair, rounded the curves of her shoulders, and poured down her arching back.

All this he imagined while starving his physical eyes with the brilliant, reddish-orange flowers of the Flame Tree shading the swimming hole; and a wild Loquat, branches heavy with succulent yellow fruit as tart and biting as George's desire.

"What am I thinking about, right now?" George said, mentally lowering the drawbridge and standing before the iron gate.

"You want to know *how* I know what you're thinking about right now," she said, with a friendly giggle. "And you're wondering if we'll see each other after today."

"Can I turn around now?" George said.

"You didn't have to look away in the first place. I'm not ashamed of my body. Why should you be?"

George shrugged and turned to face her. "I guess I wanted to give you privacy."

"And torture yourself with wondering how the light glances off my naked body?" She smiled and reached quickly for her tee shirt, suddenly in a hurry to dress. "You should raise your drawbridge before we're both embarrassed." She wiggled into the shirt and let it hang loosely over her shorts. George could tell by the seams that she was wearing it inside out. Such a unique and amazing girl. Everything about her, with or without clothes, fascinated him.

But he asked: "So, if the drawbridge is effective, how could you know I was thinking about light over your body?"

"Thoughts, George, as fleeting as they are, leave behind echoes. Especially thoughts charged with emotion."

"So how *do* you do it? Were you born with the ability? Did you inherit it from your mother? Is that the power behind her success?"

"So many questions," she said, while stepping into her sandals. Ones I'll be happy to answer. But we're out of time."

"What do you mean?"

"They're early. They said they'd be back in two hours."

"Who?"

Cerissa replied with a gaze over George's right shoulder.

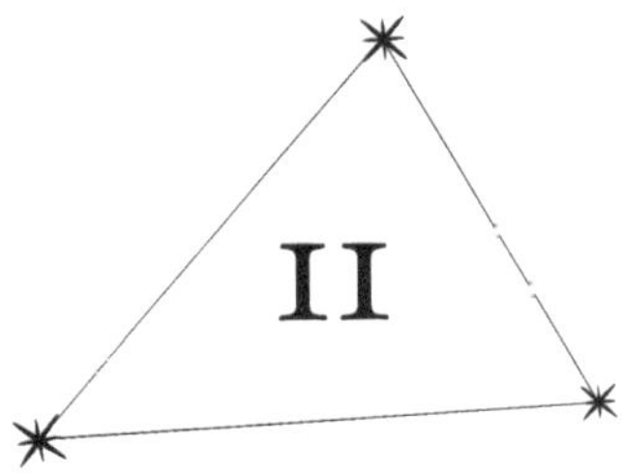


Turning around, George saw the legendary Kathryn Maxwell standing forty feet away, reins in hand at the top of the waterfall, the horses, Barry, and Glen standing meekly behind her. She had a look of molten fury on her face.

"She doesn't look too pleased to see me," George muttered under his breath.

"Sex is a big issue with her," Cerissa whispered back. "Remember what I said about not playing along."

"But we haven't done anything."

"We should have. The punishment is the same either way."

"Punishment?"

"Never mind. If she's playing games, you'll know soon enough. She's sharp too. Very strategic."

It sounded like a battle about to begin and George didn't like the look on Kathryn Maxwell's face. She had a very well-defined jaw line, like a sculptor's marble goddess, but that quality hardened her appearance—especially in contrast to her daughter's classically soft features. Kathryn was also dark, striking, her beauty more demanding. George wondered how many people she had conquered with her smile.

Mrs. Maxwell led her horse around some boulders, disappeared for a moment, then tramped down the steep terrain, around the trees to creek level. She handled her horse like a trained equestrian.

George glanced at Glen and Barry. Barry was doing his best to appear indifferent, though most likely guffawing under his breath. And Glen? Behind his customary smirk, he was no doubt thinking: *Watch out, Georgie Boy, if she has her way, your ass will be your headstone.*

Cerissa joined George at the water's edge and stood a few steps in front of him. "She promised not to make any scenes this trip," she said with a scoff. "Too much to expect." With her back to George, her shirt was even more noticeably inside out. The little white tag said: MACHINE WASH, WARM WATER.

*More like hot water*, George thought.

"George, are yer okay?" Barry called, when the group was still a good twenty feet away. After almost two days of absence, it was a natural question—considering the noticeable swelling on George's forehead; clothes caked in mud, and marginal, if any, nutrition. But in George's mind, a two-day manhunt ending with him in the company of a beautiful young woman would inspire laughter and ridicule from everyone on the island.

He decided to play into it. "As you can see," George said, "I'm fine." Keeping his dinner with Jonathan secret, he added: "But I'm pretty damn hungry."

Barry shot a glance to Glen, and Mrs. Maxwell said: "I don't imagine you're as hungry now as you were a while ago."

George stiffened under his casual posture. The memory of Cerissa's body and the sting of guilt lingered.

"What's this, the latest fashion?" Mrs. Maxwell said, indicating Cerissa's inside-out tee shirt.

Cerissa stared into the woods with a look of calm bemusement.

"It appears my daughter has found another lost boy," Mrs. Maxwell said. George didn't like the way she said "another", or for that matter, "boy".

George shrugged. After lowering his mental drawbridge, he envisioned wasps nesting under the ledge of a dark cave. Cerissa smiled, offered him a slight nod, and seemed to relish George's delight in this new and mysterious form of communication.

Mrs. Maxwell glared in classic shrew-rat style, and for much too long (even though it was just seconds), the only sound coming from the splashing water. Finally, Barry said: "There's some ugly stormers rollin' in this time a year, Mrs. Maxwell. Best not get caught in the woods durin' hurricane season. Come on, Georgie."

George started to move, but froze when Mrs. Maxwell raised her palm. "Barry, why don't you and Glen take my daughter back to the Roman Colony. Leave the horses with the other searchers and ride the tram to the mansion. I want Aaron to know right away that we've found George safe."

*For how long*, George wondered.

"Leave the horses? But..." Barry stopped mid-chew.

"Well?" Mrs. Maxwell said.

"It's just that I..." Barry lowered his eyes and looked everywhere but at the gorgon who could bite his job off. "I been considerin' that tuber on George's forehead there and, well, I think I better get on it for it gets, ya know, *in*fected."

Kathryn's full, delectable lips pursed in an ugly scowl. She turned to George and glared, dark brown eyes like two bitter almonds, raw, toxic. "Very well," she said, in a voice barely audible above the falls. "*Five* minutes."

"Yes ma'am," Glen blurted along with Barry. The two looked at each other as if they too could read each other's minds.

*Flowers' Carnival*, George thought.

Barry gestured for George to follow him to his horse, now grazing a few feet away.

Mrs. Maxwell led Cerissa to the edge of the woods, speaking in a low voice.

"Christ, Georgie," Barry muttered, as he reached into his saddlebags for a first aid kit. "A man yer age ain't never lost as long as he's got his "divinin rod" leadin' the way." He muffled a laugh and pointed to George's pants. "Yer was goin' the right direction, son, but yer shoulda kep goin'."

"Never mind that," Glen said, until now abnormally quiet. George sensed an underlying tension, something unrelated to Kathryn Maxwell. "George, are you really all right?

"Of course."

"You damn sure don't look all right."

"What are you talking about?"

"Stand still, son," Barry said, grabbing George's arm and dabbing at the wound. "Good thing I'm here, Georgie. I'll get ever' one a them stinkin' germs."

He poured alcohol onto a fresh cotton swab while sneaking a glance at Mrs. Maxwell. "I ignored yer tracks as long as I could," he said, in a low voice. "But Jesus, George, even she noticed 'em after a while. Hell, I couldn't pretend that the sky warn't blue."

"You saw my tracks?"

Glen stepped closer and pointed to Barry. "You think a trail rat like this is gonna miss the devastation you left behind?"

"What? Ouch!"

"Hole still, will ya. Ya want them critters out 'a yer face, or don't ya?

"You make it sound like I drove a bulldozer though the woods." He grabbed Barry's arm. "Jesus, Barry, leave a few germs for the next infection."

"I gotta get 'em all," Barry said.

"You're opening the wound with all that rubbing. Thanks, but enough."

"Don't blame me if yer head rots off."

George turned to Glen. "If you saw my tracks, why the hell were you ignoring them?"

"George, this isn't the time." He nodded toward Mrs. Maxwell. "But we've all been thinking. We want to talk to you tonight. Show you something."

"We?"

"A lot of us on the island. We can help you become a little more..." His voice lowered to a whisper. "A little more independent."

With images of a legless old man, drugs, and Plato's *Republic* swirling in his mind, George asked: "Do you by any chance know a guy named—?"

"Shit!" Glen muttered and backed away. "*La Puta del Sur.*"

Mrs. Maxwell had left Cerissa and was walking toward them.

Barry pressed a wide bandage across George's lump. "Ouch! Goddamn it!" George said, jerking his head back. "The wall I hit didn't hurt that much."

"Why, yer welcome, Georgie."

George took a deep breath. "Sorry. Thanks."

"It was worth ever' bit a pain I suffered, if the world be rid a one more germ," Barry said.

"Barry...Glen...!" Mrs. Maxwell called.

As the echo of, "Yes, ma'am," hung in the air, George noticed Kathryn's voice, now light, even brisk. He couldn't tell whether she was acting, or relieved by whatever Cerissa may have just told her.

"I should never have allowed Cerissa to stay behind. She's overtired and suffering from too much sun." *Both lies,* George thought. "We've wasted enough time already."

"Yes ma'am," Barry said, not foolish enough to protest again.

"I'd like to stay here and spend a few moments with George." Kathryn gestured toward the horses. "Glen, you ride with Barry. I'll need the stallion for George."

The glower from Glen could have boiled oil, but he patted the stallion and walked silently over to Lucy, Barry's grey mare.

Barry cleared his throat. "Now, ma'am," he said, "I wouldn't shilly about too long. Them woods'll chew ya up on a no mooner like tonight."

"Don't worry. We'll be right behind you."

With a grunt, Barry grabbed the reins. "Slide on," he said to Glen. "Miss...?"

Cerissa offered George a quick half-smile and mounted. In a moment, all three had disappeared up the steep incline into the woods.

Well, the next question was: Where would Kathryn Maxwell's righteous talons strike? The heart? The head? Or was she going to spank him? Something was unresolved, and she had a remarkable knack for long, tense, silences.

She was silent now, staring.

George stared back. He had done nothing wrong. Still, murmurs fluttered in his stomach. His tongue felt like a sponge drying in the heat of Kathryn's gaze. Memories from early lessons cluttered his thoughts—parts he'd played under various guises in various Colonies (young *Antonius*, or *Toltectl*, or *Mengyao*)—all guilty of childish crimes, all terrified, all shrinking from angry mothers. He banished the images. But ache and abandonment lingered like a harsh scolding. He had never lived with, or even met, his biological mother. Older women, women like Kathryn Maxwell who would be around his mother's age, flustered him.

"You probably think I'm a wretched bitch," Kathryn Maxwell said, in the same calm, controlled voice she had affected earlier.

George remained silent, but his eyes screamed: *You have no idea!*

"Well, you're right. Especially when it comes to protecting my daughter." She stepped near enough to slap him. "Cerissa has been sleeping with a man over three times her age, a man somewhat older than her own father."

Kathryn's eyes narrowed. Renewed anger churned. George steeled himself for an outburst, but instead of speaking, she sighed. A long, deep, exhalation that ended with a droopy frown. Fear, concern, dismay, defeat, each dragged her allure to the brink of ugly. Pity replaced fear. Clearly, she believed her fantasy. But to George, the notion of Cerissa with an old man seemed comical. A fiction spawned by an over-protective imagination.

He looked away to stifle a laugh.

Kathryn continued: "I uncovered this latest affair before we left for Europe. It's dangerous. It goes beyond sleeping with her troop of local *machitos*. I'm putting a stop to it." She aimed her brows and bored skillfully through his doubts. "I almost believe you didn't bed her. But only because she didn't have time."

"Why are you telling me this?"

"Because I want you to know why you won't be seeing her again." She had the solid, no nonsense manner that was, no doubt, the foundation of her reputation. Aaron Flowers' "warlord in a beautiful body". A warlord armed with invincible eyes.

The sun drew shadows over the trees and sank somewhere behind the Medieval Colony. "It's getting dark," George said, mounting the stallion. "We'd better start back."

"Wait!" she snapped. With crossed arms and an expression both grim and rigid, she reminded George of an alabaster *ushabti*, the funerary figurines buried in Egyptian tombs. He winced at the notion of Kathryn Maxwell as his eternal, afterlife servant. *I'd rather be squeezed in* Shezmu's *wine press and swim in my own blood,* George thought. "You should know that despite who or what you think I am, I want the best for you, as does Aaron." *Fuck, I hope Cerissa didn't hear that* Shezmu *shit.* "Someday..." *I wonder if she reads thoughts from a distance.* "...you may meet Cerissa again." *Sorry, Cerissa, I didn't mean to trash your mother.* "But not until you're both ready." *I'll have to remember to stay behind my drawbridge. Just in case.*

Kathryn Maxwell mounted her horse.

*What the hell was she saying?*

George watched Kathryn ride into the woods.

He stayed as far behind as he dared.

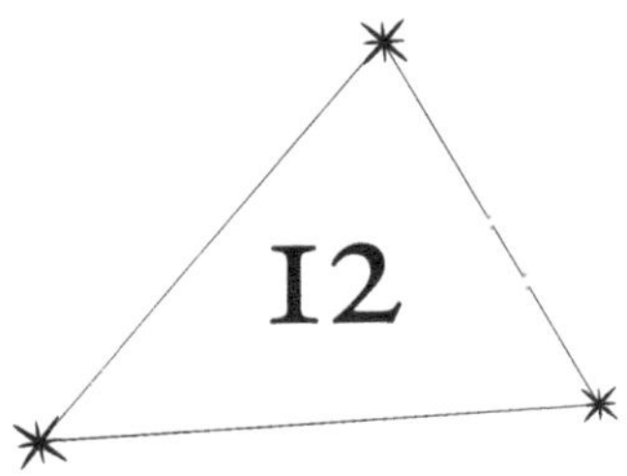

# 12

Glen's stallion was as gentle and responsive as George had hoped, and as intuitive. Unlike Kathryn Maxwell. Unfamiliar with the terrain and confused by the darkening woods, she led them east toward the Middle Eastern Colony instead of south past the Roman Colony. George rode silently behind, offered no advice or course corrections, and knew that, soon enough, they would intersect the horse trail. From there, the lights from the distant Mansion Complex would guide them home. Home. What did that word mean anymore? Was it a mud and straw hovel in the Medieval Colony, the tiled courtyard of a Grecian Colony *oikos*, or George's room in the mansion? Since Old Flowers had lied, had slaughtered the sacred Rule of Separation as swiftly as a goat during *Eid-al-Adha*, George's trust in his father's motives had been sacrificed. He didn't want to return to the Mansion Complex, face Old Flowers, his failure, his friends, or any aspect of his former life.

On the other hand, his longing to see Cerissa equaled the craving to be rid of her mother. So, when in little over an hour George and Kathryn arrived at the stables, George followed his usual practice and stayed behind to feed, water and brush his mount. Kathryn sauntered off toward the lights of the mansion while George's mood brightened.

Barry Dee grabbed her horse, snorted when she'd walked beyond hearing range, then aimed a defiant wad of chew. George smiled, but couldn't wrestle more than a couple of "Yeps", and several "Uh-huhs" from him during the thirty minutes they were together.

George left with a good bye. "Good luck", was all Barry said.

Rollins and Jonas Felty, the headmaster, were waiting for George on the porch.

"Welcome back," Rollins said. "Your father is anxious to see you."

George dreaded the encounter, but said with arrogant bluster: "Not as anxious as I am. Is he in his study?"

"Of course," Rollins said. "He wants to see you at 8:30. That gives you time to eat and clean up."

"I'll see him now."

"George, Aaron's in a meeting. He can't be disturbed."

"He'll make an exception for me."

"Listen to Rollins," Jonas Felty said, looking small and insignificant without his Socrates clothes, but still a voice of authority.

"Fine," George said, the word so drawn with exasperated breath it moaned like a hymn to sighs. "So, how was the performance of Plato's *Republic*?"

"Flawless," Jonas said, pleased with the memory if not with George. "That is, except for the missing Thrasymachus."

George shrugged. "Looks like I failed my final exam. *Adios* world tour. I'm trapped here for another year." Anger fused with self-pity diluted by shame.

Without meeting George's eyes, Jonas said: "We'll discuss that later."

"And the birthday party?" George asked, turning back to Rollins.

"No party this year, George. The end of silly pranks. Both birthday boys were unavailable."

"And what about Bruce? He's unavailable too, right?" Rollins serene as a tomb, stared without expression as George frothed. "Did Bruce return to his fictional Grand Trinity University? Resume his studies of *Immunology*?" George snickered. "Nice touch. Not that I believed it. Oh, and did he return the Chalice of Dionysus?" Now snapping sarcasm. "Or did he sell it to some antiquities dealer in New York City? That's what I would do. No more hanging around off Broadway. No more waiting in line for another audition."

"Please," Rollins said. "Let's not—"

"George," Jonas said, brows furrowed by worry, lower lip pursed with perplexity. "Are you all right? What on earth are you talking about?" Then to Rollins, "What's going on? Is Bruce the stranger who—"

"Never mind," Rollins said, raising his palm. "George was lost. He's hungry, tired, more than a little bruised. What he needs is a hearty meal, rest, and a hot shower. We'll sort everything out tomorrow."

"Fuck you," George said, pushing past them and storming into the mansion.

* * *

Thirty minutes later, after snubbing food, but eager for the hot shower (he might, after all, meet Cerissa again), and then five minutes of restless lying on the waterbed where he tried to rehearse the upcoming conversation with Old Flowers, George left his room. He went to Glen's apartment above the potting shed, but found it empty. He tried the greenhouse, the kitchen, all three libraries, the conservatory. No Glen.

He passed Old Flowers' private elevator. The grandfather clock across the hall said, 8:05. Too early, but what the hell? Aside from pots and pans clanging against the babble in the kitchen, the hallway was tranquil. Unlike George. Apparently, Rollins pursued his duties elsewhere.

George faced the elevator and pressed the first button of the five-digit access code, then paused before touching the second. A low hum signaled the rise of the elevator, up from his father's study in the sub-basement.

Glancing down the hall and struck by sudden fear, he darted down the corridor and hid in the shadow of a large walnut hutch.

*Why am I so edgy?*

A moment later, the elevator opened. Followed by footsteps retreating down the hall in the opposite direction. Peeking out, George saw Cerissa, her bearing as breezy as the blond hair flowing over a sleeveless teal dress. Seconds before she reached the steps leading to the west wing, it occurred to him to lower his mental drawbridge.

No response.

He watched her climb the gentle curve of the winding staircase and disappear from view.

*What was Cerissa doing in Old Flowers' study?* George thought, as he rode the elevator down to the sub-basement. He stood, poised, ready to face his father when the elevator opened.

Old Flowers wasn't in the study.

*I'm early. He's in the aviary, the exercise room, or the library.*

A squawk from the far end of the room.

Bernie, Old Flowers' favorite Rose-Breasted Cockatoo wasn't in the aviary. He perched, never silently, on the edge of an overstuffed chair. Muted cries from Bernie's companions in the aviary embellished the colors of the luminarium tunnel. A deck of cards splayed in an arc over a glass coffee table (the study would feel empty without a deck of cards). An oak desk stacked with hardbacks and blueprints—Old Flowers planning the next development, improvement, or renovation.

George checked the exercise room. "Father!" he called, thinking Old Flowers might be in the sauna.

Silence. No sign of Leona either.

Spiral stairs led up to Old Flowers' library. Probably reading, oblivious to the outer world, hearing aid sitting on the end table.

Empty. But for two thousand, four hundred and thirty-three volumes, many rare first editions, the rest leather and cloth bound hardcovers on a range of subjects as vast as history itself.

*That leaves the aviary*, George thought.

But only birds occupied that room.

"Aaron's in a meeting," Rollins had said. "He can't be disturbed"

*A meeting with Cerissa? She left five minutes ago.*

The aviary's service elevator (and, of course, the wall-mounted ladder located beside it—a ladder Old Flowers would use in an emergency) was the only other way out of the sub-basement.

George had arrived in the main elevator.

So where was Old Flowers?

"Christ! I forgot how much racket you fuckers make," George said, as he left the aviary. He paused briefly in the luminarium to breathe in the colors, and then walked toward the elevator, perplexed.

A click sounded behind him.

Turning, George faced the full-length mirror he had seen a hundred times. On the mirror's frame, just above his reflection, a carved wood and gilt cherub smiled amidst swirls of Acanthus leaves.

Very slowly, the mirror slid away.

"George," Old Flowers said, while the glass retracted, "you're early." A full ten seconds passed before the mirror installed into a cavity in the wall.

Old Flowers limped into the study.

A glance past his father revealed a flight of stairs plunging down a gloomy passage.

*That's one mystery solved,"* George thought. Then said: "You never showed me that one." He gestured to the secret stairway.

Old Flowers laughed, flung his arm over George's shoulders and walked him to the couch, his cane tapping the tile floor. "You boys had enough hidden panels to play with. God knows I didn't need your tomfoolery down here."

"What's down there?"

"Nothing. An old storeroom. Let me see your forehead."

"Another nothing," George said, not referring to the bruise.

"Seriously, let me see." With a grip on George's chin, Old Flowers studied the bandage. "Not Feldman's best work."

George pulled away. "Barry did it. It's fine, *now.*" He stepped back. "But I could have been seriously hurt."

Old Flowers tucked his cane under the glass table, then sat on the couch. He gathered his cards. "You mean hurt by your fall into the chamber?" he said, looking up.

Normally, George admired his father's conviction, his confidence, the vast depth of his knowledge, and most importantly, his capacity to accomplish ambitions regardless of disability or difficulty. But now, with dank memories of pain and helplessness; satyrs, terror, and hunger swirling in his mind, he faced that bemused smile with revulsion. That tilt of Old Flowers' head, eyes curious like a baffled dog, but glinting with mischief, enraged him. Apparently, George's trials, questions, and discomforts deserved scant concern.

"Of course, I mean the chamber," George said, restraining the impulse to shout. "What else would I be referring to?"

Old Flowers chuckled, further incensing George, shuffled the deck, and dealt the four aces with practiced calm. "You're far from the first person to fall into a chamber like that, you know." His expression soured. "Other than a few bruises, are you 'seriously' hurt?"

George stood in silence, hated the truth in his father's words, knew he had suffered far greater injuries in other lessons and accepted, even welcomed, blood, aches, and cuts with masculine pride.

Why did this lesson feel different?

"George, I built that chamber to exact physical specifications. It's a very sophisticated mechanism. Designed by Ancient Egyptians to train initiates, not harm them." With a wide splay of his arms, he again smiled. A gesture meant to welcome George into the secrets of ancient mysteries. "As intended, the inclined plane broke your fall. Am I right? You didn't plummet into the chamber, you slid in gently." With a wave of the hand, he gestured to George's forehead. "I'm sorry about the bruise, George, but pain can also be instructive." He turned the four aces face down. "If I were you, I'd feel honored. That chamber was copied from the Pyramid of Cheops. You're the first person in six thousand years to be trained in the mystical traditions of ancient Egyptian priests."

*Right, honored,* George thought, then asked: "What about the Rule of Separation? All these years, you've demanded separation between lessons in the Colonies and life on the rest of the island. How can you justify breaking the Rule?"

Old Flowers turned the four aces face up. They had changed into four jokers. "Because I'm sneaky, George."

"Sneaky?"

Old Flowers gathered the cards and re-shuffled. "Don't look so shocked. The Rule of Separation was created especially for this lesson. All your life, you've expected your training to come only from the Colonies. You've prepared. The last lesson of your training had to be a surprise."

*Birthday surprise?*

"All that nonsense with Plato's *Republic* was a distraction. Something to keep you busy while I prepared you for your *true* final exam." He smiled. "For the most part, your training is over."

Bernie, until now sleeping while standing on one foot with eyes half-closed—motionless, silent, like an exhibit in a natural history museum—lurched awake with a flurry of flapping wings. Crest feathers flared like a warning flag, and a gaping beak blared a deafening screech. George had never shared his father's passion for parrots, or imagined that he and a caged bird could have anything in common. Now, he wasn't so sure. "This final lesson taught me *nothing*." George said, more to the bird, than to Old Flowers.

"You escaped from the chamber."

George shrugged.

"Then you must have learned the most valuable lesson of all." Old Flowers fanned his cards in a wide semi-circle.

Weary of lessons, lectures, ancient mysteries, and most of all, Old Flowers' long, enigmatic silences, George turned from the coffee table and meandered around the study. Steadily, melancholy lifted. With each step, possibilities blossomed. *I did escape*, he thought. Modern Greece and Rome, scaling the Mayan pyramid of *Cobá*, hiking the Andes, diving the Caribbean, climbing *Volcán de Fuego* and boating across *Lago de Atitlán,* leaving Flowers Island and touring the world—all seemed doable again. Maybe Cerissa could join them. Show them the former Costa Rica and the Central American Region. For the first time since his birthday, joy and hope smothered the chamber's misery. "Tell me more about this 'most valuable lesson'," George asked his father from across the room.

The cockatoo was now rambling back and forth across the back of the couch, squawking and pumping its wings. "Very well," Old Flowers said, diverting his attention from George to the bird. "Such a spoiled rabbit," he said, lips pursed in a series of air kisses. Over the years, George had heard Old Flowers refer to his pets as "rodents", "peaches", "roaches", "mongrels", "maggots", "buzzards", "badgers", and everything but "birds"—in the sweetest, most endearing tones. Bernie answered with a shriek and a leap onto Old Flowers' outstretched arm. "There's a good little *Pierrot*," he said.

George rolled his eyes at Old Flowers' play on words, but mostly, at his father's "distinctive" nature. He paused before the coffee table. "So, I fall through a floor, land in a nightmare, slam my head against a wall, and go half out of my mind. When I finally struggle out, I meet a crazy old..." George's chariot had lapped the stump without a driver. "I mean..." Old Flowers abandoned the parrot and shifted toward George. "That is," George continued, "I think I meet a bunch of satyrs that aren't there."

Old Flowers narrowed his eyes. "Did you see Jonathan?" His voice was stern, demanding truth.

"Who?" George lied, with all the innocence he could project.

Old Flowers shook his head and stroked Bernie's head feathers against the grain. The bird bent forward and chirped in delight. "Never mind," he said to George. With his left arm a perch for Bernie and his right hand on the table, Old Flowers flipped the arc of cards face up. "So, you can't see the value in this final lesson."

"Not really."

"Or how you've conquered your latest challenge?"

"Conquered? You mean barely escaping?"

"Think. What facet of your experience enabled you to escape?"

"Fear."

Old Flowers leaned back with both arms (and Bernie) resting on the back of the couch, his expression a tolerant smirk. "Well, if that's all you learned, I guess we'll postpone your Grand Tour."

The pyramid of *Cobá* collapsed into a pile of rubble, as did the Andes and half the Central American Region. *Lago de Atitlán* drained into its mysterious outlet, and yellow bile spewed from George's gallbladder like lava from *Volcán de Fuego*. He could feel anger rising and warming his ears. "I'd like to understand," he said, keeping his tone even.

"I'm sure the memories are uncomfortable, son. But what good is learning a lesson if you don't realize what you've learned?"

George thought about his hours in the musty pit. The memory almost as bad as being there. "I wish it made sense."

"It does. Allow yourself to see it." Bernie, puffed with coddling, splayed his wings and flew to the railing of the spiral staircase.

"No, really," George said, "I..."

"Something stirring?" More a prod than a question.

"I suppose there was one thing."

"Which was?"

"It's a bit silly. But the dream I've been having for years kept flashing into my mind. I mean, images from the dream. Each image *seemed* to tell me something about the chamber."

"Seemed?"

"Okay. It told me something. The first image was the sun."

"And?"

"It led me to light, to a book of matches."

"So, you found the matches after seeing the dream image, not before?"

"Yes."

"Go on."

"The light revealed the mosaic—the monsters, the satyrs, the killing, the raping. It was sickening. But then another dream image, the dancers, flashed into my mind. That led me to the stone I dislodged in the wall."

"And your escape," Old Flowers said. "Isn't that a valuable lesson?"

"Sure," George said with a smirk. "For the next time I fall into a chamber."

With a scaly smile teasing a snake-eyed squint, Old Flowers deadpanned: "Life is a chamber, son."

George laughed.

Old Flowers never changed his expression.

"There's something else," George said. "It's still happening."

"Tell me," Old Flowers said.

Eyes closed, thoughts steadied with deep breathing, cackles, chatter, and flapping wings a fading murmur, George whispered: "It's coming into focus. The Greek hillside—knee-high grass, green with brown tips waving in the breeze—flowers, yellow Angeliki, purple Hyacinth, heliotrope. Bees humming in wild thyme. Giant poplar and cypress towering grey-green against the cloudless sky. Gusts cool my skin, tickle my forehead. Far below, a wooden flute plays a pentatonic melody. Muted notes mingle with the shrill chirps of a woodlark, then echo off granite cliffs." He paused for three pensive breaths. "The landscape is dotted with boulders, most little more than rubble, others massive enough to partially block my view of a clearing. I'm floating, or rather, thinking my way down the meadow to the clearing. Sure enough, a group of peasants, thirteen in all, are dancing. I see them in my mind's eye, right now, as distinctly as if they were in this room." George opened his eyes and stared at his father. "But I'm wide awake."

"Your dreams have crossed a threshold, George. They're merging with your years of visualization exercises. Master Chang will be pleased."

"And these merging dreams are sending me messages? Like they did in the chamber?"

"In a manner of speaking, but don't focus on the so-called messages. The true significance of this moment will not be realized for years."

"Can you be more specific?"

"Yes, but I won't be. Just know that within days of your birth, I began instilling imagery into your unconscious mind. Through verbal description, images projected on nursery walls, stories read over and over and all containing evocative references to even the minutest sensory elements of the Greek hillside dreamscape. The dream is especially vivid now, even during waking consciousness, due to some recent assistance."

"Assistance?"

George stared at Old Flowers, billionaire bird loving builder of worlds, but now focused on a trifling deck of cards. His father looked like a stranger.

"Have you spoken to anyone since your return?" Old Flowers said while fiddling with the four aces.

"Not really."

"Good. I want you to hear this from me." Placing the aces on top, he gathered the deck into a neat stack, then settled into the couch. His eyes and smile fixed on George. "Have you ever heard of belladonna?"

"Of course."

"No doubt from lessons in the Medieval Colony. It was used by sorcerers in the Middle Ages to induce dreaming." He sighed and crossed his arms. "I'm weary of justifying my methods, but in this case, I don't want you hearing a distorted version from somebody else."

"Distorted version?"

"There are people on Flowers Island, Headmaster Felty being one, that don't see your education quite as I do. Ignorance plays a role, naturally. They don't understand that I've researched everything."

George felt his jaw tighten. "I do remember belladonna from the Medieval Colony," he said. "But belladonna is the modern word. The witches of the Middle Ages called it Deadly Nightshade."

"Well, you know how dramatic folklore can be," Old Flowers said, dismissing the notion with a wave. "Everything is deadly this, and deadly that."

"It's still a dangerous alkaloid."

"I wouldn't say danger—"

"I would!" George blurted. "And it was supposed to be your little secret." He glared at Old Flowers, this stranger in the familiar body. "But Glen ate half of my *dose* and the whole island found out."

Old Flowers leaned forward and jabbed the air with his finger. "I don't pay them to judge me," he said, spitting the words through clenched teeth, a shaman hurling a curse. "It was an accident. Glen is smaller than you. He'd overdose on a cup of coffee."

Unbearable, watching his father justify the unforgivable. George again paced the study, this time trying to walk off a building rage. "So, what happened to Glen while I was rotting in the chamber?"

"You saw him. He's fine. Slight delirium for a few hours." Old Flowers regained his composure and chuckled. "Amusing, really. He thought the island was under attack. He fired flares at my yacht and it went up like a stack of kindling."

"You call torching your yacht 'slight delirium'? Was I 'slightly delirious' when I saw satyrs eating dead babies?"

"Now I wouldn't..."

George thought about waking in pain and confusion in Jonathan's quarters. "If that was 'slight delirium', I'm glad I didn't eat the entire roll. I'd be dead!"

"Nonsense. The belladonna helped you contact the dream state, nothing more. Dreams can't hurt you. Stop talking about death."

"Did I hallucinate slaughter on those walls?"

"I—"

"Was the chamber a mosaic of blood and evil?"

"If you saw something on those walls, it must have been there."

"I can't believe anything you say. You drugged me and threw me into a pit."

"George, this is the after-shock from the lesson."

"The lesson, the lesson. I'm just a goddamn experiment."

With a low chuckle and a sad shake of the head, Old Flowers smiled. "We're all experiments, George, don't you see?"

George reached under the table, raised his father's cane, and smashed it through the glass table.

"George!" Old Flowers screamed, shielding his eyes from flying glass.

"Here's the result of your experiments," George yelled back. "How do you like me?" Stomping to the elevator, he kicked the doors when they didn't open immediately, then rode up to the main floor.

Aaron Flowers studied the sparkle of glass littering the floor.

The mirror slid open. "I'm worried," Rollins said, stepping from the hidden stairway into the room.

"You saw it all," Aaron said, brushing shards from his smoking jacket. "I told you George would come early in defiance of my orders. That he would experience a sudden rage." He gestured to the shattered table.

"Indeed, you did," Rollins said, walking to where George had thrown the cane and handing it back to Aaron. "The boy is a remarkable talent. A real breakthrough." Demonstrating an obsession with cleanliness, Rollins stooped and began filling his pocket handkerchief with broken glass. He looked up. "What is Cerissa's role in all this?"

Old Flowers answered with a shrug and a grumble. This conversation was over.

Rollins dumped a handful of shards into a wastebasket and returned for more. "She knows nothing about our work here," he said, also obsessively persistent.

"Nothing wrong with a little innocence." Aaron said, leaning on his cane and stepping over the glass. He perched Bernie on his arm and limped toward the aviary. "The next phase of George's training begins tomorrow."

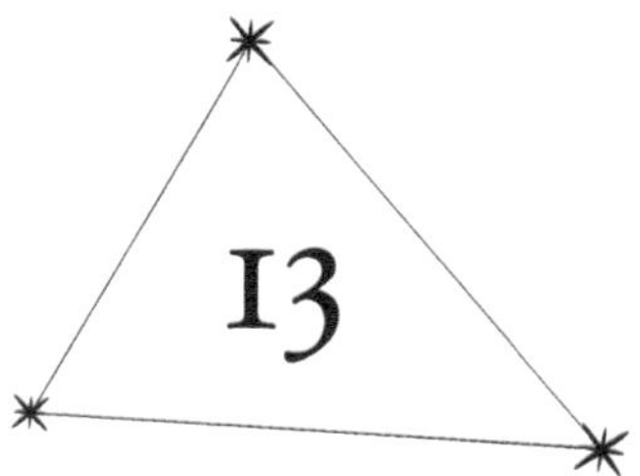

By the time the elevator opened, George's anger had vanished, as suddenly and inexplicably as it had appeared.

Mechanically, he walked down the hallway, feeling lost and alone in a brightly lighted corridor crowded with marble, plaster, bronze, wood, and ivory residents. *Artemis Ephesia*, Goddess of Lydia, a plaster replica scaled from its original height of forty feet, down to four, but still displaying twenty-one breasts, eggs, figs, or priest testicles—George was never sure which, but he had studied all theories. An *Aphrodite* (with arms), half a dozen *Kouros*, statuary of nude male youths, perfect athletic ideals bronzed, not by sun, but by bronze. Opposite them, *Kore*, their young female counterparts. Beautiful, but emotionless, draped in elaborately painted gowns and sculpted in marble to transcend the world's hardships.

A voice whispered. "George, over here." Glen stepped out from behind a full-sized granite *Fortuna,* goddess of good, or bad, luck.

In a daze of confusion, dismayed by his actions in the study, muscles tense, throat dry, jittery from the after-effects of Deadly Nightshade, George faced his best friend as if meeting him for the first time. This new Glen had a wider, even pug nose; the dimple on a receding chin, deeper. He appeared shorter, not midget short, but so slight and wiry he looked more elfin than usual. For the first time, George saw a garden gnome, muscles as taut as Roman braids, conditioned by digging, hauling, pruning, and planting. But what unsettled George most were

Glen's eyes. No longer glinting with joyful schemes or hinting at new adventures, this gaze was earnest, even candid. An expression as rare as a *Khufu* statue.

"What's the matter?" Glen said, "you're crying."

"No I'm not," George snapped, then rubbed his eyes and felt tears. "Fuck, I don't know what I am." He slumped in the shadows behind the lofty figure of *Augustus of Primaporta*, this replica neither marble nor bronze, but humble plaster. "Maybe I'm sad," he said, wiping his eyes with his shirtsleeve. "Maybe these are the tears of rage. Maybe I've lost my mind."

"That Fil-lon-chi bitch," Glen said.

"It's not Kathryn Maxwell. It's Old Flowers. I wanted to kill him. For a second, I hated my own father. I smashed his fucking coffee table."

Glen squeezed George's shoulder. "He told you about the drug."

"Yes."

"Well, I give him credit for that. Too bad you're the last one to know." Glen stepped into the corridor, glanced in both directions, and seemed satisfied that no one was around. "I'll be honest. I enjoyed the drug."

"What?"

"I did. It put me in a very unusual, but wonderful, state of mind. I became a warrior." Imitating the statue, Glen raised his arm, index finger aimed at the future. "Like him," he said. "If Augustus Caesar was a drug-crazed *fida'i* assassin." George laughed. "Seriously. The drug gave me a feeling of unlimited power, and purpose. Only I could save the island."

"Too bad it was all in your mind," George said.

"Yeah, leave it to reality to get in the way." He smirked. "What I *hated* was being tricked."

"The cinnamon roll was meant for me."

"Still." He faced George, again with that unusual, even aberrant (for Glen), seriousness. "But I realized something from the experience. I finally saw what you've been going through all these years."

"What do you mean?"

"Besides the drug, did Old Flowers tell you anything?"

"About what?"

"Look, I told you at the waterfall that I had something to show you. Before that, I promised you the ultimate birthday surprise. Well, tonight you're in luck."

*Good, or bad?* "Why all the mystery?" George said. "Can't you just spit it out?"

"It's not that simple. Nothing's simple." Glen paced the corridor, hands in the pockets of his cargo shorts, head lowered, weighing options. Finally, after enough pacing to make George want to nail his feet to the floor, Glen flung back his head, sighed, and stretched toward the ceiling. George heard a vertebrae pop in Glen's neck. "Then that's what I'll do," he said, if not to George, then to the gallery of statuary. "I have to start somewhere."

George almost blurted, *What the hell are you talking about?*

"I lied when I told you that I never met my father," Glen said. "Partly because he's not worth ruining a good conversation." He looked up at Augustus Caesar and mused: "I wonder what this guy's dad was like." He scoffed. "So, I met my so-called father for the first time when I was eleven years old. His name is Elliot, but he wants everyone to call him "Marcos". I remember thinking, 'So, you're the miserable bastard that couldn't handle the pressure.'"

"What do you mean?" George asked.

"I mean two years after I was born, my mother died on Interstate 81. Fluke accident. The car in front of her lost control, hit a wall, and smashed into her. Instant death at 70 MPH."

"Jesus," George said.

"I didn't hear the story until years later. Old Flowers told me. Anyway, my old man tried to pawn Sara and me off on various relatives, but the family was so poor they owed *dirt* money. Nobody could take us. He literally abandoned us at the orphanage."

"Why did he come back into your life?"

"Why else? My grandmother died and left her house to Sara and me. Worth maybe a few thousand credits. The piece of shit must have bribed, or more likely, exasperated somebody at the orphanage. Somehow, he got our records. He found Sara first. She had just married Randy, shortly after her eighteenth birthday. So, my old man hunts her down, gives her some hard luck shit, plays Mr. Remorseful, wants to make up for all the pain he'd caused, and blah, blah, blah."

Of course, Randy spotted a fellow scum sucker, so Marcos never got anywhere with Sara. But she told him, and now I wish to hell she hadn't, but she tells him that Aaron Flowers, yes, *that* Aaron Flowers, had adopted me. Must have seemed to Marcos like falling into the motherlode."

Mansion employees just finishing supper gathered in small clusters near the front entrance. Laughter and banter echoed across the marble floors. Someone switched off the lights, first in the dining room, then the kitchen. The corridor dimmed to its nightly setting of broad shadows between pockets of bright, museum lighting. George, in the dim silhouette behind Augustus Caesar, leaned against the wall. Glen sat cross-legged next to the marble pedestal. Both waited for the last "Good evenings" and "See you tomorrows", and the final thump of the great oak door.

Silence.

"So," George asked in a low voice, "how did Marcos even get to Flowers Island?"

"He didn't. But, thanks to the kindness and generosity of Old Flowers, I traveled to Dicksuck City, former state of Pennsylvania."

"What?"

"Actually, Dickson City. But the name evolved as the city decayed. I regretted the trip as soon as the cab pulled up to Marcos' three-story fleapit. Still, I climbed those shit-stained stairs." He closed his eyes and squinched, the memory like a migraine no drug could soothe. "Georgie, imagine the worst *insula* in the Roman Colony, get a vomit-covered junkie to live in the entryway, throw in a family of crackheads that never stopped arguing, wallpaper that looked and smelled like piss, blood on the handrails, roaches, and less ventilation than a crypt, and you have it—Marcos' building.

"His apartment was 2B, and I remember thinking: *I want* to be *anywhere but here.* Then I saw the hollow-eyed ghoul who answered the door. I'm serious, George. I woke the guy up at one in the afternoon. He lived like a vampire. His dawn was 5:00 PM., his night a foul chain of smoke and butts. With beer, of course, always some Australian lager in a huge can. But at least the place had electricity. Probably nicked from the nearest power pole. It was hell. Every night straight through until 4 or 5:00 AM Marcos would watch T.V..."

*Watch television all night long!?* George thought. *People do that?*

...and act like an unsung "Rock Star". I guess, years ago, he'd played with some L.A. band nobody's ever heard of." Glen shook his head at the wonder of human delusion. "Just long enough to master the clichés—the ballistic hair, the full body tats, the slow, burned-out rocker drawl, the insider slang, the shabby tales of groupie tail, the managers and agents that leeched on his innocent soul and fucked him out of his big break. Every angle of a jaded life a caricature of music."

"All this time," George said. "I've been studying history. But I knew so little about yours."

"You may as well hear the rest," Glen said. He shifted to a more comfortable position and stared at the ceiling, expression distant, or bemused, memories floating in the air like dust motes. "Amazingly, the bastard hadn't lost, destroyed, or pawned his guitar. He could even string some decent riffs together. Of course, he had to perform for me. Try to win me over. But he couldn't finish a three-minute song. He'd start in, get really cranking, then eight bars later, just stop. Take a drag on a cigarette, which for three days I never once saw him without, then a slug of beer, another drag, another sip. Then play a few more bars, then stop again and whine about how the whole fucking world was out to get him. More beer, and an unsmoked cigarette smoldering on the edge of a coffee table. Just another burn.

"Then he'd strum some chords from a completely different song, mutter about the wife who died and left him burdened with responsibilities—buying food, dealing with landlords, paying taxes, figuring out how to use a bus schedule. When the pity ran dry, he'd fiddle on some random strings, and stop again. Blah, blah everything wrong with life was somebody else's fault, and the drugs, especially the ones that fucked up his brain. As if a gang named Crystal, Smack, and Blow tied him to a sofa and forced themselves into his body. They, not he, ruined his life. But, luckily, he found a doctor who specialized in helping the oppressed. Certified "disabled", Marcos collects a monthly "pittance" earned fair and square, in his telling, from working at CostMart for a year or two back in the nineties.

"This went on and on, George, worse every day till the very end of my three-day journey through the inferno—before finally getting to the heart of the matter."

"Which was?"

"I'm sure you can guess." Glen cleared his throat, raised his voice to a whine, and mimicked his father's rocker inflections. "'Son, now that you can vouch for me, do you think your godfather could loan me some wallet for a used trailer? And maybe an old Chevy to haul it? What's a few grand to a multi-billionaire?'

"Seems," Glen said, "Marcos was looking to get out of Dicksuck City and move to a tiny village in New England. Get away from scumbags and dead ends, focus on music, form his eighth, or ninth, band. I forget which. He had so many great ideas, some guaranteed hits, and with his credentials any musician would love to play with him. With the right guys, he could break into the mainstream and pay back the loan with interest."

"Jesus," George said.

"Yeah," Glen said. "But none of that speaks to the main point, the main lesson you might say."

"Which is?"

"Besides the fact that being with my *real* father was the worst three days of my life, the main lesson is: Look Closer." Glen paused, as if expecting George to say something. When George remained silent, he went on. "I could have just waved goodbye and hated my biological father. Despised him, chewed on the betrayal, felt disgust that his DNA was flowing through my veins. Instead, I realized that if that useless parasite hadn't deserted Sara and me, we'd still be living with his junkie friends in some rat-infested flop house. Old Flowers would never have found me in that orphanage, and I wouldn't be living on Flowers Island."

The turn in the story from sinking misery to gravity reversed, purged the last of George's gloom. Anger shattered like a glass coffee table.

"The point is, George, maybe your situation is just the opposite. You've always idolized Old Flowers. Maybe you should look closer."

"Seriously, how could I not know any of this?"

Glen stared, his silence saying: *"I think you're about to find out."*

Commotion from the service elevator at the far end of the corridor. Steps, and the rumble of a housekeeping cart. "*God kväll, pojkar*," Ebba said, as she wheeled into the shaft of light beaming over granite *Fortuna*.

"*God kväll*, Ebba," George and Glen said together, knowing that if she was speaking Swedish, she was playing "Ebba" today.

"I would kill for one night with that woman," Glen whispered when Ebba was beyond earshot.

"As you've told everyone a dozen times," George said with an "in your dreams" eye roll. "But you've never specified which woman."

"Ebba, of course."

"What do you mean, 'of course'? Why not Chiara, Cressida, Celeste, or some other character she plays?"

"It's a tough choice. But when I saw Ebba in *Wild Rainbow*, I knew she was the woman of my dreams."

"Seriously? And how in hell did you see *Wild Rainbow*?

"Look. I know I'm talking bullshit. Truth is, I'd be happy with one night of friendly conversation. But the woman is an enigma." Glen turned from George and stared down the corridor, transfixed by Ebba's unsexy trudge toward Old Flowers' elevator. "Maybe that's why I find her so fascinating."

"I think the feeling will pass," George said.

"That's what I thought. Until I met an actor who downloaded all her films. The woman's a cult icon."

"I'm not sure what that means."

Glen pondered the question. "It's the modern equivalent of worshipping *Faustitas*."

"The goddess of *livestock*?"

"No, forget the cattle. I'm talking about a goddess, or in this case a celebrity, with a small but devoted following. A minor celebrity in the Roman Pantheon, but still worshipped and still a goddess."

"I had no idea you were so smitten."

"Watch *Wild Rainbow* and judge for yourself."

"Now downloaded to *your* laptop."

"Of course."

"When did all this happen?"

"About three years ago."

"Three years you've been carrying this torch?"

"I don't like that expression."

George studied the figure at the end of the corridor and tried to imagine a goddess dressed in a maid's tunic, bent to a floor of broken glass, vacuuming, dusting, hauling the debris to Waste Processing. Indeed, she was a beautiful, middle-aged woman, still thin, agile, and energetic, still blessed with radiant green eyes and a clear complexion. Luxuriant auburn hair, lightly streaked with grey and often coifed in a Swedish crown braid (at least in her "Ebba" character) lent her a royal air. But a goddess with a floor mop? George wondered if protecting a herd would suit her better. He turned back to Glen. "When Ebba starred in *Wild Rainbow*, she must have been, let's say, closer to your age."

"Oh, so I'm only fixated on youthful beauty? Is that it? Fuck you, Georgie. Ebba doesn't need youth. She's funny, smart, a brilliant cellist. An actress dedicated to her craft. Her range is extraordinary."

"You know a lot about someone you've barely met."

"Ask anyone. She's a legend. Elegant and poised one day—"

"Okay—"

"...and tempestuous the next. She's immersive when playing a beggar, a fieldworker—"

"Okay, I—"

"...relatable as nurse, or murderous, or chambermaid. She's—

"All right, all—"

"...so gorgeous, she's not afraid to look ugly. I really think—"

"Stop! I believe you," George said. "Jesus. You're the "fan" in "fanatic". He paused for a calming breath. "Maybe she *is* extraordinary. I've seen her acting in the Colonies, but she's never a character I can interact with. Always a noblewoman, an abbess, or for all I know, expressing some deep emotional resonance while hidden under a *burgha*."

"Not funny," Glen said, his gaze sharp as a chisel. He crossed his arms and leaned back in stony silence, in his mind, building her temple.

"And then," George continued, "when she's here, she's over at the *Pergamum* buried in some research project. I rarely see her. I saw her even less when she worked at the marina."

"You see her almost every day," Glen said.

"Bullshit," George said. Then, "Oh, I get it. You're saying she's such a masterful performer, and so brilliantly disguised, that she blends into our everyday life."

"Ebba, Chiara, Cressida, Celeste are some of the *female* characters you know about. She plays many others, and *men*."

"So what you're really saying is—"

"We should go." Lurching to his feet in time to see Ebba push the cleaning cart into Old Flowers' private elevator, Glen glanced down at George. "Maybe I shouldn't have told that Marcos story. The guys will be pissed."

"What guys, and why would they be pissed?"

"They need me for the second half."

"Half of what?"

"Come on."

George followed Glen down the corridor to the kitchen. After peering around to see that nobody was watching, they passed through the swinging double doors and stepped into darkness. "Wait here," Glen whispered. Tentative steps, and the sound of some utensil sliding across a metal table. "Shit!" Drawers opening. Metal clatter. Rummaging. A click as light from a headlamp beamed over rows of pots and pans, all hanging from stainless steel racks. "You never know when Miss Ruth might wander by. If she spots the lights on, we're cooked."

"Hilarious," George said.

"This way." George followed to the back of the kitchen and the thick metal door of the walk-in cooler. A swoosh of frigid air poured over them when Glen yanked it open. "Enter," Glen said, in a mock sinister tone. "Close the door." He flicked on the interior light.

"What are we doing here?" George said, rubbing his bare arms.

"You know how Old Flowers is about alcohol."

"Do I really have to answer that?"

"So, we smuggle it in. Give me a hand." Glen passed George cardboard crates filled with carrots, broccoli, celery; heads of lettuce, ears of corn, leeks. "Help me with this." They scooted bins of potatoes to one side. "We have to keep this shit in the same order we found it." He peered around a stack of milk crates, stepped over a short stack of cartons filled with lemons, and then squeezed into the far corner of the walk-in. "Good thing Miss Ruth is too fat to get back here," Glen said, smiling. "Ferd's got our system down to a science. He's one of us."

"One of us?"

"You'll see."

"Jesus, if this is one of your pranks."

"Ha! Grab this." He passed George two cases of beer. "Imported from a tiny brewery on the mainland. All done very craftily." Glen snickered.

George didn't get the joke.

After meticulous replacement of every carton and bin, they switched off the light and closed the door.

Outside the kitchen, Glen said: "Now comes the fun part. You carry the beer and I'll scout ahead."

"Where are we going?"

"Christ, you're worse than *Tomás de Torquemada.*"

"You're really enjoying this, aren't you?"

"I always enjoy being with you, Georgie. But ease up on the inquisition." He cupped his hands around George's ear and whispered. "But if you insist, we're going to the third floor of the North Wing, to the closet at the far end of the hallway."

"The closet next to the stairway leading to the Observatory?"

"I said no more questions."

"Fuck you."

Glen laughed. "That's the one. Inside the closet there's a trap door leading down."

"There is?'

"You just don't listen. Everybody is waiting. Come on. Watch for Rollins."

Still wondering what this was all about, George followed Glen as he led the way to the North Wing. "You go to all this trouble to drink beer?" George whispered.

Glen hissed back: "There's a lot more to it than that, *Tomás*. You'll see. Just...shhh!"

Behind them, from the far end of the corridor, the sound of Old Flowers' elevator.

"Shit!" Glen said. "She's finished already. Give me one of those." He grabbed the top case. "Follow me and don't shake it up." Raising the beer above his head, he dashed away, using bent arms to absorb the shock of his motion.

*This is absurd*, George thought, but he did the same.

Glen turned the corner, and slid to a stop a few feet from the main floor library. A swath of light shone into the hallway from the wide-open door. "Damn," Glen muttered. "The wheels of the cleaning cart rolled steadily closer. "Seriously, we can't let *anybody* see us with beer." *The Tempest* by Jean Sibelius poured softly from the library. "We'll never drink again. Even worse, we'll lose the Trine."

"What?"

George rested his beer on the floor and peeked into the library. Miss Ruth sat on a sofa, facing the open doors. "Georgie," she said, smiling and patting the couch. "Come sit for a minute."

"Good move, George," Glen whispered. "Now what?"

"Hi, Miss Ruth," George said with a wave. He turned to Glen. "Take the beer to the storage closet. I'll meet you there." Then, stepping into the library while closing the door, said: "Haven't seen you since before my birthday..."

* * *

Ebba Lundgrin stepped into the corridor just in time to see George and Glen scrambling down the hallway. Before turning the corner and vanishing from sight, the boys reminded her of Egyptian water-carriers, but without the balance, grace, or poise. She smiled, guessing that George was taking another stride into his new life. A life she must learn to view with even greater emotional and material distance. Fitting, because she viewed her own life as a vista, a broad expanse of limitless possibilities.

It hadn't always been that way.

In the beginning, she was a child star. What her mother, Ida, called, "A dear in the footlights" (Ida was always more enamored by her wit than those forced to endure it). With help from Ted, her industry connected father, an American sculptor turned Makeup Designer, and of course, Ida, failed actress and Swedish Hair Stylist obsessed with celebrity, Ebba aimed toward stardom. "You, my dear, shall have a real career," Ida told her daughter, while scorning an industry that cast her aside after a two-episode role in *Hem till byn*, Sweden's longest running and most popular TV series. "Yours is a special talent."

She proved her mother right as Beatrice, the youngest of three sisters in *The Scandalous Nanny,* when she eclipsed the larger roles by sheer force of cute. The public adored her and dressed their daughters in "Beatrice" smocks, and "Beatrice" curls. Critics acknowledged the "sparkle" she brought to the film, but restrained their praise.

*Chocolate Wonderland,* a film adaptation of a Broadway musical, appreciated smiles and charm, but depended on the dance and vocal skills Ida had force-trained on darling Ebba.

But it was the drama of *Fly My Kite*, the British story of a girl torn from loving parents during the Second World War, her escape from servitude and eventual reunion, that exposed Ebba to international acclaim. Critics swooned. Agents sharpened their pencils.

Ebba's life swirled like dust in a whirlwind. Too much advice. Too many demands. Too soon. Too oppressive.

Too disconnected from her true passion—music.

From the moment Ebba could climb a piano bench, she had loved her parent's baby grand. Barely beyond baby herself, she began formal lessons at age three and performed Chopin's *Mazurka in B-flat Major, Op. 7.* at her first recital, age five.

The performance astonished, not the audience, but her parents. It not only ended a season of delicious torture, but displayed to the world another facet of Ebba's preternatural focus, persistence, contempt for the boundaries of limited technique, and most telling of all, her willingness to torment others with countless hours of practice, practice, practice in service of her goals and with zero regard for hours, days, weeks, or months.

With time stolen from film sets, rehearsals, interviews, and public appearances; lost in the fever of musical exploration, Ebba had, by the time of her recital, mastered a plodding, dirge-like interpretation of Chopin's lively *Mazurka*. Not dismal enough to spin the composer in his grave, but sufficiently somber to lead him there.

That was fine with Ebba. Her musical tastes were already morphing away from piano, egged on by a starring role as Agneta in *The Orphan Princess*. Her character's theme, a haunting melody rich in strings and fronted by a sorrowful cello, embedded itself in Ebba's soul.

Days after Ebba's ninth birthday, Sabine Fritz, an award-winning cellist and former instructor at the Royal Swedish Academy of Music became her private tutor.

Years ripened her and Hollywood noticed.

More good films followed, roles that revealed unexplored facets of her own character. Collaborations that blossomed into romance, travel to thrilling locations, sets and themes worn like elegant gowns. Artifice birthed a galaxy of talent. Movies ached. Pushed. Infuriated. Revealed. Art taught her about tools, machinery, cooperation, empathy. Movies refined her knowledge of prosthetic makeup, a hobby she had long enjoyed with her father. Age a decade, fatten cheeks, bulge a nose, maim features or glorify them.

Then numerous artistic peaks. Quality films, standards of achievement by which she judged her more mediocre efforts.

Then average pictures that exploited fame to earn a fortune.

Even a few terrible films, exercises in pointless motion that soiled story and character with incoherent ego vomit—for her, a career low, for too many others, their summit.

All crowned with one savage, glimmering diamond—*Wild Rainbow*, Ebba's undisputed masterwork.

Famous, acclaimed, hailed as a brilliant, risk-taking actress with a bottomless range, Ebba gravitated to theater where critics praised her work in settings as diverse as the *Göteborg Opera*, the Booth Theater, the *Palacio de Bellas Artes*.

Fundamentally shy, rousing as she matured to the curse of beauty and charisma, the torture of high cheeks and low esteem, she created a guise. A persona that ensnared with a wink and crushed with a frown—a façade with a taste for *mota*, coke, ketamine, London elites, and the incomprehensible gibberish of "Ket night" revelries.

That method served her.

Until bloody urine crashed the party.

Spent, confused, wandering the dawn near Canary Wharf, feeling like a flea on the Isle of Dogs, her Chelsea boots splashed into an oily puddle. There, reflected in the rainbow ripples, a thin film, a shallow puddle, a colorful veneer.

She called her agent. She wanted to act, needed to, but refused all offers. "Benoit wants you for a remake of *Scarlet Street*," the agent said. "David Evans is staging *Esther* and thinks you're ideal for the lead. Curious? Tempting? Well, if not theater or film, what?" She answered with a well-practiced, captivating calm, and that gaze, so inscrutable and adored. "That's it?" the agent said. "Silence? Do you juggle, darling, I could book a clown gig at a three-year-old's birthday party." Then a chuckle. "Maybe busking. You could play cello on street corners." Encouraged by her smile, he added: "Or dress in rags and play a bag lady." Another teasing chortle. "I hear they need cheap-jacks at Piccadilly Circus?"

Her smile waned. She leaned forward with both palms pressing the desk. "You've always looked out for me, Milton. But this is the best advice you've ever given." Eyes moist and teetering on the cusp of never to return, she smiled and said: "I'll miss you. But I no longer need your services."

That afternoon, she fired her manager (with a generous severance) and instructed Bailly, Weishair, Seymour, and Co., her accounting firm, to divest all investment portfolios, land holdings, and retirement accounts. Retaining one savings account with a balance of $123,516 credits, she combined the divested funds with the cash reserves from another half-dozen bank accounts and directed the firm to create a non-profit endowment fund for the benefit of the Loki Clan Wolf Sanctuary, a facility located in a remote region of the former state of New Mexico. A charity she had long supported.

With savings, income earned from interest, and whatever residuals trickled in from prior film and television work, she moved to Italy and enrolled in The Umbra Institute. Already fluent in Swedish, English, and French; she studied Italian, Art history, Sculpture, Research Writing and Methodology, Archaeology, Creative Writing Through Literary Models, Ancient History, and of course, Cello.

She earned a Master's of Art degree five years later.

By now, at age thirty-one, public curiosity had waned. Thanks to leaping off the celebrity escalator, refusing interview requests, reclaiming Eloise Van Laeke, her birth name and the name she had always used on legal documents anyway; cutting her famous hair and changing its color; using her collection of wigs, prosthetics, and theatrical make-up to, at least, mute her beauty, at most, alter her appearance completely—even (against all feminine instincts) age herself by shadowing and contouring the hollows of her temples, eye sockets, and cheekbones, she managed, over time, to engineer a low key lifestyle.

Slowly, fame drained into the Sea of Obscurity, and at the same time, employment opportunities flooded her life. Intelligent, lovely, charming, familiar in a way people couldn't quite put their finger on, she was the kind of person people invited into their lives. She excelled at retail sales, especially women's fashion, and did so for the next two years.

She had always applied keen photographic sensibilities to exotic movie locations, producing portfolios editors wanted to publish and publishers wanted to sell. She refused, explaining that hobbies like photography, music; her short stories and the novel she had written and would never make public—all existed for the sake of personal gratification, for love of art, for the pure delight of expression.

With one exception.

She couldn't resist offers from select producers (friends she had remained close with) to act as Location Scout for various production companies. As works for hire, those photographs were never hers from the beginning. They weren't art, in her opinion, but tickets to remote Amazonian villages, glacial peaks, the *Chilean Andes, Isla de Pascua, Mui Ne* beach, Mongolian deserts, the *Taupo* Volcanic Zone, and any realm envisioned by screenwriters huffing L.A. smog, bearing London fog, or dreading the slog of a New York walkup.

Exciting months, but exhausting.

A dilemma solved by months as a waitress in the city of Lawrence, former state of Kansas, where she met an Archeology professor from KU who offered her a position as Archaeological Assistant at a dig in the former Guatemala. Which inflamed her interest in Spanish and led her to *La Academia de Antigua* and work on the school's expansion project. For a woman who, at the time, could barely order a *chile relleno* (stuffed chili), she excelled at running *hilo de cobre* (copper wire), from *el interruptor* (the light switch), to *el tomacorriente* (the outlet).

So much real life, so many fascinating people, so much to learn.

Traveling north (always with her cello) to the Baja Peninsula, she connected with *The Xerces Society* in time for their annual Monarch butterfly census. A month later, she joined volunteers and built Habitats for Humanity in *El Triunfo, Baja California Sur.* She even performed a piano and cello duet in the town's *Museo de Música*. At the post-concert pizza and Margarita dinner at *Café El Triunfo*, she met Manuela, a dive operator at the *Parque Nacional Cabo Pulmo* who taught her to scuba-dive, and later, to hunt the invasive lionfish in the Sea of Cortez.

By the following winter, Ebba (Eloise), was working as an interim innkeeper, managing small motels, hostels, and more than one bed and breakfast while the owners went on *their* vacations. And it was during just such an inn-keeping assignment in the former copper, silver, and gold mining town of Jerome, former state of Arizona, that Ebba met Michael Davidson. An author mid-book on a narrative account of events leading to the Battle of Bosworth, Michael was in desperate need of a research assistant.

"How have I never heard of Flowers Island?" Ebba said, when the subject came up the following year. Galley proofs of *Annihilation: How the Battle of Bosworth Transformed England* had just arrived from the publisher.

Michael, depressed, weary, compelled to read those 236,519 words yet again, cherished his third Scotch in grey twilight while musing about an island where past is present and antiquity breathed. "Aaron will love you," he said.

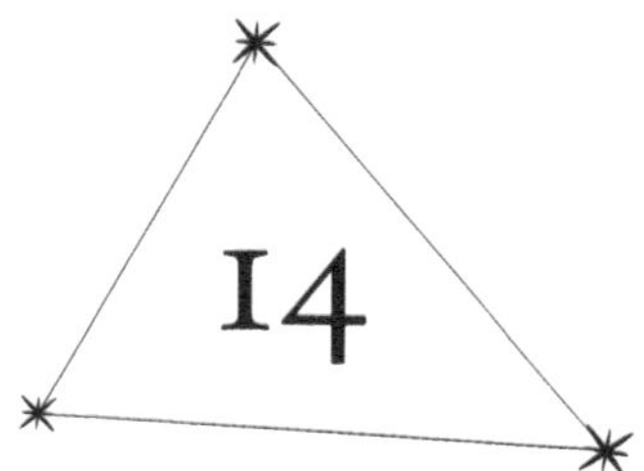

Minutes after leaving the library and his conversation with Miss Ruth, George stood in the North Wing of Flowers Mansion, gripping the brass knob of the closet door. Still suspecting a prank, or test, or even a lesson in this world without a Rule of Separation, he wondered if Glen, or Old Flowers, or even an actor in a satyr suit was waiting in the closet to scream out: "Surprise!", "You failed", or "Grrrrr!"

*I'm insane,* George thought, wrenching the door open.

Surprise.

A closet.

For another moment, he considered leaving, simply refusing to play along with...whatever this was. But instinctively, his hand probed for a light switch. Finding it where he expected, next to the door frame, he illuminated a long, narrow room with shelves stuffed with neatly folded linens and towels, boxes of toiletries, and half-used rolls of wallpaper. No Glen, but George found the headlamp on an eye-level shelf. Stretching the elastic band over his head and aiming the beam toward the back of the closet, George switched off the closet light, closed the door, and followed the trail of dirt and scuff marks to the trapdoor.

"How did I not know about this place?" he muttered to himself.

He and Glen had spent half their childhoods searching stairwells, cabinets, basements, bedrooms, attics, storerooms, and, he thought, every closet in the mansion for secret passages and rooms. Thanks to Old Flowers and his eccentric, eclectic tastes; his fondness for Edgar Allen Poe, the architecture of *Mont*

*Saint-Odile*, and even the homicidal habitations of the Murder Castle, the boys had discovered many passages, staircases, false floors, and windowless chambers in Flowers Mansion.

But this trapdoor was new, at least to George, and must have been covered in years past by carpet or its own false floor.

Why was it exposed now?

George fortified his resolve, grabbed the steel ring from its recess in the floor, and lifted. The trapdoor was heavy, but silent, with well-oiled hinges.

Aiming the headlamp into the gloom, he discovered a ladder that appeared to descend all the way to the sub-basement. Small platforms at the second and first story levels allowed access to narrow walkways that led...somewhere.

*Only one way to go*, George thought, as he stepped onto the first metal rung. Then: *How the hell did Glen carry two cases of beer down this ladder?*

He found the answer a few steps later when the lamp shined into a niche in the floor joists. A small luggage net tied to a coiled rope lay in a heap at arm's reach.

*Jesus*, George thought. *All this to drink modern beer?*

Never fond of the pepper, resin, and seawater in Ancient Greek wines, or the tasteless, heavily-diluted Roman wines, he did enjoy, sort of, the bitter Egyptian and Medieval meads. Especially after the buzz kicked in. But Aztec *octli*, the sour, milky extract that George called "cactus pus", never failed to heave his stomach.

In that context, he understood the appeal of modern brew.

But was it worth all this mystery?

These thoughts sloshed through his mind as he climbed down and down and down to the bottom rung, and finally, to a concrete floor. As he suspected, somewhere in the mansion's vast sub-basement.

Shining the lamp in both directions, he discovered another, all too haunting, long, dark corridor running along the perimeter of the mansion's natural stone foundation.

He listened.

Faraway voices somewhere to his left, and when he switched off the headlamp, a distant, ghostly luminescence. To preserve night vision, he switched the headlamp to red light and aimed the beam at the floor. Bursts of laughter echoed down the corridor. Followed by shouts and bellows.

With each slow step a counterpoint to a racing heart, George pushed forward, through hesitation, suspicion, fear that this was just another humiliating prank; through visions of chambers, terror, and isolation. Memories from a comfortable past crowded his mind with cries of danger. Urged him to walk away, now, return to the ladder, settle back into faithful compliance, apologize to Old Flowers, enjoy the comforts of lessons and learning.

Then a sound, nothing more than the squeak of his own tennis shoes, fixed him in the moment. The now, the here, body bathed in red, skin chilled, breath soured by stale air, and bitter—the taste of anger flaring in defiance of every rule, lecture, and punishment, against life on Flowers Island and the tyranny of history.

"*Ma-Con-Do!*" a voice cried out. "It's the only way to make a statement." Even pitched and echoed by the squared face of the corridor's limestone, Ferd's lisp and intonation were unmistakable.

*Ferd is one of us*, George recalled Glen saying, and each step brought him closer to the flickering glow, to Glen's "us".

"Don't be ridiculous," said another voice, clearly Headmaster Felty. "What we need now is *Pae-Ka-Lin-Chee*."

*What the hell is this?* George thought, increasing his pace to a fast walk, then a short sprint.

Back pressing the wall, mere feet from the open door, he heard Glen say: "Nope. Ferd is right. The *Poo-Paa-Loo-Choo* didn't work last time. We need a good *Ma-Con-Do*."

"But it can't be used in a situation like this." That was George's Elizabethan History teacher, Michael Davidson, the world-famous novelist and supposed father of good old lying Bruce. "I'd like to see them try the *Fa-Ma-Cho*."

Bewildered, George leaned closer to hear more.

Trained from birth in remote languages like *Nahuatl, Xhosa*, and *Chemehuevi*; as well as common idioms like *Hansa*, *Arabic*, and the Germanic and Romance languages (even dead languages like *Vulgar Latin* and *Middle English*), he had attained fluency in a total of twenty-three. Even so, he only half recognized the vaguely *Mandarin "Fa-Ma-Cho"* and *"Ma-Con-do"*. Not from his studies, but because he'd learned a similar word, *Fil-Lon-Chi*, from Glen. When George had asked about the word's origin, Glen said that he'd invented *Fil-Lon-Chi* because he'd grown bored with standard curse words like "assrabbet", "cockslaker", and "shitslicker". Glen further complained that the Rule of Separation limited his vulgarity options because it forbade the use of *irrumatio (*Ancient Roman face fucking*)*, *cinaedus (*Ancient Grecian ass fucking*)*, *metrokoites*, (mother fucking) or Ancient Egyptian *nek tchew a-a* when not in the Culture Colonies, regardless of how desperately he wanted to tell someone to get fucked by a donkey.

Fine. But why would an Elizabethan scholar use Glen's invented curse words?

"That stupid *Fil-Lon-Chi!*" cursed Headmaster Felty.

And there it was.

George thought about the countless times he and Glen had used the word—as a curse, an exclamation, a substitute for "thing", or "stuff", as a noun, an adjective—and concluded that its vast applications rendered the word *Fil-Lon-Chi* meaningless.

"Oh, no, that silly Fal-La-Po, he's trying the Nee-Keen-Dee again.' This voice was female, Kristin Urie, Glen's girlfriend whenever she was interested. She worked in the *Pergamum*, downstairs in Historical Records.

Glen's "us" had broadened.

George inched closer as Barry Dee said: "Now, Darlin', don't get yerself all pissy over that loosin' team."

"They will *not* lose," she huffed back. Barry chuckled.

"Who needs a brew?" Glen called.

"Sure," "Hit me," "Over here," voices replied.

*I either go in now, or run back to the past,* George thought.

Slipping the headlamp into his back pocket, he stepped into the light and paused at the threshold, expecting all eyes to be immediately upon him. No one noticed. Twenty or so men and several women sat in a rough semi-circle, on hard metal chairs, staring at a television. George had seen photos of televisions in the library's encyclopedias, but had never actually viewed one. And this television—its shocking color, the clarity of the sounds booming from stereo speakers, the sheer size of its screen—easily six feet wide and almost as tall—stunned George. Used to an ancient computer with a tiny, monochrome monitor and just enough power to support basic word processing (Old Flowers prohibited internet connections, cell phones, and any unauthorized contact with the outer world), George could only gape in amazement. Captivating, marvelous, enchanting, so vibrant the eye creases, brow ridges, even the pores on the announcer's face; his mustache and eyebrows, the cleft of his chin—all looked tangible enough to touch.

*This is magic*, George thought. *What an amazing birthday surprise.*

"Hey, Georgie boy," Glen cried, shattering the spell. He had just grabbed an armload of beers from an ice chest.

The words shattered *everyone's* spell. All turned from the screen and acknowledged George with smiles and waves.

"Well, well," Jonas said. "You've come to join the game."

*Game? Jonas never plays games. Jonas is always profound, even somber.*

"Come on in, son," Barry Dee said, without the slightest trace of a southwestern accent. "Glen, I bet George could use some refreshment."

*What happened to Barry? His voice?*

"Yes, join us," said a figure just now visible from behind a row of chairs. The steady clomping of wooden blocks boomed across the floor as Jonathan strode to the ice chest. "Welcome to the real world," he said, hoisting a bottle in a mock toast.

Real? Not the word George had in mind.

"Come on, George," Barry said. "You can drink a beer for antiseptic purposes. There might be germs on your forehead." The others laughed. George cringed. Barry's parody voice felt like mockery. But why? Barry was a scamp and a joker, but normally well-meaning.

"Come on, George," someone said. A sea of arms waved him over.

*These people look like strangers*, George thought.

After an awkward moment and a few shrugs and smiles, everyone turned back to the television.

Glen passed around a few beers, kept two, and joined George. "Come on. I think you could use one of these," he said, leading George back to the corridor, but not beyond sight of the television. "Georgie, relax. We're your friends."

"I have no idea what's going on. What language are you guys speaking?"

"Take a breath and have a drink. I'll explain everything." He nodded to the television. "I told you we did more than get drunk down here. Cool, right?" Glen laughed. "Right under the old man's nose."

"What is this?"

"What does it look like?"

"I know it's a television. I mean, what's on it?"

"Oh," Glen said, his attention drawn to the screen by yelps and shrieks from the room. "Well, pretty obviously, a football game. Wouldn't you agree?" His tone was sarcastic, but proud as he gestured to the television, presenting a gift. "That, my friend, is the Grand Trine."

"And that's supposed to mean something?"

"What, you don't know?" he said, half speaking, half drinking. "Come on, you're the expert on all the important shit. History this and that, philosafree, language, art, appreetiaton..." a belch "...of culture?"

"Appreciation," George said. "You're drunk."

"Fuck that. I'm talkin' about top-ranked college football. Best in the U.N." He jabbed George with his index finger. "And you... don't...know...shit. Here..." He yanked George's sleeve, spilled beer on both their shoes in the process, and pointed at the television. "Watch and learn, rookie."

Instead, George noticed the viewers. Brilliant personages like Jonathan, Michael Davidson, Jonas Felty, and Kristin Urie mingled with Charlie Doyon and Larry Parvek, skilled craftsmen and maintenance personnel indispensable to the smooth operation of Flowers Island. They, in turn, socialized with laborers like Eddie Olney, Frank Unger, and Leon Beaudry—guys who barely finished high school. George saw carpenters, accountants, landscapers, artisans, men and women from Historical Artifacts, historians from Archives, masons, plumbers, heavy equipment operators, horse wranglers, Captain Waller from the marina...

What the hell was going on here?

"There!" Glen shrieked, with splatter George felt on his cheek.

"Goddamn it, Glen, get out of my—"

"That's Coach Buffington. Check it out! Willis Buffington is the main event."

The camera panned to an ancient man, skin pale and drooping like wet leather. The coach raised his right hand. The television, with obscene clarity, displayed knobby, arthritic fingers twisted in grotesque contortion.

"He's signaling the Foo-Loo-Poo," Jonas cried, slapping his knee. "Brilliant move. I wish our quarterback was close enough to see it."

"He'll see it," Barry Dee said. No drawl, no chew hawked into an empty bottle, no chortle or guffaw.

*When he's watching football, he becomes a different person,* George thought.

"Well, there it is, Georgie," Glen said.

"There *what* is?"

"My life. If I could live it my way."

"What are you talking about?"

"Trine-style football. Winning, being the envy of the world, having everyone for a best friend. Look at the stadium. Listen to that." Deafening roars, stomping feet, banners flying as trumpets blared, bodies swaying in swarms of waving arms. "Trine players are gods, Georgie."

"Come on."

"Don't believe *me*. Watch these guys play."

"Here it comes!" someone yelled.

Everyone's gasp drew George back to the television where a player in a gold and white uniform flew over a line of defenders wearing blue and red. Stranger still, the player soared another twenty yards before landing in a perfect parachute roll.

"What the fuck?" George said, perplexed by this sudden development. "What hurled that player?"

"He saw Buffington's signal!" Jonas cried, to the group, not to George.

"Shittin' mules," Barry growled. "I could 'a bet on that one." Barry had affected his normal slang-heavy voice. But now it seemed...affected.

"What is this?" George said to Glen.

"Ah, duh, it's football," Glen answered.

"Bullshit," George said. "That guy cleared the tallest defender by three feet, then flew another twenty yards. That's *nothing* like football."

"Oh, now you're the expert?"

"No, but I've studied the game. It has deep historical roots. The version I played in the Grecian Colony was called *phaininda*. The Ancient Romans brought it from Greece and called it *harpastum*."

"Really."

"In the Medieval Colony, we played *foote balle* with stuffed animal hides or balls of rags. In that form, entire villages played against each other and the "field" was the distance between villages—through woods, meadows, over hills, across rivers and streams. Hundreds of players, both men and women, some even on horseback, kicked, threw, carried the ball, or whacked it with sticks. Even in our modified, Flowers Island reenactments, we'd beat the shit out of each other. Someone was always getting smacked with feet, hands, heads, clubs, staves, and even swords."

"Guess I missed that lesson."

"The real, historical, games were far worse. I mean fucking vicious. Some players were maimed for life, or drowned when the mob crossed a river. Others were blinded by sticks, crushed under piles of bodies, beaten, fractured, suffocated. Because the match lasted for days, sub-contests branched off the main game and families used the violence to settle feuds and punish enemies."

"Clever."

"Eventually, one village battled the rag-ball to the opposing village where they christened it 'the enemy king', or some hated rival, and the ball was "killed" by drowning, burning, or simply torn to shreds.

"Very catartic," Glen slurred.

"Cathartic," George said. "Anyway, over time, *foote balle* got so violent, damaged so much property, and diverted so many peasants away from field work, or worship, or day to day livelihoods that seven Middle Ages kings over a three-hundred-year period tried to ban it." George chuckled. "I remember Jonas forcing me to memorize a Royal Decree from 1531. King Henry VIII said: '*foote balle is nothing but beastly fury and extreme violence, whereof proceedeth hurte and consequently rancour and malice do remayne with thym that be wounded, wherefore it is to be put in perpetual silence*'."

Glen chugged the micro-brew, smacked his lips, and slapped the empty bottle against George's chest. "That's your problem, Georgie," he said. "You live in the past. The Grand Trine plays modern football."

"No," George said. "I studied how Medieval *foote balle* evolved into rugby. Then how a guy named Walter Camp modified rugby rules into modern football. How teams in the former Canada had adopted similar rules years earlier—all of it. So, don't tell me that modern football uses catapults to launch players through the air."

"No catapult, George. Just guys in shoulder pads and uniforms."

"I know what I saw."

"We all saw it. And it's not CGI either."

It took a moment for George to realize that Glen was referring to computer generated imagery, a modern technology George had read about, but barely grasped.

"What you just saw was *real*," Glen said, raising his bottle to the ceiling. He wailed like a chimp screeching a pant-hoot, a sound both primal and inebriated. "And they'll leap again, Georgie. Just watch. Or slam those bastards with a power wedge."

"And what exactly is that?"

"One guy plows through the whole defense. A fuckin' human locomotive. One guy. Scatters a dozen defenders like so many roaches. Drives their coaches ape shit."

"And you're saying these Grand Trine miracles are real?"

"Swear to god, George. Ask anyone in that room."

"How do they do it?"

"I have no idea. I just know the gods fucked up when they made me a gardener. George, *Aletheia's* truth. I'd kill to be on that team. Even for one game. Be one of the few people on Earth to learn from Coach Willis Buffington. I mean, seriously, there's some strange, powerful shit happening at Grand Trinity University."

"You've never mentioned any of this. It's all—"

"Crazy. Yeah, I know. But there's a lot you don't know about me, George. That's why we invited you here. You don't really know any of us."

"What's that supposed to mean?"

Glen clinked his beer against George's. "You're not playing fair. I just finished my fifth. You haven't had one yet."

Curious about the taste of modern beer, George tried a small sip. Enough to convince him that he wasn't in the mood for drinking.

"Ahhh," the crowd gasped.

George followed the football as it soared the entire length of the field. The receiver, as if waiting in the end zone for a kick off, caught it easily and knelt for a touchdown.

George shook his head. "Incredible," he said. "But I have a question."

Glen raised his palms. "I already told you. I don't know how they do it."

"It's not that." George studied the huge screen, again marveled at the exquisite detail, the depth of what he knew was a two-dimensional image, and the almost fairy tale window into a distant world. "I know this is amazing technology. Something I know little about. But with all the electromagnetic anomalies on the island, and being so far from the mainland, how is it possible to get such good reception?"

Glen stared as if looking at a five-year-old who had just asked him to drive forward using the rearview mirror. "It's *not* possible," he said, with a smirk. "Half the time we can't hail the marina, let alone get signals from Grand Trinity University. Jesus, George, think about it. Where would we hide some giant antenna, or a satellite dish?"

"You tell me." George pointed to the screen. "It's coming from somewhere."

"The game isn't live, for fuck's sake. We're watching it on videodisk."

"What? You mean everyone knows who's going to win?"

Glen laughed. "Of course. This game was played years ago. Before the war. Before the Northeast Kingdom seceded from the United Nation."

"What war? What Northeast Kingdom?"

"We're getting off the subject." He gestured to George's drink. "Come on, this stuff's precious. Drink or hand it over." George passed him the beer. "Thanks," Glen said, pronouncing it "tanks". All the signs: glassy eyes, drooping lids, words sliming his tongue like slugs scaling a beer trap. Thirty minutes from now, Glen would be slumped in a chair on his way to the floor. "You don't really know me, Georgie. Georgie *boy*. Shit, you didn't even know I hated those shit-fucking birds. That was a Freudian. I wanted you to see the real me. And I'm not drunk, you fucker. This is serious. I told you to prepare for the ultimate birthday surprise, remember?"

"This isn't it?"

"Hell no!"

George cringed, the thought of another surprise roiling his guts.

"I won't score points, but fuck it," Glen said. "This is important. Are you ready?"

*No*, George thought, feeling as woozy as Glen looked. "Maybe you should sit down. Tell me some other time."

"No way!" He led George deeper into the corridor and pressed him against the wall. "I need to tell you now." Squeezing George's arm and leaning to his ear, he whispered: "It's all been a fucking lie. There's *never*...I mean, ever been a Rule of Separation. Life at the mansion is just like the Colonies. We're actors, all playing roles, doing what Old Flowers tells us. You and I don't even share the same birthday."

"Fuck that," George said, pushing away. "You're drunk. You don't know what you're saying."

"My sister remembers the day I was born. Early spring. She should know, she had to wipe my ass. You were born on August ninth, not me. The birthday con was part of the plan. All part of the plan."

George slammed his palms against Glen's chest, sending him flailing to the floor. "Then that makes you a motherfucking liar," he snarled, tugging the headlamp from his pocket. "A *paid* liar!"

No longer needing night vision, he clicked the lamp from red light to white, illuminating the corridor and his first steps into vigilance and suspicion.

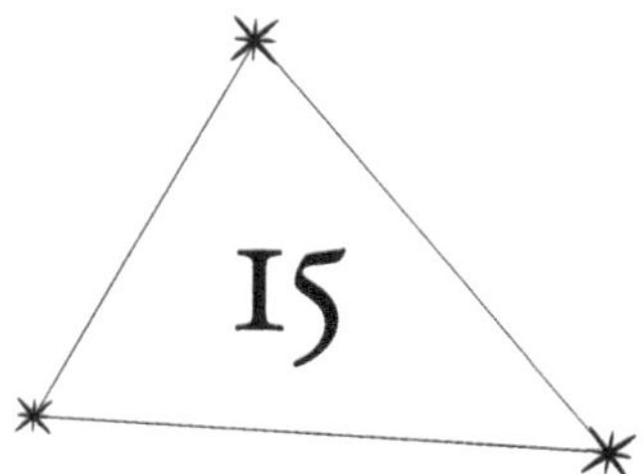

The Roman Colony. Four-year-old George Flowers stands in a crowd watching two warriors practicing the Arts of Mars; actors dressed as gladiators. The child, blinded by gleaming armor, stares up at the giant bodies. Steel slashes into flesh. A scream of pain. A flare of anger. A stream of red splashes the ground. The crowd gasps. The child surges with the tide of excitement. A lance raises, a huge body lunges, misses, hurls off balance into the crowd, his pointed helmet as deadly as the spear in his hands, lacerating the young child's neck...

"...all part of the plan...part of the plan..."

Then...

Blinding light. Crushing paralysis. Eyes staring into the light as metal claws flesh...

"...all part of the plan...part of the plan..."

Cerissa sat up with a start. The dream vanished.

*Where am I?*

Wind blew into the room. Of course, Uncle Aaron's mansion.

She leaped out of bed, flinging back the lace curtains. Dark clouds billowed over the Roman Colony. "George," she whispered, fingers caressing the right side of her neck. The dream returned. Gladiators, blinding light, metallic claws. Images mingled with real memories of surgeons looming.

Her anguish merged with George's.

She understood the echo coming from his mind and into her thoughts, "... all part of the plan...", George's pain,"...part of the plan...", his loss, "...the plan...", his aloneness, "...plan..."

"George!" she cried into the wind.

She sat on the bed and wept.

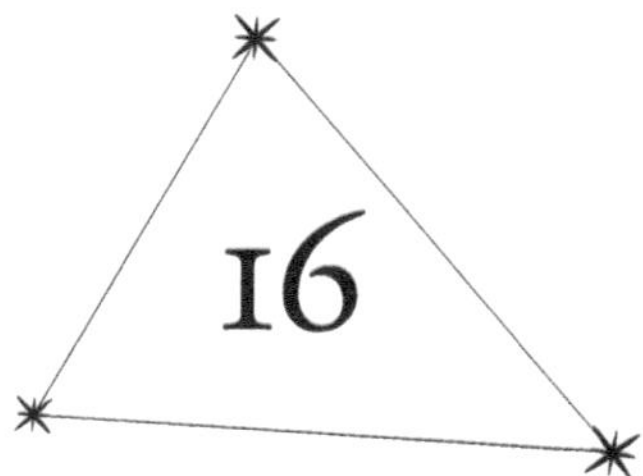

Unlike every morning George could remember, he did not awaken at dawn. Groggily, he rolled onto his side and checked the clock—7:04 AM.

*What the hell?*

Thunder crashed in the distance. Gusts blew through the veranda, rustling ivy and trembling shutters. The bedspread and sheets, normally blushed by the orange glow of the Spectralamp, looked plain and ordinary.

Strangest of all, no dreams.

Not surprising. Sleep had charted a restless course between furious tempests, churning eddies, impractical bluffs, and aimless drifting before finally bobbing on gentle waves.

The Greek hillside, peasants dancing, pentatonic melodies, all felt poisonous; noxious memories from a different life.

He listened for music beneath the howl of the storm, but that too had vanished. In its place, thoughts and images—of Glen, Old Flowers, Cerissa; memories of Culture Colonies, years of lessons, life on Flowers Island.

The Grand Trine.

Then a quote from Shakespeare: *I shall not believe thee dead until I can play foote balle with thy head.*

"The game begins today," George said to the empty bedroom. As if to accent his words, a sudden squall swirled through the room, toppled a music stand, scattered papers, and knocked a floor lamp across the waterbed, lightly grazing

George's arm. "Right on schedule," he muttered while sloshing out of bed with the lamp in tow.

Dressing in shorts, tee shirt, and sandals, he hustled to the veranda, secured the shutters against winds that in years past had stripped foliage from trees, shattered glass, ripped tiles from rooftops, and damaged any structure not made of concrete or stone. Predictable, but with astonishing variability, North Atlantic storms had sacked villages in the Aztec Colony, toppled monuments in the Egyptian Colony, and collapsed temples in the Grecian Colony.

A mere three summers ago, a suction vortex within a tornado embedded in a hurricane had sucked seawater from a shallow bay, poisoned a swath of land, and contaminated a lake while the mother hurricane scoured the island with 150 mph winds and torrential rains. Berms collapsed. Terraced gardens dissolved. Ponds overflowed banks and merged into rivers of mud.

Now, clammy tropical air churned below masses of white cirrus clouds, a *Faunus* Crown upon the Roman Colony foretelling more destruction.

With the last shutter secure, George grabbed his knapsack from the closet, stuffed it with his thickest sweatshirt, a pair of hiking boots, and a few essential toiletries. From the old metal trunk where he kept his salvaged treasures, he removed a diamond studded jewel case filled with gold coins. The weight surprised him when he lifted the knapsack onto the closet's top shelf. He hid it with a flannel shirt and left in search of the only honest person on Flowers Island.

Downstairs, the mansion bustled with activity. Rollins stood in the eye of his own storm, shouting orders, directing the flurry of workers as they darted back and forth carrying hammers, ladders, lawn furniture, ropes, tarps; anything that could tie down, or needed tying down.

"George!" Rollins cried, before George could sneak past. "I was on my way to see you." *Following today's script*? George thought. "There's been a change of plans. Mrs. Maxwell and her daughter are leaving."

An anvil dropped on George's mood, and *his* plans. "Leaving?"

Two men on the ground and two on ladders were shuttering the mansion's huge bay windows. The activity distracted Rollins just long enough for George to take a few tentative steps toward the front door. "Hold on, George. I've got a task for you."

*And I might pretend to perform it.*

Rollins called to three servants, empty-handed for the moment, but clearly on a mission. "Try the garage if you can't find them in the tool shed." He turned back to George. "Somebody misplaced the library shutters. How is that possible?"

*In fiction, all things are possible,* George thought, while smirking at the thespians scurrying through his father's playhouse.

"If people would just do as they're told, this sort of thing...never mind. I need you to take a message to Captain Jacobson."

*Jacobson*? Alarmed, George said: "He's not foolish enough to fly in this storm."

"He's smart enough to keep his job," Rollins said.

"And where exactly would the copter be going?"

A violent gust blew through the open front door. "Ghastly wind," growled Rollins, covering his nose with a handkerchief, red to disguise the blood. An authentic moment. Hemp fields, grown to provide rope and fabric for the Culture Colonies, bloomed in August, and the pollen tortured Rollins for weeks. "Beastly wind could stir up the sons of Makalos." He coughed, a phlegmy, gargling hack that only a maestro could fake. Truth serving invention. "I'm sure you recall the summer of '08..." Rollins paused mid-sentence, then turned away, a tribute to suffering, stagecraft, or both. "Bloody God!", he said, with a series of undignified sniffs. "Sorry, Master George. I was saying, do you remember in 2008 when the roof of the south wing flew halfway to the Grecian Colony? Well, this is predicted to be another..." He stopped, brushing the air with his hand. "There's work to do."

"You didn't answer my question," George said. A glare from Rollins. George tried a different angle. "Why can't Mrs. Maxwell just wait it out?"

"She should. But I never argue with Kathryn Maxwell. She always has her reasons. She's with your father now, finishing last minute business."

"Before risking three lives?"

"I don't think it's that serious. We still have several hours."

"And, of course, hurricanes are so predictable."

"As is your sarcasm," Rollins said, while massaging his temples and frowning at George through a squint. "Fine. If you must know, and you didn't hear this from me." He glanced around, timing the beats, milking the *caesura* for maximum effect. "There's been an incident with Cerissa. It's imperative that they leave this morning."

George expected none of these liars to go off script, least of all Rollins. But maybe a minuscule truth hid between the lines. "What kind of incident?"

"Kathryn is afraid the storm will trap her." Evasive non-answer, but possibly true.

"At least the island is a safe trap," George said.

Rollins kneaded tormented sinuses, for both relief and effect. "Yes, yes, I know. She's being impulsive, maybe for the first time in her life."

"Then someone should—"

"Enough," Rollins said, leading George to the front door. "Ours is not to reason, and all that. Let's guarantee the safest possible journey, okay?" George glowered in protest, but Rollins carried on. "Naturally, we can't reach the heliport by radio, so take an electric cart and drive down there. Tell the captain that Kathryn has changed the plan. He'll be flying them *ahead* of the storm. To Portsmouth, not Bermuda."

"That's ridiculous!" George said, genuinely concerned for Cerissa's safety. If this wasn't some trick, some lesson, or some performance designed to manipulate him to some unknown end, it was reality performing farce. "Portsmouth is beyond the copter's range."

"Nonsense. I've made the trip myself."

"Barely maybe, and definitely not in these winds."

"You know, George, you should practice those relaxation exercises you learned in the Asian Colony. I believe you're becoming irascible." *Shove it up your irasshole*? George thought through clenched teeth. "Don't worry," Rollins said with a dismissive wave. "Captain Jacobson knows what he's doing. Now go." With a mild shove, he pushed George out the door, then shouted into the storm. "We wouldn't want them leaving without a brimming tank of petrol."

With that, George found himself standing on the lawn, as angry as the ceaseless winds.

*No way is Cerissa boarding that copter.*

Affecting the stride of a man with purpose (and hoping Rollins was watching), he followed the sloping grounds toward the garage. He stopped when the hedges of the maze shielded him from sight. Skirting the perimeter, he ran to the guest quarters.

Two minutes later, he had climbed the back stairs of the West Wing. Several rooms in this part of the mansion were reserved for guests, but special guests always occupied the sumptuous *Hestia Suite*, so named for the Greek goddess of the hearth. Laughingly pretentious from the perspective of someone who often spent months living in Medieval huts stinking of damp earth and moldy straw, or crammed into Roman *insulae* with filthy "relatives", goats, chickens, and pots of shit and piss, George nevertheless understood his father's desire to intoxicate business associates. With comfort engorged to multiple luxury bedrooms, gold-plated fixtures and mosaic tiles in "salons" too lavish to be called bathrooms; an office, library, dining and great room, a small gym, a full kitchen, and a porch garden overlooking an actual garden, the *Hestia Suite* left little room for sobriety.

George rapped lightly on the solid oak door, preferring his own knuckles to the hulking brass knocker shaped like a fist.

No answer. He tried again, louder. Still no response.

*They may be staying in another suite, in separate rooms, or already on their way to the heliport.*

With intent and as much focus as he could muster, he lowered the mental drawbridge, inviting Cerissa to hear his call.

*Cerissa, it's George. You're in danger. I'm coming in.*

Very gently, he turned the knob and found it unlocked. *I'm an intruder, a thief stealing their privacy. But this is important.*

He stepped inside and surveyed the scene.

Three suitcases were stacked against a four-piece sectional sofa. French windows gaped onto a balcony swirling with leaves, twigs, and fragments of potted flowers. Hemp curtains, gathered in tight pleats, lashed the room like cats-o'nine-tails.

Gone. Luggage packed and ready for porters.

*Shit!*

He closed the windows against the raging wind and fastened the latch.

"Are you all right?" Cerissa said.

Startled, George spun around and faced a petite body framed under the archway of the main salon. Obviously fresh from a hot bath or shower, Cerissa held a glass of orange juice and wore a cream-colored bathrobe that accented her darkly tanned skin. The serpent bracelet he had seen at the waterfall gleamed silver in the morning light and distracted him for a moment from the swollen blue-black bruise under her left eye. "What happened?"

"I didn't walk into a door," Cerissa said with a grin. "How are *you*?"

"Forget me. That looks painful."

"She's done worse."

"Kathryn?"

She gave him a "who else?" shrug and joined him at the French windows. Clouds in a dark rage massed over a churning forest. "It wasn't too bad when Kathryn had Cedric to beat on."

"Cedric?"

"My father. He's not a tall man, but he's wiry and strong and taut as a jib sheet. Her *pinche* punches were like leaves grazing a statue. I was always a softer target."

"Jesus."

"But only when Cedric was sailing. At home, he'd never let her touch me. Even if that meant hours of swallowing shit and never fighting back."

"How long has he been gone?"

"Most of my life. Even when he was present. Weeks at sea, a few days home, a bender or two in-between. Then back to, what he called: 'The horse latitudes of family life.' Followed by his classic: 'Too much duty, not enough booty.'" Cerissa faced George and toasted with her juice. "Words to drink by—whisky, neat, with a splash of more whisky." A smile, followed by a grimace. "I could go on, but I'm more interested in you."

"I'm fine," George said.

"Right," Cerissa said, and walked to the sofa. She finished her drink with a long swallow and set the glass on a mahogany coffee table. Then, sitting with legs crossed, arms in her lap, and with an expression that expected candor, said: "You should stand behind your drawbridge if you want me to believe you're 'fine'. You don't show the world, but I can almost taste your anger."

George turned back to the windows, faced the low, thick clouds, and raised the drawbridge in his mind's eye. But a moment later, he lowered it. "At least now I know what needs to be done," he said, turning back and hoping for approval.

"I'm sure you'll succeed," Cerissa said. Her tone suggested success with unintended consequences. "Not many minds enjoy your focus. To say nothing of determination." She smiled through a heavy sigh, either twinging from the bruise, or venting sorrow. "You've chosen a unique form of revenge, George. Your father will suffer."

"You think it's revenge?"

"It's obvious."

*Only to a mind reader.*

George paced the room, thinking of all the years and the thousands of actors Old Flowers had employed. His father as Casting Director was formidable, but how does one cast a mind reader?

From the coffee table, he removed a rose from the vase brought to the suite each morning, and plucked its petals one by one. When he had stripped the flower bare, he held it at eye level. "This is my life," he said, "minus the lies." He grinned. "In the Medieval Colony, "plucking a rose" meant picking up a hooker. In a later age and among polite company, a woman excused herself to "pluck a rose" when she needed a pee. So, the question is: Which version of everything I've learned and everyone I know is true?"

Cerissa smiled, then winced and lightly touched the swelling.

"It's ironic," George said. "You and I have only spent twenty minutes together. But you're the only person I really know."

"Closer to fifteen minutes, I'd say."

George settled into the cushion beside her and rested his hand within inches of her thigh. "It sounds stupid, but I feel like I've known you all my life?"

With closed eyes and a shake of the head, she leaned back. "George, if you want a life minus lies, you'll have to stop lying to yourself." To soften her words (and to prolong their first metaphor), she grabbed the naked rose and flourished her most radiant smile. "The bare truth is this, George." She waved the rose like a wagging finger. "You and your life know *nothing* about me. You don't trust me any more than you trust Glen, or Rollins, or anybody else. And I can't blame you. The deceptions around here are thicker than tar."

"But I do trust you." He even had reasons why he should. "This is your first time on Flowers Island. If I hadn't stopped at the waterfall, we'd still be strangers. You're not part of my father's plan."

"How do you know?"

"Because Old Flowers couldn't trick me into meeting you. I could have stayed on the trail and continued to North Beach. *I* decided to stop at the waterfall. *My* decision, not his."

"How do you know?"

"What are you saying? That I'm more of a puppet than I think I am?"

"None of us truly control our lives. But in your case..." She faced him squarely and stated in an even voice: "Let's just say Uncle Aaron has mastered some truly frightening techniques. I think you're part of a much greater—"

"Conspiracy?"

"I was going to say strategy. But it could easily be a design, some scheme, an arrangement. I don't know. I thought my mother was Queen of the Curtain until I came here. It's been enlightening in an opaque sort of way."

"You're saying everybody blocks you with mental curtains?"

"Or walls, vaults, dams, mountains, hedges, you name it. I get glimpses when their guards are down, but they're all very well trained."

"Even Miss Ruth?"

"Yes."

"Jesus. It's worse than I thought."

"Definitely not how I imagined Flowers Island," Cerissa said, regret deepened by an exaggerated frown.

"Or how "Uncle Aaron" described it," George said, with a subtle shift away from her. He stared down at his hands, crossed, stiff, clenched in the grip of distrust. "You've never visited, but you've known Old Flowers for years."

Cerissa shrugged. "I understand your suspicion. But would I admit to knowing your father if everything I say is a trap? A ruse to get you to trust me?"

"You might," George said, with gaze narrowed. "Maybe acknowledge the acquaintance out of fear that I'd find out later. Or, declare the friendship openly to convince me that you're trustworthy."

"Or," Cerissa said, "maybe I've *never* met Old Flowers. But I told you I did as part of a plan to get you to trust me so I could trick you into chasing an invisible bunny down a phony rabbit hole."

"Ouch," George said. "I'm sorry. I deserved that." His sigh became a groan, then a breathy growl. "Christ. My mind is a fucking mess."

"Quite the opposite," Cerissa said, reaching for his hand and holding it to her chest. "Yours is the most unique and intriguing mind I've ever known. But, at the moment, it's a bit confused."

"That's an understatement."

"Still, you're clear enough to understand that no amount of talk will convince you to trust me." After a gentle pat, she lowered his hand. "Am I right?"

"Trust," George said, with a wry grin. "From Old Norse *traustr*, meaning: Strong. Then *traustr* evolved and became *trusten* in Middle English, a language as dead as everything I believed about Flowers Island."

Amused, Cerissa offered George a half-smile and leaned back against the cushions with a palm cradling her chin, attention focused, eyes vivid and curious. Long, uncombed hair, feathery wisps gushing over shoulders, nape, and sofa, gleamed like a halo under overhead light.

*Traustr*, George thought, the word in his mind sounding like advice.

"Go on," she said.

"Well," he continued. "I trusted the bogus Rule of Separation. Trusted my phony pals and their lying smiles. Teachers trained me like a carnival animal and I trusted them. My own trusted father, scheming, manipulating, molding my brain, designed the perfect what...prodigy, curiosity, freak? They're all swindlers and hypocrites. In it for the money, or the science experiment; to curry favor with a billionaire, punch up a résumé, fulfill a thesis assignment, write an article for some fucking magazine. Or maybe just for sport, a vacation from boredom. Come to Flowers Island and collect stories to tell friends back on the mainland. I wouldn't know. My so-called friends are all here, living a false life and giving me fake history lessons. I've known them for years without really knowing anything, and now, every one of their two faces are unrecognizable. So, yes, I can trust—their treachery."

She pressed close, knees touching his leg. Warmth flowed between them, for a moment, dazing him with the scent of lavender. Outside, rain drenched the world. Inside, doubt withered the soul. "That's one of the saddest things I've ever heard," she said, with a sigh. "I'm so sorry. Maybe I can help."

"Really?" George answered, meaning: *I doubt it.*

"It involves reading my mind."

"What?"

"To trust me, you need to see me, George. Know my deepest secrets, learn the truth for yourself."

"I thought you were being serious."

"I am. Uncle Aaron has trained you well, conditioned your mind for his own purposes. But if you're willing to own it, that training belongs to you."

"I was never trained to read minds."

"True, but look at it this way. If an athlete builds muscles, develops coordination, balance, focus, flexibility; gains confidence, learns discipline, and applies positive mental imagery, he or she can become a superb runner, gymnast, skier, climber, or can, within reason, master any sport they desire." She paused and cocked her head. "Would you agree?"

"Of course."

"You've never directed your training to reading minds, but you possess the fundamental skills—concentration, the ability to clear the mind, receptivity. Are you willing to stretch those abilities?"

"You make it sound easy."

"It isn't. But you've already done most of the hard work. You've mastered the piano, for example. That developed concentration over many years. You've also cultivated a photographic memory. Was it easy to corral your thoughts when you first started working with Master Chang? Did you accomplish that overnight?"

"Of course not," George said. He thought about Master Chang, that noble and wise soul, or was that too an act? How the *sensei* flourished on one meal a day, owned three robes, a needle, and a water strainer. How life in a monastic cocoon offered few material rewards, no distinction, and even less incentive to lie, cheat, or delude. Was that a role an actor could play for years?

"George?" Cerissa said.

"Sorry. I was distracted by thinking about the man who trained me for years to overcome distraction." They both laughed. "But to your point, yes, some of my earliest memories are temples in the Asian Colony, learning to clear the mental chatter and focus on a single line of thought. Then we worked with images, a bird, an apple, a pebble, whatever, and tried to see the object clearly in the mind's eye. I'm still working the techniques, but you're right. I practiced *ekaggatā*, single-mindedness, for years."

"So here we are," Cerissa said. "I'm inviting you to look beyond my mental curtain. Share my thoughts, discover my secrets, reveal my cravings and needs."

"Why would you expose yourself like that?"

"First, because *I* trust *you*. Secondly, that would make us even. You've already done much the same for me."

"I have? How? We've known each other for fifteen minutes."

"You'll soon understand that, when it comes to mind reading, closeness is more important than nearness. We also find each other very appealing." With the back of her fingers, she lightly brushed his cheek. "With your eyes, you saw me as naked and vulnerable as I saw you with my mind. That made me happy. From the moment we met, I wanted to know everything."

George smiled and released his gaze from hers, his attention drawn to a fold in the bathrobe and the way it opened to reveal a glimpse of nipple. Embarrassed, he raised his eyes and again noticed the scar on the right side of her neck. A trace of a hint of a clue.

"Besides," Cerissa continued, "your imagination is so vivid your thoughts are like watching that television you keep dwelling on."

"You can see that, right now?"

"Clearly. And the conversation with Glen you replay over and over."

"You amaze and terrify me."

"I'm the Wonderful Wizard of OZ," she said with a giggle.

"So, to unveil your secrets, do I knock over your screen like Toto, or use a crystal ball?"

*"Que es tan adivina,"* Cerissa said, smiling (That is so fortune teller). "Neither. Try this. I'm picturing an image of myself. Can *you* see it? No, wait! I have an idea."

Beaming, (and so sensual George considered raising the drawbridge to hide an ambush of lusty thoughts), Cerissa dashed to some other room in the suite.

*She is beautiful, goddamn it. I am attracted. I'm not going to hide it.*

Honesty and Cerissa—two sides of the same craving.

A drawer slammed. Objects clattered. In bare feet, Cerissa padded back to the sofa, sat opposite George with crossed legs, and wrote something in pencil on a small notepad. After a moment, she tore out the page, folded it, and placed the sheet on the mahogany coffee table. "Now," she said, green eyes twinkling mischief. "Close your eyes and relax. Calm the mind. Open to my thoughts."

"Okay."

"Tell me what you see."

"Blackness," George said.

"That's a start."

A long moment passed.

Sensation diminished to calm, focused breaths.

Outside, turbulent gusts rattled the shutters, but *ekaggatā* ignored distractions.

"I'm picturing an image of myself," Cerissa repeated. "Can you see it?'

"No," George replied. "I see an image, a person, but it's not you. There's a woman sitting in a high-backed chair. Wild grey hair, face aged, crow's feet around the eyes. She's holding a playing card. No, that's wrong. This card is larger, lots of color, crammed with symbols. Must be tarot."

"Can you tell which card, or suit—wands, pentacles, cups, swords? Perhaps a card from the Major Arcana?"

"The image is blurred, but I'll guess again and say Major Arcana. The symbols are too elaborate to be a minor card. Sorry. I can't be more specific."

"I think that's my fault. Give me a second to focus."

After a short period of deep inhalations; serene, controlled breaths in stark contrast to the storm's restless bluster, George said: "Ah, the Wheel of Fortune. I see Anubis, the sphinx, the four fixed signs of the zodiac. Everything is clearer. The old woman is sitting before a small table. There's a crystal ball."

Cerissa chuckled. "I couldn't resist."

"But I'm not seeing you," George said. "Who is this person?"

"It's how I imagine my older self."

"You're still so beautiful," George said.

"Ha! I chose the wrong card. I should have imagined The Fool." She nudged George's thigh. "Okay. Let's see if you passed." She handed him the folded paper. "What does it say?"

George stared at the note before speaking. "Old woman on throne holding the Wheel of Fortune. Crystal ball on table." He looked up, saw hints of blue in clear emerald eyes, insight behind vision, youth masking antiquity. Was Cerissa a Grecian *sibyl,* a Roman "looking at birds", a seer of sacred things in an Aztec *temescal*—all three?

"No, George, I'm just a girl," she said with mild rebuke.

"Right, sorry," George said. "My mind is wandering and I keep forgetting that you're in there, or rather here." He pointed to his temple.

"You can raise your drawbridge. I won't be offended."

"I think I should. This is still a little mystifying."

"Just please, don't glamorize me. As in: 'Don't dress me in magic or enchantment.' I'm a normal person with ordinary yearnings and piles of defects."

"Hardly."

"True, Fabiana, my nanny, teacher, and *bruja*, opened the world to young eyes. My mother would say, too young. Maybe I've seen too much and grew up too fast. But Fabiana also taught us compassion. She warned against prejudice. Encouraged empathy. She trained us to look beyond surface thoughts and fleeting motives. She said, 'Ego masks weakness' and 'Cowards can be heroes.' She used to laugh and say that science calls the brain "grey matter" because human nature is black as a sailor and white as a sail." Cerissa scoffed. "She obviously knew my father. And her favorite expression was: *'Bueno sirve el mal de bueno'.*"

"Good serves the evil of good?" George said, confused. "That makes no sense."

"Exactly," Cerissa said. "She loved spinning our minds, and always away from judgement and labels."

"This Fabiana sounds like a remarkable woman."

"*Como, Glinda, la bruja buena del sur,*" Cerissa said. "If we're still in OZ."

"Obviously not," George said, indicating Cerissa's bruise. "Your mother did that during an argument about someone named Conrad."

"Good. You've seen beyond the fortune teller. Keep looking."

"Fabiana wouldn't be pleased. I'm judging your mother and questioning her motives."

"Then let's go back to yours," Cerissa said.

With a slight squirm, George said: "You're referring to the 'revenge' against my father."

"Yes."

"All right, I'm angry. I've been used and manipulated my entire life. I don't even know why. But it's more than revenge. This will be the first step into my own destiny."

"Destiny?"

"Destiny, fate, free will. Living my life without Old Flowers pulling my strings."

"And your plan will guarantee that?"

"I'm surprised you asked the question."

"I don't know. Maybe Aaron wants to see his son as quarterback of the Grand Trine."

"Ha!" George said, the word like a clap of thunder. "Never in a million years. Me playing football is probably the one thing he *hasn't* planned."

"And to play for the Grand Trine you'll give up everything?" With a sweep of her arms she indicated the opulence, his inheritance, his home, all the marvels of Flowers Island.

"Fuck yes! I keep seeing that television. That room full of actors, users, and liars. Then I see myself standing in the corridor. The freak. Everybody's puppet. I feel hatred for my best friend, for the father I thought I knew. I realize now that there's more to *my* life than Culture Colonies and Old Flowers' version of the past. I'm leaving Plato, Marcus Aurelius, and the Aztec *Ometeotl*. The wealth, the privilege, the elite education in a billionaire's playground—it all sickens me. I'm going to discover a larger world, the greater world of the *common* man."

Cerissa smiled. "And you expect to find your 'greater world of the common man' at a football game?"

George slumped back into the sofa, the cushions enveloping him in scant comfort. He said in a low voice: "It's an interesting place to start."

"Because you believe everyone loves football. You think football is the common thread running through all levels of society."

"It seemed that way last night. I saw geniuses watching the game, and near idiots."

"And you want to play for the Grand Trine because they always win."

"Strive for the best, as Jonas would say."

"You're also fascinated by Coach Buffington and his strange powers."

That brilliant, frightening mind! *Yes, goddamn it!* he thought. *All that and more.* Then calmly: "What do you know about the Grand Trine?"

"I know they're the team from Grand Trinity University." She regarded him with a strange look, inquiring, but also challenging. "Tell me what else I know about Grand Trinity University."

George steadied his mind and waited for whatever surprises her thoughts would reveal. Like a wave splashing a sleeping body, he flinched. "Really?" he said.

She raised her brows and shrugged.

"*You're* enrolling at Grand Trinity University?"

"Doesn't make me look less suspicious, does it?"

"That can't be coincidence."

"Maybe it can. I learned two years ago that Grand Trinity had the best Parapsychology Department in the United Nation. I wouldn't be the only mind reader there. Unfortunately, the university is now part of the Northeast Kingdom. Which, of course, makes them the enemy. My biggest challenge will be finding a way across the border."

"Glen mentioned something about this Northeast Kingdom. A war. A secession."

"That's a long conversation, George."

"Fine. I can learn the details later. I'm just thinking, coincidence or not, maybe we could travel to Grand Trinity together."

"I can't."

"Why not?"

"Several reasons. The helicopter to Bermuda, for one. Or is it Portsmouth now?"

"That's what Rollins told me, but it's an insane plan. Way too risky."

She glanced across the room at a desk clock embedded in a cube of glass. "We're scheduled to leave in less than two hours."

"Your trip may be delayed," George said, raising the drawbridge.

"I saw that. What are you planning?"

"Something I'll keep to myself. Don't worry. Nobody will get hurt."

"Whatever you're scheming won't matter. I can't even think about Grand Trinity until I find out what happened to Conrad."

"I don't understand."

"He's a dear friend and mentor. In some ways, another father figure. Mother is convinced we're having some sordid affair. It's absurd, but that's not the worst part."

"Should I ask?"

"You saw how she is. Yesterday she was sure *'que tú y yo habíamos dormido juntos'.*" She laughed. "Naturally, I'm being polite. My mother's translation would be 'that you and I had fucked each other stupid'. She's convinced I'm a *pornai* of Athens, available to all, denier of none."

"That *is* bad."

"Not really. The worst part is whatever she did to Conrad. I can't read her and she won't be specific. She just said she 'eliminated' the problem. That's when I called her *endija de puta* and she hit me."

"Eliminated. Like paid off, had fired, kidnapped, deported, hurt, even killed?"

"I really don't know. That's the problem. She's maniacal about "protecting" me. Tries to shield me from anyone she considers "unacceptable". She forces me to hide my life, sneak around, and do the very things that drive her crazy. God help anyone close enough to become a boyfriend."

"At the waterfall, she called your lovers a 'troop of local *machitos*'."

"Yes, that's one of her favorites. Though, in fairness, she's not always wrong. Unlike her, I've never had hang-ups about sex. She hates men, thanks to my father. I love them, probably for the same reason. Of course, I'm safe and selective, but I relish sexual pleasure and enjoy it frequently. Have since age 13 when I graduated from pleasuring myself to oral, then on to actual fucking. Orgasm is Life Force, in my opinion. Cosmic energy pouring through every pore. I'll always enjoy it with whomever I please, owe no apologies, and use it to caress the core of my being. I guess you could say my clitoris has deep roots."

George stared, astonished. "Are you sure you've never lived on Flowers Island? You're like an amalgamation of every woman, culture, and lesson I've ever studied, only authentic."

"That's a high compliment. The opposite of glamorizing. Though I suppose it's okay if you find me a little enchanting." She smiled. "Just not magical. I'm an ordinary girl looking forward to the moment you undress me."

"I await that extraordinary occasion. But for now, I have a plan."

Cerissa pointed to the French windows and frowned. "I know."

"It'll work."

"George, I'm tempted to go. Just to spite my mother. But we can't steal your sailboat in this weather. Look out there. It's too dangerous."

"We don't sail the boat to the mainland now. We only go one nautical mile, as far as Little Flower. Dock there and wait out the storm."

"What's to prevent them from catching us with the helicopter?" George reinforced the drawbridge. "George...?"

"I'll take care of the copter. That leaves the *Valdaquez*, my sailboat, and the yacht. Glen took care of the yacht. Cerissa, I know this island. A storm hits and magnetic residue lingers for days. A week can pass without *any* radio contact. By then we'll be on the mainland."

"Then what?"

"Anything you like. I have treasure. Gold and jewels I've salvaged from shipwrecks. You can hire a detective and find out what happened to Conrad. Or you can come with me to Grand Trinity. It's your choice."

Cerissa gently stroked his cheek. "Oh George, adventures with you would be amazing. We could truly discover worlds together." George's heart pounded with renewed fury. "But, don't you see? That's the problem."

"No, I don't see."

Her hand followed the line of his jaw, to the tip of his chin, then back, then slowly down the left side of his neck until her fingers rested on the scar. George stiffened. "Why didn't Uncle Aaron have this cosmetically removed?"

"It happened when I was a child, during a lesson in the Roman Colony."

"Yes?"

"It's simple. There were no plastic surgeons in Ancient Rome."

"It couldn't be removed later?"

"Not without violating his so-called Rule of Separation."

"And what about me? Doesn't it seem strange, and absurd, that I have a scar on the opposite side of my neck?"

George groaned. "Yes."

"Well?"

George stood; walked to the window, and stared out at the storm. The farce of life on Flowers Island glared back. "Another reason to leave this circus."

"Maybe my mother has been lying, too. Years ago, she explained the scar by saying that surgeons had removed cysts from my neck. What if there were no cysts. What if they put the scar there."

"Why? So I'd recognize you?"

"Yes. If we stay together, we could be following their plan."

"Not if we lead our own lives."

For a moment, fierce gusts spoke for them.

Finally, Cerissa said: "Maybe you're right. Maybe we can fight back."

"I can't live another day here," George said. "Your home life doesn't sound that great either."

"It's not," Cerissa said. "But consider this. They may frame our escape as a kidnapping. Don't forget. I'm still a minor. Though I'd leave anyway just to piss Kathryn off, scare her shitless, and show her that hitting me has consequences."

"If we're caught, you can pretend you're a stowaway."

"You're reading my mind," Cerissa said with a smile. "Okay, I'll go. But when we reach the mainland, I'm returning to the former Costa Rica. I have to find out for myself what's happened to Conrad."

"I understand," George said with more than a hint of regret. "Regardless, you can't go like that." He pointed to the bathrobe.

"I can be dressed in two minutes," she said while dashing into the dressing room.

In the distance, lightning lit the underbellies of monstrous clouds aimed directly at the island. Time was running out. And as happy as he was that Cerissa would be joining him, her presence added complications. A disappearance before Kathryn's departure would compel Old Flowers to send searchers combing the island. The sailboat would be harder to steal.

As things stood now, only the underground tram, running full speed, could get them to the marina before the full force of the storm arrived. Somehow, George had to guarantee that no one used the tram to chase after Cerissa.

And then, there was another, even greater problem.

As he stood overlooking the west garden, images from the past flooded his mind—Colonies, friends, Old Flowers; everything that had given purpose and meaning to his life; everything he would, in a few hours' time, leave. It may all be bullshit, blatant lies, and illusion, but he needed to know *why*.

With the lies shattered, answers like "teaching, a well-rounded education, hands-on experience with culture and its development," all rang hollow.

Somewhere, deep in his soul, he knew he couldn't live an authentic life in the Greater World of the Common Man without understanding the counterfeit past.

An explanation existed.

Old Flowers never destroyed. He built, created, expanded.

Thunder crashed in the distance.

Only one place could hide the answer.

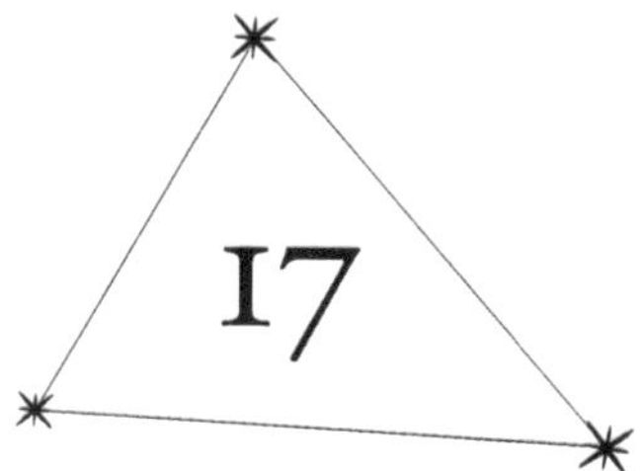

George crouched at the edge of the maze to prepare for his upcoming performance. *I can play this game*, he thought.

Before leaving Cerissa, he had drawn a map detailing the most covert route to a storeroom in the basement of the *Pergamum*. If she left via the West Wing's back staircase, followed specific garden paths around the maze while blending into the bustle and chaos of the storm, prudently followed the winding stone walkway through the marble pillars of a minimalist recreation of the Hanging Gardens, past fountains, along terraced orchards of date, almond, olive, and walnut trees, and entered the *Pergamum* through the rarely used south portico, she could find the storeroom and wait for him there.

"Are you kidding?" Cerissa had said. "I wandered into the *Pergamum* yesterday. Spectacular library, maybe the most beautiful I've ever seen. But I was lost thirty seconds after passing the Circulation Desk. So, assuming I succeed through your maze of directions, how do I find the basement, let alone your storeroom?"

"Good point," he had said, while considering options. "You'll have to do what everyone does in a library."

"Read?" Cerissa said.

"No. Ask the librarian."

"To show me the storeroom?"

"To guide you to the sarcophagus. It's on the basement level along with a collection of Egyptian artifacts. The storeroom is nearby."

"What if it's locked?"

"Rooms are rarely locked around here. A bigger problem might be Kristin."

Who's that?"

"The librarian. I'm assuming she won't leave the building after she helps you, but I'm concerned that somebody asking about you might come to the library."

"Okay. Assuming all this assuming works out, what do we do when you return from your mysterious errand?"

"We'll be a short walk and a flight of stairs away from the sub-basement," George said, evading her insinuation. "And fifty feet from the *Haji Bektash Veli* terminal.

"And if the tram isn't there?"

"Don't worry," George had said, hiding that very fear behind a reinforced drawbridge. "The tram is stationed there between Colony lessons. Except during emergencies, it's rarely used."

Cerissa, mindful and perceptive even absent a mind full of everyone's thoughts, had replied: "Then hurry back before finding me becomes urgent."

George had promised to join her in thirty minutes.

Unfortunately, that was before spending his first fifteen minutes getting to the heliport and telling a relieved Captain Jacobson that Kathryn Maxwell had changed her mind about traveling in such dangerous weather.

That lie left the captain happily in his office while George snuck into the hanger, found a tool box, removed cowling and access panels, and leaned into the engine compartment. Using a pair of dikes, he then cut out a three-inch section from the lead wire feeding the igniter box. Even someone foolish enough to try a splice would fail.

Now, having just parked the electric cart, and dripping wet from running through the rain, George opened the mansion's door to a pool of island employees. As expected, Rollins stood on the verge with an ebony clipboard, checking off lists of completed tasks and assigning more. "I gave Jacobson your message," George lied, as Rollins sent a platoon of workers to the stables. More were delegated to the greenhouses, others to the residential cottages.

"Uh, huh," Rollins answered while ordering the last personnel to sweep the grounds for, what he called, "Any potential projectiles".

With the first breath after the last close of the massive oak door, George said: "I hate to say it, Rollins. But there may be one more problem."

"Really?" Rollins said, looking up from his notes.

"I wasn't sure what to do, so I thought I'd check first."

Rollins, noticeably fatigued, eyes blood-shot, nostrils raw and puffy, appeared barely able to maintain his long-practiced, though mock, patience. "What is it now, George?" he asked, straining under the last straw.

"Well, I stopped by the stables to see if Barry needed any help." Something about all this lying gave George a strange new affinity with people he had known his entire life. "You know how skittish the horses get in this kind of weather."

"Quite."

"Yeah, well the horses are okay." At least George assumed they were.

"And?" Rollins said, like a man watching an archer slowly draw a bow. "What's the problem?"

"Maybe nothing," George said, eyes narrowed, siting the arrow. "I know she's a nature worshipper, and very independent." Finding the target. "And maybe she's like me and enjoys the thrill of a good storm, and maybe—"

"Master George," Rollins blurted. "Whom are you talking about?"

"Cerissa. I just saw her walking into the woods."

"What!?" Rollins said, as the arrow hit the mark. "When?"

"I don't know. Fifteen, maybe twenty minutes."

"Bloody lunacy! The helicopter is practically idling." With most of the staff tasked with other duties, Rollins marched down the hall to the kitchen, cleaved open the double doors like Heracles standing between pillars, and cried: "Ferd! Come at once."

Just then, the elevator opened and Old Flowers, joined by the daughter-slapping *La Corporada*, limped to the foyer.

"What's all the ruckus?" Old Flowers asked. Then addressing George. "Feeling better today?"

"Yes sir," George answered, with a false smile and a downward glance.

"Hello George," Kathryn said.

*Vete a la mierda. Mal parido, perra (Fuck you! Your birth was a mistake, bitch)* George thought, the first Costa Rican curse that sprang to mind. But then he realized that, sure, Kathryn was a bitch, but if her birth was a mistake there would be no Cerissa. So, he added another Costa Rican classic: *Se jodió tu bicicleta (Your bicycle fucked itself)*, meaning: You're about to lose control of this situation. *Lo cierto* (how true!)

"Quickly," Rollins said to Ferd. "I've just sent a crew to the stables. Go there and help Barry saddle a dozen horses. George will be along shortly."

*I will?*

Ferd dashed away.

Old Flowers demanded: "What on earth is going on?"

"I don't see our bags," Kathryn said at the same time.

Rollins heaved his shoulders and sighed. Converted in seconds from Heracles to Sisyphus. "Glen just took a luggage cart for your bags." Then, to Old Flowers: "The issue is Cerissa. She's run off to the forest."

"You can't be serious," Old Flowers said, alarmed.

"She was seen near the stables twenty minutes ago," Rollins said. "But she won't go far in this weather."

Kathryn clenched the leather strap of her purse. "I'm not so sure," she said.

"Not sure?" Old Flowers glanced from Kathryn to Rollins, then back. "Teenagers," he scowled.

George repressed the urge to laugh. How delightful to see, for once, Old Flowers as the miffed marionette. Kathryn looked less than delighted herself, and pale, almost as white as her knuckles.

"Don't worry, Kathryn. We'll find her," Old Flowers said. An empty assurance.

Rollins turned to George. "You know the terrain better than anyone. Lead a team to where you last saw her and start there. Glen can take another group and comb the woods between here and the Asian Colony." He glanced at Old Flowers and a subtle, but definite communication passed between them. "Now George," Rollins continued, "if, or rather, when you locate Cerissa, remind her of the many dangers. Convince her, for your sake, to return to the mansion."

*It's for my sake now?* George thought. Then verbally, simply to annoy Kathryn, said: "What about the luggage?"

"What?" Rollins said, with a look that screamed: *You're more irascible than I thought.* "Let's not be glib. Hurry to the West Wing and find Glen. Leave the bags. I'll collect them myself."

"No, no, don't bother with that," Old Flowers said to Rollins. "I want every available body dedicated to finding Cerissa. You round up more volunteers. Kathryn and I will go up later and deal with the luggage."

"On my way," George said, darting off to the guest quarters. When the main elevator opened on the third floor, he spotted Glen at the end of the hallway, heading toward him with the Maxwell's luggage. "Here goes," George muttered under his breath. At a fast, but not too fast pace, he walked to the cart, grabbed onto the metal bar, and began pushing it in the opposite direction. "Change of plans," he said.

"Really?" Glen said, perplexed. But he let George take the cart.

"Yeah, the Maxwell's aren't leaving just yet."

Glen eyed George with his customary smirk. "Who decided that, you or them?"

For effect, George looked away like a child caught in a lie, then muttered: "Is it that obvious?"

"It's what I would do. Delay Mrs. Bitch until it's too late."

"That's the general idea."

"But mainly," Glen continued, "you want Cerissa here long enough to diddle her trinket." Glen grinned. "Does she know about Jenny?"

"Fuck you."

"Save it for Cerissa," Glen said with a snicker. He grabbed the bar and helped. "George, about last night. I—"

"Forget it. There isn't time." George was far from forgetting about last night, but the moment required a convincing "good buddy" routine.

"Fine," Glen said.

A few rooms from the *Hestia Suite*, Glen pulled back on the cart. "Hang on."

"What?"

"I'm fuckin' brilliant, that's what."

"In my nightmares," George said.

"You want delay? I've got it. I had an idea when we passed that housekeeping closet." He pointed down the hall. "Wait here. Give me thirty seconds."

*This better be good*, George thought.

Glen returned with a pair of pliers and an adjustable wrench. "We loosen a couple nuts and skew one of the wheels. If Rollins checks, he'll see why it's taking so long."

"Jesus, Mr. Brilliant," George, the good buddy, said with an "ah shucks" accent. "Nothin' obvious 'bout that there sa-bo-tage."

"You have a better idea?"

"Yes. First of all, Old Flowers and Kathryn are coming to collect the luggage, not Rollins."

"They are?"

"So, we just flatten a couple of tires. If anyone asks later, you say it wasn't noticeable until you loaded the cart." Glen crouched down to hiss air from the tires, but George stopped him. "I'll do that. You need to talk to Rollins."

"What the hell for?"

"You're leading one of the search parties."

"What search party?"

"Cerissa had a fight with Kathryn and ran off into the woods."

"Seriously?"

"Your team covers from here to the Asian Colony. Mine starts at the stables."

"Then why bother with this cart shit? No Cerissa means no departure."

George had his own reasons. "Every little delay counts," he said.

"When did you see her?"

"About fifteen minutes ago."

"Alone, in this storm?"

"Yep."

"Then I'd better get going."

George bled air from two of the tires and dashed back to the main elevator. He didn't go inside. Instead, he hid in a linen closet and cracked open the door just far enough to peep at the elevator.

Minutes passed with thoughts focused on Cerissa—their escape, a life together at Grand Trinity University, their future after graduation—but always returned to the library and Cerissa in a dark storeroom, waiting, anticipating, George's thirty minutes stretching to forty-five, then sixty.

Would her patience hold?

A ding from the elevator.

Old Flowers and Kathryn stepped into the corridor and walked slowly toward the *Hestia Suite.*

When they turned the corner, George rode the elevator down to the second floor, waited for the door to open, and then pulled the "stop" button, freezing the car in place.

*That should slow Old Flowers down.*

The staircase brought George to the ground floor and a strangely deserted hallway, dark and shuttered against the storm. As a final precaution, he walked to the front door and peeked outside. There was Rollins on the lawn, gale force winds whipping the fringe of a balding head, the tails of his frock coat thrashing in all directions. Always and everywhere, organizing, managing, overseeing, this time with four students George recognized from the Plato's *Republic* lesson. The students nodded and turned toward the stables. Rollins, just to be sure, watched after them, and then struggled through the storm toward the greenhouses.

So much for that obstacle.

The beeps of the five-digit code seemed abnormally loud when George punched the keypad on Old Flowers' private elevator. The ride down stretched the seconds.

A ding, then the rattle of metal doors.

Chirps and screeches from the aviary.

His image in the full-length mirror hiding the secret passageway.

And, thankfully, Leona, either hunkered down in her cozy suite of underground rooms, or more likely, topside and helping the others.

With the tips of his fingers, he traced the edge of the mirror's ornate wooden frame, searching for a latch, a button, a catch. He poked at the gilt cherub, yanked on the carved Acanthus leaves, pressed the adjacent paneling with his palms. He tugged the base of a sconce next to the mirror and even lifted the candle.

Nothing.

With the tip of his shoe, he tapped along the hardwood baseboard.

A click.

The mirror slid quietly, and slowly, into the wall.

But now the stairs he had seen before seemed steeper, darker, the distant gloom cold and ominous. He hesitated. Was this exploration worth the delay? Was Cerissa reconsidering her decision to leave? Would Old Flowers return and find him snooping in a private storeroom?

*If I don't follow this hunch, I'll regret it forever.*

Resolved to accept the consequences, he stepped over the threshold and down the first two steps. A metal latch at shoulder level presumably opened and closed the mirror from the inside. To test the theory, he yanked downward and watched the mirror glide back into place, divulging its true nature.

A one-way mirror.

Old Flowers had lied, again. He hadn't been surprised to see George when the mirror opened yesterday. He could have been spying from this secret stairway the entire time.

"He wanted me to find this so-called 'old storeroom'," George said to the echoing walls.

*And I'm going to find out why.*

Pale light from the study barely illuminated the first few steps, but it did reveal a fixture with a single bulb mounted on the ceiling. *Where's the switch?* George wondered, before realizing that the light must be sound activated. He clapped. Nothing. He whistled. He said: "On", waited a second, then tried: "Light" and squinted at the glare above him. Word recognition. The Mansion's central computer monitored this passageway.

The stairs descended to a small landing and an unlocked metal door with a narrow window at eye level casting a distorted reflection of his face.

Stepping through, with only the bulb at the top of the stairway guiding him, he again called, "Light!" and activated a second bulb as the first bulb dimmed.

"Some storeroom," George said, his voice resonant in the nearly empty space.

This new light came from a brass lamp with a cobwebbed shade. It sat on a small, oval, white-oak end table. Next to it, a red velvet easy chair, the room's only other furnishing.

"Of course," George said, to a dark tunnel branching off the main room, a tunnel he had no interest in exploring. "What is the point of all this?" he asked himself, aloud. The words bounced off shadowy walls, adding eerie to the silence. Chill pressed around him. Memories from the chamber crept from the dark with taunts and fears. He wanted to leave this empty exercise, and had even turned to do so, when he noticed a photo album on the lower shelf of the end table.

Crouching, he grabbed the album, brushed dust from the cover, and opened to the first photo.

Two men, circa 1930's or 40's, wearing stylishly tailored suits. They were smiling, shaking hands. Behind them a crowd of factory workers threw hats into the air. A newspaper clipping, below and under the same plastic film, explained the photo with a headline:

ARMS BARON DEDICATES NEW FACTORY

"Arms baron?" George said, standing.

Yellowed by age, printed in a tiny font, and reflecting the lamp's dim light, George strained to read the text. *Do I really want to see this*, he thought, knowing that Old Flowers with characteristic drama, mystery, and sophistication had pointed, guided, and no doubt, manipulated him to this spot, to this moment? Surely, anything George discovered here would serve Old Flowers, not George. Yet, any window into his father's motives could assist George in his new life.

He sat in the chair and held the album under the lamp.

The clipping chronicled a happy day in the lives of Joseph and Aaron Flowers, father and son, a day marking the opening of the Flowers Corporation's twelfth armament development and manufacturing plant. The new facility was expected to boost the corporation's annual arms production to over a billion tons.

"A billion tons?" George said, bewildered. He had never heard of any war material manufacturing plants owned by the Flowers Corporation.

Turning the pages, he noted that the photographs were in reverse chronological order. Aaron Flowers appeared younger and younger the further George delved into the album. There was a graduation photo from the Harvard class of 1940, with a smiling Aaron Flowers looking barely out of high school. Earlier photos showed him standing next to a woman George recognized as his grandmother.

A blank page separated the first section from the second.

Here, George found more clippings, and a long article that chronicled Old Flowers' rise in the Flowers Corporation. The story spoke of the years before World War II, the war effort, and the increasing wealth and influence of young Aaron Flowers. Dubbed, "The Baby Baron", he had streamlined and re-organized entire divisions of the company. According to this reporter, Aaron exercised a genius for recognizing genius, surrounding himself with brilliant minds. He slashed from the corporation's bureaucracy the entrenched and unimaginative, ending policies that stifled invention and innovation. He introduced new manufacturing techniques, upgraded machinery, plunged the corporation to new levels of debt.

All this, Aaron Flowers had accomplished while still in his mid-twenties.

But when the war arrived, the Flowers Corporation was ready.

George poured over the photographs, tried to grasp in a few minutes the hidden events that had shaped his father's life.

Reaching another blank page, he turned to the third section and a new, bold headline:

ARMS BARON KILLED, OLDEST SON CRIPPLED IN BOMB BLAST

VIENNA. Billionaire arms baron, Joseph Flowers, 67, was killed today when a bomb exploded beneath the rubble of the *Militärmuseum Grafenwöhr.* Seven persons, including eldest son Jonathan Flowers, were injured in the blast...

"Jonathan," George gasped. "*Uncle* Jonathan."

"...I give your father purpose...remind him of the past...your destiny is written..."

"My destiny," George said aloud.

The article stated that Jonathan Flowers was among a team of engineers sent to Austria to assess damage and assist the government with reconstruction plans. According to the clipping, an unexploded bomb was set off by heavy machinery working in the area. The force of the explosion dislodged a concrete slab that crashed down upon the engineers and their party.

The article gave no explanation for Joseph Flowers' presence on the tragic day.

George turned another page, then another, found many blanks and nothing more. The chronicle of Aaron Flowers' life ended in 1946 with the death of his father and the dismemberment of his older brother, Jonathan.

"So that's it," he said. "Guilt. And I'm being groomed to, what, somehow make everything right? Bullshit. I won't do it."

Then the thought: *But is any of this real?*

"Stop!" he cried, waving away the notion. His own guilt felt as cold as the concrete walls.

*How fake is Jonathan's mutilation?* George thought. *Did he counterfeit a life of pain and isolation? I've lived in the Colonies he designed. Seen his miniature world.*

George felt the unmistakable weight of reality. This room, its story sealed in time, was no illusion.

Then a voice, or a feeling. Perhaps a fragment of imagination, something, calling to him.

Cerissa.

George dropped the album on the velvet chair and ran for the stairs, lunging up the steps two at a time. At the mirror, he gripped the latch and stopped cold.

Movement. In the study. Kathryn Maxwell and Old Flowers.

*La Corporada*, partially shielded by the branches of a rubber tree, waved her arms like a frenzied conductor, voice trilling panic. Old Flowers gestured back, but dismissively, and stepped into the luminarium, eager for the sanctuary of the aviary.

Kathryn knew not to follow.

George used their turmoil to open the mirror, step through, and slink behind the lush potted plant next to the elevator, pressing the "up" button on the way by.

Kathryn jabbered as Aaron retreated. "With a world of communication systems, why do you leave Flowers Island in the dark ages?"

Silence, the predictable response from Aaron.

George leaned out and pressed the "up" button again, an instinctive, but futile exercise.

Kathryn persisted. "A few phone lines, say from the Mansion Complex to the Marina. Or to the stables. Think how much faster we could mobilize a search party with just a normal amount of communication."

Not a word from Old Flowers as purples, golds, greens, and aqua marines showered his body.

"A private phone system," Kathryn called into the tunnel of colors. "The two-way radio just isn't adequate."

"Adequate?" Old Flowers said, hand on the doorknob and still not facing her. "The wireless is *too* adequate. I can't contain rebellious mouths, let alone phone lines." Still talking to the door, and fury rising in his voice. "Really, Kathryn, do you think it would stop there? First a private line to the marina, next a communal cable to the mainland." He turned. "The last thing I want is more communication. Things work fine just as they are." Old Flowers sounded much like the bureaucracy he had deposed years ago.

"Really, Aaron," Kathryn huffed, a rare defeat. She turned when the elevator dinged. "George?"

"What?" Old Flowers said.

The elevator closed, seconds later opening to reveal the main corridor—and Rollins.

"George?" he said. "What the devil? You're supposed to be finding Cerissa."

"Found her," George lied. "Haven't you heard? She's down in the study with Old Flowers and her mother."

As if crushed that a significant event could happen on the island without his knowledge, Rollins said: "In the few minutes I spent in the greenhouse you found Cerissa and brought her here?"

"No. She came back on her own."

"Thank bloody god," he said, weary, sniffling, and miserable. "I hope they're ready to leave. I prefer a tropical storm to Hurricane Kathryn." He stepped into the elevator as George stepped out.

"By the way, George, good news," Rollins said, removing his handkerchief. "We've re-established contact with the Marina, at least for now." *Great*, George thought, *the last thing I need is the marina crew, alerted and waiting, when the stolen tram arrives at North Beach.* "According to the latest reports, the storm has slowed and may be veering south. You'd never know it after walking outside, but it's safer for the Maxwells." He stared down the bridge of his nose. "Feel better now?"

George's smile sank with the elevator.

As he raced down the hallway, George guessed he had sixty seconds before Rollins, Kathryn, and Old Flowers were on his trail.

Turning the corner, he darted down a seldom-used corridor and entered the mansion's trophy room. Sad, humiliated beasts, pedestal and full body mounts, bared fangs in deference to Joseph Flowers' ego. Like George, Old Flowers hated this room, and worse, his surrender to nostalgia and his father's memory. But today, George stuffed his disgust and thanked *Fortuna* for this convenient grandfather shrine, and especially, for Joseph's 19th Century French Antique Oak gun cabinet.

With the base of a floor lamp, George shattered the glass and removed a twelve-gauge shotgun. From a box of dove and quail shells he found in the bottom drawer, he inserted three rounds, crawled out the window onto the lawn, and ran through the howling wind fifty yards to the north wing. There, tucked behind Glen's barely manicured hedges, sat the electrical transformer that supplied power to the mansion's living quarters.

Raising the gun to his shoulder, George hoped that his three pursuers were still strategizing in the study, or, if they had entered the elevator, were between floors.

That kind of luck might delay the chase for hours.

He clicked off the safety, aimed dead center, and blasted once, twice, three times.

He sprinted for the library.

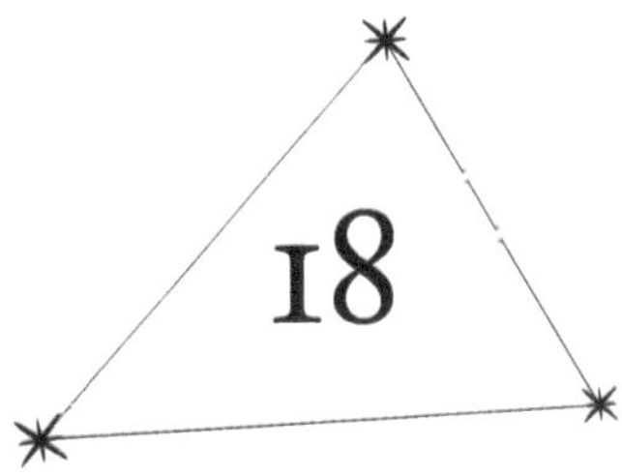

# 18

As he had advised Cerissa, George entered the *Pergamum* via the Hanging Gardens and the back entrance.

Cool, dry air, and warm, LED radiance greeted him. Being a large, multi-story building with significant lighting, ventilating, and air conditioning needs, for both humans and the stacks; as well as various archival and rare book collections stored in special enclosures under strict temperature, humidity, and airflow conditions, a separate transformer supplied power to the *Pergamum*. An even larger transformer, located in a concrete utility vault at the sub-basement's railway substation, fed power to the underground tram.

With the storm raging outside, island residents that were too old, had finished, or were not tasked with last minute preparations, opted to "rough it out" in one of several reading rooms. Seldom library quiet, these rooms often hosted boisterous talks on bizarre, esoteric subjects, and emphasized those studies rarely discussed in mainland libraries. Topics like public masturbation celebrations in Ancient Egypt, New Zealand's semen drinking Sambian tribe; the energy drink Ancient Romans brewed from goat dung, and using urine as mouthwash. Ancient Grecian *gloios* always inspired lively discussion. As did *gloios* collectors, slaves or low-born individuals employed by *gymnasia* and bath houses. After using a curved metal *strigil* to scrape *gloios*—oil, sweat, and filth—from the bodies of naked athletes, they sold the accumulated *gloios* to physicians for a variety of medicinal purposes.

Today, while George strolled through the vast reading room on the *Pergamum's* main floor, two historians debated the merits of Ancient Mongolian wisdom. One, quoting Genghis Khan, said: *"A man's greatest pleasure is to defeat his enemies; to drive them before him, to take from them that which they possess, to see those whom they cherish in tears, to ride their horses, to hold their wives and daughters in his arms."*

George stifled his laughter. He didn't recognize the man's voice, but he couldn't be part of any lesson. Yet, the man's words, the timing, this moment, fit so perfectly. George had just trapped three people underground, lied in his finest fashion, destroyed valuable property, and worse, was prepared to destroy a lot more. Did that make him a modern-day Mongol? He was, after all, on a rampage "defeating his enemies".

Then the second historian said: *"But be brotherly to one another and live in friendliness, making the whole great people walk on the road of the true state and of the law for the sake of attaining honor and glory."*

The Great Khan had uttered those words too, wise words.

Maybe George was acting rashly, wildly, too much like a barbarian. Maybe he should reason with Old Flowers, work out some compromise.

But then he thought about the lies, years of manipulation, his father's guilt and himself as the sacrificial lamb.

*Why can't Genghis Khan make up his fucking mind?*

Voices receded into the background as George followed the far wall, toward the stairway leading to the basement. No one was near this corner of the library, so he crept unnoticed through the door, down the stairs, to the storeroom where, hopefully, Cerissa patiently waited.

*What if she's not here*? he thought, grasping the doorknob.

Opening the door, expecting the worst, he was almost surprised to see Cerissa sitting across the room on a stack of boxes. The only light came from the open door. "I'm sorry," George said, contrite. "I didn't expect you to hide in the dark." Groping to his right, he flipped the light switch.

"We heard you coming, George," Glen said with an almost sinister laugh.

"What the...?" George gasped.

"I love it," Glen said. Then to Cerissa: "I told you the surprise would be better in a dark room. Jesus, George, the look on your face." He laughed again, this time with less menace. "That's gotta be worth at least three points, Birthday Boy."

"What are you doing here? How did you know?"

Glen waggled both head and finger. "Georgie, Georgie, Georgie," he said. "You told me. That lie about seeing Cerissa walking into the woods fifteen minutes before chasing me down in the hallway? Might have worked. But I saw her walking toward the library at the same time."

"And now you're going to report us?"

"Of course." Glen paused; staring from George to Cerissa, then back with calm, piercing eyes. "It's my job, you understand. Old Flowers taught me to be responsible, to take orders without questions."

George felt his Mongol-self tensing. He glared at a liar, yes, traitor, certainly, lifelong manipulator, undoubtedly, but subduing the much smaller Glen would exercise George's worst impulses. It would upset Cerissa and potentially harm his oldest confidant, companion, and comrade.

*I can't do it,* George thought.

Then Glen said: "But, lucky for you, Georgie, I don't work for Old Flowers anymore."

"Since when?"

"Since before I invited you to the Trine room. I can't lie anymore. I quit. Old Flowers doesn't know it yet, but I'm through with Flowers Island."

"Really? And where will you go? What will you do?"

"I've got these," he said, raising his hands. "I'm the best Fil-lon-chi gardener in the world."

"Maybe the best *Fil-lon-chi* gardener," George said with a wry shake of the head.

"Besides," Glen said. "I'm going with you."

"Actually, you're not."

"I am," Glen said. "And here's why." He glanced at Cerissa. "She and I had a nice chat, and I think your plan can work. But there's one major flaw."

"And what's that?"

"The storm. The pressure is still dropping, George. If this becomes a hurricane, you'll sink the *Valdaquez.*"

"Bullshit. We motor safely to Little Flower and wait it out."

"Maybe. But then what? Sail 400 miles to the mainland? Solo? Don't be stupid, Georgie. You need a second mate."

"He's right, George," Cerissa said. "I've sailed a few times with my father, but rarely beyond sight of land. I don't know your boat, or the waters, or why I even agreed to join you. I'm not usually this impulsive."

"She's talking sense, Georgie."

"I'd never do anything to endanger your life," George said. "I hope you know that. Besides, thirty minutes ago, Rollins said the storm has slowed. There's still time. The tram can get us to the marina in less than twenty minutes."

"He's right about that part," Glen said.

"Of course, it's your decision," George said to Cerissa. "But Little Flower is an excellent asylum harbor. We anchor and shelter in the old radio shack."

"I've seen that shack," Cerissa said, her tone dubious.

"It's sturdier than it looks and survived many a hurricane," George said.

"Then Glen *is* coming?" Cerissa said.

"It *will* double the safety factor, so sure. But when we get to the mainland, he's on his own." With a smirk, just short of a sniff, he added: "Besides, now that I'm leaving, he doesn't have a job here anyway."

Glen lowered his gaze, looking small and sad, the lost orphan he would have been, but for the patronage of Old Flowers.

George regretted his cruel words.

"I deserve that, George. None of us have been honest. But after the drug, and the chamber, we knew Old Flowers had gone too far. Despite everything, we are your friends. We'd never do anything to hurt you."

"I'd like to believe that," George said. "But I'm not sure I can."

"Then I'll prove it." He gestured to a small, hard shell roller bag sitting on the floor behind him. "While we were waiting, I ran to my room and packed a few things. I didn't waste space on underwear and socks."

"Fuck," George said. The tension, running around the mansion, discovering his father's subterranean past, all had distracted him from practical matters like grabbing his own knapsack.

"You are traveling a little light, George," Cerissa said. She pointed to her own suitcase.

"I'm sorry," George replied. "The gold, the jewels, my clothes. Everything is back in my bedroom."

"Don't worry," Glen said. "I've got plenty for all of us. You may cut me loose on the mainland, but if you change your mind, we can still tour the world. You're welcome to join us, of course," he said to Cerissa.

George turned to Cerissa. "Are you still feeling impulsive?"

Cerissa remained silent, her gaze thoughtful and distant.

"I promise you this," George said. "If we get to the marina and find rough seas and raging winds, we scuttle the plan. But if Rollins is right and the storm is passing to our south, I'm leaving."

With that, George grabbed Cerissa's suitcase and pointed to the sub-basement stairs. Glen followed.

When they arrived at the *Haji Bektash Veli* terminal, George darted into the tramway substation and energized the 600-volt DC overhead wire. A minute later, he had uncoupled the trailing cars from the drive engine. "All aboard," he said, noting the strain on Glen's face when he lifted the bag to the first step. "What the hell do you have in that thing?"

"Trinkets," Glen replied.

George helped him muscle the suitcase up the steps and into the storage rack. "Christ, it weighs a ton. You must have packed an entire shipwreck. Okay, close the door. Next stop, North Beach Marina."

Glen latched the door as George pushed the throttle forward, gradually sending power to the traction motor. A dazzling headlight sliced into the darkness as the tram gained speed. "At full throttle, we should make it to the marina in just under twenty minutes," George reminded them. "I hope the dock crew won't be waiting."

The tram sped north through the network of caverns under the island. On flat stretches, they clocked a top speed of fifty-two miles per hour, but mostly, their journey mixed slow, tortuous climbs with short, thrilling, descents.

During the trip, George told Glen and Cerissa everything he had learned from Old Flowers' photo album, about his earlier visit to (Uncle) Jonathan's living quarters, and how he had trapped his father, Rollins, and Mrs. Maxwell in the study after blasting the mansion's transformer with a 12-gauge shotgun.

"You're a regular Count of Monte Cristo," Glen said, laughing. "If we don't escape, we'll end up in a Medieval dungeon."

They were in the middle of an arduous climb to the highest point of the journey, when the tram lurched to a stop. "Shit!" George cursed, as the air brakes locked automatically and prevented them from sliding backwards.

They sat, nose upward, in total darkness.

"I guess Old Flowers escaped from the study," Glen said.

"Now what?" Cerissa said. "We're trapped."

"But only two, maybe three, miles from the Medieval Colony," George said. "From there, we hike overland to the marina."

"Do you have a flashlight?" Cerissa said.

"Of course. In my knapsack." He imagined her eye roll, then spoke to Glen. "I don't suppose *you* brought one."

"Didn't think I'd need it."

For a moment, silence was thicker than dark.

George fumbled under the engineer's seat, found a tool box, sliced his finger on something sharp while scavenging through it, but came away with an old-style tube flashlight. Clicking it on, he discovered it to be like every other flashlight he had ever really needed—so dim he could barely see his hand. "This won't help," he said, flicking the light off to save what little power was left. "But I have an idea. *If* we can find some rope, or wire, something like that."

"Okay," Cerissa said.

"What do we do with rope, George," Glen said. "Pull the tram to North Beach?"

George ignored him while groping for Cerissa's hand. "Here, hold the light high. Glen, check under the seats and look in that first aid kit. I'll double check the toolbox."

The light didn't dim to a useless orange glow for a whole sixty seconds. But after that, it reminded George of a setting sun seen through the wrong end of a telescope.

"No rope, no wire," Glen said. "Just surgical tape and a huge roll of gauze."

"That should work," George said, climbing down from the cab and helping Cerissa. "I found an extension cord. It's not very long, but hopefully, long enough."

"Long enough for what?" Glen said.

"Very clever, George," Cerissa said.

"Thanks."

"You two wanna let me in on the secret?"

"Maybe," George said. "Are there scissors in that first aid kit?"

"Of course."

"Cut a dozen roughly four-foot strips of gauze."

"*Ja, mein Anführer,*" he said, never fond of orders from George.

For the next several minutes, Glen passed strips to George. He, in turn, handed one end of each to Cerissa. "Okay, Cerissa, join your ends together." George did the same. "Now pull taunt and twist clockwise." Standing opposite each other, they wound the gauze until the strips tightened into one three-foot length, not as strong as rope, but close. George wrapped the ends with surgical tape.

They repeated the process until they had three "ropes".

"Gee, Georgie," Glen said, crawling carefully down the steps with the suitcase thumping behind. "This is fun, but I don't get your plan."

"We tether together with these makeshift ropes," George said.

"Then what? We can't see."

"George was counting on you to lead us on your knees," Cerissa said with a smile in her voice.

"Too bad I have other plans."

George laughed. "Don't worry, no crawling. Grab this." He searched for Glen's hand and gave him one of the ropes. "Tie this to one of my rear belt loops. Cerissa, when he's done, take the free end and tie it your front loop. Glen ties to Cerissa."

When they finished, George said: "It's super important to stay between the tracks."

"Why?" Cerissa said.

Glen answered for him. "There's not much verge on some of the curves coming up. One false step, or a clumsy trip over a rail, and we splat to the bottom."

"Oh," Cerissa said, understandably nervous.

"Thanks for tying us together, Georgie."

George ignored him. But to instill confidence, he double checked Cerissa's knots. "Sorry. We have to leave your suitcase."

"I know."

"You can help carry mine," Glen said.

"Don't listen to him," George said. "Are we ready?"

Holding the extension cord, George led the caravan to the front of the tram. With a wide, arching motion, he hurled the female end up toward the power cable, hoping to loop it over. He failed. The cord banged against the cable on the second attempt. The third try missed also. But with the fourth throw, he felt the cord loop over the cable, just barely. "Let's move forward a few steps," he said. "I need to create some slack." By whipping the cord with gentle, waving motions, he teased the cord further over the cable and down to within reach. "Got it!"

"You crazy bastard," Glen said.

"This will guide us safely within the tracks."

They struggled up the incline, movements slow and tedious. Every fifty feet or so, or whenever they came to one of the cable's support bars, George had to stop, unhook the extension cord, shuffle a few steps until he was sure he had passed the obstruction, then re-loop the cord and continue. The steep grade slowed them to a near crawl.

With the awkwardness of three bodies, lashed together, tugging and jerking each other to complicate matters, the climb quickly became exhausting. They needed a rest every few minutes.

"We won't beat the storm at this rate," Glen said.

They had walked for almost an hour, uphill, when finally, they rounded a tight bend and crested the highest point of the cavern. George yelled: "We're doing great!" He had to shout above a roiling tumult. In the darkness below, an underground river emptied run-off into the cavern, splashed against the limestone walls, soaked clothes, and pelted their closed eyes with a maddening spray. "Now it's a gradual slope down to the Medieval Colony!"

With a loud scoff, Glen bellowed: "I know exactly where we are! Why don't you tell Cerissa about Stygian Falls? She'll be thankful she can't see!"

Cerissa cupped her hands and called out, "Go ahead, George, tell me! You've been standing behind your drawbridge for the last fifteen minutes. I've been wondering why!"

"What are you talking about?" Glen said, with a sharp tug on the rope.

"Never mind," George called back. "I'll explain later."

"Tell me where we are, George."

George released his grip and the three huddled against the noise. "You're better off not thinking about it," he said. "Just pretend we're winding down the side of a mountain."

"A shear precipice is more like it," Glen said. If George and Cerissa couldn't feel him shudder, they could hear the tremble in his voice. "My ass tingles every time I travel this section of track. It's sick! Four men died here laying track. It's a million miles straight to Hell if you step one foot too far to your left!"

"Oh," Cerissa gasped.

George grabbed Glen's shoulder and pulled him closer. "Give her a break, you fuck." Then to Cerissa: "Don't listen to him. We're safe as long as we do exactly what we're doing – staying between the tracks."

"I know," Cerissa said. "How are your arms holding up?" The extension cord, when looped over the cable, barely dangled within reach of his weak, tingling arms."

"A little numb," he admitted. "But they'll be..." He stopped. "What's that?"

"What's what?"

George strained to hear. "Do either of you feel that vibration?"

"It's the falls," Glen said.

George opened his eyes as light splashed across the cavern ceiling. "Shit! Off the tracks!"

Fifty feet away, the re-energized tram crested the rise and thundered toward them like a blinding avalanche.

Screaming, the three bodies lurched, tangled, yanked the ropes, tripped, flailed, and landed in a heap onto hard, wet rock.

Clatter

Gust

Whoosh went the tram.

"OhAhOhAhOhAh!! Glen's cries mingled with Cerissa's wails.

George tried to scream, cry really, but gasped instead with lungs winded by a flat landing.

The tram snaked around the falls and rounded a corner.

Gone.

Calm...weightless...relief.

Stygian Falls, deafening before, but now a comforting roil, its mist cool on fevered skin, on cold rocks and hard ground that, in this precious moment, felt warm and loving. "We're alive," Cerissa breathed into George's ear. Both guzzled air down to the molecule, drank in the sacred gift. Fingers touched legs, caressed hair, cuddled arms. "Thank the gods," George said, with short wheezing breaths. Tingles of charred adrenalin sparked through his body.

Slowly, hearts and breathing settled, emerged from panic.

Peace, happiness, gratitude for every—"Mother of rancid fuck!" Glen screamed.

George cringed, acknowledged the crime, accepted the blame.

"You almost goddamn killed us!"

"I know," George said, wincing at his own stupidity.

"You've done some lame ass shit, Flowers. But this deserves a trophy."

"What did he do?" Cerissa said, rising to George's defense.

"No," George said, feeling more than ever like a rampaging Mongol. "He's right. It never occurred to me to pull back the throttle."

"Oh, my god," Cerissa said. "The tram will crash."

"Or worse," Glen said, with dark insinuation.

"You two," she said. "There'll be nothing left of that poor marina."

A short titter from Glen, then a moment of bleak silence.

"Well," George said, moving from grim speculation to practical matters. "We lost our guideline. Guess I'll be the one crawling the tracks."

"George," Cerissa said.

"I'm joking."

After a moment's thought and a bit of practice, he contrived a technique of sliding his right foot along the rail nearest the cavern wall, while hopping along on his left. Dangerous in total darkness, and a good way to break an ankle, but they didn't have much choice.

Cerissa and Glen didn't just follow along. They developed a rhythm, kept slack between each other and George, and tried not to knock him off balance.

And with each skid forward, Stygian Falls dimmed; from rumble, to babble, to murmur.

"So," Glen said, the reprieve from noise too precious to waste on silence. "Why do you think they turned the power on?"

"I've been wondering," George said, between slip and sway, "the same thing. Only one reason I can think of."

"They got through to the marina."

"Yep."

"They cut the power so we couldn't sneak in. Then they alerted the dock crew and sent us right into their arms."

Cerissa said: "They were pretty sure we wouldn't leave the tram."

"They wouldn't have," George said. "So they couldn't imagine otherwise."

"They think we've surrendered," Glen said. "That we'll glide peacefully into the *Theoi Halioi* terminal and hang our heads in shame."

"Yes, and what a relief."

"What?"

"They won't be surprised when the tram comes barreling in."

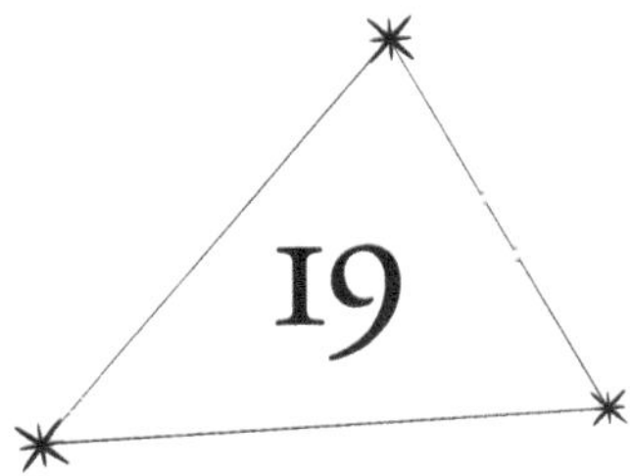

# 19

A stranger could stand fifty feet from Captain Waller's North Beach Marina office and never see it. He could climb a jagged, forty-foot man-made cliff for a better look at Little Flower, and as he cast his eyes over the water to the tiny island, not realize he was standing on the roof of the dock crew's living quarters. The same was true of Nile's radio room, and the kitchen, the workshop, and the warehouse.

The Rule of Separation.

Because Flowers Island had only a two-mile strip of beach, the Ancient Greeks needed it for launching expeditions to the *Ionia* Islands. The Romans used it to cast off the men-of-war's that would sail against the Carthaginians. Ramses III lined the same beach with Egyptian archers to prepare for the onslaught of the invading Sea Peoples.

A normal, modern marina, one that featured dozens of berths, a yacht club, restaurants, sky villas, and penthouse apartments, wouldn't fit comfortably in such a versatile past.

Still, Flowers Island required some version of a modern marina—one with a supply depot, floating docks for Aaron's yacht, George's *Valdaquez*, and other visiting vessels; underground garages for heavy machinery, living quarters, offices, a marina heliport, a canteen; boat hoists, repair shops, a refueling station.

So, Aaron Flowers disguised the complex to look like the surrounding cliffs. Hollow cliffs. Dotted with mounds of monolithic boulders. The *Theoi Halioi* tram terminal (named for the sea deities of Ancient Greece) was located beneath.

A thirty-foot concrete loading ramp at ground level, and perpendicular to the tracks (sloped toward the beach to keep rain and spray flowing away from the facilities, but not too steep for a wheelchair or forklift), was revealed by opening a sliding door made of special, lightweight, artificial stone.

Reggie hunkered in his windbreaker, apart from the others, at the beach end of this very loading ramp, smoking his sixth, or was it his seventh, cigarette (*oh hell, countin' the damn things is harder than quittin'*)? And though he stood inside and well under the roof of artificial rock, the large sliding boulder-door was open, allowing rain-drenched wind to blanket everything with mist.

Reggie turned from the gusts and scanned the loading bay, its ceilings high, domed and cavern-like, but not dank and gloomy. Warm, full spectrum lighting built into the artificial stone softened the hard textures and *bestowed* (Captain Waller's word) "an agreeable ambiance to subsurface living".

*If you say so, Captain,* Reggie thought. *Wouldn't wanna pollute your "agreeable ambiance" with cigarette smoke.*

With his back to the wind, he flicked the butt and watched it flutter up the ramp, buried his hands in the pockets of sun-bleached Levis, and monitored the doings on the platform of the *Theoi Halioi* terminal. His partner, Coz, as sucked up to Captain Waller as the man's underwear, smiled and nodded like a bobble-head monkey.

*Fuckin' ass mint. Always doin' favors and draggin' me along.*

Captain Waller, and Niles, the other dockhand, and a guy whose spiky nose and flaky skin made him look like a beached sand shark, bellowed laughs that bounded off the solid, but agreeable, walls.

*Don't stand too close, Coz old buddy, Waller can put a man to work faster than a sailfish.*

Reggie studied the floor to avoid catching the captain's glance. *Doin' my part,* he thought. *Not happy, but ready to play nursemaid.*

Maybe staying on at Flowers Island wasn't such a good idea after all.

The day before yesterday, after his covert sightseeing trip, Coz had anchored the *Sea Maid* at the North Beach Marina. By then, drug-crazed Glen had been subdued and the helicopter had flown Kathryn and Cerissa to the Mansion Complex.

Part of their fee included a full tank of fuel, but they got more. "Stay for the day and relax," Captain Waller had said. "Maybe have the doctor take another look at that hand." Coz had grumbled a bit, at that point, still pissed about having to surrender his camera's SD card. But Reggie had said: "Hell yes." Not pleased by the prospect of Doctor Feldman poking at his wound, but by the drugs that came with him. Reggie even dreamed about money, and a more permanent relationship with the Flowers Corporation.

He was quickly disappointed.

"Promotion to island duty takes years," Niles told Reggie. "You gotta do more than scrape barnacles and polish brass around here. You gotta show acting talent and pass a bunch of history tests."

*What?*

Reggie spewed a deluge of questions. "Sorry, that's all I can tell you," Niles said. "Just thought you should know, so you don't go dreamin' about gettin' a job here." Too late. Niles slapped a huge palm across Reggie's back. "But, who knows? Maybe we'll use you guys again. Next time our regular transport captain gets sick. In the meantime, enjoy the scenery."

Why not? Yesterday had been nice. Blustery and nice. But by sunrise this morning, Reggie and Coz knew they wouldn't be sailing back to Bermuda.

"Maybe we'll wait out the storm," Reggie said to Niles. "If you don't mind."

"You'll have to ask Captain Waller, but with the way you were losin' at poker last night." He punched Reggie lightly on the arm. "Besides, we can always use a couple of extra hands."

So, here Reggie stood, like the friggin' shore patrol, waiting to arrest a bunch of runaway kids. *Christ, I got better things to do with my time.* He considered another cigarette, and guilty, even retrieved the butt he'd mechanically cast onto the ramp. But quitting ought to be serious. An exercise in character. Torching one up every ten minutes looks too much like regular smoking. At least wait thirty minutes. Best to look professional and donate a couple of hours to whatever these crazy bastards are up to. Show the captain I'm grateful for last night's steak. And, of course, the cigarettes. Against the rules and everything.

Reggie turned around and squinted at the thundering whitecaps. *This could be an ugly one*, he thought. The sky twisted itself into black knots. If he looked real hard, he could see angry faces staring from the clouds, Gods scowling at the Earth, aiming their spears—*Holy Christ almighty! I'm getting all paranoid. It's only a storm. It'll pass. Where in hell is that damn tram? Ha, that's funny, damn tram.*

"Hey, Reggie!"

Reggie jerked back, startled.

"What's the matter?" Coz said. "Scare you?" He scoffed. "I just came over to bum a cigarette."

Reggie grinned up at Coz, a six-foot-four narrow beam sailor, sturdy as a spar, crony and shipmate, a cruise-racer to Reggie's tugboat. As always, especially when he tried not to, Reggie noticed Coz's two front teeth. One was slightly longer than the other. Reggie looked away. "Hi, Coz," he said. "Take 'em all. I'm quittin'." Reggie passed him the cigarettes. "Where's that damn tram?" he said, trying his rhyme. Coz didn't laugh, and that stung a little, but at least he didn't have to see the tooth.

"According to the captain..." Coz gestured to the platform where Captain Waller and Niles were waiting, "...any minute now."

"Good. Let's get this over with. We didn't come here to baby-sit." Reggie struck a match for Coz, shielding it from the wind and singeing a finger in the process. "Fuckin' cigarettes," he scowled, pleased with himself for snuffing another bad habit. "So, what's your guess, Coz?" Reggie asked. "You think little Miss Maxwell's runnin' away with the boss's son?" He snickered. "Or maybe *Mrs.* Maxwell?"

"Either wouldn't bother me," Coz said. "If I were the boss's son. Which I wouldn't want to be right now. But no, it's not the older one. The captain says it's three kids. He didn't go into detail. Something about not riling the boss. They're pretty strict around here, I've discovered, real disciplined. They don't cross the line, no matter how much you buddy up."

Reggie glanced at the captain and Niles. Both leaned toward the tracks, both peered down the tunnel. "Yeah, I noticed." Then, surprised: "Hey, what's goin' on?"

Captain Waller and Niles were suddenly dashing from the platform toward Reggie and the loading ramp. "Run!" Niles screamed.

"Shit!" Coz cried, muscle and fear launching him down the ramp.

Rumble poured from the tunnel.

Turning, Reggie lumbered after Coz, onto the beach and into the rain. Then, feeling safe, (while bent over, panting, and huffing out aromatic hydrocarbons) he looked back toward the terminal.

Captain Waller and Niles had just rushed past.

Coz was leaping foam and skirting the surf like a kiteboard.

A streak of silver whisked by as Reggie strained to see.

Three seconds later, tremors shuddered the ground, metal shrieked, synthetic cliffs collapsed, artificial boulders caved one after the other into the captain's office, then into the repair shops, and on to...

"The fuel depot!" Captain Waller screamed.

Silence.

At least from the humans.

The wind still blustered. But the ten-thousand-gallon fireball, and the explosion, and the marina reduced to tangled metal and molten rock, never happened.

Instead, seconds passed. Shock choked conversation. No one could imagine anyone surviving that crash.

Meanwhile, rivulets seeped from ruptured gas and diesel tanks, through fissures, along ridges of twisted metal, down toppled blocks of masonry, and onto the loading dock where it slowly flowed toward the first spark of panic—the spot where, while dashing away in terror, Coz had dropped his cigarette.

Still smoldering, and even aroused by the wind to cherry-red, the glowing ember lacked the sustained 500° F necessary to ignite the fuel.

The cigarette drowned in a puddle of gasoline.

Not so the dangling overhead electrical wire.

Ripped from support stanchions when the tram jumped the buffer stop, shredded in spots, and arcing at 35,000° F, the bare wire sparked and ignited a pocket of fumes in the *Theoi Halioi* terminal.

Not even the Sea Gods could stop *that* explosion.

Reggie, only a hundred feet away when the storage tanks detonated, ran through downpours of flaming cinders, bits of red-hot metal, and screamed when embers landed on his windbreaker, burned through, and blistered his shoulder. "Son of a re-fried bitch!" he squealed, slapping at his clothes while flying down the beach like a keel slug shot through a blowgun.

Niles was crying: "Oh, my dear, dear, God."

Coz wondered if his careless cigarette had caused the explosion.

Captain Waller had slumped onto the sand a safe distance away. "It's not our fault. There's nothing we could do. Nothing. It all happened so fast. What could we do?" He covered his eyes with his hands. "Those poor stupid kids. Those crazy, crazy kids. How am I going to tell Aaron Flowers?"

Reggie watched wind lash flames into the heavens.

Plumes of acrid smoke blended into the storm.

*What a shame,* he thought. *A beautiful girl like Cerissa.*

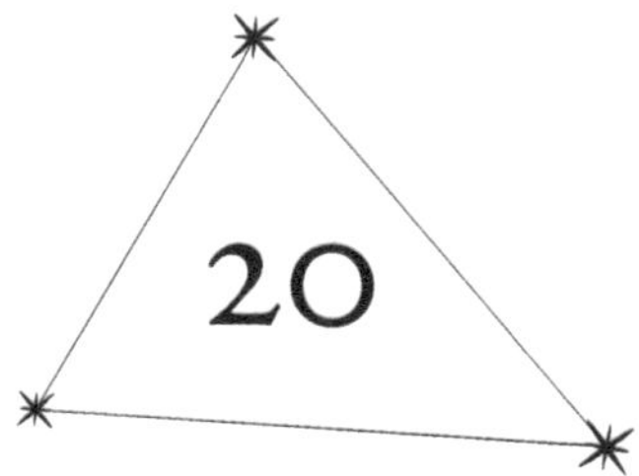

# 20

About three minutes after a thunderous boom echoed through the cavern, a cool, gaseous wind blew over George, Glen, and Cerissa.

"Phew!" Glen said. "I hope you're right, George."

"About the dock crew?"

"Yeah. If they were waiting for us, and saw that the tram wasn't slowing down, they probably had enough time to escape before the explosion." A mortal silence, made more oppressive by the stench of burnt gasoline, hung in the air. "On the other hand..."

"They were waiting," George said. "They had to be." Words dropped into a well of wishful thinking.

Trying to sound positive, Glen said: "Captain Waller takes his responsibilities seriously. If Old Flowers ordered him to intercept us, he'd pitch a tent in the terminal."

"You're right," George said, eager to believe Glen's assurance. Accident or not, death was never part of George's escape plan. Even the possibility chilled him.

Glen sneezed, once, and again. "Jesus, that stinks. You know, George, you're getting good at destroying things. You'll do well in the real world."

"You're such an expert."

"I've been to the mainland."

"Big deal, so have I."

"Without supervision?"

"Well..."

"Twice, maybe three times? Always with your father like some tourist. To you, the real world is just another colony. You have no idea what it's like out there, does he Cerissa?"

Cerissa, still making George uncomfortable with long lapses into silence, didn't immediately answer. Finally, she said: "George is probably in for a few surprises."

Glen laughed. "A few?"

"Ready for another shift on the rail?" George asked.

"Sure, anything to get rid of this suitcase."

The three-person caravan re-arranged the ropes so Glen could take the lead. When they had settled into a comfortable rhythm; Glen sliding his foot along the top of the rail, George and Cerissa half-skipping, half-walking behind him, Glen said: "Information, George. That's what makes me an expert."

"On smuggled beer and football?" George said, sarcasm floating in the gloom.

"Wrong. We get magazines, a few anyway, even some newspapers."

"Where?"

"From the crews on our supply ships. We even have a sort-of mail service Old Flowers knows nothing about." He paused. "We know the world and we're glad to be safe on Flowers Island."

"Bullshit," George said.

"Really? Ask Cerissa. It's ugly bad in the Latin American Region. Am I right?"

"It depends," Cerissa said.

"That's not an answer," Glen said, stabbing the air with a bitter, vocal tang. "Do George a favor and tell the truth."

The rope slackened. George bumped into Cerissa's back. Glen, caught off balance by Cerissa's sudden stop, jerked to the ground.

"Fuckin' son of a bitch!" Glen screamed. "What was that?" He was addressing Cerissa. "You almost broke my tailbone!"

"Are you all right?" George called into the blackness.

"George will discover *his own* truth," Cerissa said, voice cold as the cavern walls.

George shivered. Her tone was cutting, jagged, ruthless.

"The world is *not* what you read in magazines." Minus velvety features, delicate smiles, and loving eyes tempering her words, Cerissa sounded eerily like her mother. "What do *you* know about truth, anyway?" she said, disdain etched on every syllable. "You read tales of disease, war, and starvation. See photos of children covered with vermin. Some reporter writes about an orphanage, about dying babies, watered down milk, a world sharing poverty."

Glen shuffled to his feet. "Exactly," he said. "You said it better than I could. See what I mean, George?"

"No." Cerissa said. "I believe what my friend Conrad once told me. He said: `Hopeless poverty is no nearer the truth than the lavish parties of the hopelessly rich.'"

"You'd know about the hopelessly rich," Glen sneered.

"Enough," George said. The ropes tightened as Glen stepped as far from Cerissa as the tether would allow. Cerissa, equally repelled, crowded into George's arms.

*I need to end this,* George thought.

He stepped back from Cerissa. "Okay," he asked, "where is the truth?" A sudden image, himself, wearing a *chiton* in the Grecian Colony, asking the same question to Socrates.

In a blessed return to her natural, pleasing voice, Cerissa said: "The truth is in the orphanage, George. With the old women swinging blankets to dust flies off the children." She paused. "It's on the tennis courts of the rich as the ball flies back and forth and someone chances to wonder if life is really as easy as it seems."

"Christ," Glen said. "You could play Gautama Buddha in the Asian Colony."

"Knock it off," George said. "Let's keep moving." He picked up Glen's suitcase.

"George, I don't presume to know the truth," Cerissa said. "But it angers me when people are one-sided. Glen is wrong. The world is not horrible. But Glen is right, too. Sometimes beauty and decency are hard to find."

George closed his eyes to marvel at the old soul in Cerissa's young body. Who is this person? Who chose her to carry the burden of everyone's thoughts. What must it be like to live with such a curse? "Every colony taught a variation on that same theme," George said. "There is no single truth."

"Of course," Cerissa said. "I hope someday you'll be lucky enough to realize it."

"Oh, I think..." He sighed. "Never mind. This is sounding like my last three months in the Grecian Colony. All that got me was disgusted. Point is, I've made my decision and nothing will stop me. Not even the truth." George wondered at his curious phrasing. He had meant to say: "I mean, my goal is the truth."

"My goal is to get out of this hell pit," Glen said. "I feel like a fuckin' mole. My eyes will explode if I ever see light again."

George remembered the chamber. "I know what you mean."

They continued down the gradual decline, slowly, clumsily, and without speaking, each too tired, or irked, to talk.

Finally, Glen blurted out: "Light! Do you see it? It must be the Medieval beacon."

The beacon, if it could be called that, was a fiber optic tube, several hundred feet long, and three inches thick. Hidden behind a parapet at the highest point of the belfry tower, the tube gathered sunlight, beamed it down through thick stone walls and into the cavern, finally appearing as a brilliant point of light above the terminal entrance. Simply to avoid using electricity, Old Flowers had installed similar beacons in the underground terminals of each Colony.

George strained in the darkness, barely able to tell if his eyes were open or closed, let alone see light. "I don't know," he said. "I think I see something." He saw nothing. But after the tension and arguing, what harm could come from being agreeable? Even if it wasn't the truth. George chuckled to himself. In this case, Glen's happiness transcended truth, and as far as George was concerned, Glen could imagine seeing a knot of medieval hell toads and George would happily concur.

*Of course, I see them*, George would say, *big, slimy, ugly ones.*

But fifteen minutes later, even Glen stopped believing "the light around the next corner".

"I was hallucinating," Glen said, laughing. "Aftereffects from that damn cinnamon roll."

George shuddered.

"Or hell toads," Cerissa said.

*You're always in my mind*, George thought to Cerissa.

"How the hell do *you* know about hell toads?" Glen said, surprised.

"From a class I took in medieval literature. My friends and I played a game called, Hell Toads."

Behind his mental drawbridge, George thought: *You're quite the little white liar.*

"What?" Glen said, now even more amazed. "In Costa fuckin' Rica?"

"Sure."

"Come on," Glen said. "It couldn't be the same game."

To demonstrate, Cerissa deepened her voice, added evangelical fervor, and preached: *"And to increase their pains, the loathsome hell-worms, and toads and frogs that eat out their eyes and nostrils—"*

"No way," Glen interrupted. "George, did you tell her about hell toads?"

George didn't have to lie. "Are you kidding? I've known Cerissa for a day. The subject of hell toads never came up."

While George imagined Glen gritting his teeth in frustrated silence, Cerissa remained quiet, waiting for her strategy to unfold.

Glen said, testing her: "In your game, did you choose somebody to play the preacher?"

"Oh no," Cerissa answered with perfect confidence. "The game wasn't formal. Wherever we happened to be, if we saw someone lying, or stealing, any sin would do, we'd pull them aside and tease them with the dreaded *Hell Toad Damnation*. It's a curse from an old book called *Medieval Europe*."

"That's the book," Glen cried. "Unbelievable."

*She's reading you like a book,* George thought.

"Hey Georgie..." Glen's tone had already brightened. "Remember the time Ferd ate that whole cheesecake? Jesus, what a *follis*. Anyway, we cornered him in the kitchen and lashed into the *Hell Toad Damnation*.

"I remember."

Glen affected his own, fiery, preachy voice: *"And for the sinners, the loathsome hell toads shall eat out their eyes and nostrils, and adders and water-frogs, not like those here, but a hundred times more horrible..."* His sermon choked on hilarity. "God almighty fuck," he said, coughing. "I still can't believe those assbaggers!" Now Glen was laughing so hard, George thought his lungs would bleed. The absurdity of the Medieval church, their fear baiting, and the terror campaign inflicted on congregations by robed lampreys too lazy to hoe the fields, but smart enough to milk their kneeling sheep—always gave Glen a hellfire laugh. He needed a minute of sliding along the rail to calm his titters.

"Okay, I can do it," Glen said, laughter decaying to chuckles. "God, what fucking idiots humans are." Then a deep, ecclesiastical, breath: *"And they shall sneak in and out of the mouth, ears, eyes, navel, and at the hollow of the breast, as maggots in putrid flesh!"*

All three shrieked with laughter.

George couldn't decide what was funnier: the fire and brimstone of Medieval priests, or Cerissa boring into their minds, like a hell toad, finding a way to make Glen laugh.

Merriment slowly subsided, worn away by the slow grind of half-stumbling in a gloomy underworld.

"There it is," Glen said, certain this time. They had rounded the right bend and the comforting glow of the Medieval beacon welcomed them. "Finally," he said, increasing his pace.

Less than ten minutes later, they had cast off their ropes and were climbing the fiber optic lighted stairway to the surface.

A wooden door at the top of the landing announced their arrival with squealing wrought-iron hinges. Damp hay, mold, tunics, cowls, scapula, shit buckets and wild urine; sick unwelcome memories clung to the stone walls, more vivid with each step and thick as the fetid air. "Welcome to the monastery of the Medieval Colony," George said, dropping Glen's suitcase on the tile floor. He rubbed an arm that felt stretched to the ankles.

"Whew," Glen said. "Bet this brings back memories."

"Too many. I hated almost every minute of the months I spent here."

"*Almost* every minute?" Cerissa said, always alert to nuance.

George led them through the chapel, to the edge of the courtyard. They gazed out into grey curtains of rain, compared to the cavern, nearly shimmering with radiance. "Yes, *almost* every minute. I wasn't suited for the rigid order of monastic life. This prison of devotion. Talking was discouraged, of course, except to God. Joy, laughter, smiles not aimed at heaven, all forbidden. The routine was torture. Eight times every day we held services, between laboring for hours in the workshops, or the fields. Then scripture study, naturally, then making copies of old Latin writings. Every day, day in, day out, no variation, no break in the rules. Horrible life. At least for me."

"Except," Cerissa said, with a gentle nudge.

George shrugged. "Except for vespers." He indicated an archway leading off the chapel. "Through there, down another tunnel. I won't take you because it's just another huge, dark, empty room. But that's where we performed the nightly vespers." A smile, tentative, like longing for something despised. "It was sickening, but magnificent," he said, wistful. "We all wore hooded robes, of course, so you couldn't tell us apart. And we all carried the same long, beeswax candles. Then every night, we'd chant liturgical hymns. Fifty men at each end of a vast, echoing chamber. A hundred voices crying out, the candles beaming, each like a soul shining into infinity."

"Fuck me," Glen said. "They wanted you to believe that?"

"It sounds ridiculous, but that's how it felt."

"It must have been beautiful," Cerissa said.

"It's the only thing that kept me going."

"Speaking of going," Glen said. "You're stalling. Are we chanting vespers or leaving?"

"Leaving, but I still have memories."

"So do I." Glen said. Rain pummeled the earth, bouncing on the ground like dancing beads. "We may drown before we make it to the marina. What's the plan?"

George pointed toward the Medieval spires and spoke to Cerissa. "The horse trail is beyond the spires, about a mile west of here. That's the easiest way to—"

"Not that way," Cerissa said.

"Why not?" Glen spoke with renewed irritation.

"They'll be on the horse trail."

"Nobody's following us in this weather," Glen said.

"Are you sure?" George asked her.

"Why are you asking her?" Glen said, almost spitting the words. Then to Cerissa: "What the hell would you know about it?"

With that, he stepped into the rain and crossed the monastery courtyard, glancing back when he reached the stone archway of the monastery walls. Waving for them to follow, he unbarred the high carriage doors, let the wind do most of the work opening them, and marched deeper into the wet and fury.

"What's—" "George—" They blurted simultaneously.

After an uncomfortable silence, George said: "I've never seen Glen react to anybody like he does to you." He gestured to the suitcase. "He actually left here without his treasure."

"It's heavy and he knows you'll bring it." Cerissa crossed her arms with a sigh. The wind, or Glen, had chilled her. "I'm sorry about my lecture in the cavern. I over-reacted to Glen because I was afraid."

"Why?"

"I haven't been totally honest."

*More truth.*

"In what way?" George asked, not sure he wanted to know.

"About Glen. He pretends ignorance about mind reading, yet builds a mental wall." Water leaked through the thatched roof, splashed into several eccentric tributaries, flowed across the irregular tile, and merged into a puddle at the chapel's lowest corner. Pelting rain sounded like a thousand rats scurrying overhead. "Glen may still be working for Old Flowers," she said. "I know you don't want to believe that."

Now a tiny figure framed by the archway, Glen crossed the first of several abandoned wheat fields. "I don't," George said. "Not after I've made up my mind to trust him."

"He may be leading you into a trap."

"Is that what you believe?"

"It's just a feeling. Like now with the horse trail. My mother, Uncle Aaron. They feel close. We lost our head start in the cavern."

"I know. And the sad thing is, Glen was right. I am stalling. Or rather, something is holding me back. The closer we get to the marina, the more I have to force myself to keep going."

"Earlier, you said you felt compelled to leave the island."

"I did. I do. But something is trying to exert its will."

"Something?" Cerissa said, gaze keen, piercing, mysterious; a riddle solving a puzzle. For a long, uncomfortable moment, the rain was the only sound. "You don't want to say it, do you?"

George massaged his temples, an excuse to avert his eyes. "No."

"But you know what it is."

"Yes."

"Say it. Make it real. Fight it."

George groaned. "I don't want to believe it."

"Denial won't help."

"All right!" He paused for a string of calming breaths. Then: "My father has found a way to program me. A way to make me think things, feel things, see things. The technique is connected to my dreams and he tested it in the chamber."

"You were drugged."

"The drug was a trigger. And I think the dreams link to my music, my Colony lessons, the subliminal programming he's used since my birth, everything, my entire upbringing."

"Are you sure it's all bad? Look at what you've gained—the languages, the virtuosity, the knowledge."

"But it isn't mine. Not if I don't control my own will. Right now, for instance, I feel like I can't leave Flowers Island. Like you said, only hours ago, I felt compelled to."

"That's normal. You're struggling with doubt."

"No. This feels like the chamber. Like a force sweeping over me. Strings jerking me like a puppet. Buttons running a machine."

"George, no," Cerissa said, soothing him, hugging him. "You're not a machine. You're a warm, wonderful person. A powerful, unique person."

"A unique freak," he said, with a forced grin. "I'm too different, too much like a hothouse orchid, rare, sheltered, conditioned. I want a normal life with normal friends and normal problems. My life can't atone for Old Flowers' guilt."

Cerissa kissed him and stroked the back of his head. "George, I wish you could hear what's in the minds around you. All my life I have." She led him to an old wooden pew, splintered, but still solid. Gently, she seated him next to her. "We all have someone, or something, that influences our minds. Responsibilities to our parents, rule of law, God, society, even our image of ourselves."

George looked up. "Don't forget the unconscious mind and its assorted compulsions." He raised his eyes to the chapel's arched ceiling, plaster between rough-hewn beams painted with images of seraphim, saints, monks, and Madonna. "I faced many deviant compulsions here," he said. "And in every other Colony. But it's one thing to know they exist, another to live with them."

Cerissa smiled. "Most people would agree. You may be more "normal" than you think."

"Maybe." He kissed Cerissa's forehead. "We're a few miles from North Beach. We'd better catch up."

They ran into the rain after Glen.

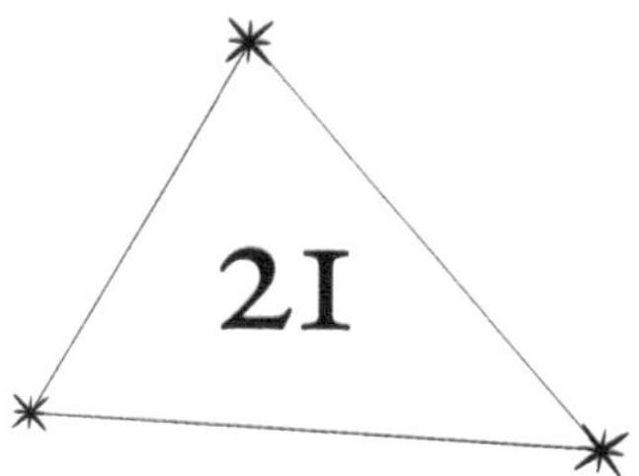

# 21

Within minutes of reaching the horse trail and entering the rocky highlands, the Medieval Colony disappeared under a gray shroud. Winds howled from the warm and deadly waters of the southeast, battered them on the higher ridges, and slid them flailing across muddy trails. "Are you okay!?" George screamed, as wind knocked Cerissa down and lodged her between two boulders. Yes, she had nodded while struggling to right herself.

Blinding rain hammered their heads like a modern version of Ancient Chinese water torture. Trees bent under gale force winds. Branches cracked. "Grab my hand," George said, helping Cerissa onto the trail. "Stay low," he advised, face pressed close to her ear. "Hold on to the suitcase."

Glen's treasure, until now a precious, but weighty burden, increased its value with every step by offering ballast against the fierce gusts. With both George and Cerissa gripping the handle, they lugged the suitcase up the trail, plopping it down like an anchor with each step. Then repeat. Again, and again, painful, slow trudging to the crest of the ridge. Then, almost as slowly, they descended to the relative shelter of the woods.

"Let's rest," George said when the trail led them to a dense copse of casuarina trees, a species famous for its resistance to wind and salt. He dropped the suitcase and slumped to the ground.

Cerissa snuggled into his arms. "Are you all right?"

George sighed, content for the brief time he could hold her. "This baggage feels like the thirteenth labor of Heracles. But it saved our asses up there." He bowed his head to exhaustion and the sopping ground.

"It must weigh a ton."

"No, just the heaviest forty pounds on Earth." With arms crossed over her chilled and saturated body, he flexed his aching muscles, trying to regain strength and banish the prickling burn. "It wasn't too bad three hours ago, but after a few miles..." Wind whisked by, taking his words with it. "Sorry I got you into this," he said, wanting to whisper, but settling for soft words into sopping hair.

"I don't mind a little adventure," she said, her voice still cheery despite the mud, strain, worry, and pain.

"Unfortunately, adventure ends at the marina. I failed after all. No boat should sail in this weather."

"There'll be another chance."

"I hope so." Then: "You're shivering."

"We should keep moving. I can help with the suitcase."

"That won't be—"

"Really. Let me try," Cerissa said, squirming out of his grasp and springing to her feet.

"I just need a short rest," George said.

"We don't have time."

Expression stern and feet set, she grabbed the suitcase with both hands and struggled for a grueling fifty feet before George stopped her.

"Maybe we can both take an end," he suggested. But the steep, muddy, often winding terrain made sharing the load awkward and dangerous. "Here, I feel better now," George said, grabbing the handle. "Glen and I dived for years to earn this treasure," he said. "Too bad it's heavy as a load of bricks." He laughed, trying to, at least, lighten his attitude.

As they continued the trudge through the woods, pausing briefly to rest, George focused on a single consolation:

*At least my burden is worth its weight in gold.*

Thirty minutes later, battered and drenched to the depths, George and Cerissa stood on the cliffs overlooking the once beautiful North Beach marina. "Holy shit," George gasped, surveying the smoldering rubble.

In the distance, far below, what remained of the marina had sunk into concave heaps. The dock crew, thankfully alive, stood near the wreckage with shovels and picks. Beyond, in the choppy waters of the harbor, three boats were anchored: Aaron's yacht, reduced by Glen's flare gun to a blackened, listing hulk; a forty or fifty-foot cabin cruiser George had never seen before; and the *Valdaquez.*

Even on a calm summer day, the sailboat would be challenging to steal. But with Captain Waller, Niles, and two strangers standing outside, three thieves swimming to the *Valdaquez* would be stupidly obvious.

"Not easy to steal your sailboat, after all," Cerissa said, no doubt reading George's thoughts. "Maybe a fatal flaw in the plan."

George agreed with a shrug.

A voice called out: "Over here!" Turning, they saw Glen, fifty feet off the trail, standing under a craggy shelf of rock. The notch offered protection from the wind and rain, and better, he had wedged pine branches and saplings, probably blowdowns, into the mouth to shield the entrance from view.

Glen ducked inside.

"He's been busy," George called to Cerissa. His arms felt like two soggy logs. His thoughts screamed: *Shelter.* "After you."

The climbing, fueled by relief, seemed easy. Slabs of granite jutted out of the mountain like steps, and soon they had squeezed into the small refuge. "Grab that branch, George," Glen ordered. He weaved the limb among the others, but left a small opening, a window of sorts, to view the marina. "Nobody can see us," Glen said proudly, "but we can see them." He smiled, settling back on a flat rock. "Exciting climb, eh Georgie?" For once, not sarcastic. "We've spent years hiking these hills, but never in a fuckin' hurricane." He chuckled, eyes focused on the suitcase. "Thanks, guess we're both forgetting our stuff today."

Glen's hair, knotted and plastered into soggy strands, hung in his eyes like some shaggy sheep dog. Even Glen's dopey smile looked stolen from a contented puppy. Did years of fun and friendship, pranks, jokes, boyish adventures and schemes make forgiving the lies too easy? Maybe. But how, exactly, do you hate your best friend?

"Other than dodging your turn with the suitcase, why are you so damn happy?" George asked.

"You didn't notice?" Glen bent back a branch and pointed to the marina. Captain Waller, wearing the sailor's cap that never left his head, and the two other men George didn't recognize, huddled in a tight group. One held a shovel, the other a rake, and the third a long pinch bar. A fourth person, surely Niles, was using the backhoe to tunnel into the wreckage. "Those poor bastards are poking through the ruins," Glen said. "Why would they do that in the middle of a storm?" He didn't wait for an answer. "They think we were on the tram." Sick as it was, or because it was sick, Glen bellowed out a sinister chuckle. "Think they'll find the bodies?" Followed by more laughter.

"It must be miserable for them," Cerissa said, maybe referring to the dock crew, perhaps to Kathryn and Old Flowers. Even in a tight embrace with George, she had barely stopped shivering. Now, she shuddered again.

Undaunted, and milking the moment for every drop of morbid glee, Glen said: "It's a good thing we're dead."

"Jesus, enough," George said, his tone sharp.

"Okay," but with a laugh. "I was just kidding." He gestured to the angry sea. "Look at that water."

Rising seas crashed into the reef. Winds slashed foam like deadly scimitars. "You know, George," Glen went on, "I honestly believe that two outstanding sailors like ourselves..." A light punch to George's arm and a return wince. "Sorry. Like I said, two competent sailors could guide that sailboat safely through even those waves. But not that wind. Not even the short trip to Little Flower."

"I wouldn't even try," George said, watching the waves crash onto the sand, the *Valdaquez* rock in choppy water.

"Little Flower is so close," Cerissa said.

"One mile may as well be a million," George said.

"Maybe right now," Glen said. "But the storm will pass. That's what I meant when I said it's a good thing we're dead. What's the hurry?"

"I thought of that," George said, still wanting escape, fighting the urge to stay, needing to leave the island, but still holding back while trying to scheme a way forward. "Then I saw the backhoe." Again resigned, he spoke to Cerissa: "About a mile from here there's another artificial mountain. Much bigger than the marina. The cranes, bulldozers, excavators, front loaders, all the trucks and machinery used to build the Culture Colonies are stored there. When Old Flowers arrives with more men, we'll see a lot more heavy equipment. If they dig out the tram before the storm is over, they'll discover we weren't on board. Ten seconds later, they'll guard the sailboat and that will crush our final option."

"Well," Glen said, "looks like you've got it all figured out. No sense hoping the storm will let up before they excavate the tram."

"Oh, I'm hoping," George said. "Just not willing to gamble on a foolish move."

"We'll see," Glen said, leaning out the opening. "We also have another problem."

"I know. The cabin cruiser," George said. "If we were to board the *Valdaquez*, we couldn't let her follow."

"What are you suggesting, George?" Cerissa said.

"I don't know."

"That's the *Sea Maid*, the boat that brought us to the island. Two nice, *innocent* sailors own it. That boat is their whole life."

George groaned and ran his fingers through matted hair. "I should never have gotten you into this."

"I agree," Glen said.

George glared, but before he could speak, a horse neighed in the distance.

"Unbelievable," George said, after peering through a gap in the branches. Old Flowers, Kathryn Maxwell, seven island employees from various departments, and oddly, Ebba, sat on horseback in heavy rain gear. They stared over the cliff at the devastated marina. Smoldering ruins and apparent death stunned them to silence.

"I think that's Ebba," Glen said, concern topping curiosity and betraying infatuation. "What's she doing here?"

"Playing another role," George said. "Seeking adventure, maybe looking for a wild rainbow, perhaps dusting the furniture." He chuckled and shrugged. "It's Ebba."

For the next several minutes, George and Glen peered out behind separate openings. Cerissa slumped against the cave wall, head lowered, eyes closed.

"What are they doing?" Glen whispered in George's ear. In such wind, he could have shouted.

"I don't know. Maybe they're in shock."

Then, "Holy shit, maybe she *is* human," Glen said.

Kathryn Maxwell had grabbed Aaron's hand. Her shoulders heaved. Face contorted and sobbing, she barely resembled *La Corporada,* let alone the invincible Kathryn Maxwell. Instead, they saw a woman, a mother whose gentle tears had defeated phobias, slaps, and rage.

"All of you!" Aaron Flowers yelled, voice resonant, thundering, its own brand of storm. "Get down there and help the dock crew."

Except for Ebba, the island employees obeyed, leaving the parents with pain.

George's anger crumbled under the weight of their anguish. He wanted to leap from the hiding place, screaming: "We're here, we're alive!"

But as those thoughts raced through his mind, he felt Cerissa's touch. "No, George," she said. Sad, swollen eyes, hair gnarled from the rain, elfin smile contorted into a pout, yet still, the most beautiful woman he had ever seen. He wanted to end her suffering too, pull her into his heart and comfort her forever.

"*Puta de mierda*," Cerissa said, shattering romantic visions.

"What?" George said. Had Cerissa just called her mother a fucking whore? "What did you say?"

Cerissa glared through the branches, looking ready to spit. Her dark temper matched the fuming anger of the billowing smoke.

Stunned, George pondered Mrs. Maxwell, weeping over the death of her beautiful daughter, then back at the beautiful daughter, cursing her mother. "I don't understand you," he said. "One minute you're bleeding for the world, the next you won't forgive your own mother."

Cerissa scoffed. "Forgive?" she said. "Look who's talking." As if entertained by a joke she didn't need to share, she grinned while shaking her head. "Poor George, I hope the real world doesn't devour you along with your innocence." Glen snickered at that one. Cerissa continued. "In the real world, George." She indicated her mother. "It's fatal to be fooled by appearances."

Feeling suddenly exposed, George raised the mental drawbridge. "I don't understand," he said, glancing at Glen to avoid those blazing eyes. Even Glen looked wary.

"George," Cerissa said, "if you could tune into my mother's thoughts, do you know what you'd see?" Her voice, deceptively soft, even calm, belied a beauty strained by turmoil. That delicate soul harbored a secret pain. "Seriously. Do you have any idea?"

"Not the slightest," George said, truthfully.

"Cerissa closed her eyes, fighting tears. "Conrad. You'd see Conrad." With a swift, defiant gesture, she brushed hair from her forehead. "Kathryn is cruel. She's vicious. She's desperately in love with Conrad."

For a demented moment, George wished he *had* been in the runaway tram. Chills slithered under his skin. He sensed, or imagined, frightening power in Cerissa's gaze. "Are you saying she's crying for happiness?" George said, ashamed for even asking.

"I think relief would be a better word. Her ordeal is finally over. She knows she won't lose another love."

"I don't...," George said, shaking his head. "You've lost me."

A moment of uneasy silence stretched to a minute, then two, Cerissa's eyes averted from George, her mother, the storm, the world, and into whatever inner realm offered comfort or meaning.

When she finally spoke, bitterness tainted her sweetness, resentment, her innocence. Too worldly to be so young, the view into Kathryn's mind cracked what had always been a fragile, but hopeful, acceptance of human nature. Now, as if chasing Cerissa's shadow father, her mother had doubled the betrayal.

"Forgive me for unloading on you, George. Or you..."She indicated Glen with a nod. "But this moment, this cave, my mother overlooking the site of my supposed death and dropping her guard for the first time in years. *¡Dios mío!* What a sight behind all that armor. I almost wish I *were* dead."

*Good thing wishes aren't real,* George thought, behind his drawbridge. *We'd both be in that tram.*

Then followed another, even longer, period of silence. To George, a tense stretch of time measured in infinite seconds, to Cerissa, he supposed, an epoch on the path to acceptance. He didn't relax until she offered him a feeble smile, sat up with shoulders back, head up, and unsnarled, as best she could, her frazzled hair. She looked daunted, but ready to talk.

George braced himself.

"As you may have noticed, George, my mother is an all or nothing person. She sees her goal and attains it at any cost. Her revenge is heartfelt. Her love is fierce. She once adored my father in her all-encompassing way, and I believe it was the only time she was ever truly happy.

"Then an accident happened—me." She smiled, but beauty couldn't hide sadness. "My father is a voyager, George, with all the props: A small fleet of broken down ships, questionable cargo, even a loyal band of followers.

"When he met my mother, he dreamed of sailing the world with his gorgeous Kathryn. For him, life is mystery, exotic ports, glamorous, outlandish, not necessarily decent or even sane people, and most of all, freedom." She paused to study George's face. "If my father sounds cliché, like a character in a third-rate adventure novel, I've succeeded in describing him perfectly."

With a wink and a lowered drawbridge, George thought: *How did a cliché spawn an original like you?*

She smiled, saying: "In fairness, at least he's genuine; a bona-fide, worthless, dashing rogue, free of chains and any desire to be more than what appears on the surface. Naturally, a pregnant lover was the only cargo he refused to haul. When my mother wouldn't "fix" me, he cast her off like a tangled net, and for all intents and purposes, disappeared."

"Where does Conrad fit in?"

"Over the years, my mother developed other relationships. Fascinating men she could hunt, capture, and destroy."

Cerissa lowered her eyes, and again, lapsed into silence.

After a few moments, in a voice George had to strain to hear, she said: "All her lovers shared at least one quality with my father. One might possess his looks, another his wild criminal nature, another his shrewd sense of business. I pitied them, and even warned a few. But they never listened to a silly girl. A jealous girl starved for attention and wanting her daddy back. Of course, one by one, as if symbolically murdering my father piece by piece, Kathryn enticed them into her world and left them in ruins."

"My kind of woman," Glen said, his voice so dry he didn't have to waste a smirk. "And if you two haven't noticed, they've gone down to the marina to join the others. We can leave this hole now."

"And go where?" George said.

Glen shrugged and turned away.

"Go on," George said to Cerissa.

"Well, then came Conrad. He was nothing like my father, and I think the attraction surprised her. Maybe she sensed his power and the way he walks through crowds and starts everyone staring." Cerissa sighed, weary from the memory or the arduous trek, worried for Conrad, depressed by her mother's treachery, or perhaps, George hoped, relieved to be away from Kathryn Maxwell and eager to begin a new life. Then, brisk as wind, a surprising and playful smile. "My mother *hates* poetry, but she *loved* Conrad's," Cerissa said, with wonder akin to discovering that Kathryn spoke *Chemehuevi*. "But then, mother was never herself when it came to Conrad.

"So, in the beginning, when Conrad and I became friends, she encouraged him to visit. Later, when mother realized that Conrad would never have any interest in her, she forbade me to see him. That's when she accused him of manipulating me into sex. For a while, things really got sick."

"*Is* Conrad your lover?" George asked, none of his business, but he had to know.

"Maybe on some level. I'm not sure." An evasive or mystical answer, or both. "My mother is certain, of course. She's wondering now if Conrad will change his mind and see her in a new light. She's pathetic and infuriating."

"Are we through with the melodrama, for fuck's sake?" Glen said, after spending the previous ten minutes fidgeting, scratching in the dirt with a pointed stick, and rolling his eyes whenever their conversation interrupted his boredom.

Cerissa and George ignored him. "The point is, George, I *am* leaving Flowers Island. If my mother is longing for Conrad, he can't be dead. And now, the thought of living with her..." Idly, she leaned over and picked up a pebble, passed it from hand to hand, and then flicked it through the branches. "I'm gone," she said.

George considered his next words carefully. He despised Kathryn Maxwell, the abuse, the callous self-interest, the ruthless, efficient scheming, and worse, loathed giving Cerissa a reason to return to Costa Rica, but still said: "And if Conrad is alive, but kidnapped or shanghaied?"

"Then I'll find out," Cerissa said, expression severe, gaze steady. "On my own and away from my mother, her assistants, her cronies, and the tentacles of the Flowers Corporation."

"Does that mean you're coming with me to Grand Trinity?" George asked, his tone betraying a surplus of hope.

"Whoa, wait a minute," Glen said, suddenly animated. "What's this about Grand Trinity? Aren't you going on the world tour?"

"That was before—"

"The Greek Islands, Georgie, Egypt, Madagascar, *Rapa Nui*. We mapped it out. You may not want me along, but that's always been your dream."

George glanced from Glen to Cerissa, then back to Glen. "No," he said.

"Since when?" Glen kicked the suitcase, hard. It didn't budge. "That's full of salvaged gold. You'll be off the island. What's the problem?"

*Everything,* George thought.

Things like renouncing an entire upbringing, abandoning home and collaborations with brilliant people; hiking the hills, studying the birds, the flowers, the trees; salty air on a blinding day; the beach, the surf, salvage, shipwrecks, underwater caverns. Roles in the Colonies, painless, challenging, all amazing and revealing the wonders of culture and life through the shifting lens of language and custom. And the concert grand; sculpted and elegant as Grecian bronze, resonant as Medieval fresco. The *Pergamum* and its universe of books. The maze, the gardens, the stables, the mansion's corridors draped in masterworks, granite gods and marble goddesses, daily declarations of genius and infinite possibilities.

And, of course, surrendering to reality and banishing the dream of a world tour.

*What's the problem?*

"Nothing," George said. But after last night and the television." He held his breath. "I'm enrolling in Grand Trinity University." He exhaled, and in a half-whisper, said: "And I want to be quarterback of the Grand Trine."

If George's head had cracked like an egg and revealed an alien being, Glen would have looked less surprised. "What?" he said, eyes darting from George to Cerissa. "Is this you?" As if to say: 'Only a woman could fuck a brain so quickly'. Then back to George. "The Grand Trine? Are you fucking shitting me?" No sound but wind whistling through pounding rain, and perhaps the clamor of confusion banging against Glen's panic. "Come on, George, I've done my share of kidding, but this is no time for jokes."

"I'm not joking."

"Quarterback? George, you don't know shit about the game. The *foote balle* you played in the Medieval Colony..." He paused to digest his disbelief. "No way you're going to Grand Trinity to fuck up my team. You'd kick a field goal and call it a hand off."

"I'll learn."

"So, what is this? Love? Trying to impress the new girlfriend? I know it's been a while since Jenny."

*You had to mention Jenny*, George thought, annoyed that his thoughts weren't hidden behind the drawbridge.

Glen stormed on, as relentless as the wind. "I get it. People go crazy when they *think* they're in love." He aimed his glare at Cerissa. "But why can't you see that your girlfriend is wacked."

"Fuck you," George said.

"Me? What do you call someone who thinks she's reading minds?"

"A mind reader," George said.

"Bullshit. Her real power is having you convinced."

"Shut up."

He sneered at Cerissa. "So, he's your ticket away from a bitch mother." He scoffed. "Nice scheme on short notice."

"It was *my* idea to leave the island," George said, fuming. "I asked *her* to join *me*."

"Or maybe *your* idea was you reading *her* mind." He cackled at the depth and breadth of his humor.

George saw another dimension. "Nothing funny about a paid liar," he said.

"I..." Glen managed, before slumping into silence.

"Don't you have anything to say?" George asked, turning to Cerissa.

"No."

"Don't you want to tell him to go to hell?"

"No."

"I need some air," George said, embracing the absurdity of the notion. He pressed through the snarl of branches and into way more air than he needed or wanted. Still, he felt curiously serene in a downpour of burning rain and flaying hair, knowing, beyond doubt, that swirl and bluster teetered on the brink of equilibrium.

*Balance*, he thought, remembering his favorite piano composition, *leads to the* Serenity of Solitude.

And serenely alone he felt, hidden behind a massive boulder, swaying in the rhythmic gusts. Even for a few fleeting minutes and steps away from unsettled emotions, George found a peaceful center. Eyes closed, time flowing unmeasured, symphonies of wind and rain rising to crescendos of fury and virtuosity, George barely noticed the steady, measured, and changing tempo.

Of the squalls.

And a sudden, inexplicable, quiet.

Rain, easing first, then vanishing.

"My ears are still ringing from the wind," Cerissa said, stepping outside. "But it's gone. The storm is over."

Above, a patch of blue. Sub-tropical sun warmed their skin. "No," George said, standing with renewed vision. "The eye is passing over the island."

Glen joined them behind the boulder and all three peered down at the marina. "I was out of line in there," he said to Cerissa. "I'm sorry. George has been planning that trip for so long, I just..." He looked away. "That's no excuse. I'm an asshole."

"George needs to go his own way," Cerissa said.

"We all need to go," George said. "Now."

"One second," Glen said, darting back to the nook. He emerged with the suitcase. "When we get to the mainland, one way or another, you two need to stay together."

"We'll decide that later," George said.

"Still, take this." He dropped the bag at George's feet. "My collection of finger ingots. Consider it your real birthday surprise."

"I've already had too many surprises," George said.

"Then reparation for years of lies."

"You're not a war criminal."

"Okay. It's my contribution to your new career as quarterback of the Grand Trine."

"You're not going to give up, are you?"

"No, take it. There's enough gold to start a dozen new lives."

"We can deal with this later," George said. "Come on, we've got maybe an hour before *Tempestas* closes her eye."

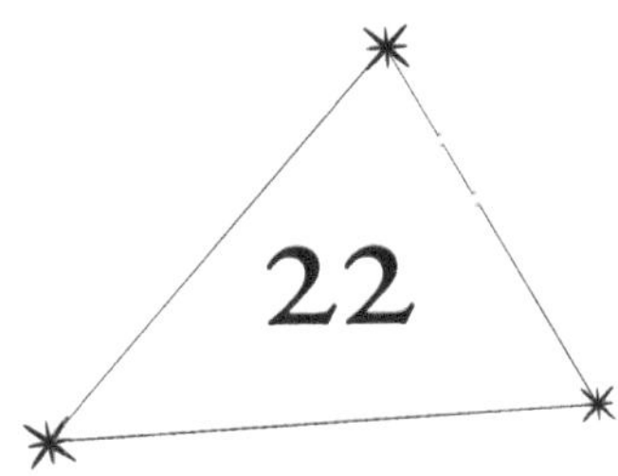

Below the cliffs, at sea level, the air was still and eerie white, a pungent mix of burnt diesel and briny mist. Aaron Flowers, always leading by example and never afraid of grime and sweat, labored with the dock crew, his team of riders, and the two marooned sailors, Coz and Reggie, in a largely psychological rescue exercise. Each either worked a shovel, swung a pick, or employed a crowbar to clear away fractured chunks of artificial rock from the fringes of the shattered marina. Niles, manning a small backhoe and making actual progress, tunneled straight into the slurry, scooping buckets of mud, probing with the claw, picking with the thumb, piling hunks of re-enforced stucco and mangled wire mesh into heaps taller than the cab.

"I want that dozer over here!" Old Flowers called, as he directed the caravan of heavy machinery just now arriving from the Construction Storage Cavern. "Clear paths for the other machines."

Niles backed away.

A Case CX160 excavator belched and clattered to the mouth of Niles' tunnel, scooped up serious buckets of rubble, and crawled along the newly revealed loading ramp, toward, what everyone hoped was, a void, cavity, or fissure that might lead them to the tram. Two additional excavators duplicated the effort, both approaching the *Theoi-Halioi* terminal from different angles.

Meanwhile, Niles steered his backhoe to the beach where a three-person crew loaded random debris into the front loader.

Human excavators ended their all but useless picking and digging, straightened their throbbing backs, and gathered behind the CX160, hoping.

"Keep low," George whispered over his shoulder. Cerissa and Glen crouched behind and followed George from boulder to boulder. They had backed away from the cliffs and circled the knoll behind the marina. Now approaching the cliffs from the opposite side, they risked detection by anyone scanning the eastern bluffs.

In the harbor below, the *Valdaquez* was anchored a few hundred feet off shore. So too the burned wreckage of Aaron's yacht, and Reggie's *Sea Maid.* Yet neither offered significant cover. "They'll see us if we try to swim to the *Valdaquez*," Glen said.

"Watch for loose rocks," George answered, evading both the rescue crew and Glen's comment.

Fortunately, most of the workers clustered near the primary tunnel, some distracted by the bang and grind of the clawing arm, a few chatting, and many still working shovels to impress Aaron Flowers. But too many bodies, knowing how the boss would react to modern artifacts uncovered in the sands of *Mycenaean Greece*, scoured the beach in cleanup details.

"This way," George whispered, their destination a tongue of rock directly opposite the *Valdaquez.* "Watch your footing."

"Okay mom," Glen said.

George ignored him, reached down for Cerissa's arm and pulled her in one swoop over a rocky crest. Glen handed up the suitcase. "Don't drop it," Glen said, smiling.

"I'd like to offer my sincere condolences," Reggie said, walking up to Kathryn Maxwell with a barely applied shovel. She orbited the main activity with her smart phone, taking photos—and ignoring Reggie. Embarrassed, Reggie fumbled through his pockets for a cigarette, knowing he had none, and when the pseudo-search could no longer occupy his dignity, hovered like a stray dog begging for scraps. *Fucking bitch*, he thought, denying he ever saw beauty in a woman whose evil black hair dangled in vile strands over a disgusting yellow rain coat. Eyes aiming the phone, and a sharp, chiseled nose looked waspish, ready to sting.

*I'm not your dirt*, he thought. *You can't just sweep me away.*

He attempted another token expression. "I'm sorry for your loss," he said, persistence a substitute for genuine sympathy. "If there's anything I can do. Anything at all."

"Thank you," Kathryn said, finally granting him an audience.

"Well, I just thought..." Reggie froze when her gaze chilled that pesky bone just above his asshole. The one that tingled when he climbed the ratlines to the topgallant sail and looked down. His eyes darted to anywhere but her face. "At a time like this, you know, well, it helps to have a..." He almost said friend, but changed to "...sympathetic acquaintance."

"If you don't mind, I'd rather be left..." She turned to look at whatever had grabbed Reggie's attention. "What is it?"

"Nothing," he said. "I think the storm is building." He snuck another glance over Kathryn's shoulder, to a spot on the cliffs where he was certain he had just seen movement. "Yep, my bad knee is better than any weather report," he said, returning to Kathryn. "I can damn near predict the wind speed with that left knee." He chuckled, but of course Kathryn the Lionfish just floated away. "Well, you take care, Mrs. Maxwell," he called after her.

*Slime shark whore!* Reggie thought as he walked back.

But, by the time he returned to the excavation, Reggie had replaced pride with something much more interesting.

Slowly, he eased away from the others, found a pile of charred debris to poke at with the tip of his shovel, and kept his eyes focused on the cliffs. *I know I seen somethin' up there.* A moment later, he saw it again. *Damn.* He glanced around to see if anybody noticed him noticing. *Shit, there's somebody climbin' those cliffs.* He strained his eyes. *More like three somebodies.*

For appearances, Reggie tossed a few shovels of mud over his left shoulder. Everyone else, including Aaron Flowers, was too busy really working.

Kathryn Maxwell, head bowed, stared at the smartphone.

As casually as possible, Reggie worked his way along the perimeter of the wreckage, toward the harbor, until he reached the dock where Coz had tied their rowboat.

*I'll get a job out of this yet*, he thought, *and a substantial reward.*

Easing the boat through the choppy water, he glanced toward the work party and realized that Coz had spotted him. *Shit!* Coz stared with a disgusted glare. Reggie waved, smiled, and placed two fingers to his lips in a pantomime of smoking. Coz shook his head and returned to work.

"Hey, hey," Reggie muttered to himself. The *Sea Maid* was anchored fifty feet from the *Valdaquez*. "This is gonna be easy money."

* * *

Glen tugged on George's shirt. "Somebody's rowing to the sailboat. And the wind's picking up again."

"I noticed. We're almost there."

"Wait a minute. What about the guy on our sailboat?"

"He's not going to the *Valdaquez*," Cerissa said.

"How do you know?" Glen said, with interest, not snark. "Did you read his mind?"

"No, I recognize him. That's Reggie, one of the sailors from the *Sea Maid*." She turned to George, eyes inquiring, wary. "George, what's your plan for Reggie's boat?"

"Nothing that will harm your sailor." He hadn't even considered sabotage with someone on board. "This is the place." He peered down the jagged rocks, then pointed to his left. "With that outcropping between us and the marina, we should be able to climb down unnoticed."

Glen said: "If Old Reggie doesn't see us."

"If," George said, even less inspired than his two friends.

They started their climb down the crag, three hundred feet above the water.

Reggie heaved alongside the *Sea Maid*, tied the rowboat, and climbed the ladder to the deck. Inside the cabin, he found a pair of binoculars and trained them on the three climbers. "Yes sir," he said, imagining the thrill of sailing the new monohull keelboat he would buy with Aaron Flowers' reward. "Time to set the trap." He would leave the rowboat tied conspicuously to the *Sea Maid* so the three runaways would think he was still aboard, then swim to the *Valdaquez* unnoticed.

Aaron Flowers would be grateful beyond his wildest generosity.

With a final look through the binoculars, he fixed on Cerissa. "It's gonna be hard givin' you back to your sea snake mother," he said. "But this is strictly business."

He slipped quietly overboard with the binoculars dangling down his back.

"George," Cerissa said, peering over the cliff. "We're trapped."

"Good work, *Hawkeye*," Glen said, referring to the Indian guide in James Fenimore Cooper's, *The Last of the Mohicans*. "You've led us right into the bear trap."

George looked left, then right, then down as far as he could safely lean. "Sorry," he said.

"Now what?" Glen said. "After all this shit?"

The water was thirty feet below, splashing against the cliffs. "We jump," George said. "Like the *Quebrada* divers."

"Don't confuse the issue," Glen said, with a quiver in his voice. "My Spanish is broken, at best."

Both George and Cerissa laughed.

"What's so goddamn funny?"

"You just made a Spanish joke," Cerissa said, still chuckling.

George explained: "*Quebrada* means "gorge" in *Español*. On the cliffs of Acapulco, *La Quebrada* Cliff Divers leap into a gorge, soar down a hundred feet, and dive headfirst into the sea."

Cerissa added: "And many have suffered "*la pierna quebrada*", a broken leg, in the process. Because "*quebrada*" also means "broken".

"So," George said, "you can dive into a *quebrada*, suffer a *quebrada* leg, and do it in *quebrada* Spanish."

"Not very grammatical," Cerissa said, "but funny."

"I'm glad you're both amused," Glen said, eyeing the churning seas. "But those rocks look deadly." As if to exclaim the point, waves bashed those very rocks, splashed up the cliff walls, and coated them with mist.

"Don't worry. We're jumping feet first at thirty feet," George said. "Scary, but not deadly." He stared up at the clouds. "We don't have time to find another way. We either jump, or we stay here and hope the storm doesn't blow us off the mountain."

"Fuck your don't worry," Glen mumbled. "You're still an asshole."

"I'll go first," Cerissa said.

Glen glared at her, then at George. "What about the gold? It's not going to float to the sailboat."

"I'll take care of it."

"Great! Say 'hi' to Neptune when you touch bottom."

"Listen," George said, turning toward the marina.

"What?"

"Nothing." He cocked his head. "That's what caught my attention. Hang on." He crawled a few feet to peer around a boulder. "I don't see anyone or hear the excavators."

"Unlike us, they're sane," Glen said. "They know what's coming. They've probably been carving out some shelter. Either that, or they broke through to the terminal and will hunker down there." He glanced at the darkening sky. "The eyewall is close."

"I should go first," George said to Cerissa. "Watch how I do it." George pointed to the water. "It may be shallower than it looks, so jump right before the wave hits the base of the cliff."

"Jesus fuck!" Glen said.

"Leap out as far as you can."

"This is nuts," Glen said.

"Feel free to stay behind."

"I'm going, goddamn it."

"Then cut the shit." George said, feet inches from the edge. He stared down.

"Well?" Glen smirked.

"Next wave." But the next wave came and went.

*I've jumped from higher cliffs than this*, he thought.

He braced himself, grabbed the suitcase, and leaped.

Water blasted up his nose and icepicks stabbed his ears. But when he hit bottom, he let go of the suitcase, shot up, and gasped for air. Through salt-blurred vision, he saw Cerissa leaning over the edge, ready.

*Quick, find a landmark.*

Straight ahead, a cone-shaped rock covered with seagull droppings.

Swimming a few feet toward the sailboat, he turned around and treaded water while waiting for Cerissa. A wave lifted, and gently dropped him. *Okay, take this one.*

Cerissa waited too long.

*Come on. Now!* He waved with both arms: *NOW!*

She leaped, splashing into swirls of foam, and surfaced, unhurt. Glen held his nose and followed on the next wave.

"Let's go," George breathed over the water.

Reggie watched the whole performance from the *Valdaquez*. Turning from the cabin porthole, he grumbled, "Silly ass kids."

He hid in the clothing locker.

When George, Cerissa, and Glen approached the tip of the outcropping blocking their view of the marina, George, in the lead, stopped. "Shit! Back up a bit." He turned and paddled after them, out of sight. "I caught a glimpse of some guys. Wait here."

Bobbing, and with nose at water level, he swam to a large rock at the base of the outcropping. Workers had climbed into the cabs of the three excavators and were moving them into formation near the excavated tunnel. Returning to Cerissa and Glen, George said: "They're circling the wagons. Blocking the tunnel against the storm."

"Meaning?" Glen said.

"They're back outside. We can dog paddle here until they leave, or swim underwater to the *Valdaquez*. Your choice."

"There's no time, George," Cerissa said. "We still have to sail to Little Flower."

"I agree. Blow your co2, dive, and swim like hell." After five powerful exhalations, George dove toward the *Valdaquez*.

The others followed, surfacing every twenty feet for a quick breath, then back to furious swimming.

They arrived on the starboard side of the sailboat, hidden from view. "Jesus," Glen said, panting. "Too much scuba, not enough free dives."

George heaved his body up over the rail, and crouched down. "Here." He lowered a ladder into the water. Cerissa climbed aboard, then Glen. They crept along the deck and ducked into the cabin.

"You've got a few minutes to rest before we leave the harbor," George said to Cerissa. "There's dry towels in the locker." He turned to Glen. "Check for any provisions."

"Why? You left the most valuable provision underwater."

"The other day," George said, with more patience than Glen deserved. "Before you freaked out and torched the yacht. Did you get a chance to do what you said you were going to do?"

"What was I supposed to do?" Glen shook his head to drain water out of his ears.

"We were going to dive the *Temperance*, remember?"

"Shit. I didn't get around to filling the tanks."

"Too bad," George said. He grabbed a BCD and regulator from the under-seat storage and checked the tank pressure. "About 200 psi," he said, frowning.

"Sorry," Glen said.

"I hope you're just diving for the gold," Cerissa said.

"What do you mean?"

"I don't want you to sink the *Sea Maid*, or even damage it."

"We can't let them follow us. I have to do something."

"You've already destroyed the marina." She turned to Glen. "You've burned the yacht. Don't drag Reggie and Coz into your devastation."

"You're right. I'll get the gold and we'll leave. If they follow, we just outrun them. I hope."

"George, don't be stupid down there," Glen said. "Watch your air. Though I doubt you're worth more than a half-mil in gold bullion."

"Fuck you."

George snugged his weights, adjusted his mask, and splashed into the water moments before Glen opened the clothing locker. "Jesus!" Glen cried, leaping back.

"Reggie?" Cerissa said. "What are you doing here?"

"I've come to discuss a little business."

George surfaced well behind the outcropping and about twenty feet from shore. The currents had carried him toward the marina, quite a distance from the gold-filled suitcase. To compensate, he swam parallel to the beach for a good minute, pausing a few feet to the left of the cone-shaped seagull latrine. The general area, certainly, but below him roiled water so murky with churned up sand he considered it less than zero visibility.

*Damn!* In only seconds, he had drifted away from his marker.

Brutal new currents and likely to get worse as the eyewall approached.

With a few solid strokes, he aligned himself again, emptied his lungs, and sank slowly into the gloom. With no visibility, only pressure on the inner ear confirmed he was sinking. He swallowed, tensed his jaw, heard his ears squeak, felt the pressure ease, and surrendered to the weightless void.

Fins touched sandy bottom. Then his butt and the line he had tied to his weight belt, the added bulk helping the currents knock his body off balance. The pressure gauge, even held inches away, almost vanished in the swirling silt. Now reading well below 200 psi, the needle hadn't pinned, yet, but it lurked in the red. *Find the suitcase,* he thought, calm, preserving air, fingers probing the soft sand. No suitcase. More sediment. No suitcase. Arms back and forth. Nothing.

Re-surfacing, desperation hinting at a hopeless quest, shocked to discover that he had again drifted twenty feet past the cone-shaped rock.

Fighting fear and the current, he swam parallel to the cliffs and, this time, thirty feet beyond the marker rock before again descending to the ocean floor.

Arms wide, drift diving across the sandy bottom, searching, exploring, straining to see beyond his fingertips, he knew within seconds that he had wandered too far.

Again at the surface, he checked the gauge. Barely enough pressure to lift the needle above the pin, 50, maybe 75 psi. A precious few breaths, but enough for one more try.

*It's got to be there. Forty pounds of gold doesn't drift, even in these currents.*

He sank to the bottom again, this time trying a blind, groping, zig-zag maneuver. Nothing. On instinct, he swiveled his body to the right. Nothing. Then to the left. The same; sand, rocks, small patches of coral, more sand, more rocks...

His right flipper brushed against...something.

Turning, he groped in a wide arc and smacked his hand into a hard object. A rock? Then yelled, "Yes!" into the regulator when his hands swept over a flat, imitation alligator skin surface.

He had discovered gold. But compared to lugging, finding was easy.

He tied the line to the handle and allowed it to play out behind him as he swam to the surface.

*I'm halfway there,* he thought.

*But with nowhere near enough line.*

The *Valdaquez* lurched and rocked in the blossoming winds.

Down, down, he sank into murky grayness, using the line to guide him back to the suitcase. Then, half swimming, half kicking against the ocean floor, he trudged forward, imagining the sailboat in his mind's eye, needing direction, demanding to see the *Valdaquez*, willing the image to become clearer, and clearer, until it crystallized into perfect focus.

Time must have passed, but not in George's awareness. In this waking dream, time and the rules of space served imagination. In the distance, the sailboat floated above him in perfect detail. With his mind's eye, he could even shift perspective and see the *Valdaquez* as if he were swimming on the water's surface. Then, as easily, return to the underwater point of view, but with clarity, as if diving on a perfectly calm and sunny day.

And all the while, a background awareness of the physical world, mainly, the regulator resisting his demands for air. Down to what he knew were his last few breaths, still, he rejoiced. Barely twenty feet from the *Valdaquez* in his mental vision, he watched as the hull grew closer in proportion to his forward movement.

Then oddly, his mental perspective shifted again. A figure underwater struggling against the cross current, tugging a line tied to a suitcase, as if viewed by someone standing on the deck of the *Valdaquez*.

*I'm seeing myself,* George thought with surprise and bewilderment.

Then again underwater, looking up with his mental vision and seeing the bottom of the sailboat directly overhead. According to the dream, if he surfaced now he would bang his head on the bow. So, he swam to the right, to the anchor line, and reached out to grab it.

The shock of touching it shattered the vision.

Current lifted his body. Dark murky swirl returned to his face mask.

But his physical hand did indeed grasp the anchor line.

*How?*

Clinging to the free end of the line, he surfaced. "Glen," he called in a muted voice. "Glen."

Cerissa came to the rail and lowered the ladder. As she grabbed the line George handed her, then his fins, she glanced quickly toward the cabin. "Where's Glen?" George asked, body churning in the waves while squirming out of the BCD. "This tank is too heavy for you."

"Don't worry. I've got it," Cerissa said, lifting the tank with a good push from George.

"We need to leave," George said, climbing aboard and dropping the tank in its slot. "The eyewall is near." He sank to the deck. "God, I'm exhausted. And the most amazing thing just happened. I—what's the matter?"

Reggie opened the cabin door.

"Oh," George said.

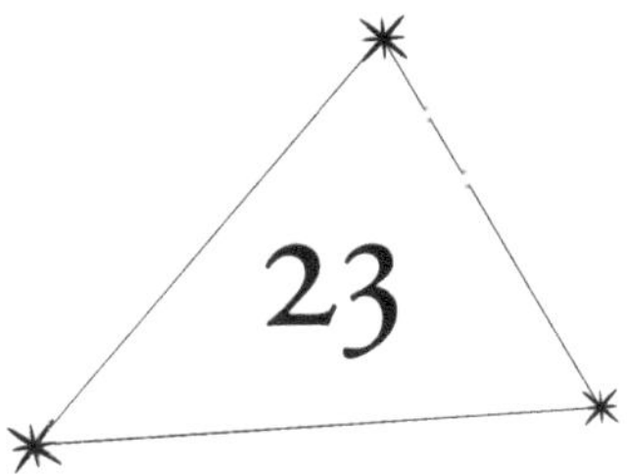

# 23

So, this is the guy who wasn't rowing to the *Valdaquez*. Maybe Cerissa *should* have read his mind.

"You must be Reggie," George said, grabbing the line from Cerissa. Reggie held, but wasn't aiming, George's Orion 12-gauge flare pistol. The 6-flare bandolier dangling below the pistol grip held 5 flares, and since neither he nor Glen had ever fired the gun, the missing flare must be chambered in it.

"Are you seriously threatening to shoot us with that thing?" George said.

"Nobody wants that," Reggie said. "I was thinkin' more about gettin' a certain somebody's attention." Still, his tone implied that flares as weapons weren't out of the question. Glen, not only absent, but noticeably quiet, was literally subdued behind him. He sat in the cabin, on one of the berths, hands behind his back and forehead bleeding.

"What the fuck did you do to Glen?" George said, his step blocked by the raised flare gun.

"Not so fast," Reggie said. "That little Chihuahua came at me. Ask Cerissa. Nearly brained me with a frying pan."

"You didn't have to punch him so hard," Cerissa said.

"And you're trespassing on our boat," George said.

"Just hold on," Reggie said, gesturing for George to join them in the cabin. When George and Cerissa were seated across from Glen, George still clutching the line, Reggie leaning against the galley and smiling like their new best friend,

Reggie nodded toward the beach. "Your old man would be mighty relieved to know you're alive," he said.

"No doubt," George said, faking his own smile. Then to Glen: "Are you okay?" Blood crusting on Glen's forehead made his well-tanned face look even darker. That, or simple rage. He glowered at Reggie and strained against the duct tape binding his wrists.

"Whatever you do, George. Don't let this fucker take my gold."

*Your gold?* George thought.

"I ain't no thief," Reggie said. "I aim to earn that gold."

Gusts blew in through the open porthole, a threat as menacing as the black fog crawling down the cliffs.

"She's coming," Cerissa said, referring to *Tempestas.*

"We're running out of time," George said to Reggie. "What do you want?"

"Simple," Reggie said. "I swim back to the *Sea Maid* and guarantee she can't follow. There's a dicey starter on the diesel. I can fix things so even Coz won't suspect."

"Not good enough," George said. "Captain Waller and Niles can repair anything."

"Then I'll break the compass and fuck up the GPS."

"Don't listen to this lying shit fucker," Glen said, and spit on Reggie's jeans.

Reggie cocked his arm, but held back. "If my hand weren't gimped, I'd wreck your face." he said.

"Fuck you!" Then to George: "Do *not* bargain with this prick." He launched a kick that grazed Reggie's shin. "He'd fuck abalone and call it his sister."

Glen's nose crackled like a dry leaf. Not once, but three times as Reggie's awkward, but uninjured left fist pummeled Glen's face.

"Stop!" Cerissa screamed, as George lunged at Reggie. An attack thwarted by a wave that heaved the boat in a sudden roll and knocked George off balance. The split-second Reggie needed to rear up and aim the gun.

"Back up! Both of you," he said, waving the pistol to port, then starboard. "I tried to be reasonable. Now I gotta be mean."

As if to accent the threat, the wind, blowing the opposite direction it had before the calm, lashed across the stern. George teetered as the sailboat rocked in the water. "Take this," he said, snatching the line attached to the suitcase. He had dropped it while springing at Reggie, and now the churn threatened to drag the line out of the cabin. "It's about to get sucked overboard."

"I will," Reggie said. "Hand it over and step aside." He backed up to the companionway with the flare aimed at George. "Sorry way to treat a new friend," he said to Cerissa. "But not me. I'm riskin' prison by lettin' a minor escape." Then to George: "You have my word. The *Sea Maid* won't leave the harbor."

*Sure,* George thought.

"Yeah, right," Glen muttered, voice distorted by burbles of blood and snot.

George opened a drawer and passed the first aid kit to Cerissa. He turned to Glen: "You and your goddamn mouth."

"And my nose," Glen said, barely able to form words. "Don't let him escape, George." More of a groan than a phrase.

"There's ointment, scissors, bandages, Tylenol." The boat rocked and heaved in the roiling seas. "Cut him loose and try to fix him up without injuring yourself. There's Dramamine if you need it. We're getting underway."

Balancing with arms wide to catch himself from slapping against the walls, George climbed through the companionway to the deck. Reggie had just reeled in the suitcase. "Keep low, goddamn it," George said.

Reggie ducked into a crouch. "Christ, this thing weighs a ton." Rain and greed dripped off his face. Then, as if suddenly remembering that his rowboat was tied to the *Sea Maid*, added: "Shit, how the hell am I gonna get this to my boat?"

"That's your problem," George said.

"I ain't throwin' it back in the water, sonny, and I ain't leavin'."

"Fine." George said. He staggered back to the cabin and removed three life jackets from the footlocker. "For the survival of your new fortune," he said, eyes searing from salty spray or scorn. Quickly, he and Reggie fastened two jackets around the suitcase; the third was clipped to the handle as a safety. "Use this as a tow line and leave." With his dive knife, George sliced away most of the line. *Or stay aboard and we'll keelhaul you,* he thought, before cramming the remaining forty feet into an empty pouch of the Finholder.

"Well, Cortés," Reggie said with a snide salute. "Good luck conquering the mainland." His grand triumph of sarcasm.

He threw the suitcase overboard and jumped in behind it.

The diesel cranked over, sputtered, hissed, cranked again, then fired to life. George raised the storm jib and retrieved the storm anchor.

Steering the *Valdaquez* out of the harbor, determined, despite everything, to anchor in the sheltered coves of Little Flower, so close and still visible in the mist, bouncing up and over the tortured seas, in blinding spray, seeing the towering clouds looming ahead, *Tempestas* staring through the eyewall—and thinking, after all this, one meaningless thing: *When will they notice?*

It took longer than he would have imagined, though the *Valdaquez* had barely motored to the fringe of the barrier reef. Horns blared. Voices yelled. "There!" he thought he heard someone scream.

He couldn't be sure because waves, deafening as thunder, crashed the hull.

Gripping the tiller with all his strength, George glanced back at the marina. Sure enough, there were Old Flowers, Ebba, and Kathryn Maxwell, out of the tunnel, and running, walking, and in the case Old Flowers, hobbling to within ten feet of the water. The old Puppet Master stared, cane in hand; shocked maybe, relieved maybe, and angry, but never defeated.

The next moments exploded with gestures, wind-smothered commands, and scurries of activity. Bodies dove into the water and swam to the *Sea Maid*. Reggie had boarded only moments before, but instead of ducking below to sabotage the engine as promised, he stuffed the suitcase into a storage hold, covered it with a piece of canvass, then leaned on the rail to await the swimmers.

"That pig!" George heard Cerissa wail from the cabin. She must have been watching through the porthole.

The *Valdaquez* sputtered on, toward the only passage in the reef, the one opened by the earthquake of 1755. Waves bounced the bow up, to the crest of the seas, then slammed it down, into the troughs, a tedious cycle as violent as it was useless. The propeller barely touched the water. *We'll make it*, George thought, Little Flower enticing in its proximity. *Just clear the reef.*

But the sailboat bobbed like a child's toy, harrowing listing followed by stomach-churning plummets. Fierce winds turned water into birdshot, stinging every inch of exposed skin. Seas crashed over the transom, the bow, the mast, and battered him to a crouch in blinding, suffocating waves.

All the while, the world grew darker, thicker, grim as a shipwreck.

"George!" Glen screamed, leaning, really swaying, against the double cabin doors, forcing them open, then forsaking them to the wind.

"What are you doing?" George screamed. "Get back inside." Rivulets of blood mixed with spray and poured off Glen's chin.

"Turn around!" Glen screamed back. "We're too late."

A huge swell bashed the boat, reeling it violently onto its side, and then righting it again in almost the same motion. "Mother of god!" Glen screamed, clinging to the rail.

"We couldn't turn around if we wanted to!" George cried. A giant sea lifted the boat to its crest and dropped her suddenly into a deep trough.

Glen clamped onto George's leg. "You lose my gold and now you're going to drown me? We won't get through the reef! We're too fucking late."

Fingernails dug into George's flesh. "Enough!" George screamed, kicking out of Glen's grasp. "Get below or clip onto a safety line. Either way, shut the fuck up!"

With almost impossible speed, fog blanketed everything. The reef was somewhere ahead, completely invisible, waiting to shred the hull into soggy splinters.

George spoke to his imagination: *We can do this.*

*We?*

He closed his eyes.

Focused his mind.

Imagination answered.

*The passage exists in both worlds.*

In his mind's eye, the fog disappeared. Seas calmed. Sun shined. The *Valdaquez* sliced through clear waters. Through the prism of imagination, George saw the reef, not ahead of them as he had thought, but below them this very moment. They were safely in the passage, now, but were starting to veer too far starboard, straight toward a deadly island of coral. Instantly, he turned the tiller starboard, veering the boat to port and away from danger.

The sailboat carved through a clear channel with plenty of leeway on each side. *I've done this so many times before. There's a jetty of reef two hundred feet on my port side. Beyond that, it's open sailing.*

The dream spray felt cool on his imagined skin. Looking up, he squinted into the sun, then back to the crystalline water. Guided by perfect visibility, George saw the coral jetty long before it became dangerous. He turned the tiller hard to port, swerved the boat to starboard, and watched the jetty pass. Ahead, less than half-a-mile away, the pink beaches of Little Flower gleamed in the sunlight.

*We made it.* George beamed. *We made it.*

Pain shattered the vision.

"What?" George cried, his first waking concept not pain, or waves over the bow, or dark fog strangling light, but time. Had the dream been like a lifetime revealed in a flash, mere seconds stretched to minutes? Or had the dream clocked time as truly as a belfry tower?

Another blow to the face, this time over the right eye.

This time.

*Why*...smash...*obsess*...smash...*over*...smash...*time*?

"Stop!" George cried, that very same time idling in a single second, a frozen likeness caught in an open shutter, a portrait, a body, rammed against the stern rail, tiller under an arm, head flinching from pounding fists. "Stop!" George cried again, time roused to action. "Are you insane?" At the same moment realizing that Glen had unclipped from his safety line and was free to attack from any angle.

Another blow, weak and glancing, then Glen on his knees reaching for the tiller, his mangled face, sneering, close, ugly, a grimace scowling with feral rage, then instantly gone, crushed under a wave.

The boat pitched.

Hurled Glen, and knocked George from the tiller.

"Glen!" George screamed and watched the flood of the wave skip his friend across the deck.

Flailing, grasping for a stanchion, a grab bar, a cleat, *Valdaquez* tilted like an awning tumbling torrents over the rail, Glen managed: "Geor—"!" before deluge crushed his words.

Knowing that the next wave could toss that slight body overboard, George lashed the tiller, cast off his safety line, and crawled, stanchion to stanchion along the rail, crouching low against the crashing seas and feeling a sick, weightless plunge whenever the boat heaved to port and swamped the deck with punishing waves.

The *Valdaquez*, riding forty-foot seas, raced down their face to a thunderous shotgun splash, lurched up into sea and fog, groaned, screeched, and shuddered from every bolt, rivet, and screw, *Tempesta*s crushing the boat in her deadly grip with George and Glen holding on for near death and screaming at the top of their panic.

George pulled the line from the Finholder. "Grab this!" he screamed, in this wind a whisper into a pillow.

Glen ignored him and cowered, head down, hands death-gripping the metal stanchion like a whimpering child on a plunging roller coaster.

"Glen!" This time jamming the line in Glen's chest.

Delirious, wounded, bleeding; Glen's screams demanded action, but he was unable or unwilling to move. Prodding and yelling failed, along with threats, anger, and trying to yank Glen's body from its desperate cling.

Frantic, and driven by friendship, George lunged at Glen with a *kata-ha-jime*, one of the many *shime-waze* martial arts blood chokes he had learned in the Asian Colony. With his left arm behind Glen's neck, right forearm front, George pressed for five seconds against Glen's carotid artery and felt Glen slump into his arms. In less than double that time, George wrapped the line around Glen's waist and began crawling across the deck.

"Cerissa!" he cried, when he had dragged Glen six feet to the brink of the companionway.

The double doors opened and a stricken-looking Cerissa pulled as George pushed Glen's body down the three steps and into the cabin.

"Fil-lon-chi Christ," George said, as he slammed the doors, and felt, at least for a brief, delusional moment, warm, dry, and safe. His skin shivered under sopping clothes. The *Valdaquez* buckled to starboard and smacked his head against the cabin wall. "Fuck!" He tripped over Glen's body when the boat lurched back to port. "I have to get back to the tiller," he said, wobbling to his feet. "We're adrift." Glen shook slowly out of his stupor and was trying to stand. "None of that, you little bastard," George said with a foot on Glen's back. "Hand me the duct tape," he said to Cerissa. They secured Glen's hands and lifted him onto the berth. "The stupid shit smacked his head when the waves washed him across the deck. I doubt he'll be much trouble." A gash on Glen's scalp oozed ever more blood through comically matted hair. His left eye, now a bloated, purple slit, wasn't so funny. Thanks to Reggie, Glen's nose, once pug and almost dainty, had transformed into a broad, red, poisonous toadstool, excruciating to see and worse to endure. Still, Glen had yet to whine or even groan. "Whatever you do, don't let him leave the cabin."

"I don't suppose you have anything stronger than Tylenol."

"Afraid not. We have that Dramamine I mentioned."

"I know. It's the only reason I don't look like Glen."

George smiled while staggering back to the rolling deck, the grueling tiller, and the sickening reality of the *Valdaquez,* floundering in a raging sea—and Little Flower, lost in a shroud of mist.

Sad, George unleashed the tiller and grabbed it hard, struggling to keep the boat at a right angle to the wind. All the while, he felt like a gambler risking his and other's lives for a very uncertain pay off.

*Too late for regrets*, he thought.

Only focus, endurance, and the compass mounted on the aft bulkhead could guide the *Valdaquez* in a general westerly direction.

And, if *Tempesta*s was kind and luck prevailed, they might even make landfall—somewhere between the former state of Florida, and the former state of Maine.

During the next few hours, the mist cleared enough to allow George to see over the crest of each incoming swell, to the one beyond. That feature not only relieved him from the stress of near-blindness, but helped him guide the boat straight into each sea, to slice through it and avoid a dangerous wall of water on his broadside. After a time, the incessant glide up, over, and down the waves lulled his mind into an unexpected and monotonous calm. *How can I be this resigned?* he thought. *So close to death, I can feel* Kymopoleia's *clammy breath.*

He mused on the surge of imagination that had leaped up like an obedient dog and guided him through the reef. He wanted a vision now. Of calm. Of sky. Of these waters on a summer day.

He even focused his mind and tried to conjure those images.

Nothing.

*Do I have to be on the edge of panic?* he wondered, dreading the grey already darkening to black, the loss of even this meager light.

*But would imagination respond to his fears, clear the skies, and display Polaris to guide him west?*

Not likely.

But minutes later, a gift.

A fuzzy white ball in the western sky. Devoid of color and passing too quickly, it assured George that somewhere on Earth life wasn't an endless series of rolling swells and numbing winds.

He smiled.

But, of course, light followed sun into the sea, along with momentary hope.

Soon, everything was black.

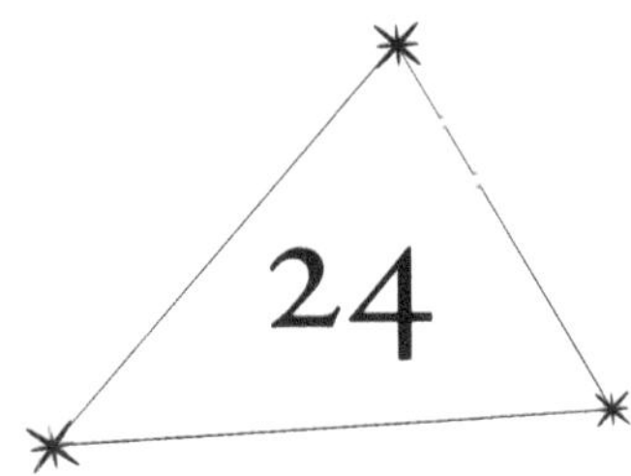


Cerissa opened the companionway doors. Under the hazy glow of the two overhead lights behind her, George saw Glen lying on one of the two folding berths, hands taped behind his back.

"It's still pretty rough out here," George said, his voice hoarse, weary.

Cerissa paused on the second step of the companionway and pressed against the sides to steady herself. "I'm not a sand crab, George," she said, her voice more rueful than offended. "Until he realized I was no substitute for a son, I sailed with my father." She scanned the restless seas, black on gloom and bottomless dark, seemed awed by the spray lashing the deck, and then finally rested her gaze on George. "You look very tired." The wind had deadened George's hearing, making Cerissa's voice sound dim and whispery. "Anyway, Glen wants to know if I can release him."

George scoffed mid-squirm and repositioned the seat cushion under his aching butt. "Is he finally convinced we won't hit the reef?"

Cerissa shrugged.

"Bad joke," George said. He relaxed his grip on the tiller. But only long enough for a deep stretch. "We have to turn him loose. I can barely keep my eyes open."

A few minutes later, the doors opened again and Glen leaned out. "I'll take over," he said, without meeting George's eyes. The cabin light shone from behind, casting a misty halo over Glen's head. But there was nothing angelic about Glen's appearance.

"Be my guest," George said, voice flat, too exhausted for anger, annoyance, or any emotion beyond relief. Standing, he stared at stiff, claw-like fingers too cramped to straighten, walked on legs that felt like stilts, ignored the spasms fluttering his muscles.

Without a word or mumble to Glen, George entered the cabin and collapsed onto the nearest berth. He tried focusing on Cerissa, saw only a blurred outline through squinting eyes, shook his head and slumped onto the pillow. "No one should ever be this tired," he said, as Cerissa massaged his shoulders, working her way gently to the biceps, then down the arm.

He was asleep before she reached an elbow.

Back on the *Sea Maid*, Reggie dreamed of new-found riches. Of course, the fifty-thousand credits Aaron Flowers was paying for the *Sea Maid* charter would have to be split with Coz. But Coz knew nothing about the suitcase—and he wasn't gonna know.

Reggie grinned, thoughts soaring beyond fantasies of monohull keelboats, and gliding full-sail into catamaran, even schooner dreams. *Hell, right place, right time, and quick on my feet.* And with twenty-five-grand added to the gold-filled suitcase, this voyage was looking less and less like a suicide mission.

"Is the radio working yet?" Aaron Flowers asked Captain Waller. Aaron had just emerged from a state of total concentration—on the map he was studying—and hadn't heard Captain Waller notifying the Coast Guard of their position only moments earlier.

"Yes sir," Captain Waller said, sharing a glance with Ebba, one of the quietest and spookiest women Reggie had ever seen. Not that she wasn't a looker—even more than Kathryn Maxwell, thankfully left behind on account of sea sickness. But scary like a blue angel, an exotic-looking, but beautiful creature that eats other poisonous fish, stores their venom in spiny fins, and stings like a Portuguese man o'war. And like this Ebba, or Eloise, or whatever they call her, nobody can agree on the creature's name. Is it a blue angel, a blue dragon, or a sea swallow? Is Ebba/Eloise a blond with long curly hair, a butch-cropped brunette, or a wild, freckle-faced redhead? In the last four hours, she'd appeared as all three, on purpose, like a taunt, as if trying to throw the true owners of the *Sea Maid* off balance. Make it easier to hijack their boat, lure 'em in with big money, then kick 'em off the wheel and swap in a new captain. Though Waller's hard to fault, being a decent skipper and all. Still, Coz can pilot a storm. Reggie's better than most able mates. And the *Sea Maid* ain't some scarlet wench that can be brought to back for a few thousand credits.

Well, normally.

"The Coast Guard is on alert?" Aaron Flowers asked.

*Alert?* Reggie thought. *We're talkin' Flowers money. The Guard probably picks up his laundry.*

"And the secondary beacons?" Aaron said.

"Nothing yet, sir."

While mainly looking out the window, Reggie snuck occasional glances at Aaron Flowers—when he could take his eyes off Ebba (Eloise don't have quite the exotic ring). The old man sat across the cabin at a large drop-leaf table, lost in what must be deep and expensive thoughts.

*Christ! If you saw that bastard on the street, you'd never figure him for a billionaire.*

Reggie took a risk and stared for a moment at Aaron's determined jaw, the eyes that burned below a mane of shock-white hair, the lines etched into his face like war decorations.

*Well, now that you mention it, the man does have a certain air about him. Hell, he's probably got a billion airs.*

Reggie chuckled at his private joke.

Aaron Flowers, caught by the sound of laughter, looked across the room.

Reggie cleared his throat and looked away.

Aaron returned to his map.

Reggie returned to schooner fantasies, or should he consider a small, but impressive yacht?

*Yep, things are gonna be different now. I risked my life earnin' that gold. Shit, before the storm eased a bit, I thought we were goners chasin' after them kids.*

But, like iron to a lodestone, Reggie's attention again locked on Aaron Flowers. *Pretty soon we're gonna have the same job, Old Man—spendin' your money.* He chuckled.

Captain Waller sneezed, drawing Reggie's attention. *Son of a bitch runs my boat like he owns the damn thing.*

Then to Coz, sitting under the forward porthole, on the settee that ran the length of the cabin. Still picking his way through another ancient novel, this one in Spanish no less, probably that guy Ureña he's always talking about, and reading at the pace of a three-year-old after six years of studyin' beaner.

*Jesus, wasted time on a useless dream.*

"Ha," he muttered to himself and returned to Aaron Flowers. *Yes sir, that guy's never scraped a knuckle, sprained a back, or slaved a day in his life. In good shape for it, too. Fuckin' a, I can do that kind of work.*

He laughed out loud.

Again, Aaron Flowers glanced up.

But this time, Reggie sensed trouble. The billionaire wasn't looking away. He reached for his cane and walked across the cabin to Captain Waller. Now joined by Ebba, all three muttered and nodded heads, pointed fingers at spots on the map, their words blown by wind and slapped by seas. After a while, Ebba resumed her stoic watch at the starboard window. Aaron turned toward Reggie. For a cripple, and not a young one, Mr. Flowers handled himself well in a rocking boat. His piercing eyes and confident aura could frighten a bull shark.

"You seem to have found a way to amuse yourself during this very uncomfortable and difficult time," Aaron said, peering down at Reggie. "Please. Share it with me."

Reggie stiffened.

*Me?*

"Ah, it ain't nothin', sir," he said, aiming for bluster, but drooping like a tattered sail. "I just remembered an old joke."

Aaron brightened, eyes like waters cleared of sharks. "A sailor's joke?" he asked, smiling.

Reggie relaxed. *This guy ain't so bad,* he thought. "Yeah," Reggie said, buoyed by Aaron's charm. *Maybe Aaron Flowers and I can become friends. The* Sea Maid *could be his regular charter.* "Yeah, that's what it was, Mr. Flowers. An old sailor's joke."

"Wonderful!" Aaron said. That voice. That luminous smile as bright as his white, even teeth. "I love jokes. Let's hear it."

*Oh*, Reggie thought, *joke.*

His mind went blank as a fog bank. *Joke. Joke. Sailor joke?*

"Ahhh...," he said, with a beef tongue. A tongue left to parch in a desert canyon. "Well..." Horror slithered under his skin. It poisoned him with irrational fear.

*He knows! Aaron Flowers knows about the suitcase!*

"Is something wrong?"

Those eyes knew.

"No," Reggie said. Then, "I mean, sir. No, sir."

"You're acting strangely. Are you ill?"

"Yes," Reggie said, thankful for the ready excuse. "Not feelin' great. No, sir."

"Sea sick?"

Carried along and willing to agree to anything Aaron Flowers said, Reggie blurted: "Yep. That must be it, sir."

"What?" Coz shot back from across the room.

"I mean no, no, sir, not never," Reggie stammered.

"May the devil fetch me," Coz said, no doubt using the antiquated curse to impress Aaron Flowers, which, of course, steamed Reggie's barnacles. "I knew I misheard you, Reggie." Then to Aaron: "I'll tell you one thing, Mr. Flowers. Reggie's been so full of beer he's puked from delight, but I've never seen the man seasick. And we've been through storms worse than this, haven't we Reggie?"

"Yes sir, Mr. Flowers," Reggie said. "We can handle any kind of storm."

"Then why did you say you were seasick?"

"I wasn't thinkin', I guess."

"Then what's wrong?"

"Nothin'."

"You said you were sick," Old Flowers persisted. "You couldn't tell me your joke."

"I—"

"You weren't at the tunnel when George left the harbor."

The tactical shift pierced Reggie's soul, lanced his ever-swelling lies, and opened a gash for the flow of truth. "No sir," Reggie answered.

"Where were you?" Old Flowers said, his gaze trained.

"I needed a cigarette."

"And where did you smoke this cigarette?"

"Here, sir. On the *Sea Maid*, sir." Reggie swallowed. Not easy in a throat lined with sandpaper. *I need beer, or Vodka, fuck, I'd settle for water.*

"How long were you smoking aboard the *Sea Maid*?"

*The devil is fetching me!* Reggie screamed in his spinning, terrified mind. Then: *Fuck you, Coz, and your goddamn novels,* while Aaron Flowers loomed, blocked the sun, the world, all of life with his monumental calm, and those horrible billions of airs that nobody should ever fuck with and a glare that told Reggie: *I'm whittling you down and there's nothing you can do about it!*

"Uh, well, sir, I guess I was aboard about thirty minutes, maybe more."

"Smoking your cigarettes."

"Yes, sir." *And breaking your island rules, I know, I know.*

"And you didn't see or hear any activity on my son's sailboat?"

"No, sir." *And you don't believe that for a splash.*

"How good is your hearing?"

"Well—"

"He can hear a mosquito shit," Coz said, stepping closer. "Come on, Reggie, tell us a sailor joke. You always remembered the good jokes before." Now they both loomed. "Why were you smoking, Reggie? That's no way to quit."

"It ain't that easy," Reggie said, anything to change the subject. "I figured I could—"

"How much treasure did my son give you?" Old Flowers said.

*Jesus! He's known all along.* "I ain't got nobody's treasure," Reggie said, floundering in a maelstrom of deceit, but still clinging to a final raft of lies.

Aaron Flowers turned to Coz. "You may be interested to know that my son and his friend Glen have earned every dollar they've ever spent. They're in the salvage business. Over the years, they've amassed a modest fortune by diving shipwrecks." Aaron peered at Reggie like a scientist studying Earth's lowest life form. "Make no mistake. The boys would carry resources to cover obstacles." Old Flowers limped back to his table and sat down. His gaze fixed on Coz, then on Reggie. "Coz, I think your partner was their first bribable obstacle."

Coz leaned into Reggie's face, seething. "So, you made a deal without me." A huge fist cocked like a hammer, ready to strike. "Show me what they gave you. Now!" Reggie stared up, smug, anchored to lies. "Show me, goddamn it, or I'll throw you to the sharks."

"Bullshit," Reggie said, Coz a mere rope burn compared to Aaron Flowers' thumb screws. "You can't threaten me. We're equal partners."

"Really? Seems like you're working alone now." When Coz straightened, his head almost scraped the cabin ceiling, a quality that had always unnerved Reggie. Now, that towering figure and those broad shoulders seemed flat out menacing.

"He don't know what he's talkin' about," Reggie said, before turning to Old Flowers. "All due respect, Mr. Flowers."

"Well, I suppose we should find out," Coz said. Now *he* turned to Old Flowers. "What do *you* think, Mr. Flowers? Is it murder when a lying thief slips and falls overboard?"

Old Flowers smiled. "In Ancient Rome, a soldier who deserted his post, perhaps for a cigarette, or who stole from a partner, that is, a fellow soldier, received the *fustuarium supplicium.*"

Reggie said: "There weren't no cigaret—"

"That sounds painful," Coz said, cutting Reggie off with a glower.

"It was death by cudgel," Old Flowers said, tapping his cane on the cabin floor.

"Sharks are quicker," Coz said, grabbing Reggie's collar and raising him a foot off his chair. He slammed him down. "Fifty-fifty my ass, you pig shit! I always forked over my half!"

Reggie blubbered something incoherent and surveyed the cabin, found no solace from Captain Waller, not even a glance from Ebba, cringed when his gaze met Aaron Flowers', and finally landed on Coz and more venom than a sea wasp. "I was gonna tell ya the whole story," he said, lathering the lie with pleading. "Soon as things cooled down."

"Sure you were, Shark Bait," Coz said, hoisting Reggie by the arm and shoving him toward the door.

"Cut it out!" Reggie cried with a fruitless squirm.

"Remember that guy you laughed at?" Coz said, palm smothering Reggie's face and pressing him hard against the bulkhead. "The one with the shark-bit stumps? Now you'll know what it's like."

"Ah...kay," Reggie cried, the snivel a strangled sob from the corner of his mouth. "I talked to the kids." Coz eased his grip. "They didn't give me nothin'. I was gonna tell ya the whole story!"

"Sure you were. Now here's my story." A fist slammed Reggie's stomach, fast and brutal.

Buckled, choking, gurgling on bile, staring up through tears at Coz, immense, threatening, aiming another blow and serious as, well, a fucking shark attack— Reggie quit. The lies. The fantasies. The life of riches and ease.

But not soon enough.

Coz was already dragging Reggie across the deck and bending him over the rail. "Say hi to Jaws," Coz said.

"Stop! I'll show you!" Reggie screamed. "I'll fucking show you."

Coz stepped back. "You piece of slug shit," he cursed. "You've got one minute." He slammed the cabin door.

Defeated, Reggie shuffled to where he had hidden the treasure and flung the canvas aside. Raising the polypropylene hatch, he grabbed the suitcase and trudged back to the cabin like a man carrying forty pounds of regret.

"Looks heavy," Coz said. "I wonder how much you were going to cheat me."

Reggie plopped the treasure on the floor, dropped to a squat, and removed two of the three life jackets. *We coulda' been friends*, he thought when his eyes met Aaron's. He couldn't look at Captain Waller, and sure as fuck not Ebba, and Coz he kept at a wary distance, safe in his fringe vision, as he unlatched the metal hasps and opened the suitcase.

"What the fuck?" he muttered, voice so inaudible he may have only thought the words.

Coz stepped over to the suitcase. "Really?" he said, surprised, confused, suspicious. Without further comment, he crouched to one knee and poked around at the row of bricks. When he was satisfied that they were indeed common bricks, he said to Reggie: "Jesus loving Joseph from hell, you're either the biggest liar on earth, or the stupidest bastard I've ever known." He walked back to his seat.

It was too late for Reggie to seize the day, but he definitely plucked the moment. "There, you see?" he said, rising from a squat to a man. His voice oozed glee and vindication. "I told you it wasn't nothin'." He turned to Old Flowers.

"You were ready to beat me to death." Then to Coz: "And you nearly launched me to the sharks." He kicked the suitcase. "You want your half? Take it!"

"Go to hell," Coz muttered.

With that, Reggie gathered up the suitcase and stomped to the deck. Rage at being duped by a bunch of kids churned his bowels, but he stopped himself a split second before throwing the suitcase overboard.

*Wait a minute,* he thought. *I can still put the blind on all these assholes.*

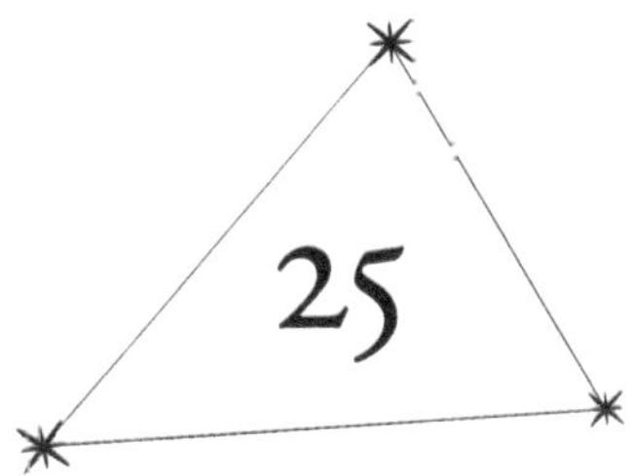

Cerissa emerged from the cabin with a duffel bag slung under her right shoulder. She dropped it at Glen's feet. "Is this what you wanted?"

"Yeah, thanks." Stooped over the tiller, hair matted with dried blood, arm various shades of black and blue, Glen now added circles of fatigue to a face horrid enough for *El Día de los Muertos.* "Now that things have calmed down a bit, we should take some safety precautions."

Cerissa unzipped the sack, and strained to see its contents in the first gray whisper of dawn. "Scuba gear?" she said.

"And look what I found." He raised the hatch on the stowage hold aft of the tiller. "I forgot we had these."

"Forgot?"

"I knew we had two extra tanks. I just thought they were empty. Look. They both have tank caps. That means they're full."

"Really."

"Then sitting here for the last two hours, I had an idea."

"Okay."

Glen sighed, closed his eyes, and yawned, a sight both pitiful and frightening. "I can't do this much longer. I'm beat to shit and can barely see straight." He shrugged. "Sorry, but you have to take over."

"I can't," Cerissa said. "I'm not experienced. What if I'm not strong enough to steer."

"You are."

"You should come up with a better idea."

"That's not the idea."

"Then what?"

"George just needs a couple more hours of sleep. Then he can take the tiller again. I'm serious. I can't go another ten minutes."

In truth, Cerissa marveled that Glen had persisted this long. His right eye was swollen shut, his left reduced to a narrow slit. She could only imagine what slamming across the deck had done to his ribs and muscles. "I believe you," she said, trying not to stare at his mangled features. "But I'd kill us all if a wave washed over. Even wearing a safety line."

"I know it's a risk."

"Of course. With you and George below deck, anything could happen."

"Which brings us to my idea."

"You want me to wear a tank."

"And a mask and a thin wetsuit. I want you to be safe and comfortable. I've been sitting here choking on seawater. It sucks, but I'm used to it. The seas are high, but if you aim straight and don't turn the boat broadside, we just ride up and over. Like we're doing now."

He looked away, and especially in profile, his features reminded her of catfish dough, the bloody, pasty mass used by the boys in Costa Rica to catch freshwater suckermouth. Empathy softened her antipathy. "I can probably do that," she said.

"That's the spirit. The mask will keep saltwater out of your eyes. The wetsuit will keep you warm. The regulator will be inches from your mouth if the spray gets bad."

"Sounds reasonable."

"You'll be clipped into a safety line, and even if you *did* wash overboard, which won't happen, the wetsuit is buoyant as hell. Without a weight belt, you'll float like a cork. Even the tank will float."

"I'm not a wimp," Cerissa said. "I just don't want to endanger our lives."

"Believe me, you'll be saving them."

"We're not exactly brimming with options."

"I'm afraid not. Two, three hours tops. From there, George and I can take shifts. I'll stay with you for the first half-hour. Give you some pointers. Make sure you're comfortable with the boat. Don't worry. The *Valdaquez* is a sweetheart. She'll treat you right."

"I hope so."

"Okay, try this stuff on. Here..." Glen leaned over and reached into the sack. With a yank, he removed a thin wet suit.

After squirming into the gray sharkskin suit, Cerissa glanced down at the creases and bulges.

"A little baggy," Glen said, with a chuckle. "I'm a size or two bigger than you."

Cerissa folded the cuff and slipped the serpent bracelet back over her bare wrist. "You don't go anywhere without that bracelet, do you?" Glen said.

"It's become my good luck charm," she said, shyly. "It's beautiful and exotic. Just like Flowers Island."

"That's cool. I wish I'd brought a few mementos. My life on the island was always...never mind." With one eye squinting forward, and one hand on the tiller, he poked around the fins and pulled out a BCD. "This holds the tank," he said.

"It looks like a deflated life vest," Cerissa said.

"In a way, it is. Push this button and it inflates." While the boat rocked and lurched, he helped her lift the tank from the stowage locker and cinch it to the BCD. "Now the regulator," he said with a grin. Together, they fumbled with the knobs and hoses, and opened the main air valve. "There, just like I thought," he said, reading the pressure gauge. "3000 psi. You're more than good to go."

After a few moments of struggle in the dim light, Cerissa managed to squirm into the shoulder straps of the BCD. Glen snugged the cummerbund, the straps, and clipped the pressure line to the inflator hose. "If a wave washes over the boat, lean forward so the tank won't hit the back of your head." He smiled. "You saw how high the seas can get."

"It seems a little calmer now," Cerissa said, voice, even to her, sounding strained and worried.

"Yeah, a little. The winds are dying down. But we're still rolling over twenty-foot seas. When it gets a little lighter, you'll see what I mean."

Cerissa sighed. "I hate to imagine anything terrible happening. Not after we've made it this far." Glen pressed the purge button on the regulator. The sharp hiss silenced and startled her.

"Okay, let's get you into position." Glen lashed the tiller and stood to help Cerissa maneuver her tank-laden body to the navigator's seat. When she was settled, he released the tiller and allowed Cerissa to take control. "You're doing great. Watch the compass and veer west. That's it, tiller starboard, boat goes to port, tiller—"

"I know," Cerissa said. "Cedric taught me that much."

"Perfect. Keep doing what you're doing. Aim directly at the wave. Up and over, up and over. Keep an eye both starboard and port. Seas can build from any direction. Never get hit broadside." He snapped his fingers. "A big sea hitting our beam could capsize the boat—just like that!"

After a few more minutes of assisting, Glen stood and said: "Finally!" his tone edgy, curt. Cerissa suspected pain he could no longer keep to himself.

He wobbled to the companionway and closed the cabin door.

Alone, steering a boat in seas she never imagined sailing, let alone navigating, Cerissa fueled confidence with a healthy measure of panic. To get comfortable and acquainted, she took a few deep breaths of compressed air, then removed the regulator and allowed it to dangle on the strap below her chin. "I've got this," she said, voice more confident than she felt.

The *Valdaquez* bobbed and splashed over the ocean, even bounced on occasion. Wind clanged the rigging, and at times, the boat shuddered so hard, she feared pieces would break away and fly into the seas.

When, after twenty minutes of exhilaration and feeling in control, guiding the boat west and safely through the very grand and magnificent waters that had seduced Cedric Maxwell and deprived her of a father, Cerissa understood. At least the allure, if not the addiction.

At that same moment, as if to prove that exhilaration and control are less than fleeting, Glen opened the cabin door.

He stepped onto the deck and proved himself the pissant she knew him to be. "You piece of shit," Cerissa said, reading the thoughts behind his lowered barricade.

"You've done well," Glen said, through what remained of his smile. "You deserve a glimpse into the plan." He had suited up in another set of scuba gear and stood with arms wide, as if to embrace the sea.

"Your plan disgusts me."

Glen laughed. "It's not my plan. I merely play my humble role. As do you." He looked to the east. "This has been my command performance. Now, the sun is rising, and it's time for us to die." A hearty, bellowing laugh, followed by a deep breath of fresh, ocean air. "It's great being on the sea again," Glen said, breathing out the words like a long gasp. "George and I used to have so much fun sailing." He shrugged. "But, as they say, all things must end."

"I'm not playing along," Cerissa said.

"Too late. Old Flowers is years ahead of you. This boat, for example. Designed by the finest nautical engineers in the world. The *Valdaquez* is part of the plan. Everyone is part of the plan. He'd never take chances with George."

"Chances?"

Glen pointed to the bracelet on Cerissa's arm. "That's another example. A beautiful, very stylish beacon."

"What are you talking about?"

"Read my mind. My wall is down."

"I'd rather swim through a sewer."

Glen laughed. "Fair enough," he said, bowing in mock reverence. "I'm a despicable liar. But you need to know that you've been wearing that bracelet for just this moment. If you want to live, you'll let me show you." Walking over, he grabbed Cerissa's arm, and twisted the bracelet until it clicked. It separated into two parts. On the inside face of each half was a tiny button. "There," Glen said, pushing one of the buttons. "I've just activated another transmitter. There are three beacons on the *Valdaquez,* and we each have our own."

Cerissa's expression flared. She wrenched her arm from his grasp, crying: "Fuck you! Get away from me!" Glen froze, still leaning over her, still holding half of the bracelet, and watched as she cast the other half over her left shoulder. "You manipulative bastards. There go your plans."

Glen took a step back. "That was stupid. You've just decreased our chances by fifty percent. I'm keeping this half and you'd better hope we don't get separated." He stretched the neoprene collar and stuffed the bracelet securely into his wetsuit.

"What do you mean 'separated'?"

"I'll tell you." But instead of explaining, he ignored her and dug around in the duffel bag. "Here it is," he said, removing a broken safety line. He reached under the rail and detached the line he'd been wearing earlier. He threw it overboard. "This will be a nice touch," he said. He then clamped the broken safety line to the boat and surveyed the horizon. "The light is perfect. So is the fog."

"Rot in hell," Cerissa said, leaving the tiller. "I want no part of anybody's plan."

"But you wanted me to explain."

"Get this tank off my back."

"Relax. We won't be in the water more than a few minutes."

"What?"

"My half of the beacon will guide the *Sea Maid* right to us. But now, thanks to your temper, we have to stay together."

"What the hell are you talking about?"

"Remember to inflate the BCD when you hit the water. There, that button I showed you."

"Hit the water? I'm not going in the water!"

"You have no choice."

"Oh, yeah?" Cerissa yanked on the cummerbund, but it wouldn't release. So too the clips of her shoulder straps. "What have you done?" she cried.

Glen smiled. "Look at that," he said, pointing to the unmanned tiller. "You make my job so easy." He reached down and unclipped the boat's drogue anchor.

Now completely adrift, the boat turned, lurched into the seas, and heaved Cerissa against the bulkhead. In an instant, she lay on her side, dazed, looking up, the tank anchoring her to the deck.

Glen steadied himself with a grab bar and watched the *Valdaquez* list to port. "Our disappearance will blend perfectly with your natural air of mystery," he called into the wind. "Everything will be so believable. Like the rest of your story." He fixed his gaze on the turbulent seas, and smiled. "I really enjoyed the part about your 'dashing rogue' father. You have the kind of imagination Old Flowers loves."

"It happens to be the truth, you shit!" she cried up to him.

"Really? Well, I guess truth has its uses."

He turned his back to her, a moment's reprieve from engorgement and seeping eyes, from purple swelling to black, from bloody snot. Sickened by his bloated lips, gruesome in triumph under a tumorous nose, she hated that face. Despised the smirk. Loathed the rotting soul under features, battered and ugly.

Glen leaned into the wind, beamed his delighted grimace, and faced a dawn coated in fog. "Beautiful," he said.

The tiller flailed with the sea's whims. Cerissa struggled against the tank and the pitching boat. "Our helmsperson deserted her post," Glen said. "Anything can happen now."

Cerissa reached up and grabbed the rail, trying to right herself. In the growing light, giant seas menaced from all directions. Glen clenched the opposite rail, rolling with the pitch, pleased by the waves bashing the beam.

The *Valdaquez* turned about, her broadside facing the seas.

"Get ready!" Glen screamed. "I hope the *Sea Maid* is close. This next sea looks huge!"

Cerissa screamed: "No! George—"

The sailboat dropped, sudden, violent, an elevator plummeting.

A monstrous wall of water, higher than the mast, towered above.

Cerissa's scream drowned under the roar.

"Use your air—now!" Glen cried, shoving the regulator into his mouth and biting hard.

The wave crashed across the deck.

Glen and Cerissa catapulted into the sea as the mast slammed below water line.

The boat careened, floundered, upside down.

* * *

From pleasant dreams of cresting and falling, George awoke to flying chaos, screamed as his body hurled through the air, and gasped when it slammed into the opposite wall, then, "Ooohhh," when he hit the ceiling, now the floor, with a brutal thud.

"Cerissa," he said, dazed and raising to his elbows. "Glen?"

Struggling to his knees, he heaved a cushion off his back, then clambered to the wall fighting for footing. Water surged in from the shattered skylight as the boat righted itself in a slow, groaning swivel. "Glen! Cerissa!" he screamed, grasping for anything solid, the boat turning, George slipping to his knees and sliding down the wall and into the opposite berth. Secure, at least for the moment, he held the support chain and hoped the boat would stabilize.

Instead, the *Valdaquez* shuddered. A sickening, dispiriting jolt, followed by a sharp pop, and creaks, first aft, then port, then starboard, metal twisting against fiberglass and squealing like rusty brakes. Then gone in an instant, replaced by wind and rushing water and seas pounding the hull, more water through the skylight, and inches below the berth, water flooding up through the floorboards.

"Fil-lon-chi fuck!" George cried, a breach of the forward bulkhead all but certain.

Minutes from now, the cabin would flood and swamp the boat.

Leaping off the berth, he opened the stowage locker and pulled out the duffle containing the four-person, *Viking RescYou* life raft—not easy in churning waters and a listing boat.

*We'll need food, water,* he thought. hurling the duffle onto a still dry shelf and searching cabinet to cabinet for provisions. A leather bota, water, probably stale, but drinkable. Full jar of peanut butter, four of Miss Ruth's pemmican bars, a can of vegetarian beans, and a tin of dried raisins. Also from the galley, a Leatherman multi-tool, a spoon, the flare gun, a flashlight, and a cloth bag to hold it all.

With the life raft slung over his shoulder, he waded to the cabin doors.

Jammed.

"Glen!" he screamed, pounding on the doors. "Cerissa!"

The handles turned, but nothing, pushing, or even slamming with his shoulder budged that immovable barrier. Had something fallen into the companionway and blocked the doors?

Water surged to his waist.

Splashing to the middle of the cabin, easier now that the boat had listed closer to centerline, George gazed up at the skylight hatch. Shards glittered back, but broke away when battered with the galley's fire extinguisher. Even better, the flooding had slowed.

*The hull must have breached high, just below the rail.*

Pushing aside debris and the clog of floating cushions, George balanced on the berth and shoved the duffle out the hatch and into the fog. The cloth bag followed. Chilled, fatigued, adrenalin quivering every muscle, he clenched his teeth and squirmed through the skylight hatch, grazed his chest in the process, but emerged under grey skies and next to a mast that looked like a giant, broken toothpick.

Hurling the provisions, then the *Viking RescYou* duffle, into the companionway, he turned in a full circle and scanned the misty sea. The *Valdaquez* turned with him, adrift in towering swells, rudderless, lost, alone.

Anything on deck had been swept overboard, including Glen and Cerissa.

"Cerissa! Glen!" George called over the water. At best, he could see a hundred feet into the fog. "Cerissa!" They could be nearby, floating, unconscious, hidden by foam and swirl. "Glen!" A frantic, disbelieving voice screamed into the water. "Cerissa!" A faint response. A female voice, distant, calling his name. Real? Imagined? "Cerissa!" he called again.

But after long minutes of straining to hear.

Nothing.

Crawling along the listing rim of the cabin, he worked his way aft, to the tiller and Glen's safety line. "No," George cried, clutching the tattered end. "This can't be the real world."

He slumped onto the deck, knew he should find another safety line, man the tiller, steer the boat, assess damage, but why? Only names mattered. "Cerissa!" then "Glen!", looping screams, over and over, for as long as he could wail.

Another blur of hours. Alone on monotonous seas. Exiled to the edge of the world. Love and friendship gone, surrendered to a hopeless future.

The *Valdaquez* bobbed, up, and down, over the waves; steady, like breathing.

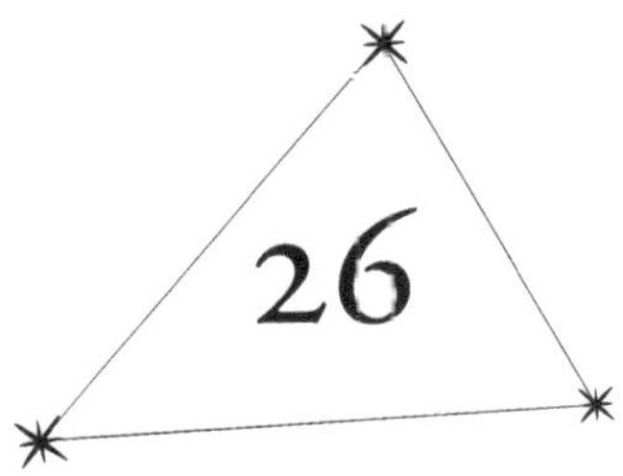


Three days later, the Outer Banks came into view.

Reggie breathed the scent of liberation, and escape, from every goddamn member of the Flowers Corporation.

*Christ, what a hive of bees. Everyone has their job. Nobody questions the need to work, work, work. Jesus, who'd wanna slave for these people? Who needs Aaron Flowers?*

"What's wrong?" Glen said, joining Reggie at the bow rail. He dangled his legs over the hull. "You're not grinning like a man with a suitcase full of gold."

Not amused, Reggie anchored his expression and scowled at the wind, mute, indifferent, a masthead of tanned leather—until temper burned his silence. *I'd love to add another lump to your collection*, he thought, searching Glen's face for a vacant spot. *You're ugly as a stonefish and twice as deadly.* Instead, he faced Glen with a smile. "Your so-called friend, George," he said, tone smug, a man without needs. "You fooled *him* with that suitcase, too. Watched him risk his life for a load of bricks." He turned away with a snort. "Real nice guy."

Glen laughed. "George swam like a champion."

"You're all puking liars," he said, eyes dancing with Aaron terror.

"Don't worry," Glen said with a chuckle. "He's below."

Still, Reggie whispered. "I'll figure out what you people are up to." He leaned close, a scurvy pirate with a dagger point. "Now, *there's* some gold."

Glen bellowed another laugh and stood. "I should have got you talking three days ago. You're a funny guy." He slapped Reggie's shoulder and walked to the sun deck.

Cerissa, alone, reading a wrinkled, decade-old issue of *Sailing World* magazine and as vexed as Reggie, sat on a folding chair glistening bronze. She shifted her body when Glen approached.

"I have news about George," Glen said, the only path to Cerissa's regard.

Cordial with Captain Waller and Coz, she barely acknowledged Ebba and her "Uncle" Aaron. Glen fell somewhere between cockroach and bilge rat. "Really?" she said, without looking up.

"He's safe," Glen said.

Cerissa stared over the rim of her sunglasses. "Another lie," she said, tone flat, indifferent, deceit as certain as sparkles on sunlit ocean. "You have no way of knowing that."

"We've known from the beginning."

Pages crackled under her fingers.

"The *Valdaquez* was designed in the former Belgium by *Etap Yachting*. Unsinkable, horizontal double hull bulkheads with a rigid foam core. You could cut that boat in half and both pieces would float."

"Does George know that?"

"Of course not. That would ruin the lesson."

"The lesson," she said, tone as fluent as spittle.

"Old Flowers even devised some clever shipwreck features."

That caught her attention. "What are you talking about?"

"Breakaway panels and penetrations, servomechanisms, remote-controlled pumps and solenoids. Basically, devices to simulate hull damage and induce controlled flooding of interior spaces."

"You sound like a servomechanism."

"Hey, I'm being honest. Isn't that what you want?"

"You wouldn't know honesty if it drowned your best friend."

"If you'd try to understand, you could be a wonderful help in our work." Cerissa ignored him. "Christ. You're a waste of my time."

*But maybe not George's*, he thought.

Sunlight slipped off perfect, smooth, oil-drenched shoulders. And that profile. If she wasn't such a snooty dreamer, she'd inspire her share of fantasy. Even her hair sparkled. It streamed in the wind like a comet's tail.

"You really believe George is okay?" she asked, breaking the spell.

"Are you kidding? George is invincible."

Cerissa scoffed. "You're delusional."

Glen sat on a deck cushion and squinted up. "You don't understand. You haven't been on Flowers Island all your life. You have room for doubt, but George believes. Consciously, subconsciously, from birth he's been trained to live, and believe in, illusion. To him, illusion is no different than reality."

"I hope those Culture Colonies work as well as you think they do. The world out there is real too."

"Of course. But George can shape the world into anything he wants."

"Just by believing?"

"If it were that easy, beggars would ride."

"Then how?"

"Old Flowers has trained him, given him the tools. The Grand Trine will teach him how to use them."

"By playing football? Is that a joke?"

"Football, or really, Coach Buffington's version of football, is another training ground. The real power is here." Glen pointed to his forehead. "It won't be easy, but when George gets to the Northeast Kingdom, to Grand Trinity University, his life will change."

"Change doesn't imply good fortune."

"That's true."

"So why all the lies and manipulation?"

"Words," Glen said. "Were you manipulated when teachers taught you the miraculous power of reading and writing? Were you manipulated into reading people's minds?"

Cerissa remained silent.

"Old Flowers is working with equally miraculous powers, unconsciousness powers. I'd try to explain, but I don't understand his methods."

"You must have some idea."

"Old Flowers says the ancients considered silence the fourth cornerstone of power. He won't teach us his techniques. Says the power could be misused in the wrong hands."

"What do you think?"

"I'm sure he's right. But that hasn't stopped me from doing a little investigating."

"And?"

"The technique has something to do with the colored lamp above George's bed, and the music that wakes him every morning. It's some special kind of subliminal programming."

"Uncle Aaron places messages under the melody and speaks to George's unconscious mind?"

Glen shrugged.

Despite herself, Cerissa smiled for the first time. "According to what I've read, the unconscious mind will believe anything it's told. It doesn't discriminate like the conscious mind. If someone could devise a way to tell the unconscious that anything was possible, I suppose it would eventually believe it."

"You said it better than I could." Glen shook his head. "You must get loads of information from poking around in everyone's brain."

"Maybe," Cerissa said.

"Well, believe what you want about our "manipulation". I just know that George has always had vivid dreams. Now, his dreams are part of his waking world, and eventually, they'll do amazing things."

"I hope you're right."

Glen grinned. "Me too," he said, looking away.

The faint outline of land appeared at twilight. In a few hours, the *Valdaquez* would drift to shore and George would step into the real world. Yet, measured against the approaching continent, he felt as significant as a speck of sand in an endless current, lost in a cycle of useless, meaningless events.

Calm seas lapped the hull, danger and terror trailing *Tempestas* to some other outrage, and leaving his mind adrift in its own gentle sway. Rise, and fall, eyes closed, surge, and ebb, asleep, awake, hours and minutes engulfed in dusky daze.

A loud thump!

Crashed awake to long, high-pitched scraping and a sudden lurch, his body slammed into the lifelines.

Dark, starlit outlines, the cabin, the rail.

Panic and instinct groping for the tiller, then just as quickly, acceptance.

*Leave it*, George thought, as the breakers smashed his beloved *Valdaquez* into the rocks.

"I'm done with Flowers Island," he called to the darkness, and held tight as the bow jammed between two massive boulders.

In the moonlight, foam and sand gleamed less than fifty yards away.

Aft, and clear of the rocks, George slid into the water and swam.

The *Valdaquez*, wrecked, discarded, symbol of an abandoned life, he bequeathed the mess to the Flowers Corporation.

On the beach, he stretched onto his back and stared at the summer night.

The swan, the dragon, and Hercules stared back.

Reggie sat on deck, next to an open porthole, until long after sundown.

Earlier, he'd overheard Ebba and Aaron Flowers order Captain Waller to follow the *Valdaquez* beacons to George's exact point of landing. Under cover of darkness, they would cruise the *Sea Maid* close enough for visual confirmation.

Using Sightmark Ghost Hunter night-vision binoculars (a toy Reggie would kill, or at least, maim for), they would confirm that George was safely ashore. From there, the *Sea Maid* would follow the coast to Cape Hatteras, fuel up, and return to Flowers Island.

*Fine,* Reggie thought. *I'll play the Flowers game. For real, and my way.*

"Hand me the starlights," Aaron Flowers said, an hour later.

With the running lights blackened, only moon glow lighted the deck. Reggie stood off, apart from the others, but listening.

"He's on the beach," Aaron Flowers said.

"Let me see," Ebba said, reaching for the binoculars. "Poor soul. He looks so dejected. I wish I could do something to comfort him." She handed the glasses back to Aaron.

"Someday," Aaron said.

"I know." Ebba eased into a deck chair, silent, almost translucent in a pale-yellow smock, a ghost in the moonlight that panicked Reggie with weird—almost draining his courage.

*You can do this,* he thought.

"I can do this," Ebba said to Aaron, creeping Reggie further.

"Of course you can, my dear," Aaron said.

"When the time is right," she continued, "I'll find George and show him my genuine self."

"He won't recognize you," Aaron said.

"In some ways, he will. Though I'll arrive with a new history. Something as far from Ebba as the Milky Way from Triangulum."

"May I suggest an impoverished childhood? A struggle from nothing to renown in arts and letters?"

"Perfect," Ebba said.

"Let's get underway, shall we, Captain?"

"Aye, aye, sir."

Reggie lingered until everyone drifted below, then snuck to the hidden suitcase. There, he cinched up the life jackets and lowered the ruse over the side. Not even a splash (if you don't count Reggie's spurt of delight). "Off you go, my friend," he almost burbled.

With more caress than shove, he launched the suitcase to shore.

"Here's my gift from those lying bastards."

True to habit, George awoke at dawn. But instead of slowly swelling music, screeching gulls awakened him. Chilly gray mist hung over the water, but George could still see the *Valdaquez* floundering between the rocks. A sad, broken toy.

Standing, stiff from the cold and still feeling the rocking boat even on solid ground, aching for food, he thought about the last three days, his meager provisions, minimal water, and the jar of peanut butter he'd salvaged from the galley. Survival would have to be more than arriving on the mainland.

Stretching, he pondered direction.

*Now that I'm here, where exactly am I going?*

He peered south down the beach, now a graveyard of ruined lawn chairs, tattered beach umbrellas, flower pots and trash, all jutting from tombs of sand. A few distant joggers weaved around tangled debris. An old woman in a neon lime slicker cried: "Casper!", then "Bad boy!" while jerking from scent to scent behind a scruffy poodle. Then north, much the same, but deserted at this hour and more commercial. Docks jutted into the water, some missing slats, others dipping into sea foam at odd angles. Steps led up from the beach to what looked like restaurants and shops, once elegant, but now dressed in naked plywood and coiffed with curled shingles.

And a hundred feet away, wallowing in garbage and lapping surf, a colorful, half-buried blob that very much resembled—

"What the...?" George said, stunned.

The suitcase?

Shielding his eyes against the rising sun, George trained his sight on the unmistakable bright orange life jackets, and the brown they enveloped.

And ran, feet digging into the sand, legs like sponge rubber, but fast, and faster still.

The sight of the suitcase triggered a memory, a dream, last night. Glen and Cerissa, alive, on the *Sea Maid*, not friendly or even happy, but talking, on the sun deck like a couple of tourists.

He fell to his knees before the suitcase and caressed its irregular, imitation alligator skin surface, proof of reality.

"Yes," he said. "Yes!"

Grabbing the handle, he dragged the suitcase out of the surf and brushed away the kelp. "Glen, how? Your treasure, somehow..."

He turned, sensing Glen standing behind him, but seeing sandpipers and oyster catchers instead, endless sand, swaying sawgrass.

Was this a miracle; like the hundreds faked in the Colonies by sham shamans, or a talisman worthy of *Tezcatcatl*, foretelling success with the Grand Trine?

*Glen, he never really lied. He gave his life.*

Unclipping the life jackets and unlatching the clasps, he opened the lid to Spanish gold, finger ingots, pure, rich yellow, the metal of faith, love, and honor.

And Destiny.

He knew now. Knew that his path, any path, was the right one.

Again, the dream—Glen and Cerissa on the *Sea Maid.*

Such a comforting thought.

But he knew it was only a dream.

# Author's Note

If I learned anything from writing a trilogy, it's that (at least for me) the first book can't truly find its place in the series until the third book is finished.

For a couple of reasons.

One, unless a writer embarks on a trilogy after already completing one or two stand-alone novels, that first book will likely share qualities with most first novels, that is, flat descriptions, clumsy narrative, amateurish transitions, skeletal, inconsistent plotting, a lack of character development, and stilted or melodramatic dialogue.

In other words: Literary garbage.

That was certainly the case with my first so-called novel, the original edition of *The Grand Trine*, copies of which I'm currently adding to piles of dry brush, leaves, and rotting wood, and calling the resulting anthology: *Bonfire of the Vanity Press.*

Secondly, trilogies are vast, covering years, even decades of various character's lives, numerous twists of plot, thematic development, flowering subtexts, etc.—all subsequent elements of the story that should spring from a fully formed first book.

Ideally.

Unfortunately, the first edition of *The Grand Trine* was far from fully formed, was finished and published long ago, and represents to me little more than writer's regret, a common phenomenon (For an interesting read, Google "writer's regret" sometime).

And when I say, "long ago", I mean completed in 1987. After years of struggle, frustration, aimless literary wandering, and back when "word processing" was a typewriter with a special "correcting" ribbon that could backspace the previous fourteen characters (yes, 14 *characters*) and overwrite them with white-out. Earlier still, *The Grand Trine* barely survived as a hundred or so hand-written pages; a thin, hardly coherent narrative outline stuffed into a loose-leaf notebook.

Editing was cross outs and additions along with circled numbers 1, 2, 3...12, 13, 14, inserted into the body of text and referencing notes crammed into the margins.

When things got too unruly, the whole mess was re-written by hand to make the text somewhat readable.

Just somewhat.

Much later, thanks to the Compaq Portable, a 28-lb. kind of movable, not really compact computer that looked like an ugly suitcase, only heavier and more unwieldy, but with two floppy disc drives and a 9" green screen monitor—thanks to that revolutionary machine, *The Grand Trine* transformed into what Ed Whalen, a retired editor from Putnam, called: "Not so much a novel as the longest prologue ever written".

Needless to say, G. P. Putnam's Sons (book publisher) had no interest in my "prologue/novel" wanna be.

And although Mr. Whalen also said: "During my editorial career, I've only read three manuscripts from start to finish in one sitting. *The Grand Trine* was one of them" (a compliment of sorts, I suppose). But, readability aside, I still hadn't written a real novel, even after years of trying.

Which explains why the manuscript sat in a drawer for the next fifteen years.

Only after a (brave?) friend asked about it, then read it, then thought it had some interesting elements and encouraged me to self-publish, did the story emerge from beneath my socks.

Too bad I was busy running a business and had zero time for, or interest in, re-writing or editing. The result was an ancient, immature manuscript published without significant changes—garbage bound in hardcover with beautiful fonts. (Again, if you happen upon a first edition of *The Grand Trine,* please let me know. The bonfire should not burn in vain).

On the other hand, maybe one saved copy could serve as a good example of a bad (sort-of) novel, or elongated foreword, or whatever the hell it is, and might help some future novelist improve his or her technique.

One man's garbage and all that, but please, only one copy.

So, there you have it. This second edition of *The Grand Trine*, this Book One re-written after completing Books Two and Three, is the novel I wish my lame writer self from the 80's could have written.

It may not be perfect, but at least it's not an overblown prologue.

Hopefully, it's also not kindling.

www.ingramcontent.com/pod-product-compliance
Lightning Source LLC
Chambersburg PA
CBHW030425310726
48979CB00009B/1617/J

* 9 7 8 0 9 7 5 4 4 6 1 2 6 *